leaving early.

Don Waitt

Two-Headed Calf Press
New York, NY

Copyright © 2010 by Don Waitt
ISBN: 978-0-9857817-2-9

First edition December 2010
Second edition January 2020

Front cover illustration by Amanda Lanzone.

To my Dad,
who always said,
Don't sweat the small stuff.

&

To my Mom,
who still says,
It will be in the last place you look.

contents.

Sunday, June 21

gun.

Laying on my side in bed with my eyes half shut, I can just barely see the corner of the blue plastic case on top of my dresser across the room.

And it gives me a strange and wondrous feeling to know that inside the case, resting on a gray foam cushion, is a brand new Smith & Wesson .357 Magnum pistol, still covered with the lightest sheen of oil.

And in the final moments before I drift off to sleep, I try to decide what will be the easiest and least painful way to use that dangerous hunk of steel and gunpowder.

To kill myself.

*   *   *

To get an accurate picture of the position I am in, you should know that it is seventy degrees in my bedroom because I like it cold, yet I am toasty warm under a blanket and a thick down comforter, with just the tip of my right foot peeking out from the covers, a thermometer to test the coolness of the air outside the covers. My head is resting on one of those special foam pillows that when you place your hand hard on the surface it leaves a full palm print.

All in all, I am quite content and quite happy.

I live in a very big house. It is midnight and my wife, who always goes to bed after me, is in one of the other rooms, either surfing on her laptop computer or watching one of the dozens of tennis matches she tapes and plays over and over. When she calls it a night, she will sleep in the guest room because I snore, quite loudly and frequently apparently. My daughter recently graduated from college and lives in New York City. Her older brother lives across town. We have an empty nest. There are two new BMWs in our driveway and a 65-inch plasma TV in the living room and plenty of money in the bank.

I want for not, need for not.

And still I think about that gun just a few yards away.

And about taking my own life.

* * *

The gun seems so out of place in this gated golf course community where crime is nonexistent and the outside world is kept at bay by multiple security gates staffed by gray-haired, pot-bellied rent-a-cops who insist on waving a hello at every car that comes through the gates. The only voices that are ever raised in anger are from golfers on the nearby greens arguing about side bets and golf shots. It's too light in the bedroom for my tastes, the blue light from the remote oscillating floor fan, the red and green lights on the cordless phone, and the swath of white light that slips around the corner through the French window on the closed bedroom door, even though we spent hundreds of dollars on some fancy blinds that look great but are too sheer to keep out the light from the living room.

On the other side of my dresser is a hallway flanked by two large walk-in closets leading to a large bathroom with the requisite sunken bathtub and separate tiled shower. There are two vanities in front of a huge wall-to-wall mirror topped by sixteen of those round lightbulbs like you see over mirrors in backstage dressing rooms. I know that when I decide to use the gun, that mirror will come in handy because it is imperative that you see exactly where the gun is pointing before you pull the trigger. I was a crime reporter for

gun.

newspapers twenty-five years ago and wrote my fair share of news stories about botched suicide attempts, guys blowing off an ear or a chunk of their scalp because they did not have the barrel of the gun pointed at the right angle against their head or because they flinched at the last second.

There are two schools of thought on the best way to point the gun, and I would often hear the cops at the police station argue back and forth on the pros and cons of those two different approaches. On one side were the cops who said you should place the barrel of the gun under your chin and dispatch that hot piece of fragmenting lead straight up through the top of your head. On the other side of the fence were the cops who favored placing the barrel to your temple and letting the bullet go from one side of your head to the other side on a nice even parallel line.

Horizontal suicide or vertical suicide?

Such a dilemma.

* * *

For me, the gun is less than twelve hours old.

I bought it earlier today on what was a sunny Sunday afternoon at one of those gun shows that take up a weekend and draw hundreds of you-can-have-my-gun-when-you-pry-my-cold-dead-finger-off-the-trigger local yokels to the community convention center. One weekend it's the miniature train collector's show and the next weekend the tables are packed with enough firepower to arm a small South African army. What's scary is that the two shows are drawing the very same people.

When I lived in Texas a few decades ago, I would drive by a small strip shopping center on the way to work every day and in that shopping center was a store with two big plate glass windows on either side of the front door. Painted on the window on the left side of the door were the words *Comics for Sale*, and painted on the window on the right were the words *Guns for Sale*.

Superman comics and Saturday night special handguns in the very same store. What a novel idea. Sell to father and son at the same time and once the son gets his fill of make-believe cartoon violence he can move up to the real deal—and still buy from the same smiling clerk. I mentioned this jarring mix of retail products to several friends who were surprised that I saw anything unusual about the situation. Granted, these were the same homegrown boys who, along with every other male in the South at that time, owned a pick-up truck with a shotgun openly displayed in a gun rack in the back window, just in case a deer happened to wander past the stoplight where they were waiting for the light to change.

I had not owned a gun for over two decades.

Because for the past twenty years I had my children in the house.

And I knew what could happen.

* * *

The first person I ever saw die was a ten-year-old kid who was accidentally shot in the chest with a 12-gauge shotgun by his older brother.

I remember riding to the boys' house in the middle of the afternoon with two veteran detectives back when I was a police beat reporter for the local newspaper. Guys I graduated from college with were starting their new jobs and learning how to work the copy machine and navigate office politics; my first week on the job I was looking at a dead body.

You never really know what direction your job, or your life, is going to take when you start out with a blank canvas just like every other snot-nosed kid at the playground. There is no question that the mayhem and violence and heartbreak and human insensitivity and incompetence that I saw and wrote about as a newspaper reporter for almost ten years has influenced every minute of my life since then. It's why I think about life and death, and now suicide, while my fellow rugrats from the playground are now thinking about 401Ks and Viagra. If I had been a florist or an accountant, instead of a crime reporter, I would not wake up every day expecting something horrible to happen and then thank God at the end of the day when it doesn't. And I wouldn't go through life thinking that, for the most part, people fucking suck.

The boy's house was one of those cookie cutter ranch homes with a brick exterior, an open carport and a tiny front yard. When we arrived, the older brother was still sitting in the living room in shock. Across from him was a couch, covered in blood, the blood sprinkled

gun.

with the white stuffing from the cushions where the buckshot had blown through his brother's chest and shredded the couch.

The TV was on and *Gilligan's Island* was playing.

On the coffee table there were two cans of soda and an open bag of potato chips. A lazy after-school snack and some TV watching had just ended because one brother was playing with his father's shotgun, unaware that a shell was in the chamber, and pointing it in the wrong direction. Accident or not, the detectives needed to confirm the chain of events and I rode with them, lights and siren blazing, to the emergency room to get a statement from the wounded brother. There were nods from the nurses and doctors who had seen the two detectives many times before as we walked quickly through the emergency room waiting area and straight into the trauma room.

Where there were no doctors or nurses.

Which seemed a bit odd.

I could see the younger brother flat on his back on the operating table. I could see the blood pumping out of his chest, straight up into the air, just like those little flat water fountains that kids drink out of at the park.

No one else was in the room except the two detectives and I.

Then another door opened and a male nurse's aide walked in, stood next to the table, reached over the young boy, grabbed a sheet that was hanging almost to the floor on the other side and pulled the sheet up and over the boy's body. Then he grabbed a sheet on his side of the table and pulled it over the boy's body in the other direction, and he continued the process until a dozen sheets covered the boy like a mummy, and I can remember vividly how the deep crimson blood would soak through each of the bright white sheets as they were folded over, and as more sheets covered the boy, the red stain of blood would get smaller and smaller until at the end, the final sheet was pure white.

I touched the arm of one of the detectives and looked at him and I did not have to say a word, the question I wanted to ask so apparent on my face, and the detective just looked at me and shook his head, and we walked out of the trauma room and through the emergency room lobby and back out into the bright sunshine of that day, and I sat in the back of the detectives' car as we returned to the police station where they would take the older brother's statement, and I leaned my head against the window and I felt the coolness of the glass on my cheek, and the two detectives never said a word the whole drive back, and even now I thank them for that.

* * *

And so, after I was married and had children, I never owned a gun.
Until today.

* * *

Growing up, guns always fascinated me, so perhaps it was preordained that I would become a newspaper crime reporter where guns, at least the illegal use of them, became such a prominent part of my life for so many years. The friends I had, once we were adults, could go months or even years where the word gun never rolled off their tongues. For me, it was part of my daily vernacular. At parties they would tell us what they thought were interesting work-related stories where the piece of equipment involved was a calculator or a postage machine, and I would follow up with a work-related story where the piece of equipment involved was a tool made simply for killing people.

Like the story about the two black guys, with guns, who were robbing convenience stores.

In the white part of town.

A big no-no.

Most of the blacks who lived in our Southern city in the 1970s lived in The Bottoms, a flatland area along the banks of a huge river that cut through the middle of the city. As long as the black residents kept their robbing, raping and killing extracurricular activities confined to The Bottoms, the mostly-white police force and completely-white city fathers did not get too alarmed. Those black-on-black crimes were investigated and arrests were made, but they were rarely mentioned in the newspaper. The Bottoms was another world that the white residents of the city knew existed, but knew nothing about, by choice.

Until two young bucks from The Bottoms realized that the cash registers at convenience stores in the nearby affluent white

6

communities held more money than the cash registers at the stores in The Bottoms. You have to give them credit for having initiative and thinking big.

I was still in high school when this was happening and it wasn't until I was a reporter about eight years later that I heard the story, told to me by a detective who had been a patrolman at that time, and who made me promise not to ever write an article about it.

There had been three robberies by the Bad Black Boys over a two-week period. None of those robberies had been mentioned in the newspaper because it just wouldn't do to get the white folk all riled up.

The police chief assigned teams of detectives to stake out a half dozen convenience stores that they thought were the next most likely targets for the robbers. He put two detectives armed with shotguns into the walk-in coolers at each of the six stores.

And they waited.

Nothing happened for three days.

On the fourth day at midnight, the Bad Black Boys strolled into one of the stores, pulled out handguns and politely ordered the cashier to open the register. Well, actually, what they said was, *"Open the register, bitch, or we'll blow your fucking head off."*

At which point two detectives stepped out of the cooler and shot both robbers dead.

And as the two robbers lay on the floor, their lifeless bodies riddled with buckshot from multiple blasts from the two shotguns, one of the detectives shouted, *"Stop police."*

When the detective finished telling me the story, I asked him if he had gotten the order of events wrong and if instead he had meant to say that the detectives had shouted *"Stop police"* and then opened fire.

He laughed and said, *"No, I told it to you right."*

Then he smiled and said, *"Wasn't that cool?"*

I realized then that when those twelve detectives had bundled up in heavy coats and hats and gloves to sit in those freezing coolers for hours on end with their shotguns in their laps, they knew exactly what their mission was. They weren't there to make an arrest.

And I had no problem with that.

You roll the dice, you pay the price.

Central to that story are the guns. The handguns the robbers used to break the law and the shotguns the cops used to enforce the law in true frontier justice fashion. Guns were the common denominator that took walking into a convenience store to a whole new level for all the parties involved.

The part of the story that has always stood out for me is the part where the one detective shouted, *"Stop police,"* after they blew away the bad guys.

I hate to admit it, but that was pretty cool. And not because they were black. I didn't care whether they were red, white or polka-dotted. They were bullies with guns terrorizing helpless store clerks. Fuck 'em.

The killing of the Bad Black Boys was never mentioned in the newspaper.

The people who needed to get the message had got the message.

From the end of a gun.

* * *

Let's talk about my new gun.

What a marvelous piece of death and destruction, all for a mere $550. And people say you can't get value for your dollar in today's economy.

As noted, it is a Smith & Wesson .357 Magnum revolver. The .357 refers to the caliber of the bullet that the gun shoots. The gun is bigger than a .38, which is usually also a revolver, and smaller than a .45, which is always an automatic. For the uninitiated, a revolver is a gun with a cylinder that rotates each time you pull the trigger, and an automatic is a gun with a clip where the bullets are spring loaded and are automatically chambered each time you pull the trigger. Or, for all you couch potatoes, a .38 revolver is what Joe Friday used in *Dragnet*, and a .45 automatic is what Neo used in the *Matrix*.

My new gun is a six-shot S&W Model 686 which comes standard with a six-inch barrel, although mine has the two-and-a half-inch barrel. It's still a heavy gun, weighing in at thirty-five ounces. That's more than two pounds of stainless steel, with an overall length of more than seven inches. It has rubber grips, a target hammer and a smooth combat trigger.

gun.

Smith & Wesson, the largest manufacturer of handguns in the United States, was formed in 1855 by two buddies named Horace Smith and Daniel B. Wesson. Their .357 Magnum gun and its unique high-powered bullets were developed in the mid 1930s when cops realized they needed more firepower than that offered by the smaller caliber .38 revolvers. So Smith & Wesson took a .38 special bullet and increased the size of the cartridge and amount of gunpowder in the shell, but, more importantly they replaced the black gunpowder that was in the .38 bullets with smokeless gunpowder, which has more than twice the velocity of black gunpowder.

People who have been shot with a .357 Magnum, at least those who have lived to talk about it, report that it is like being struck by lightning. Doctors attribute this to hydrostatic shock where a penetrating projectile with the power of a .357 Magnum bullet produces *remote wounding and incapacitating effects in living targets, in addition to local effects in tissue caused by direct impact, through a hydraulic effect in liquid filled tissues, and neural damage.* In other words, even if you are just winged by a round from a .357 Magnum, it will mess up your body to the point where each and every single organ in your body will be asking all the other organs, *Yo dude, what the fuck just happened?*

If that isn't enough carnage for your taste, you can increase the ugliness of the situation by using a special kind of bullet called a hollow point, which is designed to expand upon entering its target. The tip of the bullet has a pit, or hollowed out shape, so that when the bullet strikes a soft target, think your favorite dictator's belly, the pressure created in the pit forces the lead around it to expand into a mushroom-shape. This causes considerably more soft-tissue damage and energy transfer than if the nose was not hollow.

Hollow point bullets are also referred to as dum-dums, and if instead of a pit there are two slits in the top of the bullet, they are then called cross points. In addition to expanding so that the entry hole in your target is the size of a dime and the exit wound is the size of a softball, hollow point bullets also have the tendency to break up when they hit their target. Instead of one hot piece of searing lead tearing through a target, you now have dozens of small pieces of lead wreaking havoc on that dictator's insides.

While most police officers, and a large number of private gun owners, load their weapons with hollow point bullets, a group of countries signed international treaties in 1889 and 1907 at the Hague Convention prohibiting the use of expanding or fragmenting bullets in warfare, because they felt that the additional trauma caused by those types of bullets was *unnecessary* and *inhumane*. They wanted to make sure that any future wars we got ourselves into would be both *necessary* and *humane*. I shit you not.

Gun enthusiasts say that the most effective handgun bullet on the market is the Federal .357 Magnum 125 grain jacketed hollow point 357B which has more stopping power than any other handgun bullet.

Who am I to argue.

* * *

"Cover me," is what the detective sergeant said to me as he placed his .357 Magnum pistol into my hand and then, gripping a 12-gauge pump action shotgun, sprinted across the backyard to the fire escape ladder that led to the second story of the tenement building.

That's all he said. Just those two words. *"Cover me."*

Let me put this into perspective.

I was holding a huge fucking gun. And I was not a cop.

The sergeant was sprinting to the fire escape because it went up to the back porch of a second floor apartment, and in that apartment, the one where two other detectives were now banging on the front door and screaming, *"Police, open the fuck up,"* were two notorious bad-ass bank robbers. Considering that the two suspects enjoyed pistol-whipping tellers as much as they enjoyed emptying their cash drawers, and considering that both suspects were armed to the teeth, and considering that the consensus was that both suspects were probably high on smack, it made perfect sense for the sergeant, vulnerable on those narrow fire escape steps, to have someone watching his back.

So he chose me.

But, not to belabor the point, I was not a cop.

I was a twenty-year-old newspaper reporter. I was used to having a pen in my hand to do my job, not a giant handgun. I didn't even know if the gun I was holding had a safety switch and, if it did, whether it was on or off, and, if it was off, how to turn it on.

What I did know was this.

gun.

There was a very good chance that I was about to be shot and killed.

And not by any pistol-whipping, smacked-out armed robbers.

When the call had come in to the detective offices that the robbery suspects had been located, the two detectives now banging on the front door had jumped into their own unmarked car, and the sergeant, who was the night shift supervisor, had asked me if I wanted to ride in his squad car to watch the arrest.

I said yes. Of course.

On the way to the apartment building, the sergeant radioed and requested that four additional uniformed patrolmen meet the detectives at the scene for back-up.

And that was the problem area.

Because those four patrolmen had no idea who the fuck I was.

Which meant that if any of those patrolmen ran around to the back of the apartment building, what they would see on that dark midnight evening would be a tall, young man—who they didn't know —with a white man's bushy afro standing there in plain clothes and pointing a .357 Magnum at the back of a detective sergeant—who they did know—and they would naturally assume that I was about to shoot the unsuspecting detective and drop me on the spot.

There would be no verbal warning. Forget that shit. This wasn't some made-for-TV movie of the week. I was pointing a gun at a detective at midnight in the backyard of an apartment building in the projects.

I would be a dead man, pure and simple.

On the other hand.

I could lay the gun on the ground and hold my reporter's notebook and pen up nice and high so any patrolmen who did round that corner would see that I was not a threat, but what if the back door flew open and two pistol-whipping, smacked-out armed robbers came running out, blew away the sergeant as they rushed down the fire escape, and then saw me standing there with a .357 Magnum laying at my feet?

I would a dead man yet again, pure and simple.

Talk about a rock and a hard place.

They didn't cover this shit in Journalism 101.

As I was trying to decide which headline for the next day's newspaper sounded better, *"Armed reporter accidentally shot by*

gun.

police officer" or *"Hero reporter shot and killed by pistol-whipping, smacked-out bad guys while trying to save detective,"* I heard the front door being kicked in, followed by loud shouts and yelling, and then one of the two front-door detectives walked out onto the back porch and signalled with a thumbs up to the sergeant that the suspects had been arrested.

The sergeant climbed back down the fire escape and put his hand out to me for his gun.

"Oh my God, don't ever fucking do that again," I said, handing him the weapon.

"Why?" he asked, a mischievous grin on his face.

"What if one of the patrolmen had come back here?"

"So."

"They don't know me."

"And?"

"I'm pointing a gun at you"

"Oh. Good point."

He was still grinning.

"That could have been awkward," he said.

"You think?"

"And a little nasty too. For you, at least."

"It's not funny."

It must have been. Because he laughed then, and he kept on laughing in his cruiser all the way back to the detective offices.

* * *

Guns don't kill people. People kill people.

Well, let's be honest, having a gun makes it a lot easier.

Certainly a jealous husband or a redneck who I cut off in traffic can kill me with a knife or a baseball bat or a garrote, but in those instances I have a chance to get away because the wronged party has to get right up next to me to accomplish his task and I have to sit there patiently while he stabs away with the knife, or flails away with the bat, or tries to slip a cord around my neck. With a gun, though, he can shoot me from fifty feet away as I climb out the bedroom window or try to speed away in my car.

Everyone agrees that guns are rather impressive instruments of death. You don't use them to flip a burger on the grill or to hammer

12

gun.

in a nail. So, pretty much their entire purpose is to kill living things. And since a very minute percentage of gun owners use guns to hunt wild animals for the Sunday dinner table, I think most people would agree that guns are primarily used to, well, kill other people.

When our founding fathers said that every Tom, Dick and Harry had the right to bear arms, I think they had something completely different in mind than what we have today.

What they had in mind were those muskets where you had to pull from your pocket a cartridge, which was a spherical lead bullet wrapped in paper that also held some gunpowder; then tear off the end of the paper and pour some of the gunpowder into the priming pan behind the half-cocked hammer; then pour the rest of the gunpowder and the lead bullet and the paper cartridge case down the barrel of the musket; then draw the ramrod from the musket and use it to ram the wadding, bullet and gunpowder down the barrel; then return the ramrod to the hoops under the musket barrel; then cock the hammer all the way back; then take aim; and then shoot to kill. A friend of mine made this point at dinner one night where everybody was served and finished eating their dinner salads in the amount of time it took him to pantomime the whole, lengthy process of loading and then shooting a single shot from a musket.

"See my point," he said.

What we have today are automatic pistols that can shoot eighteen bullets and kill eighteen slow-moving school kids caught in the crossfire of a gangbanger drive-by shooting in less time than it took for one colonist to load his musket and take a shot at, and probably miss, one British Redcoat. I still recall the Luby Cafeteria mass killing in 1991 when George Hennard drove his pickup truck through the front window of a Luby's in Killeen, Texas and proceeded to shoot twenty-three people to death and wound another twenty with a Glock 17 semiautomatic pistol, which can hold seventeen to thirty-three rounds, and a Ruger P89 semiautomatic pistol, which holds fifteen rounds, before turning one of the guns on himself. My guess is if he had been using a Brown Bess 1771 musket he would have been able to cap only one senior there for the early bird special before the rest of the seniors would have beaten him to death with their canes and oxygen tanks while he was trying to load a second cartridge into the musket.

gun.

So, in hindsight, our founding fathers needed to be a little more specific about what they meant by the word *arms*.

Technically, a F117 Stealth Fighter Jet and a M1A1 Abrams Tank are arms, but we don't let Uncle Fred fly or drive either of them to his son's Little League game. We have no problem, though, letting Uncle Fred put a Taurus Judge pistol, which can fire both .45 Long Colt bullets and .410 shotgun shells at the same time, into his car trunk next to Junior's baseball glove and cleats when they head to the next ballgame. Because you never know when the umpire might make a bad call.

There are only two things in this world that can kill you instantly —a car wreck or a bullet from a gun. Granted, you can be in a plane crash, or get struck by lightning, or be eaten by an alligator, but those occurrences are few and far between. And you can die from a drug overdose, but that is a death that is the end result of an earlier action that you took. And heart attacks usually occur after you've knowingly not taken care of your body for a substantial period of time. So for unplanned, how-the-fuck-did-that-happen, instantaneous violent death, you're looking at a car or a gun. Worldwide, over a million people are killed in auto accidents and over a half million are killed by firearms every year. So in the time that it took you to read this short paragraph two people were killed in a car wreck and one person was shot to death somewhere on this planet.

Owning a gun is like owning a Siberian tiger. Both have the capacity to kill your next door neighbor, so perhaps you should be a little more careful about how you play with them and where you leave them laying around. I think it's a privilege and not a right to own a gun. So I wholeheartedly support gun laws. In fact, I don't think anybody should be allowed to own a gun.

Except for me.

* * *

Buying the gun today was an impulse decision, although the thought of ending my life by my own hand is something I have been seriously considering for the past year. If a friend had not invited me to the gun show, I would not now be in possession of such a fine instrument of death. Perhaps there were some unknown forces at work that put me in a position to find and buy the gun and propel what was once just a stream of hazy thoughts—*Should I?*—into a definite plan of action—*Yes I will!*

So buying the gun has forced my hand.

What seems strange to me is that over the past year, the only time I thought about killing myself was when I was in bed, just before I fell asleep. It never crossed my mind during the day, or when I was drinking, or when I was driving to the store, or when I was stressed at work. I only thought about it, and still now only think about it, after I have slipped under the covers. Perhaps because that's my quietest time of the day.

So, the questions to now be addressed as I lay awake in bed each night under those toasty covers before the onset of sleep are the new questions of when and where, and even how. Because it's not quite as simple as it sounds. There are many details to be worked out. It's not unlike planning ahead for a big trip out of the country. Or out of this world.

So, where do I do it? At home or somewhere else?

When do I do it? In the morning after a hearty breakfast, or at night after watching a great movie?

What do I wear? Do I shave that day or not? Do I leave a suicide note, and if so, what does it say? Do I have a will, and is it up to date? What does my life insurance policy pay out, if anything, in the event of a suicide? Do I get rid of my hidden porn collection? Do I give my Mom a call to tell her I love her? What about my wife and my two children?

And, despite buying the gun, there is still possibly the question of how. Is a shot to the head truly the best way to go? What about jumping off a bridge, slitting my wrists in a bathtub of warm water, taking an overdose of pills, stepping in front of a speeding train, hanging myself in the attic?

There are so many options, and I am sure that each of them comes with its own set of pros and cons.

I need to get busy.

Today is Sunday, June 21. My birthday is on June 30. I decide that will be the Magic Day. Which means I have nine more days to *pull* the pieces together.

Before *pulling* the trigger.

Cute.

gun.

Say what you will about police officers, and I agree there are a fair share of them who are Satan incarnate, but the vast majority of them are good men and women who are honestly interested in helping society. They see a side of humanity, or inhumanity, that regular citizens will never see or even comprehend, and they have some strange, twisted desire to right the wrongs. In many ways they are the garbagemen of our society. I say that not to demean what they do, but instead to point out that every day they have to get their hands dirty handling human trash, just like the guys do who pick up our household trash every week.

What all cops have in common, both the good cops and the so-so cops, is that they really, truly dislike bad guys. It's a game to them. They are the Good Guy Team playing the Bad Guy Team. Many times we, the general public, don't even realize the game is being played, or that when it is, often neither side is playing by the rules.

My second month as a police beat reporter I wrote about some Dickhead who couldn't be happy staying home at night watching *The Carol Burnett Show* like everybody else in the city was doing. By the way, that was a fucking funny show. The first time I ever got stoned on dirtweed pot was when I was fourteen years old and I came home and sat on the couch with the rest of my family to watch that show and I laughed and laughed and laughed at the craziness of Carol and Tim Conway and Harvey Korman. Unfortunately, I laughed just as hard during the commercials, which brought a raised eyebrow from my Dad and a little father-son chat in my bedroom after the show. But even Dad waited until after the show before reaming me out. That's how funny that show was.

Back to Dickhead.

He would dress all in black, slip on a dark ski mask, arm himself with rope, a flashlight and a handgun, and then drive to the largest public park in our city just after midnight. Slipping into the park's main parking lot with his car lights off, he would wait in the back until there was only one car left in the park with a couple inside making out. He would creep on foot up to that lone car, jerk the car door open, pistol whip the man, tie him up, rape the man's date, and then steal their wallet and purse. He was a busy little fucker, what with committing battery, rape and robbery all in one night's work. He had done this twice already over a three-week period.

Our crusty, take-no-prisoners police chief, the same one who took care of the black armed robbers who were venturing out of the hood to hit white convenience stores, was not happy. Twice was two times too many.

There would not be a third time.

This was long before police departments had SWAT teams or trained snipers. The chief sent word through the ranks that he wanted to know which of his officers were avid deer hunters, which ones owned their own .30-06 Remington hunting rifle with a high-powered scope, and, of those officers, which one was the best shot. Of the 200 police officers in his department, about 199 of them fit the bill, but he narrowed it down to one officer and said to him, *"Son, how would you like to spend some time in the park?"*

You probably already know how this story is going to end.

The department had several married couples where the husband and wife were both cops, so the chief chose the youngest of the couples, had them put on street clothes, and then drive their personal car to the park just before midnight. *"When you get there, start snuggling,"* said the chief. He positioned a half dozen detectives around the perimeter of the park who could communicate by walkie-talkie radio with the decoy couple.

The couple was armed, but trying to fire on an assailant from inside the tight confines of a car would be risky, which meant that, for the most part, they were just sitting ducks. So the police chief took his deer-hunting police officer and placed both he and his rifle on top of a hill that overlooked the park.

And they all waited.

They didn't have to wait long.

On the second night of the stakeout, a car with its headlights off slipped into the back parking lot of the park. There was no movement from the car for twenty minutes. Then the car door quietly opened, and a dark figure slipped out and walked quickly toward the driver's side of the decoy car.

And when the man in black was thirty feet from the decoy car, the deer-hunting police officer proved that he was indeed the best shot in the department. From more than one hundred yards away, he fired one shot from his .30-06 Remington hunting rifle and blew the man in black's head clean off.

Dickhead never knew what hit him.

They found a handgun under his body and nylon rope in his back pocket. And probably a pre-rape erection that was rapidly shrinking.

What I love about that story is the black and white of it.

There was a problem.

And to solve that problem, our city didn't need defense attorneys and prosecutors, or a fat lazy judge, or hardworking people having to take time off to sit on a jury, or news stories about how Dickhead was only like that because he wasn't potty-trained properly and his mother didn't love him, or hundreds of thousands of taxpayer dollars to pay for a trial and multiple court appeals and prison incarceration.

One .30-06 bullet took care of the problem.

In a single night, while most of the city was sleeping.

A gun can be a great problem solver.

Depending on who's holding it.

* * *

I really like to read books.

I like gangster movies and sports betting and punk rock and scotch on the rocks and fast cars and powdery drugs and big boobs and lemon meringue pie, but what I like the most, the very most, is reading books.

It started with Dr. Seuss, went to the Hardy Boys, on to Jack London and Louis L'Amour, on to the classics from *Grapes of Wrath* to *The Old Man and the Sea*, on to unappreciated gems like *Flowers for Algernon* and *A Canticle for Leibowitz*, on to guilty pleasures from the likes of Elmore Leonard and James Ellroy, and then on to true crime books and autobiographies, and it has just never stopped. My guess is I have read at least one book a week for the past forty years. Except for *War and Peace*. I mean, really, who has a year of their life to spare.

For the record, *The Catcher in the Rye* is the greatest novel ever written and I don't even want to fucking argue with anyone about that. And if every person on this planet was made to read *The*

gun.

Sneetches by Dr. Seuss, who for my money was as much of a prophet as Ghandi or Martin Luther King or that Jesus Christ dude, there would be no more discrimination or hate crimes or wars on this planet.

But I digress.

When I was first married, my wife and I moved into a tiny rent house where I built a bookshelf out of cinder blocks and planks of wood, and I filled the bookcase with the books I had accumulated over the years. I continually added to the bookcase with books I bought at garage sales, books that family and friends passed on to me, and the occasional book that I would buy brand new when I had the money.

Over the years, as my wife and I went from rent houses to houses that we owned, and as the houses got bigger and nicer, so did the size and quality and number of the bookshelves, and every single book I had ever owned made it into whatever the newest bookcases were, because I never threw any of the books away. When I finished reading a book, I would put it back into the bookshelves. I would stand in front of those bookshelves and look at all the books, both the ones I had read and the ones I had not read yet, and think about how they would be there for me to enjoy again and again in the years to come. They were my personal treasure chest full of escapes and adventures and journeys that I could look forward to enjoying as I slipped into old age.

But when I turned fifty, I stopped doing that.

After that, when I finished a book, I would bring it to the office and give it to a young guy who works for me who also likes to read. I even went through my bookcases and pulled out all the books I had already read and gave them away.

I had come to the sad realization that I was a half century old and I was no longer walking up the hill. I was now walking down the hill. I didn't need those books any more. I didn't have enough time left to re-read them.

Walking up the hill, I had been living for the future.

Walking down the hill, I was living the future.

I used to only buy paperback books. When a great new hardback book came out and I finally had enough money to buy whatever I wanted, I would still wait for the paperback version, because it just didn't seem right to pay three times as much for the exact same book.

That was then. Now I buy the hardback book. I don't have time to wait for the paperback. Who knows what could happen between now and then. For me, words like *later* and *tomorrow* no longer have any significance.

And this has nothing to do with suicide. I started giving books away three years ago, long before the suicide serpent raised its head.

Now when I look inside the study that has my beautiful polished wood bookcases, I see more and more gaps on the shelves where books used to be, and those gaps are slowly being filled by my wife with framed photos and other knickknacks.

I know that one day those bookshelves will be completely empty of books.

Being here for that day doesn't interest me.

*   *   *

Because I was a young whippersnapper of a reporter, and I had an honest interest in police work, and I could hold a conversation, the detectives kind of adopted me as their mascot and I spent many hours each night hanging out in their offices. As a journalist I was supposed to distance myself from the people I wrote about so that I could be impartial and tell it like it is. But you attract more flies with honey than with vinegar, and I tended to scoop reporters at the competing daily newspaper because I had an in with the detectives.

I worked the three pm to midnight shift at the newspaper which were the same hours that the evening shift detectives worked. Most of them were in their mid to late twenties, and they wore plainclothes and investigated rapes and murders and robberies because they had showed potential and initiative when they were patrolmen and had been promoted to investigations. The evening crew was comprised of eight detectives and one shift supervising sergeant. The evening shift detectives would sleep until noon, get up and have lunch and then watch reruns of *The Three Stooges* on TV before going to the police station. They loved that show. They were like frat boys in the detective office, albeit frat boys with huge guns.

The young detectives would walk around their offices doing Curly's *"nyuck, nyuck, nyuck"* voice, running their hands down their faces and then pretending to bop each other on top of the head or doing the two-finger eye-poking thing. Two detectives would get into a pretend argument until one detective would pull out his gun and point it at the other detective and say in his best Moe voice, *"Why, I oughta ..."*

Eventually the chief of detectives banned any more Three Stooges impersonations in the detective offices. It wasn't because he didn't have a sense of humor. It was because one night when a detective pulled his gun out and did the *"Why, I oughta ..."* thing, his 9mm Browning automatic went off right in the offices, blasting a round just an inch past the hip of a fellow detective and through the wall of the main reception area. Everyone breathed a sigh of relief when they realized the detective had not been hit. But then, being the perceptive investigators that they were, they looked at the bullet hole in the reception wall and realized that behind that wall was a row of six small office cubicles, and they looked at each other, mentally ticking off who was there and who wasn't, until one detective said, *"Where's Robert?"*

Like a scene straight out of *The Three Stooges*, they all scrambled to the first office, poked their heads inside, saw that it was empty, and also saw that there was a bullet hole in the wall of the adjoining office. So they repeated the process, seeing the same bullet holes in each office wall, until they got to the fifth office, where they found Robert sitting at a desk, rubbing a red welt on the left side of his head, and saying, *"What the fuck?"*

So that ended the nyuck, nyuck, nyuck.

* * *

I do most of my thinking when I am in bed before I fall asleep. Some times I think too much and it takes me forever to go to sleep. But my decision to vacate the earth's premises is an important one and I know I need to get organized, so tonight the sleep faeries will have to wait.

I decide that when I go to the office tomorrow morning I will make a list on my computer of all the questions that need to be answered and all the things that need to be done, and I will assign each of those items to one of the nine remaining days that are left in my ten-day plan. I think about what to call the text document that I will be typing the need-to-do daily items into because *Things To Do To Kill Myself Easily and Painlessly* is not very subtle, and not a title I want anyone at my office to see on my computer screen. They might jump to conclusions.

I decide to just call the document the *Taking Care of Business List*, or the *TCB List* for short. Seems appropriate to me. I realize that this whole thing is going to take a lot of research and some serious planning.

Which is fine.

Because I love a project.

* * *

The detective offices where I spent most of my time did have black patrolmen, even black detectives. They also had a few female officers, but no female detectives. Don't be ridiculous. We're talking the Deep South.

On the evening shift there were two black detectives who were moderately friendly with the other white detectives but never engaged in their fraternity antics. They spent most of their time hanging out with each other. One was older, in his forties, and built like a middle linebacker. He had a huge scar on top of his bald head, courtesy of a minor race riot he waded into as a patrolman, and though he was always smiling and laughing, he was one tough motherfucker and so had the respect of all the officers, black and white.

"I'll snatch a grown man clean out of his shoes" he said to me once, smiling the whole time. Not sure how or why that subject came up, but I certainly believed him.

The other black detective was younger, in his mid twenties, and rail thin. He couldn't have weighed more than a 140 pounds. He was a Vietnam vet and he never smiled. It took over a year for him to warm up to me, which meant that after a year he would occasionally say hello. I once wrote in a newspaper article that he had the look and the personality of a sharp knife.

As expected, the two black detectives mainly investigated crimes in the city's black community. I would ride with them every

gun.

now and then on calls into a strange world of open beers in brown paper bags, alleyway dice games, and big assed hookers in tight stretch pants. On one call we arrived at a dive bar to find that patrolmen already had five black guys handcuffed and leaning against the outside wall of the bar. The suspects were actually standing a good three feet away from the wall with their hands cuffed behind their backs. The patrolmen had bent all of the suspects over at the waist and then leaned them forward until just the sides of their faces were pressed hard against the rough concrete wall.

"That's a rather unusual position," I said to the older black detective.

"That's how we roll down here."

"Why?"

"Because if any one of those assholes gets lippy, then you just kick their feet out from under them and their face slides all the way down the wall. Quiets them down real quick."

"Oh."

He explained it as casually and as matter-of-factly as your local butcher would advise you on the best way to cook a rump roast.

The black cops had to be tough as nails in this Southern city. They caught it from both ends. Many of the department's white officers were either full blown racists or still had remnants of generations of Deep South prejudice flowing through their veins. Shared blue blood not withstanding, the black officers would still be called nigger behind their backs by some of the white officers. On the other side, many of the black citizens that they swore to serve and protect despised them for working for The Man. Shared black blood not withstanding, some black citizens would call them the White Man's nigger behind their backs. Jackie Robinson may have received all the accolades for breaking the color barrier in Major League Baseball in 1947, but try breaking barriers by being a black cop in a Southern town in the second half of the 20th Century without the support of the world media. *"It ain't easy, brother,"* the older black detective said to me one time when I asked him about it.

At the bar, as the older detective questioned the men leaning with their faces against the wall, the younger detective talked to a middle-aged black man sitting in the front seat of his car in the parking lot. I was standing on the passenger side of the car, and through the open window I could see the butt of a gun sticking out from under a newspaper on the passenger seat. I tried to get the attention of the detective on the other side of the car to warn him. He knew I was motioning to him, but he just ignored me.

The man in the car answered the detective's questions, then started his car, backed up and drove off.

I started to open my mouth and the young detective said, *"I know. The gun."*

"But ..."

"We know him. He owns a store. He carries the gun for protection. He's no problem."

"Oh."

The thin detective smiled. First time ever that I saw.

"What do you think I am," he said, *"a fucking rookie?"*

* * *

I think about those cops and guns stories from my past as I lay in my bed looking at the blue plastic gun case on my dresser. What appeals to me about the stories is how police officers remedied situations in a timely manner without procrastinating or having to jump through a million hoops by seeking city council approval or doing a public opinion poll.

And they usually resolved the problems with a gun.

I see the parallels to my own current situation.

I can handle this on my own. I don't need to ask anyone for permission and I don't need to survey family and friends. I have a gun. And I can buy a bullet.

It is at that moment in my thought process that I hear three words.

"Don't do it."

I freeze under the covers.

I don't move an inch.

I slow my breathing.

A voice just said those three words. Somebody just spoke in my bedroom only a few feet away from me. And there is no one in the room but me. I say out loud a single word in tentative question form.

"What?"

There is dead silence for at least ten seconds, and then.

gun.

"I said, don't do it."

Fuck me running, who is talking to me?

Even as I ask myself that question, I know that the words I am hearing, I am not really hearing with my ears, as in sounds made that ripple through the air, but that instead I am hearing the words in my head. But I also know that I am not saying them. Someone is saying them to me.

"Come again," I say.

"I said don't do it. What are you, fucking hard of hearing?"

I sit up in bed and look around the room. As I thought, all alone. Except for Boudreaux.

Boudreaux is my three-year-old Miniature Pinscher. At night he sleeps in his dog cage under the TV stand in the corner of the bedroom, the front of his cage facing the end of my bed. I get out of bed and lay down on the floor and look through the narrow metal bars on the door of his cage. His head is laying on his two front paws. His eyes are open. He is looking right at me.

"Are you talking to me?" I ask, feeling very, very foolish.

"Yes."

Oh shit.

"Why?"

"Why not?"

"You're a dog."

"So."

"You can't talk."

"Says who?"

"Why now?"

"I didn't have anything to say before."

"And now?"

"You're thinking about killing yourself."

"And?"

"I'm not a big fan of that idea."

"Why not?"

"I'll tell you tomorrow. I'm going to sleep now."

And then Boudreaux closes his eyes.

I lay there on the floor staring at him as the seconds tick by, until he opens just one eye and says.

"You're freaking me the fuck out. Go back to bed."

Which I do.

Monday, June 22

dad.

When I wake up the next morning, Boudreaux, or Boo as I call him, is sleeping in my bed. His body is under the covers in the spot where my wife usually sleeps and his head is laying on the pillow. He is on his side so his face is looking right at me. His eyes are open. It's a very strange sight, and was quite startling the first few times it happened, but now it happens almost every morning and I am used to it.

Boo, as I mentioned, is a Miniature Pinscher, which means he looks exactly like a full-grown Doberman Pinscher but is actually the size of a stuffed animal. He weighs a mere ten pounds and stands about twelve inches at the shoulder. Contrary to popular belief, Min-Pins, as they are called, are not from the Doberman Pinscher family but instead are actually from the Chihuahua breed of dogs. But don't tell Boo that; in his mind he is a huge strapping canine, not a tiny toy dog. He is chocolate in color and wears a red and black custom-made leather dog collar with sterling silver conchas on it. I wear a bracelet made out of the same materials.

I tell everyone Boo is my second son.

He's the best dog I've ever had.

dad.

Every morning while I am still sleeping my wife lets Boo out of his cage and walks him outside where he takes care of his business in our large front yard. Then, like a shot, he beelines it inside and jumps into my bed, no mean feat, considering that the top of the bed is three feet above the ground which means he has to jump three times his height to get into the bed. He burrows under the covers and sleeps until I wake up.

I look at Boo. He looks at me.

"Okay," I say, *"say something."*

Boo looks at me unblinking.

"Come on. You were talking to me last night. Say something."

Boo yawns.

I feel like an idiot. I am an idiot.

I get up and get ready for work.

Which basically means a two-minute shower and a quick shave, no breakfast and then into the car with Boo, who goes to work with me every day and rules the office from his perch on the couch in the open office foyer. He ignores me all day, terrorizes any visitors to the office and enjoys his frequent walks outside by one of the girls in the office. At about six pm he will saunter over to my office, plop down in the doorway and stare at me with that it's-time-to-go-home-motherfucker look until I finally get up, grab my car keys and head for the door. Then it's back in the car for the drive home. Boo has his own custom, padded dog seat on the passenger seat of the car. Usually he just sleeps until we get home.

Every now and then I let him drive.

* * *

I am still mad at my Dad.

For dying.

It's been more than thirty years and I'm still mad.

When he died I wasn't mad at God. Because I don't believe in God, which is really a whole other story that involves a yellow bathroom, a cracked toilet seat and an Archie comic book. It might be an interesting story to tell one day in the unlikely event there is someone out there curious about why I don't believe in the existence of a supreme being. But for now, for the sake of this story, let's just

dad.

say that God, either the real one or the non-existent one, is off the hook on the subject of my Dad.

I wasn't mad about my Dad dying; I was mad at my Dad for dying.

There's a big difference.

* * *

My Dad died when he was forty-eight years old. He had a heart attack while playing racquetball. I know, sounds ridiculous doesn't it? Playing fucking racquetball. Hitting a little black ball with a shortened tennis racket inside a closed-in room. Racquetball. That's what killed my Dad.

My Dad was an Air Force pilot. In the Vietnam War he flew more than a hundred secret missions, code named Phyllis Ann, over the Ho Chi Minh Trail, and earned the Distinguished Flying Cross after taking artillery fire on one flight and bringing his crew and the plane home safely. The planes he flew were C-47s, affectionately known as Gooney Birds because, though they looked goofy like an albatross, they could take a lickin' and keep on tickin'. Later, they were rechristened as Puff the Magic Dragon because of the three huge Gatling guns they carried that could shred dense jungle foliage and enemy soldiers with equal aplomb. He flew KC-135 Stratotanker planes that were half the size of a football field, held tens of thousands of gallons of jet fuel, and re-fueled fighter jets while they were both in the air traveling at about a million miles an hour. Every few months he would go live in a bunker on the runway at the Air Force base for a week with his flight crew where they would be "on alert" with other tanker and bomber crews, waiting for the President to call and say, *"Alright boys, fire the engines up and go over and drop a few hundred nukes on those commie bastards."*

He lived through all that.

And on March 2, 1980 he died playing fucking racquetball.

It's not even a popular sport.

The only thing worse than telling someone your Dad died playing racquetball is to have them ask, *"What's racquetball?"*

A friend of mine's father was gored to death by a bull. So I don't feel so bad. Well, I feel bad for my friend, but it makes the whole racquetball thing a little easier to swallow. I mean how can you not

dad.

help but laugh when someone tells you their father was gored to death by a bull. Really, what are the chances?

Most people probably say, *"That's horrible. I'm so sorry."*

But what they really want to say is, *"No shit, how did that happen?"*

Adam, one of my son's friends, is a good-looking kid with an English accent. My son thinks the accent is a bit suspicious considering Adam only spent a few years as a child in England. But he puts up with it because Adam is a fun guy and a bit of a character.

Adam and my son and some buddies were getting drunk on cheap beer late one night at a college apartment party that had spilled into the front yard when, as usually happens, a car filled with other young men slowly drove by and the insults shouted between the two groups soon evolved into a rumble. Where it went wrong from there no one can say, although perhaps Adam said something with that funny English accent that didn't sit well with one of the local rowdies because that chap went back to the car, grabbed a three-foot-long machete, and buried it in the middle of Adam's forehead.

Which, of course, brought an abrupt end to the melee.

As well as a hasty trip in a blood-soaked car for Adam and his crew to the emergency room. Adam has a memento from that night in the form of a three-inch scar that goes from his eyebrows straight up to the middle of his hairline, making him a cross between James Bond and Al "Scarface" Capone.

I presume Adam has already reconciled himself to the fact that he can never run for President. Try explaining that scar at one of the debates. It must be aggravating to know that for the rest of his life, whenever he meets someone new, at some point the big question is always going to pop up, *"So Adam, I don't mean to pry, but how ..."*

My niece also has a scar. Hers is on her left cheek from a bite from a pitbull that she got when, as a toddler, she wandered into the middle of a dogfight which, I am now ashamed to admit, was occasionally the featured entertainment at backyard barbecues out in the country where I grew up in the Deep South. That's not quite as interesting as the machete story, but it's still a pretty cool story, much cooler, I think, because she's a girl. Every guy would love to have a scar with a great story attached to it.

My niece, by the way, is a pretty young woman now, and the scar is barely visible so it's not like she was disfigured, but I'm sure she is still reminded of that day every time she looks in the mirror. Or maybe not. I have two earrings in my left ear which I know for a fact are there, although whenever I look into a mirror I never notice them, so after all these years it is possible my niece no longer sees that faded scar.

Wouldn't it be nice if as easily as our minds can choose not to see things that our eyes actually see, our minds could do the same thing with the memories that cause us pain?

In the scheme of things, dying while playing a sport is not too bad, at least as compared to being gored by a bull.

Still, if I had my choice, I would have preferred a different exit for my Dad.

* * *

Do I blame my Dad for dying?

Yes.

Hate to say it, but yes.

My Dad never did anything half-assed. He always played to win. The day he died he was playing racquetball with the nineteen-year-old son of a business associate. Apparently the kid was pretty good because my Dad was playing hard. There was no way he would let a kid beat him. So instead of spending an hour getting some good exercise he pushed himself too far and his heart exploded.

Great, thanks Dad. Because you had to be a winner, you made a loser out of me, and Mom, and my little brother, and my three younger sisters.

That's one of the reasons I'm still mad at my Dad.

* * *

When we get to the office, Boo quickly trots through every cubicle to see who's already at work and who's not before grabbing his spot on the couch while I get my coffee, close the sliding glass door to my office, turn on my computer and start to work on what needs to go onto the *Taking Care of Business List*.

What I do for a living really isn't all that important. Let's just say that it still involves writing and publishing of a sort, and it makes me a nice sum of money, but it's not something that fully interests or satisfies me any more. It's a chore. A boring chore.

I own the business so at least I don't have a boss to kowtow to. I have nine employees and some of them have been with me for more than ten years which of course means that they think of this office as their second home and not necessarily a place of business. I'm too nice. I don't crack the whip enough. My friend John owns a similar type of company and reminds me all the time that these people are not my friends or relatives, they are my employees. *"Fuck them. Make them fear you. Don't worry about whether they like you or not."*

He's got a point. There's no question in my mind that over the past twenty years I could have made more money if I had been a stricter taskmaster. Then again John has very few employees who have stayed with him for more than a few years, and I'm fairly sure that the ones who are still there stick pins into dolls with his likeness when they are at home.

I have another friend named John who is more like me as far as being a boss. He too thinks he could have made more money if he wasn't so damn friendly with the staff.

Both Johns may pop up again, so for the sake of clarity I will refer to the *"fuck them"* John as *Mean John* since he is Italian, he is from New York, and he is the spitting image of infamous Mafia killer Sammy "The Bull" Gravano, and he loves when I point that fact out. The other John, for obvious reasons, we'll call *Happy John*.

They say that a good friend will help you move, but a true friend will help you move a body. Mean John would do both for me, but he would be much more excited about the moving the body option and, truth be told, would actually feel left out if not included in the earlier part where the person in question actually became a body. Happy John would help me move some furniture, but that's where he would draw the line.

Happy John, who has never met Mean John but has heard me tell many stories about him, guarantees me that if they met, Mean John would like him immediately and become his good buddy. I tell him that I doubt that very much. There is a world of difference between knowing how to lift a heavy coffee table using your bent legs instead of your back and knowing how deep the hole should be

dad.

and how many bags of lime you would need for, let's say, a six-foot-two, 220-pound guy who has really pissed you off.

That said, if I was an employee I would much prefer to work for Happy John.

I open a Word document on my computer, label it *TCB List* and then start typing things I need to do over the next week.

The first line I type is, *Get me some bullets.*

* * *

I refer to my Father as *my Dad*, not as *my Father*.

What else would I call him? I would never say to you I am going to visit my Mother. Instead I would say I'm going to visit my Mom. If we shared a friend, say a really strange guy named Harold, I would not say I was going to visit a friend; I would say I'm going to visit Harold. Father and Mother are descriptive terms; Mom and Dad are their real names, at least to me.

Sometimes I call my Mom Grammy, since, after all, she is the grandmother of my two children. When I do call her Grammy in public, it just pisses the everlasting shit out of her.

"Goddammit, I'm your mother not your grandmother," she'll snap.

Which, if you are standing there when she says it, can be as funny as hell because my Mom is actually just two inches shy of officially being a midget and I am six-foot-two-inches tall and weigh 240 pounds, or almost an eighth of a ton if you want to get technical. So when that little dynamo gets wound up and has to tilt her head back ninety degrees to lay down the smack-down on her laughing giant of a son, it is a site to see.

My Mom is from New England, she was born right after the Great Depression, she was raised by a kind and gentle Italian father and a Irish mother who made Nurse Ratched look like Mother Teresa, and she gave birth to five children who she often raised on her own while married to a globe-trotting military man. Which, naturally, means she is the most opinionated, tell-you-what-she-thinks, it's-my-way-or-the-highway person in the world. I'm kind of like that too. The whole acorn doesn't fall far from the tree thing.

Like any child spawned by Italian and Irish parents, she is a good practicing Catholic who would eat shards of glass before

dad.

missing a Sunday Mass. But that doesn't mean she can't swear like a sailor, or that she won't give her opinion to anyone, no matter what their stature. If she met Jesus Christ himself, she'd say:

"Come on Jesus, put your shoulders back and push your chest out; your posture is horrible. You're an important man, so act the part. Let's wash that hair and trim that beard, and when, Lord Almighty, was the last time you brushed your teeth?"

My Mom is big on making a good appearance. So when I call her Grammy in public she is concerned people will think I am her grandson, and since I am fifty-four years old, she does not want those people to think, *"Damn, that woman must be ancient."*

She's got it all wrong, though. Instead, I think people would look at me and then look at her, and think, *"Damn girlfriend, if that old fucker is your grandson, you be lookin' good for your age."*

It's all in how you look at it, I tell my Mom.

But she's not buying it.

* * *

When my Dad died, my relationship with my Mom changed.

I became somewhat cold to her.

I had to.

She had breakfast with my Dad that morning. And that afternoon he died. In the middle of a normal sunny day, he died. The most important person in her world, her rock, kissed her in the morning, got in his car, drove off, and never came back. She was only forty-seven years old.

Her world ended before dinner time.

And I saw my Mom about to get sucked into a black hole of despair. It was like I was standing against an old-time brick well filled with cold, dark swirling water that was being sucked down into the bowels of the earth, and my Mom was in the middle of that water. And I knew that if I did not reach down and grab her hand and pull her up, she would be lost forever. And the way I grabbed her hand was to be as cold and dark as that swirling water.

I was there for her, yes. I moved back to our hometown with my wife and I rented a house and I got another newspaper reporter job and over the next four years I had a son and a daughter, her first grandchildren, and I was there for holidays and little home repairs.

dad.

I gave her my presence, but that was all.

If she got teary-eyed, if she started to talk about missing my Dad, if the spark in her flickered, then I turned my back on her. I would not talk about my Dad. I would not share, or partake in, her misery.

One day the security guard manning the outside reception desk at the newspaper where I worked buzzed me to say I had a guest. Even thirty years ago newspapers were smart enough to have security measures in place to protect reporters from nut-jobs. It took a federal building in Oklahoma being blown up and two passenger jets bringing down the Twin Towers before the rest of the world woke up to the fact that there are some not-so-nice people breathing the same air as us.

"I think it's your mother," said the security guard.

I walked out and found my Mom in the lobby. She was crying. It was about some ridiculous thing. Maybe her change oil light was on. I don't remember. I do know it had nothing to do with her car. The loss of my Dad was just killing her. I walked her outside.

"Don't ever do this again," I said. *"Go home. Deal with it."*

And I watched her slowly walk away to the parking lot.

That tiny little woman.

And I fucking hated myself.

Thirty years later I can remember that day like it was yesterday. I can tell you what the concrete landing and stairs looked like, what the color of the sky was, what the damp air smelled like, what the sounds of the cars driving by were like, and what my Mom's face looked like when she realized, finally, that her oldest son, her first-born child, was not going to be her new rock and that the grief she had was hers and hers alone.

I didn't know any other way to handle it.

We have never spoken about that day, and I like to tell myself that, whether it was cowardice on my part or a stroke of genius on my part, it was because of how I acted, or rather did not act, that played a big part in her eventually coming to terms with my Dad's death. I'm sure that's wishful thinking on my part and does not pay enough homage to how strong that tiny little woman was, and still is.

The best I can hope for is that my actions helped speed up the process.

If not, then there is a special place in hell waiting for me.

dad.

* * *

After just randomly typing a list of all the things I think need to be on the *TCB List*, I then take time to assign each of the items to one of the remaining nine days on my ten-day plan. Some things make more sense to do during the work week and others make more sense for the weekend.

All in all, I am surprised at how few items there are on the list. This killing yourself thing is really not all that complicated.

The list I come up with is this:

MONDAY
—*Make* the *Taking Care of Business (TCB) List.*
TUESDAY
—*Do research on suicide in general.*
WEDNESDAY
—*Research pros and cons of different types of suicide, settle on one.*
—*Shopping day, buy what is needed for the suicide method I select.*
THURSDAY
—*Get legal and financial affairs in order.*
—*Find out about my life insurance and how they pay out on suicide.*
FRIDAY
—*Plan my funeral.*
—*Get totally drunk and fucked up that night, last chance to party.*
SATURDAY
—*Decide where to do it, time of day to do it, what to wear.*
—*Throw away my porn collection and anything else embarrassing.*
—*Fire up the slow cooker for a sumptuous meal.*
SUNDAY
—*Make "just saying hi" phone calls to family and friends.*
—*Write my suicide note.*
MONDAY
—*Have last staff meeting.*
—*Go out for a great lunch.*

dad.

—Take Boo for a walk.
TUESDAY
—Do it.

The schedule looks good to me. I get another cup of coffee and ask some of the staff where we are ordering lunch from today.

I hope it's tasty.

I only have so many meals left.

* * *

Over the next thirty years after my Dad died, my brother and my sisters and I delivered to my Mom twelve grandchildren and we soon all scattered to the four winds, as did my Mom who moved to Florida and the condo life and days of sailing and turning brown as a berry in the sun. She never remarried.

"How could I?" she would say. *"No one could ever replace your father."*

And she was right.

He could not be replaced, but he could be forgotten.

At least that's how it seemed to me.

Considering how much his death impacted my Mom and my siblings and what a basket case my Mom was initially, as the years went by I was surprised at how seldom as a family that we spoke of him. I can only remember us going to his gravesite two or three times. Even today I can only find one photo of my Dad in my Mom's condo. Perhaps the hardline approach I had taken with my Mom, and which through osmosis had trickled down to my brother and sisters, had been too successful. The irony is that as they all got stronger, it became harder for me.

And that's when I started to have the dream.

It was always the same dream, at least once a month, every month for years and years and years.

I am in the kitchen of the house where I grew up. My Mom is making dinner. My brother and sisters are there. I am the age I was when my Dad died, twenty-three, and my siblings are spaced two years apart, which means the youngest is only fifteen years old. The late afternoon sun is still coming in through the windows of the small kitchen. Mom is at the stove and my sisters are setting the table for

dad.

dinner. My little brother is in the den watching TV. I am leaning against the kitchen counter.

It is always exactly like that.

Every single time.

The door opens and my Dad walks in.

And everyone is surprised. Nobody moves. Nobody says a word.

And I feel my body just burn up with hate.

I am so mad.

I can't get the words out fast enough.

I yell at my Dad. I demand to know where he has been, why he left us.

He always gives me an answer. I can never remember what that answer is, but I know that it never makes sense. It doesn't add up.

And then I wake up.

And if I touch my skin, it is actually hot. There is so much anger in that dream that it changes my body temperature. Sometimes I can go right back to sleep, other times I lay awake. Either way, in the morning when I wake up again, I am angry for the rest of the day.

After about ten years, I told my Mom about the dream.

"I never dream about your Dad," she said.

"Never?"

"Never."

And then she talked about something else.

Quid pro quo.

The dreams went on for almost twenty years until I went to see a psychologist for a drinking, and an occasional drugging, problem that was getting out of hand and threatening to end my marriage. It was my wife's idea, not mine. Although, to be honest, I actually enjoyed it because, well, I love talking about me.

It only took a few sessions to identify what my substance abuse problem was. Basically, when God, who again I will agree exists just to make another point, was handing out doses of moderation to the line of souls about to be zipped down to earth, I was in the bathroom taking a leak. The end result of not being there for the recommended dose of moderation is that, in my mind, if one piece of chocolate cake tastes good, then the whole cake will taste even better. Which is why I can't stop at one scotch on the rocks; I want to

dad.

drain the bottle. And I can't stop at one line of coke; I want to snort through a few eight balls. And if I have the chance to bet $10 on a hand of blackjack, why not bet $1,000 on that same hand. You get the idea.

Together the shrink and I quickly deduced that I don't have a death wish, I don't want to sleep with my mother, I wasn't fondled as a child by a pervert relative, and I was not improperly potty-trained. Basically, I just have the tendency to be a fuck-up every now and then, and also a tendency to forget that I am now a grown-up and should act accordingly.

Once that was nailed down, the good doctor asked me if there was anything else bothering me.

So I told him about the dream.

The doctor took a nice long pause and said, *"In the dream you are very angry with your father?"*

"Yes."

"You are very mad at him?"

"Yes."

"Well, why don't you tell him that."

"Say what?"

"Why don't you tell your father you are angry and mad at him."

"He's dead, Doc."

"No, tell him that in the dream. Just talk to him."

Wow. This shrink is crazier than me.

But driving home, I told myself I would try it. The next time I had the dream, I would tell my Dad how angry and mad at him I was.

* * *

I must have told my Dad.
Because I have never had the dream again.

* * *

A few days after my Dad died, my Mom sent my brother and I to the airport to meet the father of the kid my Dad was playing racquetball with the day he died.

"He has something to give you," my Mom said.

dad.

I had no idea why we were meeting him at the airport since he lived in the same city as us. It seemed strange then and it seems strange now.

The guy looked very uncomfortable. I'm sure he didn't want to be there any more than we did. Airports are cold and lonely places. They don't seem real. They are more like purgatory, a place where nobody stays for long and nobody knows anybody. It was spooky being there meeting a man we didn't know at all to discuss someone we knew very well.

The man handed us my Dad's wallet. Why the hell did he have the wallet? You got me. I'm telling you, the whole thing was weird.

He told us that my Dad was a great guy and that he didn't suffer. He must have been there when it happened because he said they tried to give my Dad first aid, but that he pretty much died right after he hit the floor and that there was spit coming out of the side of his mouth. I remember that part, the part about the spit, the most.

Why the fuck did he have to mention that? What the fuck did that have to do with anything?

I always picture that guy driving away from the airport, banging his hands on the steering wheel and saying out loud, *"You idiot, why did you have to mention the spit?"*

Driving home my brother and I were quiet, until my brother said, *"What a fucking jerk."*

We both smiled. It was the first time we both felt normal since my Dad had died. The rest of the world might be screwy, but we were okay.

In my Dad's wallet was an old business card that he had printed up when he was in Vietnam. The front of the card listed his squadron and other Air Force jargon, but on the back, in a nice script font were the words:

"I may not be as good as I once was,
but I am as good once as I ever was."

And he wasn't referring to flying a plane.

That business card has been in my wallet ever since.

Also in my wallet is a scrap of pink index card paper that had been attached to a gift my daughter gave me when she was very young. Scrawled in hard to read green ink, it says:

"Dad, don't open this box until you're sad and lonely,
feel unloved or miss someone."

dad.

I needed that card the day at the airport.

* * *

I tell my kids stories about their grandfather as often as I can.

In the beginning, I would tell them a story and refer to him as Grampy, but it would always ring hollow. My kids know and love Grammy, but they don't know anyone named Grampy. They've seen his photos and they've heard stories, but that's the extent of it. They are more familiar with their dentist than they are with the man who was their grandfather.

So now, I just say my Dad when telling the stories.

My children are very smart and perceptive and loving, so when I tell the stories they feign an interest because they know it's important to me. They ask questions and they pay attention to my answers, but I know that it's really just to make me happy. Only I know how much my two children would have enriched my Dad's life, and only I know how his humor and his strength and his understanding would have enriched their lives.

My kids are incredible.

And their grandfather was incredible.

And they never got to meet each other.

Which sucks.

And that's another reason I'm still mad at my Dad.

* * *

My Dad was my father first, and my friend second. To my kids, I think I am their friend first, and their father second. Sometimes I think that's good and sometimes I think that's bad.

When my Dad was on alert one time, driving around the Air Force base in his green flight suit in a government truck with a huge red light on top that he would flip on if the base sirens went off to signal all personnel on alert to rush to the tankers and bombers on the runway, he had me meet him and we drove to the base gym to play, of all things, racquetball.

I was only fifteen at the time, so he was forty. Idling at a stop sign, he turned to me and said:

dad.

"You know, here I am an Air Force pilot, ready to jump in a plane and go bomb Russia, and I own a house and two cars and two TVs, and I have bills to pay, and I have a wife and I have five kids, and yet deep down, in my mind, I am still just a fifteen-year-old kid. How the hell did all this happen?"

Wow.

Part of me was like, *Whoa dude, you're the Big Guy*, you're in charge of my entire world, don't go getting all funky on me, and the other part of me, for the first time ever, saw my Dad as a person, not as a father.

I realize that the closest my kids will ever get to knowing their grandfather is by what they see in me. The things I say, the things I do, my take on life, the advice I give them. My mantra, which my children know by heart, is to question everything, to trust no one, to believe that anything is possible, to plan for the worst and hope for the best, and that when it's all said and done, when the chips are down, nobody, and I mean nobody, cares more about you than you. Always look out for Number One, and you are that Number One.

I was driving to the store with my daughter when we were both the same age that my Dad and I were when he made his observation about still feeling like a fifteen-year-old. I had just told what I thought was a wickedly funny story, always with a clever moral attached, and after laughing uproariously and patting myself on the back, I said to my daughter:

"You know, I wish I could clone myself so I would have someone just like me to hang out with."

To which my daughter said:

"No you don't, Dad."

"Why not?"

"Because he would drive you absolutely crazy."

I love my daughter.

* * *

It's now 6 pm and, like clockwork, Boo walks around the corner and plops down in my doorway and gives me the evil eye. He's ready to go home. He can be such a pain in the ass sometimes. In the morning he will run back and forth like the Tasmanian Devil between wherever I am walking in the house and the back door to

dad.

our garage because he is so excited about hopping in the car and going to the office. And at the end of the day, when he sees me pick up my car keys, he will do the same Tasmanian Devil thing, running back and forth between me and the front door of the office, because now he is so damn excited about going home. I love him to death but he is one wishy-washy canine.

"Hold your fucking horses, Tonto," I say to him.

He dismisses me with a yawn. But he doesn't leave the doorway. He knows to keep the pressure on.

I check my email one last time and laugh a little laugh at one of the new emails that pop up. It's a notification that an obnoxiously expensive Ermenegildo Zegna leather jacket that I ordered online will be shipped to me in a week, with a scheduled arrival of July 2.

Oh that's not good, I say to myself.

I call the toll-free phone number listed in the email and get an Indian woman on the line, the kind of Indian who likes lamb vindaloo and not the kind of Indian who owns all of the casinos in America. She starts talking and I can only understand every fourth word out of her mouth. It's ridiculous that US corporations stress their high level of customer service and then outsource their customer response duties to people in foreign countries who sound like bad cartoon characters.

"May I, if it pleases you, ask you why you do not want the jacket of leather?" asks Miss Indira Ghandi Junior.

"No," I say. Quickly and curtly.

There's a pause and then Miss Indira says, *"Excuse me?"*

"No," I say. Again quickly and curtly.

Another pause and then she says timidly, *"Oh, okay."*

"I'm just pulling your leg," I say with a laugh. *"Go ahead, ask away."*

"Oh, thank you sir. I was interested to ask you why you no longer want to possess the jacket that you ordered?"

I know the charming but befuddled young lady I am talking to is in a call center half way around the world in a country where they worship cows and paint a dot between their bushy eyebrows. Nothing against any of that, but it does mean that nobody on this side of the pond is going to believe anything she says. Which means I have nothing to lose. So I say:

"Well, because the jacket won't arrive here until July 2."

dad.

"Is that a problem, sir?"

"Sure is. I'm planning to kill myself two days before that."

"Sir?"

"Yep. Pulling the plug. Won't be needing no jacket after June 30th."

A nice long pause, and then, *"So you would like me to cancel the jacket?"*

"Yes, please."

Miss Indira puts me on hold, then comes back on the line and gives me a confirmation number for my cancellation.

"Is there anything else with which I may help you, sir?" she asks, and by the way she says it, I know she is praying like hell that I am done.

"Just one question," I say.

"Yes?"

"How about that Slumdog Millionaire. Great movie or what?"

She hangs up.

I can be such a dick.

* * *

To make my Dad happy, I went out for the high school football team in my junior and senior years and spent pretty much the entire time sitting on the bench because I have the athletic prowess of a three-legged sloth. Say what you will, but at least from my perch at the end of the bench I always had the best seat in the house to watch the game. My Mom would still wash my football uniform after every game even though it never saw a single grass stain. Moms are the best.

"Put the bench in coach," was the chant I remember most, and it was always a one-man chant coming from my Dad standing in the bleachers with my Mom tugging at his coat trying to get him to sit down. As if he didn't stick out enough, some times he would wear one of those big Russian-style fur hats that, trust me, not a single living soul in our redneck state had ever seen before, much less owned.

"Kid, your old man is something else," the coach would say.

For a man who was very athletic, very smart and very charismatic, my Dad had a son who was none of the above. I sucked at sports, I had no girlfriend, my grades were just average, I had pimples, I wore the wrong clothes, and I had that bushy white-man afro.

How bad was I? One morning my Dad was driving me to school when he turned off the radio, fixed me with a somewhat mournful eye and said, *"Son, suicide is not the answer."*

What the fuck? Did he know something I didn't?

"You know, puberty is a hard time for everyone. Don't let things get you down. If you ever feel like hurting yourself, you just need to come and talk to your Mom or I."

Whoa Dad, it's just a few fucking pimples. They'll go away, I promise.

I was stunned. If I wasn't depressed before, I certainly was then. I didn't say a word, and neither did he, the rest of the awkward drive to school.

Luckily for me, my Mom, as usual, came to the rescue. After high school I floundered in college as a pre-med student, deciding to be a doctor to make my parents proud despite the fact that the sight of blood made me keel over. The fainting roadblock did not do me in, though. The death blow came from organic chemistry.

"Not gonna be a doctor Mom," I said.

"What do you want to be?"

"Hell if I know."

"What do you like to do?"

"I like to write."

"So be a reporter."

Which I did.

I started as a copyboy at the local newspaper my junior year in college and after three months I told the managing editor, a true gem of a man, that I was now ready to be a reporter, to which he said incredulously:

"But you're just a copyboy!"

"Yes, but I'm working on my journalism degree."

"So you don't have your degree yet?"

"No."

"Then why should I let you be a reporter."

"Because I can do the job."

And it was then that he said something that has turned out to be the best business advice I have ever received.

dad.

"You know kid, if you don't ring your own bell, no one else will. You got the job."

Which meant that for the next two years I took journalism classes to learn how to be a reporter and in those classes my fellow students critiqued copies of the local newspaper that already had my byline on the front page. Ha! Fuck all you all.

My Dad got to see those bylines and he made sure that everyone he talked to knew that his son, the pimply-faced kid who sucked at sports, was a star reporter for the local newspaper. His boy wasn't sitting on the bench any more.

But I got lucky. I got to prove myself, finally, to my Dad before he died. My little brother and sisters didn't. My Dad never knew that all three of his daughters breezed through college, held great jobs, and married and had wonderful families, or that his middle daughter was a multi-millionaire before she turned thirty. He never knew that his youngest son, the laid-back kid who loved a good joint and seemed to have no ambitions in the world, earned his doctorate and traveled all over the world.

I can't be mad at my Dad about not being there to salute the success of his other four children. I can be disappointed. But I can't me mad.

That's up to them.

* * *

If you were to ask me to tell you how my Dad's death affected my brother and my sisters, how they felt about it when it happened, how it impacted their lives over the following years, and how they feel about it today, I honestly can't say. Which is strange considering we are a close family, doing family reunion vacations every few years, swapping cards on holidays, making occasional phone calls to brag about the accomplishments of our kids. But we didn't talk about the death then, and we don't talk about it now.

At family reunions we are more likely to tell stories about Duke than we are about my Dad. Duke was the dog we had growing up who became the lone survivor still living with my Mom after all of us kids had left the nest. He was killed chasing a car. By then he was a hundred and five in people years, had cataracts, his hair had turned

dad.

gray, and he walked with a Ratso Rizzo limp, so I tell people he died chasing a parked car.

My brother did start calling me a little more often when I turned forty-seven, mainly to remind me that Dad died when he was forty-eight which meant that I only had another year to live, since as a good son I should honor my father by following in his footsteps.

"Yo Bro, you only got a few months left. Hope you are using your time wisely."

"Fuck you."

"Can I have your BMW when you go?"

"Double fuck you."

"Maybe you shouldn't be playing any racquetball this year."

Then he would laugh and hang up.

On the day I finally turned forty-nine, he called me.

"Bro, you made it!"

"Yeah, now it's your turn."

"I know," he said. And this time he had no funny asides.

My brother recently turned forty-seven so the countdown has started for him. I know, all jokes aside, that he is nervous about it, even though he's a pretty cool guy, much cooler than me because I work too hard at it while it just comes naturally to him. The fact that he looks like a young Marlon Brando and is as laid back as Jack Kerouac certainly doesn't hurt.

When we talk it's always brother to brother, never Big Brother to Little Brother. The first time he had sex, when he was a teenager, he dipped his wick where he shouldn't have. Dad was gone so he came to me for some brotherly advice.

"Sucks to be you," I said.

"Your dick is going to turn a lovely shade of green."

"And then fall off."

The reporter in me pumped him for the salacious details before sending him off to the clinic. I knew exactly where it was.

He has played pick-up basketball games and street hockey for years with a group of guys his own age who, like him, are all in great shape. During a recent basketball game, one of those very healthy, very physically fit guys said he had a sharp pain in his leg. He drove himself to the emergency room. Where he died.

"Bro, we hadn't even finished playing our game when he died. It happened that quick," my brother said when he called.

46

dad.

That's how I know he is worried about making it to age forty-nine.

It's interesting to me how entwined life and death and time are. We measure, categorize and reference the good and the bad in our lives using the yardstick of time.

My Mom and I were in the car one day when, totally out of the blue, she said, *"Do you realize I have known you as a person longer than I knew your father when he was alive."*

That made me feel uncomfortable. I didn't know why then, but I now realize it is because every son measures his life and his accomplishments by the life and the accomplishments of his father. By outliving my Dad, by being a part of my Mom's life longer than my Dad had been, I had ventured into new, uncharted territory.

I was a sailor without a North Star.

* * *

I can't remember a single word that was said at my Dad's funeral, or who else was there besides my Mom, my brother and my sisters.

All I really remember is a young black Airman who was part of the white-gloved Honor Guard that fired off a volley of rifle shots at the gravesite. He fidgeted, shuffled his feet, looked at his watch, stared off into space. I could tell he wanted to be anywhere else in the world but at that funeral. He was there in body but not in spirit.

He and I both.

* * *

On my way home from the office I stop at a local neighborhood strip joint called Jimmy's. I crack the car window for Boo who is used to this particular stop and who will sleep while I am in the club. Of course the club is owned by a guy named Albert, not Jimmy. The club is small, one of those stucco bunkers with no windows, the exterior painted a fluorescent purple and pink. The beer is cheap, the air conditioning always works and the girls are friendly if not that attractive. I'm what you would call a regular, a schmuck who comes by at least once or twice a week, usually early evening, and I'm gone after just a few beers before the craziness starts.

dad.

Some guys like sports bars or pubs.

Me, I like titty bars.

And, believe it or not, it's more about the clientele they attract than the entertainment on stage. I'm not saying you meet a better class of people at strip clubs, just a more interesting class.

Like Albert.

"That's a real sad story," says Albert, who for some reason finds me a kindred spirit and always takes time to sit with me at my favorite spot at the bar, the last bar stool farthest from the front door. Albert is old and short and stocky, but always nicely dressed in slacks and a polo shirt. He smokes constantly and talks slowly and when you look at his eyes you know there are very few things he has not done and even fewer things he has not seen.

Albert is referring to the pretty, and very thin, blonde bartender who has just brought him one of his many Diet Cokes of the night. He waits until she is out of earshot, which in this case means just three feet away given the thunderous noise that fills the club every minute of the day from opening to closing courtesy of the hard rock music blaring from the jukebox, no live DJ at this little club, and the nonstop chatter at shouting volume from both the customers and the dancers. There is an art to conversing in a strip club that involves watching a person's lips as they talk and leaning forward whenever the noise level surges.

Albert takes a sip of his soft drink before continuing.

"She split up with her husband after moving here. She has a little boy and they used to live next door to an Iranian who owns a gas station. That gas station is immaculate. Very clean, very well run. You'd have to see it to believe it.

"Anyway, the Iranian guy kind of adopted the kid, taking him to the park, to ball games. You know. Well after awhile they found out that the guy was molesting the kid. By then it was too late. The kid's head was all fucked up. Really screwed up. Nothing happened to the guy. He had a good lawyer, and there was something about too much time passing. I don't know all the details. It's really sad. Cause she's a nice girl."

Albert flips through the Fine Book, a loose-leaf spiral-bound pad with the names of dancers written in, followed by fines that Albert or one of his managers have levied on the girls for everything from arriving late to leaving early to getting a little too touchy-feely with a

dad.

customer during a lap dance. He checks several names and takes another sip of his Diet Coke. His mind seems to be elsewhere.

"I don't even know that guy," says Albert quietly, *"but every time I drive by his gas station I want to go in and blow his fucking head off."*

Which, one day, could happen.

I know from talking to a few of the other regulars that Albert did some hard prison time in his younger days. And I know that under his untucked polo shirt is a worn leather holster that is clipped to his belt and wedged into the skin at the small of his back, and in that holster is a stainless steel .380 Sig Sauer automatic.

Albert always has that gun on him.

Even when he stops for gas.

* * *

My Dad only ever yelled at me twice.

The first time was when I was in the kitchen, the same one where the dream always happens, and I was being surly and backtalking my Mom.

When I turned around, my Dad, who was three inches shorter than me but built like a middle linebacker, was standing there, his blue eyes now dark as coal.

"If you ever raise your voice to your mother again, I will knock you on your fucking ass."

Nuff said. He didn't have to tell me twice.

The second time was at the airport, the same airport where I later went to get his wallet. He had come to pick up my wife and I, and apparently I did or said something that was discourteous to my wife. My Dad grabbed me by the arm, walked me a few feet away and, still gripping my arm in that vice-like grip, between gritted teeth, he said, *"I don't like the way you treat your wife."*

That's all he said. He didn't have to say anything more.

I was more upset that I had disappointed my Dad than I was that I might have hurt my wife's feelings.

Because my Dad was, and still is, the only man I have ever looked up to.

* * *

dad.

I never cried when my Dad died.
I was too mad at him.
I still am.

* * *

Tonight is a repeat of last night. I'm in bed looking at the blue plastic gun case, my wife is watching tennis in the living room, and Boo is in his cage.
I wait.
And then Boo speaks.
"Well, well, well, somebody had a busy day."
"Yes I did."
"So are you going to tell me why you want to kill yourself?"
"No."
"Do you even know why you want to do it?
"Maybe."
"So tell me. I deserve to know the answer."
"And why is that?"
"Just because."
"That's not a good enough answer."
"What do you expect? I'm only a fucking dog."
"Stop whining."
"I'm not whining. I'm just curious."
"Don't worry. I'll tell you soon enough."
"Promise?"
"Yes, promise."
"Okay, I can live with that."
I want to tell Boo that there isn't just one reason. That it's a mix of reasons and that it's just now that they have all finally come together.
My family, friends and staff tell me that I am the Analogy King because I always tell a story or make a real life comparison when I want to make a point. Many in that group will roll their eyes when I start one of my stories because they have heard them so many times before. The one about a juicy rib-eye steak on a fine piece of china with garnish and the same steak on a floppy paper plate will draw yawns from the entire room.

dad.

In this case, it's the analogy of a stew.

My life started as a stew pot filled with just broth, everything was nice and clear and uncluttered. But as the years went by different items were slowly added to that pot. Sometimes the item added to the pot represented a time in my life that was good, like a tasty carrot when I hit that first home run in Little League. And sometimes the item added to the pot represented a time in my life that was bad, like spoiled cabbage when I wrecked the first new car I owned two weeks after I got it. The stew pot has been cooking for fifty-four years and over that time period many more items have been added to the pot, some that please me and some that displease me.

And now, because it has been cooking long enough, the stew is ready.

But not to eat.

To toss out.

Because it is full of both good and bad.

And also because there just isn't room for any more items in the pot.

It's just that simple.

I always wanted my life to be perfect. It's almost an obsessive-compulsive disorder. If I messed something up, if something bad happened, I wanted to erase that page and go back and do it again so that the pages that made up the book of my life would be perfect, each and every page. But they haven't been. My Dad dying so young was the first truly imperfect page in my book. Is his death the reason I want to commit suicide? No. It's just one of the worst items in the stew.

"Can I ask you another question?" says Boo.

I know this suicide thing has him concerned and that it's the most important thing on his mind right now. I brace myself for a grilling.

"Shoot," I say.

"Ginger or Mary Ann?" says Boo.

I smile. Boo is full of surprises.

"Ginger."

"The Stones or Zeppelin?"

"Zep."

"Superman or Batman?"

"Superman."

dad.

"The Godfather or Goodfellas?"
"Goodfellas."
"Lone gunman or conspiracy?"
"Oswald alone."
"Okay, not bad. You got four out of five right." says Boo.
"Which one did I miss?"
"I'm not telling you, Homey. You figure it out."
"Okay, I'll mull it over. Good night Boo."
"Good night owner."

I wait. I have a feeling that Boo is not going to end the day with such a nice salutation. He will want to have the last word, and the more caustic it is, the better.

I'm right.

"You know, I think I'll lick my balls before I go to sleep. Bet you wish you could do that."

"You don't have any balls. You've been fixed."

"Whatever."

lines.

It's Tuesday morning and I am at the office and I am in a good mood.

I am an organized son of a bitch and the *TCB List* says today is research day, so I turn on my computer and go to the World Wide Web.

The Internet. What a great invention. Talk to anyone in the world in real time, discover the most obscure facts at the touch of a key, start a chat site and become a billionaire, set up a sexual rendezvous with a twelve-year-old in Detroit. I'm just kidding. About the billionaire thing.

When I started as a newspaper reporter we all pounded away on manual Underwood typewriters. Computers were something you only saw in science fiction movies. It was all about the click, clack, click, clack of metal typewriter keys hitting a black ribbon. If you needed to look up a fact, you had your choice between Encyclopedia Britannica or the Colliers Encyclopedia. One set was black, and the other red. I wonder sometimes what happened to those unlucky guys who signed up as sales reps for the encyclopedia companies

lines.

the year before the Internet was launched. *"We're going to be rich, honey. I got the rights to all of Wyoming for the Britannicas!"*

We had both the Britannicas and the Colliers when I was growing up, and *"Look it up in the encyclopedia,"* was one of my Dad's constant refrains. He was also keen on us learning big words so every night at dinner he would teach us a new word. I remember him placing his glass of tea on the very edge of the dinner table and asking my little brother what position the glass was in. My brother was about five at the time so he didn't have a fucking clue. Then again I was twelve and I didn't know either.

"Precarious," said my Dad. *"The glass is in a precarious position."*

I found a way to use that word the very next day in the lunch room at school and my fellow students, like my little brother, didn't have a fucking clue what I was saying, nor were they impressed.

"How about I put your head in a pretty-curious position," said one of the football players.

Those trusty encyclopedias are long gone and it would not be prudent to pop into the local police station to quiz the cops about the pros and cons of suicide, so I do what everybody else in the world does.

Go to the Internet.

I hesitate before launching a search. If you think the government does not monitor what people search for on the Internet, then you are as crazy as a loon. If you don't believe me, do a search using the key words *homemade bomb*, *the White House* and *President's funeral*, then tell me how long it takes before there is a knock at your front door. For a second or two I worry that, if I do a search on the key word *suicide*, I too might get a knock on my door and open it to find a priest who says, *"Can we talk?"*

I figure it's worth the risk, so I type in the word suicide and hit return. And spend the next few hours reading about something that the majority of the public is totally unaware of, which is that suicide is an epidemic on this planet of ours and a lot more common than most people realize.

And here I thought I was doing something unique and special.

Silly me.

* * *

lines.

Whether or not Dean knew that the small automatic handgun I somewhat absentmindedly placed to my right temple was actually loaded is a question I have mulled over repeatedly since that cool wintery afternoon many years ago when we sat and talked on facing couches, he with a burning cigarette between his fingers and I with the smooth steel of the gun trigger between mine.

That the gun was loaded with a full magazine of .22 caliber shells, hollow-point longs at that, was a fact of which I was very much unaware. Had I known the gun was loaded, that a round had actually been chambered and was capable of being fired with just the slightest bit of pressure from my finger as it ran up and down the smooth curve of the trigger, I certainly would not have continued placing the tiny hole of the gun barrel against my head.

But I didn't know.

And for about five minutes during a lazy conversation in the living room of a comfortable but rundown two-story frame house that Dean shared with several former high school buddies, I repeatedly punctuated my remarks by tapping the gun barrel to my head in a spot just a bit forward of my ear and a bit below the baseball cap that I used to help subdue what was then a jungle of unkempt curly hair.

The subject of our conversation escapes recall, but it was apparently inconsequential enough that I felt it necessary to augment the spoken words with a nervous continuous physical action, that being a steady yet light thumping of the gun to a most sensitive part of my body, much like someone might tap their foot against a coffee table or flick a pencil into an open palm. That the object being used to placate my hyper energies was not an impotent shell of a weapon but was actually an on-line instrument of death, one that was incredibly close to spitting out a peanut-sized piece of quickly fragmenting lead into the soft inner sanctum of my head, was a fact of which I was most assuredly unaware.

But Dean knew.

In looking back on that afternoon, my thoughts, surprisingly, have not lingered on the "what if" aspect of that afternoon because now, like then, it's not really possible to acknowledge or accept the possibility of one's own early death; it's always someone else who dies in an accidental shooting, has a heart attack or is killed in an auto crash. Instead, whenever I have reconstructed the events of that afternoon, my thoughts have always been on Dean, and on whether he knew how close to death I really was. And each time I have rerun the scene in my mind, slowing it down to a single frame at a time, the strongest image has been of Dean's eyes, of a brilliant steady stare that seemed brimming with wonder and wild expectancy.

Dean knew, yes indeed.

And he waited, and he watched.

*   *   *

I get a second cup of coffee and prepare to plow forward on my Internet research. Sure would be nice if someone would bring in some fresh donuts every now and then. I could really go for a Bavarian cream right about now. I make do with a stale chocolate chip cookie that someone left in the office refrigerator. It comes to life when I dunk it in my coffee a few times.

The Internet points out the obvious.

Which is that suicide is the intentional taking of one's own life. In some European languages the word for suicide translates into English as "self-murder" or a "crime against the self" which takes the act out of the realm of something you just do to yourself, like masturbation, and moves it into the realm of true crime, like disgruntled employee murders. Personally, and it's just me grant you, I think there's a big difference between whacking off into a nice soft tissue with an open copy of Cheri magazine laying next to you versus blowing Betty the office receptionist's head off with a shotgun just because you got pink-slipped six months ago and have been pouting about it ever since.

We average 35,000 suicides a year in the United States, which is one suicide for every 10,000 people. Suicide is the sixth leading cause of death in America, but rockets up to the third leading cause of death of Americans ages fifteen to twenty-four. And I thought those were the most carefree years of a person's life. To put the annual suicide figure into perspective, consider that 42,000 people die annually in traffic accidents, which means someone dies in a car crash every thirteen minutes and someone commits suicide every fifteen minutes in this country. Incredibly, deaths by suicide actually outnumber homicides two-to-one.

56

lines.

And those are just figures for the United States.

The World Health Organization estimates that in the year 2000 approximately one million people died from suicide, which shows you that not everyone was as excited about the New Millennium as you were, since someone killed themselves every forty seconds during that entire festive year of fireworks, parades and speeches. In the last forty-five years, suicide rates have increased by sixty percent worldwide.

For every successful suicide, there are twenty to twenty-five unsuccessful attempts which are referred to as "suicide gestures" or pseudocide. I'm not sure what is more disturbing, the fact that twenty-five million, that's 25,000,000, people want to kill themselves every single year, or the fact that there are twenty-five million totally inept fuck-ups who can't do anything right.

Jimmy, why did you miss work yesterday?

I committed a suicide gesture.

Oh okay, better luck next time.

If published news reports are to be believed, celebrities who have made suicide gestures range from Mike Wallace to Elizabeth Taylor to Maria Callas to Johnny Cash to Walt Disney to Elton John, and the list goes on and on, and even includes *Father Knows Best* Robert Young. Who'd of thunk it.

Although suicide rates had traditionally been highest among elderly males—which has a lot to do with going bald, getting fat, not getting laid anymore, and having to wake up twice a night to pee— rates among young people have increased to such an extent that they are now the group at highest risk in a third of all countries. Mental disorders, particularly depression and substance abuse, are associated with more than ninety percent of all cases of suicide, which confuses me because right now I am neither depressed nor abusing substances.

Okay, sometimes I overeat.

Half of all suicides come at the business end of a gun, while twenty-five percent are from poisoning and the other twenty-five percent are from suffocating, which I guess refers to hanging yourself or sitting in a running car in an enclosed garage or falling into a vat of Swiss chocolate. The most common method of suicide for females is poisoning, although women also shoot themselves.

lines.

When I was a newspaper reporter, the cops told me if they went to a crime scene and found a woman laying in bed with a gunshot wound to the head and a gun next to her, they knew it was a homicide and not a suicide because a woman will not shoot herself in the face or the head. Women are not going to mess up that face that they've been moisturizing and putting makeup on for years no matter how damn depressed they are. Conversely, if the cops showed up at a crime scene and found a guy laying in bed with a gunshot wound to the chest and the gun next to him, they knew that it was a homicide because guys don't mess around when they commit suicide; they go straight to the cranium.

I presume that people have been committing suicide ever since that little tart Eve convinced gullible Adam to take a bite of the forbidden apple. Considering there were no firearms and no car exhaust fumes and no sleeping pills during those caveman years, and certainly no Swiss chocolate, you have to wonder what method they used to accomplish the deed back then.

Tossing yourself under the feet of an irate wooly mammoth had to be a little hit and miss.

* * *

My belief that Dean knew the gun was loaded is bolstered by more than just the recollection of that look in his eyes. Dean had my gun last, having been given an empty pistol, a handful of bullets and a rather stern admonishment not to combine the two the night before. Yet Dean had apparently done just that, loading the clip with smooth copper-plated slugs and then jacking one of them into the firing chamber before eventually leaving the gun on his coffee table. Where, the following day, I picked it up after collapsing on one of the living room couches to join him in watching a soap opera while we planned our night's activities.

To Dean it must have seemed like a second television set had kicked on when I came over that afternoon, opening the front door without a knock, striding into the room accompanied by a chilling rush of winter air, snatching up the gun and falling onto the couch in one fluid motion before erupting into idle chatter, all while Dean sat unmoving on the facing couch, his legs propped up on the coffee table. Seconds before it had just been he and a television screen alone in an empty house in the middle of an unchartered day, and in the snap of a finger there was a human being sitting across from him about to blow his brains out.

Dean and I were from the same neighborhood and though our paths had crossed over the years we had not started hanging out together until about a year before that afternoon. Geographic proximity, some mutual acquaintances, and fathers who had been in the military were about all we had in common. I was fresh out of college by way of a private high school and a secure family home; he was fresh out of a short broken marriage by way of a government equivalency diploma and a turbulent home life. My future was so open and unblemished that I didn't even realize or appreciate the beauty and opportunity ahead of me; Dean had already made the first strokes on his life canvas and they had come out dark and ugly. A handsome infant son whom he saw infrequently was a constant painful reminder, his amazingly quick growth a yardstick upon which Dean could measure his past failures and predict his future sadness.

Decadence brought us together.

We were young, not yet twenty-one, and we were from two totally different backgrounds, yet we found a common thread in our appreciation of that side of life that went one step beyond what was socially acceptable, one step beyond what was morally advisable, and one step beyond what was knowingly legal. We were night people and reveled in the opportunity to stay out as late as possible exploring every nightclub in town, preferably ones with pool tables and most especially ones boasting topless dancers.

We fancied ourselves bad boys and in accordance chose to frequent those clubs where the sight of a tattoo on the arm next to yours on the bar was not always a sure clue as to the gender of the owner, where the pool tables were only open to betting players, and where the bathroom sinks were more often than not sprayed with drops of blood. Heavy boots, faded blue jeans and black T-shirts made up our uniform of the night, and back then they hung on bodies lean and sinewy, not from workouts at fancy health clubs but rather from a diet of junk food only bought when the hunger pangs could no longer be ignored and we would count loose change to buy a TV dinner.

We'd alternate between driving my Firebird or Dean's never get busted car, a four-door Chevrolet with a Support Your Local Police sticker on the bumper and a child's seat in the back. Some nights we would borrow a friend's Harley and ride up in style on the bike, parking it next to the other scooters lining the curb at the front door of one particularly nefarious club that we favored, careful always not to touch any of the other bikes, mindful of Dean's often mentioned recollection of the night some novice smacked a scooter with his front car door and was promptly and efficiently stomped by three irate yet smiling bikers.

Dean's brother-in-law was a bartender at the club and that association provided us with a certain degree of protection from the bar patrons who would not normally tolerate the youthful exuberance that seemed to follow us into the club like a cloud despite our attempts to project a macho aura like the weekend warriors and hardcore bikers who called the bar home. We might have had the Harley and the clothes, but we didn't have the grease under our fingernails, the sandpaper palms, the swirling green tattoos, the fish-white skin hidden by sweaty clothes, the missing teeth, the uncut hair and unshaven faces.

But we still managed to fit in. Barely.

Our lack of credentials was certainly obvious to the regulars, and such a deficiency would have led to a confrontation with anyone else on a first visit, but we weathered our first trip into the club by tethering ourselves to the bar within sight of Dean's brother-in-law, who had established quite a reputation by virtue of a 9mm Browning automatic that he kept under the bar and quite often slipped into his waistband when he deemed such a move would aid him in his negotiations with an unruly customer. After that first night, we slowly eased into the flow of the bar and in time our constant presence earned us our own niche at the club, albeit one at the bottom of the totem pole. The philosophy was that if you came back to the bar after your initial visit then you knew the score, and if you knew the score then you had the chops to deal with any problem that might come up.

We didn't.

We were just crazy.

And lucky.

* * *

lines.

Around noon one of my staffers pops his head into my office and asks what I want for lunch.

It's an easy decision.

"I want the Garibaldi," I say, quickly moving an open text document on my computer desktop to cover the suicide info page in case the staffer can see my computer screen. The Garibaldi, a little slice of heaven from the Italian deli down the street, is a hard Italian bread roll packed with sopressata dry-cured salami, prosciutto ham, fontinella cheese, red roasted peppers and garlic oil. Its only drawback is that you are still tasting the sandwich ten hours later. But damn, it's good. Twenty minutes later the sandwich is on my desk and I dive in with one hand and with the other hand tap away on my keyboard to find some suicide facts good for breaking the ice at a cocktail party. I find these tantalizing tidbits.

In the United States a suicide occurs every fifteen minutes. *That's four people for every episode of American Idol.*

More people die from suicide than are killed in drunk driving accidents. *I'll drink to that.*

Males are four times more likely to die from suicide than are females, while females are more likely to attempt suicide than are males. *Which means they are horrible drivers, and even worse suicide-attempters.*

Whites commit suicide more often than blacks. *So much for racial equality.*

Suicide rates decrease in times of war and increase in times of economic crises. *Empty bank accounts are always more depressing than sending loved ones off to fight and die for oil.*

Suicide rates are the highest among the divorced, separated and widowed, and lowest among the married. *That may be a typo.*

The risk of suicide in alcoholics is fifty to seventy percent higher than the general population. *What a buzz kill.*

The highest suicide rate is among Caucasian men over fifty who are not medically ill. *Hey, that's me! I found my brand!*

* * *

Dean and I met officially at a lake party after having seen each other a number of times during our teens, but it wasn't until that party that we bypassed what had for years been an assumed mutual

lines.

dislike and discovered that we actually shared some interests, specifically bar-hopping into the early morning hours at clubs whose names we would not normally mention to friends more interested in discos and restaurant lounges. Dean's interest peaked when I told him I covered the police beat and descriptively spun a few tales of some of the sights I'd encountered while working with the cops. Sitting on the back porch of our host's lake house watching ski boats loaded with drunk partiers speeding through the night firing bottle rockets at each other, I slowly warmed the waters between us by allowing him a glimpse into a world that I ventured through five nights a week armed only with a notebook. My stock rose in his eyes as I ticked off tales of cops and robbers and murderers, and much of his open-eyed, open-mouthed wonder was due to his surprise to hear such stories spilling from the lips of someone he had for years written off as a lightweight.

As the party increased a notch in foolhardiness and one of the partiers stumbled down the porch steps and into a roaring barbecue pit, branding his bare chest with criss-cross grill marks, Dean took the ball into his court and attempted to match what he had acknowledged with repeated nods of his head were my impressive credentials with a few stories of his own. They ranged from an arrest in his early teens for stuffing his father's pistol into his pants and showing up at school for his own unauthorized version of show and tell to aggravated assaults on his ex-wife's succession of boyfriends to his dabbling in the fine art of drug dealing. As he painted pictures of ventures into terrain never traveled by myself, my interest was peaked.

Comparing notes we found that our work shifts both concluded at midnight, leaving two hours for bar hopping, and in no time at all we were making the club circuit together several nights a week. We tended to gravitate to those bars whose names cropped up in small newspaper stories about patrons whose nights didn't quite end like they would have liked, people with descriptive phrases in front of their names like "stable, but serious condition."

Every town has its Strip, a stretch of highway dotted with package liquor stores, lizard lounges and titty bars, where the gaudy neon flashes, where the parking lots spit up chunks of gravel, where the doors are heavy and solid and tattooed with locks, where the club interiors hide dark corners, where the rugs smell of spilled beer and cigarette burns, where the mixed drinks come in plastic glasses and the first gulp of draft beer makes you want to gag, where the bartender doesn't smile and doesn't expect a tip, where the bouncers are indistinguishable from the patrons, and where the guy on the stool next to you will buy you a drink and two hours later want to carve on you with a Buck knife for some imagined slight. The locales vary, the structures vary, the names vary, but there is a sameness in the people drawn to these clubs.

For us, it was the Black Knight Lounge.

It was the most enduring, the most prolific of the nasty nightspots in our happy town, unrivaled for its sleaze factor and its reputation as the raunchiest topless bar on the Strip. It was a little piece of hell packed into a small concrete building that boasted one bar, one stage and enough nightly mayhem to earn a reputation that drew like a magnet those traveling men and women who lived in the belly of the beast. Like a truckstop that through word of mouth about its good food draws truckers from across the country, the Black Knight was a fluorescent bug light that sucked in the dregs of the highways at a rocketing speed, many of them rushing in too fast and smacking headlong into the unforgiving burning lights, carried off in ambulances or leaving trails of blood-spattered parking lot gravel that morning duty police could only peer at in wonder.

And as such, it was a beacon to Dean and I.

There was no other place, no other setting, where we could come face to face with a slice of life that challenged and enthralled us. From the moment we pulled into the parking lot, our bodies went on alert. We parked within sight of the front door, never so close that our car would end up being the wrestling mat for combatants spilling out of the bar, never too far that we would give false encouragement to a robber who might feel he could ply his trade on us unobserved. There always seemed to be the briefest feeling of nausea before we opened the door, not a moment of hesitancy but more a chance for a last safe breath as one of us would grasp the heavy handle, give it a quick hard jerk and we would slip across to the other side.

Given the nature of our town, small, the nature of the club, small, and the nature of the tips, small, it was no surprise that the Black Knight tended to attract a class of topless dancer that more often amused than aroused the patrons. We were unaware that in larger cities across the country young men our age frequented

lines.

topless bars where the talent on stage was much younger and more attractive, and where the personal risk for venturing out to view the bared charms of women who chose to make a living by exposing themselves was much smaller than what we faced when we would yank open that heavy door to the Black Knight several evenings a week. It was a dangerous bar, more so than our biker joint mainstay, because at least there we knew the regulars, we knew their flashpoints, we knew who to avoid, we knew the rules.

The Black Knight had no rules.

You seldom saw the same faces, at the bar or on the stage. The club crackled with a violent energy that literally made the hairs on the back of your neck stand up, and chill bumps pop up on your arms. It was a bar where you could get fucked, fucked up or fucked over depending on who you were speaking to, how you were talking, and what you were saying. The dancers were cold, heartless women who strong-armed you for a buck tip after they danced, and strong-armed you to buy them a drink of colored water for six bucks just to slide onto the stool next to you and rub a chubby thigh between your legs. Interestingly enough, Dean and I seldom had to contend with this female flesh loansharking; undoubtedly our young foreheads blazed with signs reading "broke, not really horny, actually just here to leer."

And voyeurs we were. But not for the women, for the whole ball of wax. We saw fights. We saw drug deals. We saw fights. We saw dancers strip totally naked in a city whose ordinances mandated G-strings and pasties. We saw fights. We saw girlfriends get up from the audience and dance topless on stage. We saw fights. We saw couples grappling in dark corners. We saw fights. We saw dancers giving handjobs under the table. And we saw fights. Lots of fights.

We saw, and we watched.

Watching was everything.

* * *

If you look at a list of famous people who have committed suicide over the years, one of the first things you notice is that the majority of those people are really not all that famous.

Which might be one of the reasons they killed themselves.

lines.

There are a lot of actors and actresses and writers and authors and poets and sports figures and politicians and musicians and inventors and even Nobel Peace Prize and Pulitzer Prize winners who have killed themselves, and while you may recognize the movies they appeared in, the TV shows they starred on, the sports teams they played for, the bands they were in, their inventions, and the cities and states where they were elected officials, in most cases you will have no idea who the person is. The people killing themselves, for the most part, seem to be the supporting players.

For example, everyone knows the movie *Midnight Cowboy,* which won the 1969 Best Picture Academy Award, but do you know about the book's author, James Leo Herlihy, who overdosed on drugs? Or how about author John O'Brien, who wrote *Leaving Las Vegas* which was made into an Academy Award-winning movie, who shot himself? I could give you more examples, but you wouldn't know who the hell those peeps were, even though they were associated in some way with something famous

There are some exceptions. Truly famous people who were the best in their field but chose suicide as their final appearance on the world stage include novelist Ernest Hemingway of *The Old Man and the Sea* and *For Whom the Bell Tolls* by gunshot; poet and author Sylvia Plath of *The Bell Jar* by placing her head in an oven and turning on the gas; novelist Virginia Woolf of *A Room of One's Own* by drowning after filling her pockets with stones and walking into a river; Sigmund Freud, the founder of psychoanalysis, by morphine overdose; George Eastman, inventor of the Eastman Kodak Camera, by gunshot; country and western singer Faron Young of the prophetic *Live Fast, Love Hard, Die Young* song by gunshot; gonzo journalist Hunter S. Thompson of *Fear and Loathing in Las Vegas* by gunshot; Nirvana lead singer and songwriter Kurt Cobain by gunshot; painter Vincent van Gogh, known equally as well for his artwork as for lopping off the lobe of his left ear to give to a hooker, by gunshot; and finally, Cleopatra, the real one and not Elizabeth Taylor, possibly through the self-inflicted bite of a poisonous snake called an Asp.

There are also some heavyweights who occasionally end up in the suicide column although there is debate on whether their deaths were instead actually accidental deaths, including Brian Epstein, manager of the Beatles by drug overdose; silver screen goddess Marilyn Monroe by drug overdose; General George Armstrong lines.

Customer who some historians think saved the last bullet for himself; protestor and author Abbie Hoffman by drug overdose; actor George Reeves who played Superman on television by gunshot; and Sid Vicious of the Sex Pistols by drug overdose.

In the famous for being infamous category, you have that little prankster Adolf Hitler by a combination of cyanide and gunshot; strumpet Eva Braun who Hitler was banging at the time by cyanide; Hitler's playmates Joseph Goebbels by gunshot, Hermann Goering by cyanide, Heinrich Himmler by cyanide, and Rudolph Hess by strangulation; literal back-stabber Brutus by falling on his own sword after helping to turn Caesar into a pin cushion; that other back-stabber Judas Iscariot by hanging after he dropped a dime on Jesus Christ; happy-go-lucky Rev. Jim Jones by cyanide-laced grape-flavored Flavor Aid along with 914 of his more gullible followers; and notorious Al Capone hitman Frank Nitti by gunshot.

That may seem like a lot of famous people, but is it really when you consider all of the big names throughout history that did not make the list?

Other notables—*but can we really say famous?*— include Frances Ford Seymour, the wife of Henry Fonda and mother of actors Peter and Jane Fonda, by slitting her own throat; singer Del Shannon of the hit song *Runaway*, by gunshot; Edwin Armstrong, the inventor of FM radio, by jumping out a window; Clara Blandick, who was Auntie Em in *The Wizard of Oz*, by drug overdose and suffocation; matinee heartthrob Charles Boyer by drug overdose; Brad Delp, lead singer of Boston, by asphyxiation; Robert E. Howard, creator of *Conan the Barbarian*, by gunshot; playwright William Inge of *Bus Stop* and *Splendor in the Grass*, of carbon monoxide poisoning; comedian and actor Richard Jeni of *The Mask* by gunshot; actor Brian Keith of *The Parent Trap* by gunshot; novelist Jerzy Kosinski of the award-winning book and movie *Being There* by barbiturate overdose and suffocation; Richard Manuel of Bob Dylan's The Band by hanging; and actor and playwright Spalding Gray of *Swimming to Cambodia* by drowning. Gotta love that last one; he wrote a great play with swimming in the title and then drowned himself.

Some of the dearly departed should be applauded for the creativity of their demise. Swiss writer Niklaus Meienberg suffocated himself with a garbage bag. French inventor Claude Chappe threw himself down a well. Thomas Caute Reynolds, the Confederate Governor of Missouri, jumped down an elevator shaft. Movie actress Peg Entwistle jumped to her death from the famous Hollywood Sign in the hills of Hollywood. Actress Florence Lawrence poisoned herself with ant paste. Former Pittsburgh Steelers NFL lineman Terry Long drank antifreeze.

Let's give them all a big hand.

* * *

As firearms go, the gun that ended up playing such an important role that afternoon in Dean's living room was less than impressive, certainly nothing to compare with what we saw on the silver screen in the beefy, steady hands of Eastwood, Bronson and Connery. No, you couldn't crack an engine block or drop a fleeing suspect from fifty yards with our little black beauty, and we occasionally took a ribbing from friends who questioned whether what we held in our hand was really a gun or simply a cigarette lighter shaped like a gun. At such times we'd smile, pass the piece over for inspection and then somewhat boastfully recite the resume of the gun in question. For while our friends might plunk down hundreds of dollars at the local gunshop for mighty .357 Magnums and 9mm automatics, replete with fancy grips and shiny barrels, we knew and they knew that what they paid big bucks to own was still virgin hardware. They had the looks, we had the history.

I had bought the small .22 automatic from a detective sergeant, illegally I might add since it was a gun confiscated in an arrest that should have ended up in the evidence property room and then incinerated with the other hundreds of guns collected over the year by the police. But the sergeant had chosen to keep this particular gun, which he had taken from a robbery suspect. Such a gun could prove to be just the insurance a cop might need if one night he shot at and killed someone whom he thought was pointing a gun at him but the gun turned out to be a flashlight or a wallet or an extended finger. It happens. And when it does, and when there are no witnesses, or when the only people left standing after the firefight happen to be fellow officers, it's not unusual that a throw-down gun can appear from a back pocket or from under a patrol car seat and

lines.

quickly take its place near the outstretched hand of the newly deceased party.

I'm not saying that's what this particular detective sergeant had in mind for that little gun, but he knew that would be my deduction when he showed me the gun and yet that did not deter him. I kept my comments to myself that night when we sat in his cramped office as he pulled out his middle desk drawer and rummaged around amid the pens, blank incident reports, bullets and Rolaids before extracting the flat black metal gun with its grip of hard black plastic. Holding the gun, it could be almost completely hidden in your palm with just a hint of the stubby barrel protruding past your index finger. With your pinky finger you could push back a hook-like catch that would release the six-shot clip. My observation that it didn't appear to be much of a gun, particularly in comparison with the massive .357 Magnums favored by the detectives and worn in an array of personality revealing styles from standard-issue hip holsters to cocky shoulder rigs, was met with a hearty scoff from the sergeant.

"This automatic can hold .22 longs or shorts, as well as hollow points," he said with the same matter-of-fact mixture of expertise and admiration one might expect from a car mechanic recommending a particular brand of spark plug. *"Load this with .22 long hollow points and you've got a weapon that at close range can do as much damage as any other handguns. Yes sir, up close it will most assuredly fuck a body up."*

One didn't have to be an aficionado of police boiler rooms or late night cop shows to translate the detective's ballistics analysis. Ours was a town and a state where young boys growing up were just as likely to wield a .22 rifle or 20 gauge shotgun in a stand of pecan trees as they were to wield a baseball bat at a ball park. Ours was a town where the sight of a pickup truck without a rifle or shotgun on pegs in the rear window was an oddity, where car registration and insurance papers in glove compartments were kept suitably flattened by the weight of loaded pistols, where sporting goods stores did an amazingly brisk business in not only gun sales but all the accoutrements that made stalking and killing game so much easier like decoy ducks, camouflage jumpsuits and deer stands. Ours was a town where you knew if you shot an intruder in your home you were fine, and if you shot one outside your house then you knew to just drag his dead ass inside and you were still fine. We knew guns.

lines.

And so I knew that .22 long referred to a shell that was longer and packed with more gunpowder than a .22 short, and more powder meant more bang for the buck. And hollow point meant plenty of fragmenting, exploding lead for the buck. The gun offered a nasty combination indeed, a lot of firepower and guaranteed carnage in a weapon of deception that could easily be palmed unseen before one was just inches away from a potential victim's head.

"I just might" was the detective sergeant's answer when I asked if he would sell me the gun. Might turned into will, and the gun soon became a third companion on Dean and I's nightly excursions, placed into a gutted leather wallet and slipped into my back pocket. While there was a sense that the gun was communal property, I kept it out of Dean's hands as much as possible, nervous about a fiery temper that could become uncontrollable after a certain amount of drinking. Though nothing had ever happened to give me real cause for alarm, I had a premonition that it might not be in anyone's best interest to have Dean in possession of the gun on a night when he had surpassed his limit of alcohol and patience. Dean didn't push it, and so the gun was most often in my hands.

As it was that cold afternoon.

*   *   *

I step outside the front door of my office to smoke a cigarette. It's my tenth cigarette of the day. It's 2 pm. By the time I go to sleep tonight I will have smoked one pack of cigarettes and cracked open and made a dent in a second pack. Days that I go out partying at night I will knock back two to three packs of cigarettes.

Drives my daughter fucking crazy.

My former brother-in-law is a professional comedian and he says, *"They say that smoking will take ten years off your life. What the hell—it's the last ten."*

I like that.

Standing outside I enjoy the little oasis of my office condo and the other three condos in our development because they are surrounded by giant oak trees that are packed with squirrels. There are even otters in a small stream behind one of the condos. From where I stand, I can see a major thoroughfare a few hundred yards away that cuts through our part of the city. It's not a street or a highway, but rather something in between, and although it's always packed with traffic, my office is far enough away that we aren't bothered by the noise. So I stand on the sidewalk outside the front door, smoke my cigarette, breathe the fresh air that circles the trees, and watch a colorful array of motor vehicles streaming down the not-quite-a-street and not-quite-a-highway.

Sounds enjoyable and peaceful, doesn't it? Try doing it twenty fucking times a day, five days a week.

I really need to quit.

Cigarettes do weird things to people. The only time a complete stranger will walk up and ask you to give them something for free is when a stranger asks to bum a smoke off you. You never have a stranger walk up and ask if he can have a bite of your Big Mac, or ask if he can bang your girlfriend. So he won't sound like a panhandler, the stranger will always ask if he can "borrow" a cigarette, not can he have a cigarette. I've lent out a few thousand cigarettes in my lifetime and have yet to have one of them returned.

I worked construction one summer during my college years helping to build residential houses. Actually, I never got to hammer a single nail and instead did grunt work all day, carrying roof shingles up a ladder, toting sheetrock, digging ditches, pushing wheel barrels, and doing all those other manual labor things that reinforced, on a daily basis, my resolve to get a college degree that would land me a job sitting down in an air conditioned building.

The foreman paired me up with Old Tom, a skinny black man in his mid to late sixties with only one good eye, the other eye was glazed white from cataracts, and a voice that sounded like gravel being shaken in an empty oil drum. As a youngster, dirt poor Tom had gotten strep throat and instead of taking penicillin, which his family could not even afford, his mother had him gargle with white gasoline. Cured the fuck out of the strep throat, but ravaged his vocal cords.

There were another half dozen grunt laborers on site, and I was the only white boy in the group, which tickled the shit out of those black guys who joined me in singing *tote that barge, lift that bale*. We'd get to the job site at 7 am and huddle together to smoke cigarettes and pass around a pint of cheap vodka before the foreman arrived. I'd take my hit off the bottle as they passed it around and never once wiped the mouth of the bottle before taking my gulp.

They all noticed that, and that's why I was invited back to the huddle every morning.

Old Tom could not read or write and if you had asked him who the President was, he would not have had a fucking clue. But he was one of the smartest people I ever met.

The foreman told Old Tom and I to use sledgehammers to bust up thirty feet of recently-poured and hard-as-steel concrete sidewalk one day because of some property line error they had made. The sidewalk was made up of concrete sections that were a yard square and six inches thick. I hoisted a sledgehammer up over my head and brought it down dead center in the middle of one of the concrete squares. The head of the sledgehammer bounced up six feet into the air and it felt like I had just shattered both my elbows. And there wasn't a scratch on the concrete. I tried three more times with the same results and now my body was tingling from the tips of my fingers down to my toes.

"This is impossible," I said.

"Stand back, youngster," said Old Tom who, though he was ancient and skinny and weighed less than 130 pounds, was made up of nothing but hard scrabble sinew, bone and muscle.

He brought the sledgehammer up over his head and I watched as the head of the sledgehammer just hung there motionless for a moment, and then Old Tom gritted his teeth and his one good eye flashed with wild abandon and he brought that sledgehammer down with a thunderous bang and it split that huge slab of concrete into a dozen pieces.

"Nothing is impossible," said Old Tom, eyeing his handiwork.

He set his sledgehammer down and rested his hands on the top of the wooden handle. *"Now you try it again."*

I was not going to be outdone by an old man. I stepped in front of the next concrete square, raised the sledgehammer over my head, gritted my teeth and brought the sledgehammer down. Nothing. I tried again. Nothing. And I tried again. Nothing.

"I just can't do it, Tom," I said.

Old Tom just stared at me.

"Yes, you can," he said.

And then he stepped up close to me, looked me square in the eye, and said, rather sternly, *"But when you hit it, you hit it goddammit. Put your whole heart and soul into it, boy."*

lines.

So I did it again.

Just like Old Tom said.

And I broke that damn concrete.

I learned a lesson that day about not giving up, about never underestimating what you can do if you put your mind to it, about nothing being impossible. And I—an educated, well-to-do young white man—learned that lesson from a man who was black. And old. And poor. And uneducated. And, in my eyes, a true diamond of a human being.

The very first day Old Tom and I worked together we took a smoke break and I watched him pull what appeared to be brand new, unopened pack of cigarettes from his shirt pocket. I waited for him to unwrap the cellophane from the top of the pack, but instead he turned the pack upside down and pulled a cigarette out from a small hole he had torn in the bottom of the pack.

"Tom," I said, a little embarrassed, *"you opened the wrong end."*

He smiled at a me, a smile made up of both crooked and missing teeth.

"No, I didn't, youngster," he said.

He smiled even bigger seeing the confusion on my face.

"Listen up," he said, *"these here cigarettes is mighty expensive. I don't like givin' 'em away. So when one of dem boys comes up and asks me for a cigarette, I says to dem, 'Son, I'd be more than happy to give you a cigarette, but as you can see I haven't yet opened up the pack. Come back later.'*

"After awhile," said Tom, lighting a Lucky Strike and taking a deep, throat-rattling drag, *"they just stop asking."*

I know guys with master's degrees who aren't as smart as Old Tom.

I finish my cigarette and flick the butt into the parking lot where it joins a growing pile of other dead soldiers. Every weekend a landscaping service cuts our grass and cleans the parking lot, so each Monday morning I start fresh with no reminders of the previous week's smoking marathon.

Before I go back into the office, I look at the concrete squares that make up our sidewalk. I wonder to myself if, almost forty years later, I could crack one of those squares with a sledgehammer. I see Old Tom's craggy face in my head and I hear his white gasoline voice, and I know, without a shadow of a doubt, that I could.

* * *

We are a society that loves to give out cheesy awards, so with that in mind, I suggest these suicide peeps are deserving of their own special suicide awards, even if they aren't here to collect them.

The *Best Product Endorsement Award* is a tie and goes to English poet Charlotte Mew who drank a bottle of Lysol in 1928 and by American poet Vachel Lindsay who also drank a bottle of Lysol three years later.

The *If At First You Don't Succeed Award* is also a tie. It is shared by Japanese film idol Yukiko Okada who jumped from a seven-story building after his earlier suicide attempts of slashing his wrists and gas inhalation had failed, and by Norwegian vocalist Per Yngve Ohlin who killed himself with a shotgun after slashing his wrists and slitting his throat had not done the trick.

The *All in the Family Award* goes to professional wrestlers and brothers Chris Von Erich who shot himself in the head; Kerry Von Erich who shot himself in the heart; and Mike Von Erich who overdosed on sleeping pills and alcohol.

The *Be A Little More Patient Award* goes to author John Kennedy Toole who killed himself with carbon monoxide because he was despondent over not being able to get his book published; after his suicide his mother managed to get his book, *A Confederacy of Dunces*, published. Oh, and it won the Pulitzer Prize.

The *I'm A Real Multi-Tasker Award* goes to Jose Luis Calva who hung himself and who was described as *"a Mexican writer, cannibal and serial killer."*

The *That's What Are Friends For Award* actually goes to someone who did not commit suicide. Author J.M. Barrie gets the award for saying that his buddy Peter Llewelyn Davies was the source for the name of the title character in his famous play *Peter Pan,* but being identified as *The Boy Who Wouldn't Grow Up* plagued Davies his whole life until he threw himself in front of a train.

Drum roll please.

Hands down, the winner for *Most Creative Suicide Award* is Louis Lingg, a German anarchist scheduled to be hanged for his alleged role in the Haymarket Square riot bombing, who committed suicide by exploding an entire stick of dynamite in his mouth.

lines.

Now that takes balls.

* * *

A few months before the afternoon with the gun, Dean and I were parked outside the Black Knight, sipping warm beers as the flashing neon of the club's roadside sign blinked off, signaling the end of the evening for those night crawlers who, unlike us, had had the good fortune of arriving before closing time, before the bouncer with the three-pound crescent wrench in his back pocket began herding them toward the door. Resigned to having missed last call, we quietly smoked and drank our store-bought beer, staring out the front windshield as across the parking lot the revelers headed for their cars.

Directly in front of us, not quite thirty feet away, a tall attractive girl, obviously drunk, walked away from a group of friends and leaned against the back of an old Ford pickup truck. A girl alone would naturally catch our attention, and so Dean and I were both looking at her when we saw the truck lights come on and heard the big engine roar to life. The truck began to back up, knocking the girl to the ground, and her head lay flat on the gravel of the parking lot just inches away from the rear tire of the truck. The driver of the pickup, talking to a passenger, must not have heard the bump, nor had the girl's friends, who were engrossed in conversation on the other side of the truck.

Only Dean and I saw.

And we watched and we waited.

It was a warm night and the sounds coming through our open windows from the parking lot were clear and crisp, a mixture of drunken laughter, loud boasts, slamming car doors and what seemed like the deafening crunch of loose gravel under the fat black tires of that Ford pickup truck. Either one of us could have yelled a warning, but we didn't move, didn't say a word to each other, just watched. And when the space between the truck's rear tire and the girl's head no longer existed, when the rubber knobs of that wide tire were just beginning to press into the smooth skin of her cheek, two giant forearms slammed down on the hood of the truck. One of the girl's friends, a burly bearded fellow, had seen her legs under the truck and at the last second had pounced on the hood, a move that

74

effectively alerted the driver to slam on his brakes. The rest of the group quickly surrounded the truck, cursing the driver and pulling the unconscious, and miraculously unharmed, girl to her feet.

What was then said between Dean and I escapes recall, but in the interest of both our moral characters, I'm sure it was some exclamation of relief. Yet we never questioned each other as to why we had both neglected, or chose not, to issue a warning. It was certainly not for fear of getting involved, for we were neither shy nor loathe to enter a situation, and it was certainly not out of any desire to see carnage inflicted on another person, for though we relished frolicking on the edge of violence there was a mutual abhorrence of unjustified pain and suffering. I can only assume that on that night we sensed a clear line between participation and observation, that we had a choice between the two, and that our fascination with what had quickly and incredibly unfolded between our eyes tipped the scales to a choice that could have meant the grisly death of another human being.

When I compare the night with the truck and the fallen girl and the afternoon with Dean and the loaded gun, I see the similarities between the two scenarios and realize the power that silence can have. Within a few months of the parking lot incident Dean again had the opportunity to choose between observation and involvement, but this time it wasn't a stranger, it was a good friend, and this time the space of his action wasn't measured by dozens of yards across a parking lot, it was simply inches across a coffee table. In that parking lot we had been together, both of us wearing the cloak of anonymity and sharing in the knowledge of our inactivity. In his living room a short time later, Dean retained his status as an observer but I crossed the line and slipped on the mantle of participant, pushing a loaded gun into the side of my head. And nobody knew that but Dean.

And he waited, and he watched.

Which I can completely understand.

* * *

I fell asleep on Dean's couch that night and the next morning when I idly picked the gun up off the coffee table, something prompted me to eject the clip and I saw that the gun was loaded.

lines.

With a bullet in the chamber.

What the fuck. I could have killed myself.

It wasn't until a few days later that what had happened, or rather what had not happened, really started to sink in.

I realized then, and have seen it proven time and time again over the years, that there is a very fine line between life and death. That old here today, gone tomorrow thing. Some people's lives are hanging by a mere thread, others by a steel cable.

The first suicide I wrote about as a reporter was that of a pretty college coed who had parked her car on our city's only bridge and jumped into the deep muddy river below it. I know she was pretty because her photo was on the front page of the newspaper when I came to work. The weekend police beat reporter had written the article. That afternoon the city desk called me on my walkie-talkie radio and said they heard on the police scanner that a floater had been found in the river. It was a sunny, pleasant day. I stood on the river bank and watched fire rescue pull the coed's body from the river.

She wasn't pretty any more.

I'll spare you the details, but it's scary what happens to a body that has been in the water for as little as twenty-four hours. Driving back to the newspaper later, I stopped at a traffic light and looked over at the car next to me. A pretty blonde girl was driving. We made brief eye contact and she looked away, somewhat dismissedly. I remember wondering if she realized that beauty was truly only skin deep, and if that skin is slipping off your body because of river currents and hungry fish, then beauty is only a word.

In the newsroom everyone was laughing and talking and enjoying the day. I sat at my desk and could not get the image of that coed's bloated body out of my head. I couldn't eat anything that day.

Four months later someone else fell off that bridge. This time it was an off-duty police detective who was married with three children and who was one of my favorite cops at the station. He always had a smile on his face and was friendly to everyone, even the perps he arrested. He was driving home at midnight when he saw a car stalled on the bridge. He stopped to assist the driver and another motorist accidentally struck him and knocked him off the bridge and into the muddy river. They found his body the next day.

lines.

One bridge. Two deaths. One by choice, one by fate.
Who decides?

When I was a teenager my Dad was stationed in Central America. We lived on the Air Force Base there in base housing on a dead-end street along with eleven other families, six houses on each side of the street going up a slight hill to a cul de sac. The sun shined bright and strong every day, our lawns were spongy with thick green grass, behind our houses was a three-story wall of lush jungle that stretched for miles, colorful birds nested in trees packed with ripe exotic fruit, and you could actually watch monkeys swinging on vines from tree to tree. It was so serene and beautiful. It looked like a postcard.

And in a one-year period, three teenagers who lived on my little street all died.

One boy was killed in an explosion. One girl died of heart failure. One boy fell off a cliff.

Three out of twelve families lost a child. In less than one year.

"It was hell," says my Mom. *"I hated that place. I lived in fear every day that I would lose one of you kids."*

Forty years later her eyes still get misty when she recalls the pain and misery that blanketed our street, and the unpredictability of death's embrace.

* * *

Violet death always surprises people.

The truth is that both our entrance into this world and our exit out of this world are, for the most part, violent.

The entrance part certainly is. Just ask any woman who has given birth. I held my wife's hand and watched as little capillaries exploded just under the skin on her neck until her neck was covered with hundreds of red pin-prick dots when she summoned every ounce of power to push my son out. Caesarean sections involve blood and pain and a scalpel. Some children, and mothers, still die in the childbirth process. Add in circumcision for males and a slap on the bottom from the doctor and some might say a delivery room more resembles a medieval dungeon than a nursery school playroom.

lines.

As for the exit part, how many people actually die peacefully in their sleep?

I was walking through a nightclub parking lot with Happy John once when we saw an ambulance go by.

"You know," I said to John, *"a ride in one of those things is in everybody's future."*

"Well, that's depressing as fuck," said John.

"But true," said I.

If you are not lucky enough to die in the middle of a really great dream, and if you don't die a violent death in a car crash or a house fire, and if you don't die a long lingering painful death from colon cancer or kidney failure, then your death is probably still going to involve an ambulance and a ride to the emergency room and needles and catheters and such.

All in all, being born is not warm and fuzzy.

And neither is dying.

*   *   *

They say the only things in life that are certain are death and taxes.

Which is bullshit. Only one of those things is certain.

You can live all by your lonesome in a thatched hut in the heart of the Amazon jungle, eating papayas and drinking rainwater, and you will never have to pay taxes.

But one day you are going to die. You can fucking count on it.

Whether you're in that jungle with papaya juice dribbling down your chin or banging some overpriced hooker in your penthouse apartment in Manhattan or feeding the poor and homeless on a pilgrimage to Haiti, your card is eventually going to get punched. Don't matter what you be doing, brother, one day you is gonna die.

And that's what's so cool about death.

Life can be incredibly unfair—*right now someone is eating a dirt pancake while someone else is throwing away a half-eaten porterhouse steak*—but death is the great equalizer. In the end, it puts everyone on the same even playing field. It is truly the one universally shared experience. Death shows no favoritism, does not discriminate, and does not take bribes.

lines.

"All my possessions for a moment of time," said Elizabeth I, Queen of England in 1603, on her deathbed, to which death said, *"Sorry, sucks to be you."*

And while death is always certain, what is never certain—with one exception—is *when* you are going to die, *where* you are going to die, and *how* you are going to die. You know the beginning, you just don't know the end.

Call up your mother and ask her when you were born and where you were born and how you were born, and she can tell you to the minute when you popped out, and she can tell you what city the hospital was in where you were born, and she can even tell you whether it was a quick easy delivery or a long drawn out process that involved forceps and an epidural. She can even tell you if the sun was shining, what color eyes the doctor had, what song was playing on the radio when her water broke, and what her last meal was that day.

Now ask her *when* you are going to die, *where* you are going to die, and *how* you are going to die.

"How the hell would I know," will be her answer.

Followed by, *"Why are you asking such a silly question?"*

And then, *"Okay, what have you done wrong?"*

Which is what makes suicide so fascinating. It is truly that one exception where you can know in advance the when, the where and the how of your death. To the very minute if you so desire. It's your one chance to go from observer to participant in the game of life and death, your one chance to cross the line and take life and death out of the arbitrary hands of fate and put it into your own hands.

Think about it. There is only life and death. There is no in between. You can only have one of them at a time. They are the two most important things that will ever happen to you.

Every day you put your life into your own hands.

So, why not your death?

Just a thought.

* * *

Dean and I, visions of blondes in bikinis in our heads, moved to California about a year later, doing that whole sowing your wild oats rite of passage thing since we had both recently turned twenty-one.

lines.

We shared an apartment for a few months, but two strong personalities confined together in a tiny apartment was a recipe for disaster, and so we fought like cats and dogs. Drinking every day didn't help the situation. We'd go to a nightclub and, after Dean had a few drinks in him, he would walk the length of the bar, bumping his shoulder into the biggest guys sitting at the bar, trying to start a fight. He was a tough, angry motherfucker. He would fight at the drop of a hat.

One night Dean dropped acid at our apartment and we got into an argument about something, so I went to bed. For some reason I woke up at about four in the morning. I was laying on my back and my eyes were just barely open in the dark room. Dean had dragged a chair from the kitchen into my bedroom and was sitting next to my bed, leaning over in the chair, staring at me. Let's see, he's hallucinating on acid, he has a propensity for violence, we just had a fight, there are several butcher knives in the kitchen, and he's sitting right next to my bed staring at me at four in the morning. Not good.

I had two choices. Open my eyes all the way and startle Dean by asking him what the fuck he was doing, which did not seem like the best of ideas. Or close my eyes and go back to sleep and whatever was going to happen would happen. I chose the latter.

I moved into another apartment the next week, and a year later I moved back home and eventually got married. Dean stayed in California and then moved around the country, increasing his alcohol intake and picking up a deadly methamphetamine habit in the process. Over the next half dozen years, I would see him every now and then, and he would look worse each time I saw him.

One day I got a phone call at work from my wife in the middle of the afternoon.

"You need to come home." She sounded scared to death. *"Right now."*

"What's wrong?"

"Dean's here."

"I'll be right there."

I jumped in my car and sped home. Dean's car was parked in our driveway and he was leaning against the car, talking to my wife who was standing on our front porch. She had not let Dean into the house. Our two young children were inside. As I pulled up, my wife turned around and hurried back into the house.

lines.

I walked up and shook Dean's hand and I could see why my wife had called me in a panic. Dean was a strung-out, jittery mess. His eyes blazed red. Even I was scared.

I don't remember what we talked about, but I do remember that Dean was leaning against the front fender of his car which meant that I could see the front driver's door. And that door, from the top of the half-open window to the bottom edge of the door, was covered with still wet blood. In the middle of the fucking afternoon.

"Oh, I had a problem with a guy at a gas station," said Dean when I mentioned the door. *"Don't worry about it."*

Dean soon left and I didn't see him for many years. The consensus among our mutual friends was that Dean's days were numbered. Either the meth would do him in, or the type of people he was hanging out with would do him in, like the night a Hell's Angel stuck the barrel of a shotgun against his forehead and threatened to pull the trigger.

And then something unusual happened.

Dean stopped drinking, and he stopped drugging, and he stopped fighting. He moved back home and he got married and he had a son and he learned how to repair computers and hard drives and he got a good job and he bought a house and he became a loving husband and a loving father.

When I first heard about it, I did not believe it, and it wasn't until I went back home for a visit and I went and saw Dean and I shook his hand and I looked into his eyes that I knew that, yes, against all the odds, he had vanquished his demons and turned his life around. That made me very happy.

And when I shook Dean's hand that day, I thought of Old Tom and of what he had taught me.

"Nothing is impossible."

* * *

"So where's the rat?" asks Albert, answering his own question.

Albert knows Boo sleeps in the car whenever I stop into Jimmy's for a drink. He just likes to bust my balls by referring to my pride and joy as a rodent, and to subtly remind me not to make the same mistake I did the first week I started coming to Jimmy's when I let a few of the dancers convince me to get Boo out of the car and bring him into the club for them to see.

"What's that fucking dog doing in my bar? Get that rat out of here. You want me to lose my liquor license?" Albert had shouted that day.

"Sorry, the girls ..."

"That was your first mistake. Don't listen to them broads."

That's one of the reasons I like Albert. I don't know anyone who still refers to women as broads. Kind of sums him up, and not necessarily in a bad way.

We take our seats at the end of the bar. Albert is not in a good mood.

"You watch the game last night?" he asks.

Before I can answer, he says, *"Lost my ass on it. Took the over. Screwed up my parlay. Cost me big."*

I nod to show empathy. Gambling, particularly sports gambling, is not a loner event. You win, you want to brag to someone. You lose, you want to complain to someone. I've done my share of both. But my current project has my mind in a different type of sporting arena, so I didn't watch the game last night or bet on it.

I met Albert many years ago at another strip club where he was just the night manager when I had first come to this city to look for a house to buy. I eventually moved here and over the years I would occasionally see Albert working at other clubs as a manager. When he bought Jimmy's and traded his manager hat in for an owner hat, I made Jimmy's my main hangout.

At that first club where I met him, the club owner was a real character, an old school titty bar guy. He took Albert and myself and three of his dancers to a neighborhood Italian restaurant near his club one night and proceeded to get into an argument with Albert about some ridiculous thing. The dancers, having seen it all before, just ignored them and kept picking at their food. Other patrons, some with children, kept a nervous eye on our table as the shouting got louder and louder until the club owner lifted up his shirt, pulled a pistol from the front of his pants waistband, and started waving it in front of Albert's face. The dancers still didn't even bat an eyelash, although I thought our young waiter was going to shit a brick.

"Put that damn thing away and pass the Parmesan," Albert had said, being sure to add the word *"please"* at the end.

lines.

Crisis averted, we all ended up back at the club at the club owner's personal table in a back corner. The club featured totally nude dancers which meant that alcoholic beverages could not be served because of that county's liquor laws, but that didn't stop the club owner from sending Albert to the package liquor store next door to get him a bottle of red wine and me a fifth of Jack Daniels bourbon.

"Just keep the bottle in the paper bag when you ain't pouring," said the club owner, which I did when I wasn't liberally pouring bourbon into the cokes that the waitress brought me. An hour later the club owner called it a night, and an hour after that I decided I would have one more drink and then leave. I pulled the bottle from the crinkled brown paper bag and was surprised at how quickly and easily it came out of the bag.

Probably because it was empty.

Uh-oh.

I did a quick mental calculation.

One fifth of Jack Daniels.

Consumed in two hours.

By just me.

I'm fucked.

I tried to stand up, an emphasis on the word try. Albert rolled his eyes, pulled me to my feet, fished the rental car keys out of my pocket, asked what hotel I was staying at, drove me in my rental car to the hotel, pushed me into the hotel elevator, and then caught a cab back to the club.

The last thing I remember that night was standing in my hotel room bathroom taking a piss. Okay, I'm lying. Actually the last thing I remember was leaning a little too far back until I completely lost my balance and fell backward into the bathtub, still holding my dick and watching bleary-eyed as a plume of piss shot five feet straight up into the air and then splattered back down on me. I knew that in my awkward and slippery position I could never untangle myself before the stream had run its course, so I just laid there and laughed and laughed.

The next time I saw Albert I thanked him for the ride home and he brusquely brushed it off, but we became acquaintances and today, even though he would never admit to it, I think we would be considered friends.

lines.

"So Albert," I start to say and can actually see him wince. I know he hates it when I say those two words because it means I am going to ask him a question and Albert does not like questions. That's how I know we must be friends because he will tolerate an occasional question from me. Questions from other people he just ignores.

"Yeah?"

"Why did it take you so many years before you stopped being a club manager and bought your own place?"

Albert thinks for a minute. He knows that I know that he did some prison time. And he knows that I know it's impossible for a convicted felon to get a liquor license without working some kind of angle. So he knows what I am really inquiring about is, what did he get popped for?

It takes him a while to answer.

"I had to wait to get some things straightened out before I could get a liquor license," he says, a hint of irritation in his voice.

"What kind of things?" I ask.

"I did something I shouldn't have."

He pauses.

"Or at least I shouldn't have got caught for doing it."

He stops talking.

So I say, *"... and?"* because neither I nor anyone at the bar seems to know what *it* refers to.

Albert turns and looks at me with hard eyes. I have crossed a line. I can tell he is deciding whether to say something or just ignore me.

"What do you mean, 'and?' You asked me a question. I fucking answered it."

I realize I don't really need to know what *it* refers to.

And I wonder about that Albert and I being friends thing.

*   *   *

Laying in bed tonight I can still taste the Garibaldi sandwich. I think it's the fontinella cheese. Or maybe the garlic oil.

Boo weighs in.

"Try brushing your teeth, goofball."

"I did already."

lines.

"Yeah, well you might want to take another stab at it."

"Don't be a hater, Boo."

"That was a foot-long sandwich. You could have just eaten half of it. Why be a glutton? I'll bet your cholesterol is through the roof."

"What are you, my Mom?"

Boo doesn't answer. I slip on my reading glasses and open the book on my night stand. I wait a few moments because I don't want to start reading and then have Boo interrupt me. He's quiet, so I start reading. I turn to the next page in the hardback book and the page turning makes that very unique sound, which is just the signal Boo has been waiting for.

"Damn bro, you sure as hell pissed Albert off tonight."

"I didn't mean to."

"Well, you did. Big time."

"You know me. I'm just a curious person. I'd really like to know what he served time for."

"A word to the wise. Don't press that issue. I only saw that fucker once when he kicked me out of his bar, but one look was enough to tell me he's not someone whose bad side you want to be on."

"I hear you."

Boo goes quiet again. I wait, then start reading the next two facing pages in the book. When I turn the second page, it makes that page turning sound again and loosens Boo's tongue.

"Can I ask you a question?"

"If you insist."

"Now who's being the hater?"

"You're right. Sorry. What's on your little pea brain?"

"Keep that smartass attitude up and I'll interrupt your book reading all night long, cowboy."

"Touche. Okay, what's your question?"

"You know how your Dad dying messed up your head?

"Yeah."

"How his death is your only regret in life?"

"Yeah."

"Well, if you kill yourself, won't you be doing the same thing to your children? Is that really fair to them?"

"I've thought about that."

"And?"

lines.

"It makes me feel very guilty."

"So don't kill yourself."

I pause for a few moments and then pick up the book again. I flip it open to the last page I folded over.

"Okay," I say, *"I won't kill myself."*

"Don't play me."

"No, really. I won't."

"Liar."

Wednesday, June 24

dark.

Yesterday morning I was in a good mood.

This morning I am in a bad mood.

I have a schedule to keep and I feel like I wasted most of yesterday doing Internet suicide research.

As the *TCB List* dictates for Wednesday, I need to decide on the best way for me personally to commit suicide and then I need to get the tools I will need for the project.

Which, pain in the ass that it is, means getting a cup of hot coffee, shutting the door to my office, and firing up my computer yet again.

It may seem silly to search the Internet for different ways to commit suicide since most people already know the common methods. Still, I hit the search button on my computer because my fear is that I might miss out on some new method that beats the hell out of the old standbys. I'm looking for that new method where I slowly drift off to sleep while getting a blowjob from the Playmate of the Year, receiving a really good Swedish massage from a beefy lass with strong hands, hearing Robert Plant and Jimmy Page play a private a cappella version of *Stairway to Heaven*, smelling freshly baked chocolate chip and pecan cookies, and having the TV anchor announce that I just won a Pulitzer.

dark.

While there are many different ways to commit suicide, there are really only two ways to kill yourself, or more specifically, only two ways to get the human body to stop functioning—the physical way and the chemical way.

Physical modes of stopping human life are ones that incapacitate the respiratory system or the central nervous system by destroying one of the body's key components.

Think getting hit by a train.

Chemical modes of suicide are ones that interrupt important biological processes in the human body like cellular respiration or the ability to breathe.

Think knocking back a vial of sleeping pills and washing them down with a bottle of cheap red wine. I suggest Thunderbird.

According to the Internet, these are some of my choices:

I can slit my wrists.

This is officially known as exsanguination where the goal, through a single or multiple incisions, is to slice through the radial artery, ulnar artery, cephalic vein or the basilic vein. When I take that razor or broken piece of glass to the soft underside of my wrist, here's what doctors say will happen. *Your body will attempt to compensate with increased cardiac rate, vasoconstriction and coagulation of blood. You will experience a drop in blood pressure, increased heart rate, somatic pain and poor peripheral perfusion. As the bleeding continues, cardiac arrhythmia is likely to ensue as the body is eventually unable to compensate. If the exsanguination is allowed to continue, the resulting severe hypovolemia will cause shock, followed by cardiovascular collapse, cardiac arrest and death.*

In other words, I will fucking bleed to death.

Sounds messy and way too painful. I whine when I get a papercut. I don't want to lay in a pool of my own blood for hours and feel the pain of deep slashes on my wrists. I could do it in a bathtub full of warm water, but I would want to read while I'm in the tub, so how do I hold the book if blood is spurting out of my wrists? What book do I read, one that really interests me or one that will look cool when they find my body? What if I get to a really good part in the book and then I die? Or what if I'm still alive and the water turns lukewarm, then cold?

Also, I'd prefer not to be naked when I'm found.

So, strike the wrist slitting.

dark.

I can drown myself.

But the oxygen still in my body will make me pop to the top of the water and, best intentions aside, my body's natural tendency will be to come up for air. I don't want to have to buy cinder blocks and heavy chains, I don't want to drive all the way to the beach, and I don't own a boat. That's probably why drowning is among the least popular methods of suicide, with less than two percent of people taking the plunge.

Drowning sounds too labor intensive, so I'll pass.

I can jump to my death.

Suicide by jumping from a building or some other high point like a bridge or a cliff is not very common in the United States, less than two percent of suicides. Although, more than half of the suicides in Hong Kong are from jumping because the city is saturated with high-rises, which shows you the law of supply and demand at work.

I'm scared of heights, so that one is out.

I can suffocate myself.

In the biz, they call the plastic bag you put over your head to suffocate yourself the *exit bag*. Isn't that cute. I can also suffocate myself by using depressants in the form of inert gas to make me pass out and die from lack of oxygen. The good news is that breathing inert gas will render me unconscious and cause death without any experience of panic and discomfort. The bad news is that the inert gas you will need is helium, argon or nitrogen and I haven't seen any of them on sale recently at my neighborhood grocery store.

How much nitrogen do you need, sir?

Oh, I don't know. Why don't you just fill up this here "exit' bag.

I am going to want to smoke a few nerve-calming cigarettes on the big day and it may not be a good idea to have an open flame around inert gases that could explode.

So nixay on the suffocation.

I can electrocute myself.

That's easier said than done. Dropping my iPod in the bathtub will probably not do the trick, and I know the local prison warden won't let me borrow Sparky for an hour or so. I stuck a screwdriver into a wall socket when I was a kid and it didn't kill me, so that method is questionable. It did, however, throw my Mom clear across the room when she went to pull it out. Next time, Mom, try grabbing the plastic handle.

The goal of giving myself a lethal electric shock is to cause arrythmias, which means the contractions of the different chambers in my heart will get out of synch and my blood will stop flowing. But I can also be severely burned in a lethal electrical shock, and why the hell would I want to do that?

Nope, let someone else try the screwdriver trick.

I can jump in front of a moving vehicle.

One website says that, *some people commit suicide by deliberately placing themselves in the path of a usually large and fast-moving vehicle, resulting in a fatal impact.*

I'm pretty sure if you open a dictionary, you will find that exact same sentence when you look up the definition for *needless fucking pain*.

I rule that ridiculously painful notion out, but admit that I read on because I am intrigued by its variations.

Some people throw themselves directly in front of an oncoming railroad train, and others drive their car onto the tracks and wait to get hit. Apparently this is a much more popular sport in Europe where they have tighter gun control laws but more highly developed rail networks. Suicide by train has a ninety percent success rate, but I question if you want to be in the remaining ten percent with *massive fractures, amputations and concussion, permanent brain damage and physical disability.* If it's any consolation, studies say that, *this type of suicide may be traumatizing to the driver of the train.* Poor guy.

Your survival rate jumps to almost seventy percent if instead of a railroad train, you step in front of a subway train because trains arriving at subway stations are slowing down to let off and board passengers.

Some single-occupant, single-vehicle car crashes are actually suicides, but statistics are hard to come by because, unless the driver left a suicide note on the front seat of his new Ford Fiesta before hitting that bridge piling at eighty miles per hour, he's not doing any talking. Even if it is suspected that the driver committed suicide, unless a note is found, his death will be classified by police and the insurance companies as an accident.

Massive trauma sounds painful, pass.

dark.

I can poison myself.

This option offers a true smorgasbord of taste treats.

I can go with a fast-acting poison like cyanide. Reverend Jim Jones recommends a nice mix of cyanide, diazepam and your favorite fruit-flavored drink. He promises it will be a big hit at your next outdoor party with all of your friends. What the hell, why not invite a congressman and a few TV reporters to the bash.

I could go the whole foods, naturalist route and gobble down some Belladonna plants, castor beans, or Jatropha curcas nuts, which are all toxic, but they take forever to kill you and during the interim you are in a lot of pain, and probably still hungry.

Worldwide, thirty percent of all suicides are accomplished by ingesting pesticide poison. That's just the cockroaches getting even.

I've always been a picky eater, so forget the poison.

I can hang myself.

Looping my favorite vintage Jerry Garcia silk tie or the rope from my neighbor's tire swing around my neck, and tying the free end around a rooster weather vane would end by life either through strangulation or by snapping my neck, depending on the length of the drop. In the strangulation scenario, I am *likely to experience hypoxia, skin tingling, dizziness, vision narrowing, convulsions, shock, acute respiratory acidosis, cerebral ischemia and a hypoxic condition in the brain which will result in death.* In the snapped neck scenario, I am *likely to suffer a fractured second and third and/or fourth and fifth cervical vertebrae which may cause paralysis or death.*

I vote for option number two.

But what they forget to mention about what is behind door number two is that if the rope is strong enough, and the drop is far enough, many times your head will pop right off your body when you make that drop. I agree with the saying, *live fast, die young and leave a nice-looking corpse,* and it's hard to maintain the last part of that quote if your body is on the ground but your head just rolled across the street and down a storm drain.

No hanging for me.

I could take a drug overdose.

Now you're talking!

Overdosing is a method of suicide which involves taking medication in doses greater than the indicated levels. Been there!

dark.

Or *in a combination that will interact to either cause harmful effects or increase the potency of one or other of the substances.* Done that!

So you take some pills and fall asleep. Sounds easy enough. But while this is the most peaceful form of suicide, its success depends on the type and quantity of the medication taken. It's not an exact science, with some people having, or incorrectly thinking they have, more drug tolerance than others, which is one of the reasons there are a lot of accidental overdoses that are not suicides. Acts of stupidity, yes. Suicide, no.

Serious devotees of suicide by medication go for the tried-and-true barbiturates like Nembutal and Seconal, but it's almost impossible to get a legal prescription for them. Prescription and over the counter sleeping pills and painkillers are next up to bat, but the problem there is that drugs taken orally can be vomited back up before they have been absorbed into your blood system.

On the surface, this method sounds like a winner, but my concerns are the vomiting and that fact that, given my past indiscretions, I believe I have a very high tolerance for drugs. Plus, I really want to go out with a bang and not a whimper.

So I just say no to drugs.

I can kill myself with a garden hose.

Well, more specifically, with carbon monoxide. The garden hose simply transports the colorless and odorless gas from my running car's tailpipe into the interior of my car where I am sitting with the windows rolled up listening to Howard Stern on Sirius Radio. But if it's a colorless and odorless gas, how will I know if it's working? And the diameter of every garden hose I've ever seen is smaller than that of a car tailpipe, so now I have to go buy some duct tape to attach the hose to the tailpipe, and won't the heat from the exhaust pipe melt the tape so that the hose falls off the pipe, which means I'm getting in and out of the car? Plus I need to find an old car because the exhaust from old cars contains twenty-five percent carbon monoxide but new cars with catalytic converters only have one percent carbon monoxide which means my new car will run out of gas long before I asphyxiate myself.

Some people actually kill themselves through carbon monoxide poisoning by burning charcoal in a barbecue in a sealed room. They call it *death by hibachi*. I shit you not. That's even funnier than the *exit bag*.

I have a new car with a catalytic converter and the only barbecue grill I want to be around is one with a sixteen-ounce New York strip steak on it.

Pass.

Death by Tide.

I can drink detergent or other household cleaning agents, or I can use them to make sure I have clean clothes to wear and the house is nice and tidy on the big day.

I'll go with the latter.

I can have a poisonous snake or spider bite me.

Which I presume I can buy at the same store that carries helium, argon and nitrogen.

I can set myself on fire.

But I won't. Are you fucking crazy?

I can starve myself to death.

See set myself on fire.

I can commit harakiri.

You know, seppuku, the ancient art of preserving your honor by slicing your belly open with your own knife while wearing a snazzy kimono. To do it properly, your first cut is left to right and your second cut is a slightly upward stroke.

How about no cuts at all, Tojo.

I can blow myself up.

The Internet says *high explosives that are certain to explode and release an extreme amount of energy are often used to avoid unnecessary pain.* How convenient since it is so easy to buy high explosives, not just normal explosives but *high* explosives, at Walmart. And I need to be sure to remember to get the ones that *are certain to explode.*

Pass.

I can die in a suicide attack.

I'm not relying on anyone else. Screw that.

Or through suicide by cop.

Same answer.

I can shoot myself.

Death, says the Internet, most often results if the bullet enters above the ear, destroying the parietal lobe, which is responsible for

dark.

breathing and critical life processes. I had no idea I even had a parietal lobe, much less that it is so damn important.

It gets better.

A high caliber weapon and a proper barrel orientation to the head is likely to exert devastating high energy transfer effects: high class hemorrhage, severe rearrangement of the brain structure with permanent partial or complete tissue destruction of multiple lobes, nerve destruction and obvious skull fracture with potential bone fragments embedded in the brain.

Not sure which part is the funniest, the part about proper barrel orientation to the head, or the part about severe rearrangement of the brain structure.

Maybe the proper barrel orientation thing is really not all that funny. I read a report once from an EMT that said, *"We were called to a scene but not told what kind of emergency we had. This was late at night. A man comes walking to our ambulance holding both hands to his face. I asked him what happened. He could barely talk. He had blown off part of the front of his face. He had lost some upper and lower jaw and his tongue and nose by a rifle shot. He said he had pulled the rifle away at the last minute and that is why part of his face was gone instead of his head."*

Still, the bottom line is that I already have a gun so I don't need to go buy any rope or duct tape or poison or prescription drugs or lethal spiders or cinder blocks. And based on what the Internet has outlined, a gunshot seems to be one of the quickest and, if my aim is true, least painful of the suicide options. Hey, it's the method of choice for half the population, so who am I to buck the trend.

A gun it is.

I just need me a bullet.

* * *

When I think about it, fingers poised over the computer keyboard, so much of my life has revolved around life and death and police and crime. While other kids were reading *Sports Illustrated* at the library I was reading *True Detective*. When those kids became adults and went to work at accounting firms and insurance agencies, I rode in patrol cars with cops to crime scenes. Now, at night when they read fiction best sellers cranked out assembly line style, I read the latest non-fiction True Crime offerings.

And when they fall asleep they dream about forty-foot luxury yachts, while I have this recurring dream about me and a high-powered rifle and a university building tower, but that's another story.

One day, after I either told one of my cop stories or maybe made a personal observation, Dean turned to me and said with a mixture of awe, concern and disgust, *"You know you are one dark motherfucker."*

Which I took then as a compliment.

Later, I would realize it was a curse.

* * *

In every police station across the country, no matter how big or small, you will find an arrest book or arrest log. In my day it was a giant leather bound book with ledger pages that looked a lot like the log Ebenezer Scrooge used to write down all the amounts of money that people owed to him. Handwritten into the arrest book will be the name, address and age of every person arrested that day in that particular police jurisdiction, along with the specific criminal charge or charges that police arrested them on, and the date and time they were booked. The arrest book is like Ebenezer's what-you-owe-me book, but in this case it shows a debt that someone owes to society, soon to be paid with the currency of prison time if they are eventually convicted for the crime.

By law, the arrest book must be open to the public 24 hours a day so that the public can see who has been taken off the streets by their government, unlike in those Third World countries where police routinely snatch people off the street and just shrug when family and friends show up asking what happened to Uncle Pasquale.

In addition to the arrest book always having to be available for public scrutiny, the book must remain intact without any missing pages, and once information is written into the book it can not be changed or erased or covered up in any manner. The book is usually left out with the pages spread open and on there is room to write in about forty arrests on each page.

As a police beat reporter I routinely made the rounds of the city police departments, the sheriff's offices and even the state police offices to look at their respective arrest books to see which lucky people would become fodder for the pages of the next day's newspaper. The arrest book was very impartial. It didn't matter if you were a skid row bum arrested for vagrancy or if you were the son of a state senator arrested for date rape. If you got popped, you ended up in the arrest book. No exceptions.

The arrest book is monitored by a desk sergeant who is also the person you talk to if you don't have a phone to call 911 and instead walk to the police station to let someone know you've just been carjacked. Just like in the movies, the desk sergeant is always a cantankerous mofo who never smiles and will actually get a pained look on his face whenever a citizen walks in.

Part of my beat included a few smaller city police departments within our two county area, and one of those looked like it was the setting for that classic 1960s movie *In the Heat of the Night*. Every cop on that tiny force was short and fat, was the spitting image of Rod Steiger from the movie, and invariably was called Bubba, regardless of what name his parents had christened him with. I say *his* because there were no female cops on this particular force, and the only blacks and Hispanics ever in that building were the ones behind bars in the jail on the second floor.

When I checked the arrest book late one night at that police station, I had to do a double-take. I could not read a single word on the two open pages. Probably because they were covered, actually more like soaked, with blood, still shiny and wet.

I looked at the desk sergeant, back at the arrest book, and back at the sergeant.

He did the same, looking at me, then the arrest book, then back at me. He smiled.

But of course he did not say a word. He was enjoying himself. If I wanted to know what happened, I would have to ask. By and large, desk sergeants are all assholes.

"So, what happened?" I asked.

"What do you mean?

"The arrest book."

"What about it?"

"It's covered with blood."

"Really?"

Like I said, assholes one and all.

dark.

I didn't say another word. I would not give him the satisfaction.

Finally he spilled. Turns out two Bubbas had arrested a black guy for a barroom brawl at one of the local juke joints. While they were booking him, he kept getting louder and louder with his complaints about being arrested in general and about why the other guy wasn't also arrested in particular. Despite the fact that his hands were cuffed behind his back, the man made the grievous error of switching from complaining about his arrest to questioning the sexual proclivities of the mothers of the two Bubbas. Whereupon, one of the Bubbas placed his hand on the back of the man's head and then slammed his face into the middle of the arrest book, shattering his nose and spraying the pages with crimson blood. The man then crumpled to the ground, out cold.

"That's why the book is covered with blood," said the desk sergeant. *"And you know I can't tear those pages out."*

"How am I supposed to read who's been arrested?"

"Not my problem."

He was right. Not only could he not tear the pages out, the most he could do was wipe up the blood with a paper towel and if the dried smeared blood made it hard, or even impossible, to read the writing on those two pages, nothing could be done. Changing anything in the arrest book would be like fucking with the stone tablets the Ten Commandments were chiseled on.

Over the next few months I watched as those red-edged pages went further and further to the back of the arrest book, a constant reminder of why when you are handcuffed you should be as polite as possible to the boys in blue. I'm sure that over the ensuing months first-time arrestees wondered what those red-edged pages were, and I'm just as sure that repeat offenders standing handcuffed in front of that arrest book knew exactly what those red-edged pages were and how they got into that condition and wisely kept their mouths shut, stifling any urge to shout, *They call me Mister Tibbs!*

* * *

Everybody wants to be, or at least to feel, special.

I had thought committing suicide would make me special until I found out that everybody and their brother is committing suicide nowadays. And I had also thought that buying a cool gun to do the deed would make me special until I found out that everybody has a gun.

Guns, it seems, are everywhere.

Bows and arrows, not so much.

There are 308 million people living in the United States, and it is estimated that there are anywhere between 250 million and 300 million firearms owned by civilians in this country—and that's not counting firearms being used by police officers and military personnel. That equates pretty much to one handgun, shotgun or rifle for every Tom, Dick and Harry in America. The saying used to be *a chicken in every pot*, but today it's *a gun in everyone's hands*. Gun ownership has more than tripled in the past forty years with forty-two percent of all households in the U.S. owning one or more firearms.

Surprisingly with all those guns floating around, there are only about 1,100 fatal firearm accidents every year. Granted, there are a lot of homicides caused by guns, but the number of people accidentally shooting themselves or someone else is relatively low considering that there is almost one firearm for every person alive in the U.S.

Actually, doctors are a thousand times more lethal than a gun.

The National Institute on Aging reports that medical errors are the number one cause of death and injury in the United States. According to the NIA's report, over 780,000 people die annually due to medical mistakes. Comparatively, the annual death rate for heart disease is about 700,000 and the annual death rate for cancer is about 550,000.

The NIA report claims that over 2.2 million people are injured every year by prescription drugs alone and over twenty million unnecessary prescriptions for antibiotics are prescribed annually by doctors for viral infections. The report also said that 7.5 million unnecessary medical and surgical procedures are performed every year and 8.9 million people are needlessly hospitalized annually.

So don't worry about that dude with a gun.

But you might want to think twice before asking if there is a doctor in the house.

* * *

dark.

The same desk sergeant from the police department with the blood-stained arrest book was on duty one night as I was reading the arrest book when another Bubba walked in the front door of the police station, just chuckling away.

"What's so funny Bubba?" asked the desk sergeant.

"You won't believe it," said Bubba, catching the attention of a half dozen other officers at the station.

"Do tell," said the desk sergeant.

"Well, I was up on ol' Highway 80, parked behind that Shell gas station. You know the one?"

"Yeah."

"And this nigger in a big ass yellow Cadillac goes screaming by at about ninety miles an hour."

The desk sergeant smiled as did the other cops in the station.

Bubba, warming to his story, rolled a wad of chewing tobacco with his tongue from his left cheek to his right cheek, hitched up his gun belt a bit, and said, "So I took off after him."

"Yeah, and what happened?"

"You won't fucking believe it. When he saw my flashing lights behind him, he just pulled right over."

"You're kidding."

"Nope. He pulled over and before I could get out of my cruiser, that boy jumped out of his car, closed the door, spread his legs, leaned over and put his hands on his car roof, put his head down, and was as still as a church mouse."

"No shit. What'd you do?"

"I walked up to him and said, 'Boy, what the hell are you doing?'"

"What'd he say?"

"He said, 'Officer, I's from LA. This is how we does it out there."

"What'd you do Bubba?"

"Damn, I was laughing so hard I just let that nigger go!"

This was the same police department where a few years earlier some of the more industrious and imaginative detectives got into trouble for thinking outside the box when it came to interrogating suspects. They would take a suspect for a nice leisurely drive out into the woods, pop the hood of their unmarked police car, pull down the suspect's pants and underwear, hook one end of a set of jumper cables to the car battery and the other end to the dangling balls of

dark.

the suspect, rev up the car engine, and then ask, *"Where were you on the night of ..."*

Needless to say, they got plenty of confessions and solved lots of crimes in a rather expeditious manner simply by using a twelve dollar set of jumper cables.

They had guys confessing to kidnapping the Lindbergh baby.

But then some party-pooper blew the whistle, the Feds came in, the detectives got canned, and after that the jumper cables were just used to jump cars.

So much for rewarding initiative.

* * *

"I'm going to lunch," I tell one of the secretaries.
"Have fun."

I swing through Taco Bell and order some tacos, always crispy shell tacos because a soft shell taco is really a burrito if you ask me. I eat the tacos while driving to one of the three gun shops that are all within two miles of my office. Thats right, three gunshops within a two-mile radius. Scary.

There is one clerk in the gun shop, a weasel-faced guy wearing blue jeans, a country and western shirt, and a holster with a gun it.

Gunshop owners and clerks wearing sidearms seems so ridiculous. Granted, most criminals are not rocket scientists, but even they know better than to try to rob a store where the owner and his staff have hundreds of guns at their disposal, all laying in display cabinets whose open backs face them and not the robber. They know not to rob a gun shop whose owner and clerks are extremely familiar and proficient with the product they sell. Better to rob the Greek restaurant across the street instead where all the owner can do is bounce a gyro off your forehead.

It reminds me of when, as part of an investigative series of articles I was writing about home burglaries, I went to the huge prison in our state and interviewed three convicted burglars to get a sense from them of how they picked their targets.

"Will you rob a house if you hear a dog barking inside?"
"Hell no," they said in unison.
"Why, because you're scared of dogs, of getting bit?"

dark.

"Fuck no. I ain't scared of no dog. I'll kill that motherfucker with my bare hands," said one of the inmates.

"I'm confused."

All three inmates just shook their heads.

"Listen here," said one of the cons, "a barking dog, especially those little ones, just makes too much noise. Why do I want to jack that house with that yapping dog when there are ten mo houses on that street that don't have no dog? Man, you be buggin'. Use yo head."

I'm getting schooled by convicts.

Off topic, I asked if, in addition to burglaries, they ever did muggings or armed robberies. They looked at me bug-eyed like I had just asked if they had ever been racially profiled by the Po-Po.

"When you walk up to that guy you're going to mug, what do you say?" I asked.

"It don't happen that way," said one of the inmates.

"How does it happen then?"

"If you be walking toward me on the sidewalk, I'll smile or nod my head at you. And just as you walk past me, I'll turn and clock you right in the side of your fucking dome. And when you down on the ground, I'll kick you in the face and take your wallet."

"That doesn't sound very fair."

All three inmates looked at me like I was from another planet.

"Nigger, please," said the dog-strangling con.

In the gun shop, a young woman with an infant in a baby stroller is talking to Mr. Weasel. He looks like he's about to start drooling. The woman is attractive in a I-may-be-blue-collar-but-I-was-once-a-high-school-cheerleader kind of way. Her jeans are tight, she has a nice rack and if she were to smile, which she doesn't do the entire time she is in the gun shop, I can tell that her face would be country pretty.

"I need a gun," she says.

Because she is there to buy a gun without the help of a husband or a boyfriend, or whoever the father of her infant child is, and because she says, "I need a gun" and not "I'd like to buy a gun" I know, as does Mr. Weasel, that the only reason she is buying a gun is because of a dangerous husband or a boyfriend.

dark.

I move to the back of the shop to give them some privacy, but I still hear Mr. Weasel say, *"Now if you really want to put a man down, I would recommend this gun."*

I half expect him to then say, *"And after you shoot that son of a bitch, why don't you get a babysitter for the rug rat and come by here and we'll go grab a drink."*

* * *

The Lieutenant who ran the detective division at the Bubba police department was a relatively young guy who to me did not seem to fit in at that police department. He was certainly not a Bubba. He was tall, good looking and was always dressed immaculately in nice suits with silk ties. He was a college graduate and I spent many hours in his office talking with him about interesting subjects not related to police business. In a police station of tobacco-spitting, cowboy boot-wearing, head-bashing redneck cops, he seemed out of place.

I'm not sure how the subject came up, but one day he told me the story of how he had run over and killed a man on, of all places, good ol' Highway 80.

He was in his unmarked detective car heading to the station one morning when a young man tried to run across the highway, misjudging the distance and the speed of the lieutenant's approaching car. The lieutenant didn't see the man until the last moment, tried unsuccessfully to swerve to miss him, but ended up hitting him and killing him.

"It was an accident, pure and simple," said the lieutenant. *"But you know what the worst part is? You can only do that once. If it ever happened again, people would start to talk."*

I swear to God, that's exactly what he said.

Maybe I was wrong about the Lieutenant not fitting in.

* * *

The young woman tells the gun shop clerk she needs to think about it but promises to come back later that week to make a purchase after she gets her paycheck. We both know she won't be back. She'll forgive that asshole husband or boyfriend yet again.

dark.

As she leaves, the clerk turns his attention to me.

"I need some bullets, please."

"You mean ammo?"

I am a rube.

"Yes, ammo, please."

"For what type of gun."

"A .357."

"You want target ammo or defense ammo?"

Which translated means, do I want less powerful and less expensive bullets to shoot into paper targets at the gun range, or more powerful and more expensive bullets to shoot into a fellow human being.

I want to say, *"Well buckaroo, I'm planning to shoot myself right in the fucking head, so what ammo do you recommend?"*

Instead, I say, *"For defense."*

He turns and scans the shelves of ammo.

When I went to get a physical at my doctor's office a few months ago, the nurse had to draw blood and was having trouble finding a vein. She tried one needle and then a second needle, plunging each one in several times without success. On the third needle, blood starting running down my arm. I thought I was going to faint. Florence Nightingale was about two seconds away from having two-hundred-and-forty pounds of middle-aged man passed out on the floor.

"These needles are so big, so it's hard to hit a vein."

"Use a smaller needle."

"Oh, we have to use these. Smaller needles cost fifty cents more."

"I'll pay the damn fifty cents."

"Let me get the doctor. He's better at this than me."

When the doctor came in, he took one look at me and suggested I lay down on the examining table.

"Do me a favor Doc," I said, *"what say we splurge and use the smaller needle."*

He did and quickly hit the vein. I had bruises on my arm for the next week.

I feel the same way about the ammo that I am about to buy that I felt about those needles. I'm not going to use a cheap bullet. To hell with that. Sell me the most expensive bullets you have in the

dark.

store. When the detectives and coroner get together after my autopsy and compare notes about the gun and the bullets I used, I want them to say, *"Hey, at least he had good taste. That's the most expensive ammo you can buy."*

It's like that clean underwear and car accident thing your mother always warned you about. God forbid you were ever killed wearing dirty underwear. I never understood that frequent admonition because if my fragile ten-year-old body was being dragged under a speeding Cadillac Eldorado just prior to the left rear wheel rolling over my head and squashing it like a ripe cantaloupe, I know the last thing I was going to be worrying about was whether my white Jockey underwear was nice and clean.

Still, Mom had a point. Dead or not, you need to keep up appearances.

Before the clerk can turn back around, I recall some of the info I read on the Internet about the new gun I bought on Sunday, and so I say in a husky and authoritative voice, *"You know what? Do you have any Federal .357 Magnum 125 grain jacketed hollow point 357B ammo?"*

"Sure do," he says, grabbing a box and setting it on the counter. He looks perplexed and impressed, wondering how the rube who just asked for bullets instead of ammo could then ask for a specific, top of the line brand ammo.

"Thanks, Boss," I say.

*   *   *

Not all cop stories are funny, like the Bubba police stories, although some people might argue that jumper cables attached to gonads is really nothing to laugh about, to which I would have to say, *Oh, lighten up.*

Three incidents from my time as a police beat reporter have always stood out, and given a new meaning to the word dark for me. If you want to skip ahead, I understand. I won't hold it against you. Some people just don't want to know.

The first incident involved Polaroids.

One of the investigators in the detective offices greeted my question of, "So *what's been happening tonight?,"* with an innocent smile and a stack of Polaroids when I walked into the police station

dark.

late one winter night. The room was filled with a half dozen detectives who watched as I set my notebook and walkie-talkie radio down on the counter and began looking through the brightly colored photos, casually leaning back against the counter and shuffling through the thick photographs like a stack of cards.

The first photo was of a cute little girl, about two years old, standing up in a crib and gripping the handrails with her chubby fingers. She wore a white flannel nightgown with yellow flowers on it and she had a big smile on her round face, a face with sparkling blue eyes, framed by ringlets of curly blonde hair.

The second photo threw me.

I couldn't make out what it was, a vivid vertical slash of red surrounded by pink.

The third and fourth photos, similar to the second photo, didn't help either, and it wasn't until the next half dozen photos, when the detective taking the photos had moved further back from his subject, that the child's spread legs came into view and I realized I was seeing close up, in excruciating detail, the aftermath of a child rape.

And the room started to spin.

Oh my God, it was so hot all of a sudden in my heavy winter coat, the fluorescent lights in the crowded room were so bright, the nervous laughs of some of the detectives competed with a thunderous buzzing sound in my head, and the grotesque grin coming from the face of the detective who had handed me the photos seemed to get bigger and bigger. I felt my legs begin to buckle as I dropped the photos on the desk and walked quickly to the police station's main doors, rushing outside into the winter night where I sat on a curb and sucked in deep gulps of the chilly air.

Bam, bam, bam, bam, those photos kept cycling through my head, always in sequence, starting with the embodiment of goodness and purity and ending with vividly colored photographic proof that evil had taken on a new definition for me, that my understanding of true evil had, in just a few brief seconds, made a horrifying leap from assumption to reality.

I wanted to leave and go back to the newsroom, but I knew that if I did, then that one asshole detective would have won. And I would lose the respect of the detectives who were friendly with me and helpful with news stories. After about five minutes I walked back into the detective offices. The detective who had handed me the photos didn't apologize, didn't offer an explanation, didn't say a single word. He had made his point. He had taken a too young, too friendly, too naive reporter and thrust him headfirst into the real answer to the question of, *"So what's been happening tonight?"* He hadn't told me, he had shown me. And any attempt to soften that introduction with consoling or qualifying words would have cheapened his purpose. He had more respect for his work, for the child, and maybe even for me, to do that.

"She's alive," said one of the friendlier detectives, *"and doing okay."*

"The female vagina has an amazing capacity for stretching," said another detective in all seriousness, awe in his voice.

They handed me the police incident report which I scanned as they ran down the assault.

Mother finds infant daughter in small pool of blood, calls police, detectives question live-in boyfriend, boyfriend says child was crying so he checked on her, detectives find bloodstains on the bed on the side where the boyfriend slept with the mother and bloodstains inside the boyfriend's underwear, book him for rape, say for a little guy he was hung like a horse, say they enjoyed the look on his face when they told him what was going to happen to him when he went to prison as a child rapist.

"I hope you like the Navy," one detective had said to the man, *"because where you're going, you're going to be seeing a lot of black 'semen'."*

The detectives also enjoyed relaying the emergency room physician's assessment that the child's injuries would heal quickly and his prediction that since she was so young, she would not remember the incident. And after I left to file my story, I know they enjoyed talking about my reaction to the photos.

And though I could understand, I could also hate.

The boyfriend for doing it, the cops for showing me, and myself for pushing on that door for a glimpse of hell.

* * *

The young woman is still in the gun shop parking lot when I leave. She is having trouble folding up the stroller and getting it into

dark.

her car's backseat while balancing the infant on her hip. I help her. She doesn't smile, but she does say thank you.

I want to tell her to go back inside and buy the gun. I even want to give her the money to do it.

But I know that's not appropriate.

Just as I know what could very well be in her future.

Her dead—and her husband/boyfriend dead.

It's at this point that a Public Service Announcement is probably in order regarding murder-suicides, and I think every father with a daughter and every brother with a sister will appreciate me taking the time to pass along this PSA. If you are a woman who has broken up with your longtime boyfriend or if you are a woman who is separated or divorced from your husband, then please grab a pencil and answer yes or no to the following questions. Just write your answers down right on this page next to each of these questions.

Did your ex ever hit you when you were together?

Are you now fucking some other dude, and does your ex and all of his buddies know about it?

Is that same guy playing catch in your front yard with your ex's son and is he wearing your ex's favorite Rawling's baseball glove?

Is your ex living in a small apartment and driving a beater because that's all he can afford due to alimony and child support payments?

Did your ex ever tell you he would kill you if you left him?

Does your ex own a gun?

Does your ex listen to country music?

Okay, let's add up your answers.

This will be easy.

If you answered yes to any of the questions above, then you are totally screwed, and so here is some advice to keep you from ending up in one of those murder-suicide news stories in your local newspaper.

If your ex calls to apologize for having made your life a living hell and for the bloody noses he gave you and for having passed on to you that particularly resistant new strain of venereal disease and for hitting your children with various household objects and for taking all of your money out of savings to gamble with, and then he invites you to dinner at some romantic and very out of the way restaurant ... *Do not fucking go.*

dark.

If you look up from your desk at work and your ex is walking down the hall toward you, unannounced and holding a bouquet of roses and has a big shit-eating grin on his face ... *Quickly jump out of the nearest window.*

If your ex communicates with you in any way, be it a phone call or a voice mail or an email or a text message or a handwritten letter or a note tied to the skinny leg of a carrier pigeon, and the words *come alone* show up anywhere in any of those messages, then ... *It's time to think about moving to another state.*

Buy a gun. And don't be afraid to use it. It's easier to ask for forgiveness than permission. Wouldn't you rather be in that police interrogation room saying, *"Oops, my bad,"* than having your teary-eyed father at your funeral saying, *"She was such a wonderful daughter."*

There is a saying, *"Hell hath no fury like that of a woman scorned,"* which is true but does not really have the bite that it implies. What's the worst you can suffer at the hands of a scorned woman—a tongue lashing, your favorite leather jacket cut to shreds and tossed into the street, her telling all your friends that you have a tiny dick?

There needs to be a second part to that saying that states, *"... and Hell hath no unbridled, all-consuming hate like that of a man scorned,"* because now we aren't talking about him just cutting up your favorite Burberry sweater or telling your friends that you give a horrible blowjob. Instead we're talking about him killing you and your children and even your parents if they happen to be at the birthday party when he shows up unannounced carrying a real gun instead of a plastic birthday present gun for Junior. After shooting all of you, he'll even kill the family dog, despite the fact that he always told you he liked the dog better than you, before finally turning the gun on himself. And, of course, the last thought that will go through his pea-brain before shooting himself is always, always, always going to be, *"I guess I showed that bitch."*

Sure you did, buddy. Great job.

I take issue with the police and the media calling these incidents murder-suicides.

It gives a bad name to suicides.

They should be called *murder-murders* because they are acts of rage that involve unwilling participants, as in, *I'm pissed so I am*

dark.

going to murder my former loved one, and then I'm going to murder myself. That's got nothing to do with suicide.

Call it what it is. It's a double murder. By a coward.

Pure and simple.

* * *

The second incident involved a black eye.

Actually two black eyes.

Both on the face of a seventy-year-old man.

He was sitting in a chair in the corner of the detective offices.

"What happened to him?" I asked one of the detectives.

"He was robbed."

"Oh."

"And raped."

"Say what?"

"He was raped."

"Are you fucking kidding me?"

"No. Some muscle-bound steroid asshole broke into his apartment to steal his TV. He beat the shit out of that old guy and then raped him."

I looked over at the old man. He could not hear what the detective was saying, but he knew exactly what the detective was telling me. And the look of shame and pain in his eyes is as vivid to me today as it was thirty years ago. This was somebody's father, somebody's grandfather. He had lived through the Depression and two World Wars. He had spent seven decades on this often cruel planet and had earned the right to spend his last days in security and comfort. Not to be beaten to a pulp and fucked in the ass. That was so wrong, so unfair. What kind of cruel world were we living in.

I looked over at the old man again. His eyes met mine, then he lowered his head and stared at the floor.

"We caught the fucker," said the detective. *"Do you want to see the incident report?"*

"No."

"You're not going to write a story?"

"No."

"Good."

"I'll be back in a little while."

dark.

"Okay."
I walked to the public restroom in the police station.
And threw up.

* * *

Back at my office I place the box of ammo I bought into my briefcase and lock it. No one here needs to see it, nor does my wife when I get home.

I call my wife which surprises her. I seldom call her during the day just to chat.

"What's up?"
"Not much."
"Did you play tennis today?"
"Yes."
"Win?"
"No, dammit."
"What's for dinner?"
"Your favorite. Sweet and sour pork."
"Great."

She's right. She has the recipe for my Mom's Americanized and bastardized version of sweet and sour pork. It is my favorite home-cooked meal. I think about it the rest of the afternoon.

Sometimes in life it's the little things.

* * *

The third incident involved a three-ring binder.

The binder, almost four inches thick, was sitting on the counter in the detective offices.

"May I?" I asked the detective behind the counter.
"Knock yourself out."

The first page in the binder explained that the binder was sent by the FBI to every police department in the country and contained brief reports of murders that detectives from coast to coast could read about to see if the particulars of any of those cases were similar to cases in their jurisdictions.

"Cool," I thought.

On the next page of the binder, there were two cases profiled.

dark.

The first case was about a blanket found spread out at a lakeside park one summer afternoon in Denver. On the blanket was a bottle of wine, a loaf of Italian bread and a plate of assorted cheeses. Some kids had found the picnic set-up but did not see any people near the blanket. Also on the blanket was a huge picnic basket. Being kids, they slowly peeled back the red and white checkered cloth that covered the top of the picnic basket. Inside was the dismembered body of a young woman, her limbs and torso and head neatly arranged in the basket.

The second case on that page told of a woman realtor who had been missing for two days in Biloxi. Investigators obtained a list of houses that she and the other realtors in her office were representing and began to search them. They eventually found her body in the attic of one of the vacant houses they had listed for sale. She was naked and had been hung from one of the rafters in the attic. Her nipples had been cut off.

"This is some sick shit," I said to the detective.

"No kidding."

"Why don't they mention any arrests?"

"Because they only list unsolved murders."

The cases were printed on the front and back of each page in the binder. With two cases, sometimes three, per page. I flipped to the last page in the binder. The page number said 729.

"And guess what?" said the detective.

"What?"

"We get a new binder every month."

*   *   *

My Mom smokes. A lot. So do I. Both my parents smoked. The sound that woke me up every morning was the sound of my Dad's Zippo lighter clicking open and snapping shut. Before his feet even hit the bedroom floor. Eventually, when the flight surgeon told my Dad he had a choice to either smoke cigarettes or continue flying planes for the United States Air Force, he chose the latter and quit smoking that day.

"Hey, I don't fly planes," said my Mom, who kept on puffing.

My Mom and I like to smoke and talk. In my car one day, both of us enveloped in a gray haze of smoke, my Mom asked me how

dark.

my life was going. I don't think she even listened to my answer, because what she said was, *"You will never be happy."*

"Why?"

"Because you are never satisfied."

She was right. But coming from your mother, the person who will always know you better than any other person in your life, it was a bit of a downer.

I tried arguing the point about me never being able to be happy, and my Mom said, *"Okay then, what would really make you happy?"*

"There is only one thing I really want."

"Which is?"

"To die before my children."

My Mom looked over at me and then stared straight ahead and took another drag off her cigarette.

She didn't say a word.

She just nodded her head.

I know that is one of the main reasons that I first started to think about suicide. I have lived in fear for years that one of my children would be murdered, and if that were to happen the pain would be too much. I don't want to ever be here for that. I know that it is an irrational fear and that if I had not spent so many years as a police reporter, documenting man's inhumanity to man, I would not have worried so much about my children and the dark side of our world. But once you see that side, once you know that it truly and horrifically exists, then it will always be in your head.

I can't deal with it.

It is another ingredient in that stew.

* * *

It's Wednesday, hump day, so Jimmy's is crowded, which means Albert is in a good mood for the most part.

A slender girl with straight brown hair limps into the club with a crutch under her right arm and makes her way through the milling bodies to where Albert and I are sitting at the end of the bar. Albert's eyes light up and he quickly stands up to hug the girl and then drag an empty bar stool over next to his stool. The girl leans her crutch on the bar and Albert helps her up onto the stool. She is wearing blue jeans and a white halter top, her hair parted in the middle,

dark.

highlighting a face with big brown eyes and a smooth complexion, just a trace of pink lipstick on her lips. She is actually quite beautiful.

"So where have you been, baby? And what happened to your leg?" There is real concern in Albert's voice.

Before she can answer, Albert says to me, *"This is my favorite girl of all time. I love this girl."* Which coming from Albert says a lot. He is never effusive, much less sentimental.

"So where have you been, baby? And what happened to your leg?" he repeats, knowing the answers already.

Years of dancing as a stripper in ridiculously tall high-heels coupled with a hereditary bone condition have knocked the girl from the stage. Her right knee is shot. She tells Albert about doctor visits and yet another upcoming operation. They talk like old friends, like equals, not like former boss and employee. As she talks, the girl scans the club, commenting to Albert on the visual pros and cons of various dancers.

"How long did you dance here?" Albert asks the girl for my benefit. She danced at the club for almost five years and over those years had seen dozens of managers and hundreds of dancers come through the club. The one constant was Albert.

"Was he a good boss?" I ask.

"The absolute best," says the girl.

Albert smiles.

The girl seems so fragile with her bad leg, a waif-like creature with a quiet voice who does not look like she could weather a month, much less five years, of exotic dancing with the long hours, the crippling shoes, the suffocating cigarette smoke, the constant drinking every night, the horny customers. She talks with Albert about her two young daughters and how they are doing at school. She doesn't mention a husband. Albert tells her she is welcome to work the club's front door collecting cover charges whenever she wants.

"How much?" she asks.

"Eight, nine dollars an hour," says Albert, the sheepish tone in his voice and the pained look in the girl's eyes testament to how little that is compared to the hundreds of dollars a night she pulled down when she was dancing on stage and doing lap dances.

"I'll let you know, Albert. Thanks."

dark.

The talk stops and they both survey the club. There isn't much more to say after the reminiscing is done. The girl knows that she is out of the loop, that Albert's fond welcome and genuine concern will always be there, but that the business of dancing must go on, and as each day passes and she is no longer on the front lines for Albert, she will become more of a distant memory.

Albert pats her leg and smiles at me.

"She was always my favorite dancer," says Albert. *"We'd get a bunch of nasty bikers in here, sitting around the stage pounding their fists on the railing and screaming and hollering. Just a crazy, dangerous bunch of guys. All the other girls would be scared to go on stage."*

Albert laughs as he tells the story and the girls' eyes are bright and proud because she's heard the story many times before.

"I'd send this tiny little girl up on that stage and she'd put her hands on her hips and yell at those bikers that if they wanted to see any pussy, they better just shut the fuck up. She would. And they'd quiet down like babies. You wouldn't believe it. Just tell those badass bikers to shut the fuck right up. And they did. Nothing scared this girl."

Albert and the girl both smile recalling the memory. After a few minutes, the girl starts to get up. Albert helps her off the stool, hands her her crutch and gives her a big bear hug. As he hugs her I see his hand slip into the back pocket of her jeans and in his hand is a wad of green cash. He starts to let her go from the hug and she pulls him back for a last tight squeeze, her face buried in his beefy shoulder.

She walks to the front door.

Albert sits back on his stool and stares straight ahead as she leaves. He doesn't look sad or embarrassed. He looks resigned.

"So ..." I start to say.

"Later," he says.

I shut the fuck up.

* * *

When I get home there's a note on the kitchen counter from my wife saying she is over at one of her girlfriends' houses to have happy hour cocktails with some of the other ladies from the

114

dark.

neighborhood, and that my dinner is in the oven. I take the ammo out of my briefcase and hide it in the top drawer of my dresser under my socks.

Later that night, after dinner, after some TV, and after some Internet web surfing, I go to bed and read. When I know that my wife has fallen asleep in the guest bedroom, I get up and take the blue gun case from the top of my dresser and the box of ammo out of the top drawer. I lay them both out on the bedspread and load the .357 Magnum. Empty the gun is heavy enough, but after I add the six bullets, it feels massive. I hold it in my hand, gingerly slip my finger through the trigger guard, and point the gun at different objects in the bedroom. It feels good in my hand, very powerful, very dangerous. I put the gun back in the blue plastic case, place it back on top of my dresser, and put the box of ammo back in the top drawer.

And then I wait, because I know Boo saw everything and is about to give me a ration of shit.

"I'm pissed," says Boo.

"Why?"

"You bought bullets today. Oh excuse me, I mean ammo. And you just loaded that damn gun. Are you fucking serious? I thought this was a little game."

"It's not."

"Oh man, you think you are so important. Big monumental decision, whoo hoo."

"Why are you being so mean?"

"Because you need to get over yourself. You are not all that and a bag of chips."

"I agree. I am inconsequential. So what's the problem?"

"You are but a grain of sand."

"I don't follow you. Stop talking in riddles."

"Let me give you the DL on this shit. And listen to what I am about to say because it will put this wackness into perspective for you."

"Right on. Go ahead."

"You are just one person. You live on just one planet. That planet is in just one galaxy. And that galaxy is in just one universe. Follow me?

"Not really."

"Pay attention, then. This is important."

"Okay, okay."

"This planet, Earth, is one of one hundred billion planets in our galaxy. And there are one hundred billion galaxies in our universe. That means this planet is only one of over 10,000,000,000,000 planets in our universe. And that's just our universe; there are many others."

"Wow. That's impressive."

"Don't be condescending. With trillions of planets out there, do you really think you are the only intelligent life form? Do you really think everything revolves around you? Do you really think that your decisions impact this world or this galaxy or this universe?"

"No."

"Listen, you are just another animal. You evolved from apes. Do you ever stop to think about that? You have the same internal organs as a rat. You show the same emotions and have a slightly higher intelligence than a dolphin. Millions of years ago your caveman ancestors squatted down to shit in a hole."

A pause, then, "Just like you still do today."

Good last line. I know he's proud of that one.

"I don't think you are seeing the big picture. Go get a pen and some paper."

I go to the den, grab a pen and paper, and then plop back into bed.

"Okay, write down the number five followed by four zeros."

I do and it looks like 50,000.

"What's that?"

"That's how many years Modern Man has been around."

"Okay."

"Now write down the number fourteen followed by nine zeros."

I do and it looks like 14,000,000,000.

"What's that?"

"That's how many years the universe has been around. You humans have only been dragging your knuckles on the ground for a brief hiccup of time. The average human being only lives eighty years."

"What's your point?"

"Trees live longer than you do."

"No, the main point."

dark.

"The main point is that you are making your death more important than the big picture and you think that it matters."

"It matters to me."

"Yeah, and what makes you so special?"

"Damn, lighten up."

"Well, you're really pissing me off."

I lay back down and pull the covers up over my head so Boo can't see my face. I'm quiet for awhile, and then I say, "That was mean."

"Oh, grow up."

"I don't think I'll be able to sleep now."

"Give me a break."

Boo can't see that I am grinning under the covers.

"You know, I had changed my mind about the whole suicide thing."

I pause for a second.

"But now you've got me so depressed, I'm going to go ahead and do it."

I pause another second.

"So it's all your fault."

There's dead silence for about twenty seconds, and then Boo says, "You're a real fucking comedian, you know that."

I smile.

And easily fall asleep.

Thursday, June 25

them.

This sucks.

This being Thursday and, based on the *Taking Care of Business List*, this being the day I need to get all of my legal and financial affairs in order to make it easier on the grieving family. How boring. I hate paperwork.

It's ridiculous how much red tape there is in the world today. How many documents, how many notarized signatures, how many forms and applications, how many rules and regulations, how many laws and penalties, how many permits and licenses, how many judges and legislators and authority figures. George Orwell might have missed it by a few decades, but he was fucking spot on.

In today's world there is *us* and there is *them*.

Us might have created them, but them stopped being on the same page as us a long time ago.

I pull down the three binders from the bookshelf in my office that are labeled Banks, Insurance and Investments. Because I am an organization freak, the binders have all the details my wife will need to know about our various accounts, from account numbers to passwords to balances. I have always put everything in both our names so there should be no roadblocks in having all the accounts continue on as normal, but now just in her name alone.

I go to my file cabinet and start pulling out other items she will need and put them into specific folders that I then label.

The titles to our two cars. After next week, I won't need my car so she should sell it. Great car, by the way. It's a BMW M5, runs like a scalded ape with 517 horsepower. Only got two speeding tickets in it which isn't bad if you ask me. One of the cops reached his hand through my window and petted Boo on the head while I was signing the speeding ticket. The gall of the man. I chastised Boo severely as we drove away for not tearing the cop's pinkie off. Traitor.

The paperwork for our house. The mortgage is paid off, so I put the paperwork that shows we own the house, copies of the last few annual real estate tax statements, insurance statements, and home owners association fees statements in the folder. Home owners associations, what a grand idea. It's not bad enough that we let government control every aspect of our lives, now we let our neighbors tell us what color we can paint our houses, and we pay a monthly fee for the privilege. We are all pussies.

All our warranties, bought begrudgingly. Like a pack rat I save everything, so in this folder I put the receipts and warranties and job orders for any of the high dollar items we have bought in recent years, from plasma TVs to Cartier watches to patio furniture to having the pool resurfaced.

Computer and phone stuff. Between my wife and I, we have three laptop computers, two desktop computers, a half dozen iPods and two iPhones, all with warranties that I put in the folder along with the receipts.

Wills. We have wills for my wife, my son, my daughter and myself. In my will everything goes to my wife, with my son and daughter listed as the secondary beneficiaries in case my wife and I were to keel over at the same time. I place the wills in a folder along with my passport and my wife's passport, plus copies of our two living testament wills which state that medical personnel can consult with either of us if the other one is in a coma. Mine says to pull the fucking plug as soon as possible because for all I know I might be laying in that hospital bed in intense pain and not be able to tell anyone. I came into this world as a mammal and have no interest in going out as a vegetable. These documents could come in handy in case I botch the suicide job—remember the part about *proper barrel orientation to the head*—and end up in the intensive care unit with my son saying, *"Why's Dad's ear where his nose used to be?"*

Business stuff. I put the US copyright and trademark documents and corporate papers for the various corporations and businesses I own in a folder. My wife is a co-owner on all that paperwork as well, so it should be business as usual after I'm gone. My bookkeeper can give her all the financials. My guess is she will sell the businesses. She's never really liked my chosen field. Not many wives would. I also co-own a rather nefarious, yet legal, business in Central America with Mean John, but I doubt my wife will want to have anything to do with a business where the monthly P&L has an expense category for condoms. Hey, they just give massages there. That's my story, and I'm sticking to it.

Boo's veterinarian records. Boo is one expensive canine, what with twice a year check-ups, heart worm medicine, flea medicine, more shots than a child ever gets, and having to have his anal glands squeezed. Don't even ask me what that last item involves, but he has to have it done every time he goes to the vet and he has a big smile on his face the rest of the day after it's done. I probably would too. Reminds me of one of my favorite jokes: *Why does a dog lick his balls? Because he can.* I put all of Boo's vet records into a folder. Boo's predecessor, a mean-as-shit Min Pin named Romeo, actually had a criminal record of sorts at that same vet's office. At the top of his manila medical folder, handwritten in large block type and highlighted in yellow marker, were the words, *"Be careful. Will bite!"*

Made me proud.

* * *

My Mom and I were standing outside a Mexican restaurant one evening smoking, as usual, and talking about politics, as usual. I don't give a shit about politics because I know that one asshole in charge is no different than another asshole in charge. But I like to bring the topic up because it winds my Mom up like you wouldn't believe. Just push that politics button on her back and she's off to the races like the Energizer bunny.

That night she was on a tear about some ridiculous bureaucratic blunder and she ended her tirade by saying she could not

them.

understand how the people who are in charge could make such idiotic decisions. I have heard the same comments from my Mom a thousand different times, whether it involved the board of directors that runs her condo association, members of her town's city council, or one of her state representatives or U.S. senators. She's even global, which means other world leaders can also fall under her verbal scalpel.

"I don't understand why you are always so surprised at how inept the people are who run things," I said to her as she fired up another cigarette and nervously paced back and forth.

"What do you mean?" she asked.

"There are two reasons that that crap always happens," I said.

"Which are?" she asked, rolling her eyes.

"The first reason is that people in public office are from the bottom of the barrel."

"How so?"

"As you yourself have said, those who can—do, and those who can't—teach. It's the same with the private and the public sectors. Those who can, the people with smarts and initiative and creativity, go into business for themselves or work for a successful private company. Those who can't, the people who aren't smart enough or creative enough to run their own business or get hired by a successful private company, go to work for the government or run for public office."

"That's ridiculous."

"Is it? Who do you think is the CEO of the largest business entity in the city where you live?"

"Hell if I know."

"It's the mayor of your city."

"How so?"

"Add up all those city hall employees, policemen, firemen, social workers, school teachers, licensing and zoning officials, jail workers, city attorneys, parks and recreation workers, and on and on, and your mayor is in charge of more employees than any other business in your city. Now add up all the local tax monies he collects and the state and federal funding he receives, and he will have more annual revenues than any other business in your city. Add up all the money he spends on everything from new school buses to street re-paving

to meals for prisoners, and you will see he has more annual expenses than any other business in your city."

"And your point?"

"How much do you think your mayor makes a year?"

"Probably $150,000."

"How much do you think the guy who owns those Mercedes Benz, BMW and Jaguar car dealerships in your city makes a year?"

"Probably a couple million."

"That's my point. You've got a guy who makes less than a gas station owner running the biggest corporation in your city. How smart can he be? So, in essence, the janitor is running your city. And you're surprised at the decisions he makes. Remember what Dad used to say?"

"What?"

"You get what you pay for."

"But the mayor does the job because he wants to serve the public."

"Mom, give me a fucking break."

"It's true. Not everyone is money-hungry like you."

"What happened to your last mayor?"

Another rolling of the eyes.

"He was arrested for taking bribes."

"I rest my case."

"Okay, okay, okay," she said. "I see your point, but dammit it to hell sometimes you just irritate the crap out of me."

I know I do. And I love it.

"Want to hear my second reason?"

"If I must."

"It's because people are people."

"Can you be a little more vague?"

My Mom is no stranger to sarcasm.

"Let me paint you a picture. Think of our President ..."

"Oh, I love him."

"... sitting on the toilet, with his pants around his legs, reading the newspaper and a huge turd coming out of his ass."

"You are disgusting. I can't believe you are my son. Why would you say something like that?"

"To prove a point. We put our leaders up on a pedestal and think of them as these perfect super beings. I think this peculiar *need to have someone be in charge, someone to look out for us, someone to make sure all the wrongs are right, starts when we are infants. Parents are our first super beings, then it's our school teachers and our coaches, then it's policemen and army generals and the media, and eventually it's the legislators and elected officials who tell us the laws we must live by every day for the rest of our lives. We don't want to be in charge. We want them to be."*

"And?"

"They are not super beings. They are human beings. They sit on a toilet seat every day just like the rest of us. And it's that human part that screws everything up. They have the same faults and insecurities and self-interests that every other human being on this planet has. They lie, they steal, and they cheat."

I lit another cigarette.

"Mom, have you ever made a mistake?"

"Yes."

"Do I ever make mistakes?"

"All the time."

"Well, newsflash, the people in charge are going to also make mistakes. Let me give you the perfect example. Who is the most powerful person in the world today?"

"The President of the United States."

"Correct, and there have only been forty-four US Presidents since this country was founded. Every one of those Presidents knew that they held the fate of the entire world, billions and billions of people, in their hands, and they knew that their every move and every word would be analyzed, and that they would be written about in history books and their presidency would be studied for hundreds of years, right?"

"I agree."

"So, knowing that the fate of the free world, to a degree, was in his hands, and knowing that the world would study his legacy for centuries to come, one of our US Presidents risked everything just because he wanted a blowjob in the Oval Office?"

My Mom's eyes popped open.

"That particular President was intelligent. He knew full well the risk he was taking for himself, for his family, and for his country, but the lure of a sloppy, three-minute blowjob overruled the common

sense of the most powerful person in the world. Why? Because he was simply human."

I tossed my cigarette into the parking lot to punctuate the point.

"And Mom, to me that's a little scary."

My Mom looked defeated. And depressed.

"Let's eat," she said and opened the door to the Mexican restaurant.

*   *   *

I want to make sure my life insurance will pay off if I commit suicide, so I go to my good friend the Internet for a little research. While I do this, Boo starts barking at someone who just walked in the front door of our offices. My office is around the corner from the main reception area and I can't see out to the front, so when I yell, *"Shut the fuck up,"* really loud, which I do about three times a day, I always wonder what the person who just walked in is thinking.

There is a great scene in the TV show The Simpsons where Homer rushes into a gun store, picks out a gun and tells the clerk he wants to buy it. The clerk tells him he will have to wait a week to pick up the gun because of the federal government's mandatory five-day waiting and cooling off period.

"But I'm mad now!" shouts Homer.

The same concept comes into play if you are planning to commit suicide and want to first buy some life insurance to tide your loved ones over after you vacate the premises. Just about every life insurance policy has a Suicide Exclusion which states, *If the insured, whether sane or insane, dies by suicide within two years from the issue date, this contract will end and we will return the premiums paid. The contract will provide no further benefit.*

Which just means you need to plan further ahead.

In the old days the Suicide Exclusion had no time limit. Kill yourself at any time and your family got squat. The insurance companies defended that policy by saying they didn't want to give people a monetary incentive to pull the plug. In the mid-1800s, though, tired of being portrayed as vultures, and also after much civil and government litigation, the insurance companies agreed to limit the Suicide Exclusion to two years from the date of the policy. Everyone seemed to agree that if you bought life insurance with suicide in mind, after two years you probably no longer had the urge to end it all.

Life insurance is actually regulated by the individual states and not by the federal government, and in some states, like Colorado, it's only a one-year exclusion, so if you're in a hurry to kill yourself but want to make sure that the wife and kids get their money, you can head there for your Rocky Mountain high.

Also in the 1800s the insurance companies developed something called the incontestability clause, which limits the amount of time, again usually two years, that the company gets to uncover and object to problems with statements you made in your policyholder application. So if you told that geeky insurance dude who wrote up your policy that you did not routinely smoke crack while parasailing nude over shark-infested waters, but then you and your crack pipe and your parasail end up in the belly of a Great White shark within that two-year period, your surviving relatives are not going to get a dime if the insurance company can prove that you had that peculiar proclivity all along. After two years, though, puff away and sail away to you heart's content.

I pull a copy of my whole life insurance policy out of the stack of file folders that I will be leaving in my office for my wife. How much is the policy for? None of your fucking business. But, trust me, it's plenty for the little lady. I scan through it and find the Suicide Exclusion and see that the exclusion period is indeed limited to two years from the date that the policy was issued which, in this case, was over five years ago, so I am good to go.

In the same folder are copies of the annual premium invoices and copies of the checks I sent to pay them. The next premium is not due for six months, so there should be no stumbling blocks on the insurance front. To file the claim, my wife just has to send the insurance company a copy of my death certificate, which she can get from the funeral director, and a completed, signed and notarized insurer's claim form.

Then it's check time.

If I were her, I'd splurge and buy something nice.

* * *

them.

At a newspaper, reporters have assigned beats. Some reporters cover city hall, some cover the state legislature, some cover sports, some cover lifestyle events, some cover the crime beat and, the really fucking unlucky ones, cover the school board. I'd rather eat dirt. Every now and then a reporter is out sick or on vacation and a reporter from another beat has to fill in, which is how I found myself in an auditorium one night listening to a debate between three candidates for a newly vacated seat on the City Council. I did not want to be there.

Back in the newsroom I wrote my article and the opening paragraphs went something like this:

Three candidates for the District Nine City Council seat engaged in a lively debate before a packed crowd at the Shriner's Auditorium last night. Candidate Steve Thomas promised to push for substantial teacher salary increases so the community's children can get the best education possible. Candidate Julie Robbins vowed she would vote against a proposed sales tax increase designed to raise funds to build a new convention center for the city.

Candidate Bob Rogers wore a red tie.

I can't believe the city editor ran my story exactly as I wrote it. The next day the newspaper received dozens of phone calls from readers who said they loved the article, or, more specifically, the part about the red tie. We also received letters from readers saying the same thing over the next few weeks. The big boss editors weren't happy, though, so the city editor got chewed out and I was never asked to fill in for another reporter again. Mission accomplished.

Bob Rogers didn't win the election, didn't even come close. There is no doubt in my mind that it was my article that shot him down. No one could take him seriously after the red tie comment. That a young rookie reporter had destroyed him with just a few keystrokes on a manual typewriter was ridiculous. What Bob Rogers didn't know was that it was just the luck of the draw. I had arbitrarily picked him. I could have just as easily said that Steve Thomas simply wore a blue tie, or Julie Robbins simply wore a pink scarf.

That's the part that shows just how fragile this whole putting someone in power thing really is. If I hadn't mentioned the red tie and Bob Rogers had won, then he could have been sitting on the City Council and making daily decisions that impacted the lives of tens of thousands of people in our fair city. Instead, the voters picked someone else to make decisions that would affect their lives for the next four years, never knowing that the person they thought was best could have just as easily been the one I skewered in my article and made lose the election.

It's scary, the power of the press.

And what an asshole reporter in a bad mood can do.

The media likes to say that they are the watchdogs over the government. That it's us against them.

The truth is, the media is them.

* * *

As human beings, we become acclimated to and accepting of anything and everything.

Take taxes, for example.

We all complain about them, but we keep paying them. I am in the 35 percent federal tax bracket. That means that 35 cents out of every single dollar I earn goes to a business partner that I don't even like, and who I don't think is pulling his fair share of the load. But I put up with it, and hardly ever think about it, because that particular business partner has been putting the squeeze on me since I was a teenager and got my first check for pumping gas.

I'm used to it, just like you are.

But suppose this Saturday morning your doorbell rings and you open the door to see a huge motherfucker with a bent nose named Tony D., who says, *"Show me how much money youse made dis week."*

You hold out all the cash you earned that week in your sweaty palms, and Tony D. reaches over and takes thirty-five percent of it and says, *"Thanks, see youse next Saturday."*

And sure enough he comes back next Saturday and every Saturday after that. Don't you think eventually you would get a little pissed? Don't you think you would have some questions about why you were having to pay Tony D. thirty-five percent of what you had earned that week? And don't you think you would have some questions about exactly what he was doing with your money?

"Excuse me, Mr. Tony, no disrespect, but I'm a little pissed. I don't want to pay you any more. Does that mean you are going to bust my knee caps?"

them.

"No, don't be silly. If you don't keep paying, I'll just take your cars, then your house, then your stocks and bonds, then your savings account, and then, I may even put you in prison."

"You can't do that."

"Watch me."

"Uh, Mr. Tony, why do I have to pay you every week?"

"Because The Boys say so."

"Who are The Boys?"

"Don't be a smartass. You know who they are. They're your Boys. You voted them in. Don't you remember?"

"Not really."

"Not my problem."

"Uh, Mr. Tony ..."

"Kid, you sure ask a lot of fucking questions."

"... I'll keep paying, but can you tell me what exactly you are doing with my money?"

"Are you shitting me? We don't have to account to you. The Boys spend it however they want to. And by the way ..."

"Yes, Mr. Tony?"

"Starting next Saturday they need an extra five percent?

"Why?"

"We gots us a huge national deficit, kid."

"How much?"

"Oh, round about $1.4 trillion dollars."

"Okay, whatever I can do to help, Mr. Tony."

If you think that sounds silly, look at your next paycheck stub. And each one after that.

* * *

When you die, by whatever means, your heirs will have to go through probate which is the court-supervised process of locating and determining the value of your assets, paying your final bills and taxes, and then distributing what's left to your heirs.

If that hassle is not enough of a nightmare during a period where everyone is in mourning, then the state and federal government bloodsuckers come calling. They didn't care much about you when you were alive and kicking, but once you die they will come swooping in quicker than vultures on fresh road kill. What they want from your grieving widow and children, or that mistress you had on the side if you included her in your will, is something called the federal estate tax, and possibly a state inheritance tax, which is a tax on all of the stuff you owned before you croaked.

See, despite that old adage, you should have taken it all with you.

The estate tax is affectionately known as the *death tax* since the government can't go after those tax dollars until you're good and dead. In Great Britain they call it *death duties*, as in, hey mate, it's your *duty* to pay the Queen. If your heirs add up all the stuff you own, from property to cars to coffee cans full of silver dollars buried in your backyard, and the total is less than $5 million, then they don't have to pay any estate taxes and you can tell the Feds to go pound salt. However, if the total is more than the current 3.5 million applicable exclusion amount, then Uncle Sam will take forty-five cents out of every single dollar over that figure. Now you know where that line about taking copper pennies off a dead man's eyes comes from.

You can also avoid the estate tax vampires if your property, your business and your bank accounts are jointly owned with your spouse, and your spouse is a U.S. citizen. In that instance, no probate is necessary, and your spouse just needs to show your bank, your mortgage company and your investment companies a copy of your death certificate and they will remove your name from those accounts, leaving just your spouse's name. But once your spouse kicks the bucket, then all of the assets that you both shared become eligible for the estate tax, and with retirement accounts, real estate, and life insurance death benefits thrown into the pot, it's easier to get up near that applicable exclusion amount than you think. The federal government is lobbying to drop the applicable exclusion amount from $5 million to $1 million. Of course they are. What's taking them so long?

I hope this shit is sinking in.

Let me put it into perspective for you.

Let's say you make one million dollars a year and you never get married. That puts you in the thirty-five percent federal tax bracket, so Tony D. will come by every Saturday to collect, and at the end of the year you will have given him $350,000 of your hard-earned one million dollars. You then toil away to make that same one million dollars every year for fifty years. When you retire, you will have given Tony. D a total of $17,500,000.

Tony D. was gracious enough to let you keep the other $32,500,000, and, instead of splurging, you just lived off the interest so you could leave something to your sister's two children who always said you were their favorite uncle. Lying little shits. But by being frugal, when you die there is still that $32,500,000 in your estate. Your niece and nephew are ecstatic.

That is until Tony D. drops in, mentions the words "death tax" and tells Bippy and Buffy that they don't get to keep all that money even though you already paid taxes on it once. Nope, Tony D. is going to collect forty-five percent of that money, minus whatever the exclusion is that year, which means he'll pocket another $12,375,000.

So of the $50,000,000 you earned, $30,000,000 of it went to Tony D., aka your federal government.

Isn't that special.

I remember when they used to put mobsters in prison for doing stuff like that.

* * *

Dan and his wife are good friends of ours. We go out to dinner with them and Happy John and his wife quite often and drink heavily and happily, from when the appetizers come all the way through to when they take away the desert plates, and we talk about all kinds of stuff, with mainly Dan and I doing the talking because we tend to monopolize the conversation and believe that we know everything about everything. Which I do. Not sure about Dan.

As much as Dan likes professional sports, what he likes talking about most is how much the current President of the United States sucks a big donkey dick and how it's 100 percent my fault that the country is going to hell in a handbasket because I voted for the guy. My eyes glaze over when he starts down that road, because I have heard the same complaints from him about the previous President and about our governor and about our mayor and about the people who run our country club community and about any other people who happen to be in a position of authority and whose decisions in some way, no matter how remotely, impact Dan's life.

them.

"You gave up your right to complain," I say to Dan.

"And when the hell did I do that?" Dan will ask.

"When you abdicated the responsibility for the world around you and put it into the hands of 'them'," say I.

"Who the fuck is 'them'," asks Dan.

"Other people," say I.

"Oh, you are so full of shit," says Dan.

I explain my reasoning to Dan, telling him about the conversation I had with my Mom outside the Mexican restaurant.

To which Dan responds, *"Oh, you are still so full of shit."*

I want to tell Dan that I don't think anybody in this country, or any other country on this planet, should be able to vote until they have read a book called *Ishmael* and seen a movie called *Wag the Dog* and listened to every CD from comedian-prophet Bill Hicks.

I want to tell Dan that giving control of your life to politicians and legislators who are not as smart as you and who do not truly have your best interests at heart is only half the problem. The second half of the problem is when you let those incredibly flawed people dictate how you can live your life by allowing them to make and enforce laws.

I want to tell him, but I don't think he'll listen.

I want to say, *"If you don't believe me, try doing this."*

Try peeing in public.

Try smoking in a store.

Try not paying a sales tax.

Try spanking your own kids.

Try not sending your children to school.

Try taking a tiny pocket knife on a plane.

Try stopping someone from burning the flag.

Try buying a handgun for personal protection.

Try walking across a border without a passport.

Try shooting the man who raped your daughter.

Try arranging an abortion for your under-age niece.

Try telling your secretary she looks sexy in that dress.

Try catching a fish or shooting a deer without a license.

Try plucking cannabis, a common weed, and smoking it.

Try watering your lawn on a water rationing blackout day.

Try selling yummy home-made tamales without a license.

Try refusing to send your son to fight one of their wars.

them.

Try letting the grass in your front yard grow two feet high.
Try telling coworkers a joke involving sex, race or religion.
Try killing your own dog because he keeps biting your kids.
Try not hiring someone because of their religious preference.
Try smothering your cancer-ridden grandmother with a pillow.
Try burying that same grandmother in your own back yard.
Try taking a baseball bat to the head of a KKK rally leader.
Try saying a prayer or pledging allegiance to a flag in school.
Try sunbathing totally nude on a lawn chair in your front yard.
Try buying a beer when you are seventeen and half years old.
Try adding a room on your house without a building permit.
Try driving your car barefoot and not putting on your seat belt.
Try not giving half your hard-earned money to the government.
Try promoting someone based simply on their job performance.
Try coloring outside the lines.

* * *

If you don't play by their rules, there are three things they can do to remedy the situation. They can take your money, they can take your freedom, and they can take your life.

Happens every day.

It's called the IRS, it's called prison, and it's called the death penalty. And any one of those three remedies can quickly and easily be bestowed on you if you run afoul of their red tape.

That red tape is like the proverbial Chinese death by a thousand small cuts. Eventually you become numb to the cuts. The one time, though, that you fully realize that your life is not really yours, that it is being overseen, monitored and controlled by other people, is when a pair of cold steel handcuffs are slipped over your wrists.

* * *

The first time I was arrested I was nineteen years old, and I had a belly full of pizza.

Let me tell you, that pizza was the best pizza I have ever eaten. The place we always went to made this incredible thin crust pizza that they cut into long strips rather than into wedge shapes. You could hold the end of one of those long strips with just your thumb and a finger and it would not bend at all, that's how hard and crunchy that crust was. And they weren't stingy when it came to adding the toppings. They'd slap a thick layer of ground sausage, onions and green peppers on the entire pizza. It was like taking a bite of heaven. When I knew we were going to that particular pizza parlor, I would daydream about it all day long.

That night I was quite content with a belly full of thin crust pizza, probing my teeth with a toothpick and patting my stomach, when I walked out of the pizza parlor with my best friend, Tom, only to see a police officer beating the ever living shit out of a young guy we knew named Randy. The officer had his left hand wrapped in Randy's shoulder-length blonde hair and in his right hand he had one of those long, black, six-D-cell maglite flashlights which he was repeatedly smashing into the side of Randy's head. A second police officer had another young friend of ours named Dennis pushed up against the wall and was handcuffing him.

Did I mention that Randy, a small wiry guy who weighed less than a 120 pounds, was also handcuffed with his hands behind his back, but that didn't stop the much larger police officer from treating Randy's head like it was his own personal pinata. Randy, to his credit, never went down, and it wasn't until the cop's flashlight finally broke over his head, sending batteries flying across the parking lot, that the beating stopped.

Tom and I kept walking to my car. We were planning to go to a nearby strip of nightclubs for a night on the town. In my car, my hand on the key in the ignition, Tom and I looked at each other. We were both in college and, ironically enough, Tom was majoring in law enforcement.

"That sucked," said Tom.

"Yeah it did."

I started the engine and looked over at Tom.

"Fuck that shit," said Tom, opening the car door. *"Let's get their badge numbers."*

Seemed like a noble plan, except that the next words I heard shortly after that were, *"Take your shoes off and put your hands behind your back."*

And it wasn't Tom who was saying it.

them.

When we walked back to the front of the pizza shop, a half dozen squad cars had arrived at the scene. We couldn't see the original two Louisville sluggers so I tapped another police officer on the shoulder, which in hindsight was not the smartest thing to do, and when he turned around, I said, *"We want the badge numbers of the two arresting officers."*

"Oh really," he said, the tone in his voice catching the attention of two other cops standing nearby. *"Take your shoes off and put your hands behind your back."*

"No, you don't understand. We weren't involved. We just saw those two cops beating up our friends."

"Oh really," said the cop again. *"I'm going to tell you one more time. Take your fucking shoes off and put your hands behind your back."*

I knew that, truth be told, the very last thing in the world that cop, the one who had just pulled his own long, black, six-D-cell maglite flashlight out of the loop on his gun belt, wanted was for us to follow his orders. He was itching to step into the batter's box himself, as were the two officers now standing next to him.

Tom and I pulled our shoes off. And put our hands behind our back.

And were promptly handcuffed and tossed, shoes and all, into the back of a paddy wagon that had pulled up. Randy and Dennis were already inside.

"What's up, dudes," said Dennis. Randy, his hair matted with blood and both his eyes already starting to swell shut, wasn't in any condition to talk.

"Not much, Dennis."

"What are you guys doing in here?"

"We saw those cops beating you up and asked for their badge numbers."

"Very cool. But dumb."

"No shit."

Dennis smiled and said, *"Hang on."*

We didn't know what he was talking about until the paddy wagon screeched out of the parking lot. There are no seat belts or grab handles in the back of a paddy wagon. The floor, bench seats, sides and roof of a paddy wagon are all covered in a thick metal grating and the holes in the grating are too small to stick your fingers into. If there is nothing to hold on to and your hands are cuffed behind your back, then your body in the back of a paddy wagon, one that is taking sharp corners at ridiculous speeds and intentionally driving over every curb, is like a loose marble inside a tin cup. We bounced all over the place and every time Dennis yelled, *"You motherfuckers,"* the two cops driving in the front would bust out laughing.

At the station the cops stood on each side of the paddy wagon door and ordered us out, which can be a bit tricky when you are dizzy, your hands are cuffed behind your back, and you have to bend down to get through the small doorway. Randy took one step out and fell flat on his face, adding a broken nose to his injuries. The cops just laughed again before picking Randy up and dragging him in to see the booking sergeant, pushing Tom, Dennis and I ahead of him.

They hit Randy and Dennis with a bunch of different charges, and charged Tom and I with interfering with a police officer. They took our mugshots and fingerprints, and put all four of us in the elevator that went to the jail cells upstairs. One of the cops started razzing us, saying how proud our parents were going to be of us.

Until Tom mentioned who his father was.

And that's when the cops stopped laughing.

When the elevator doors opened, one of the cops took Randy and Dennis to a jail cell. Another cop took Tom and I to a conference room and politely asked if we would like a soft drink.

We said no, and he left.

Five minutes later the two Louisville slugger cops who had arrested and pummelled Randy and Dennis and the cop who had arrested Tom and I came into the conference room and proceeded to tell us that they were just doing their jobs, that they were really good guys, that they were sorry for having arrested us, and that we needed to realize there are a lot of bad people out there and police sometimes have to use force on bad people.

They were plenty nervous.

Because Tom's father was the base commander of the Air Force base that sat right next to the city we had been arrested in. You know, one of those huge military bases with all the fighter jets and nuclear bombs and a direct line to the federal government in Washington, DC, and tens of thousands of servicemen who contribute to the economy of the city. So when Tom's father got a courtesy call at home from the desk sergeant saying his son was in jail, Tom's father called the mayor at home who called the commissioner of public safety at home who called the chief of police at home who called the desk sergeant and told him that he and any other cop involved in our arrest was about to be re-assigned to a new beat patrolling the city dump if they did not fix the situation immediately.

Which is why a half hour later those same officers were handing us our shoes back, shaking our hands and even opening Tom's father's car door for us when he came to pick us up. A few weeks later we went to a court hearing where the judge, upon the recommendation of the district attorney's office, formally dropped the charges against us and ordered that our records be expunged.

Randy and Dennis, meanwhile, ended up doing some jail time.

Because they didn't have an important father.

To quote an old Hebrew proverb, *"The court is most merciful when the accused is most rich."*

Three things stand out for me from that night.

The first is that asking for a police officer's name or badge number may work in the movies and on television, but I would not recommend it in real life. Years later a friend told me about being arrested on drunk and disorderly charges outside a casino in Reno, Nevada. He too was handcuffed with his hands behind his back, and the massive amount of Jim Beam bourbon coursing through his body was encouraging him to verbally taunt the arresting officer until the cop's patience had been exhausted. Pausing between loud curses and pointed questions about the cop's sexual preferences, my friend leaned forward and tried to focus on the cop's name tag, before slurring, *"What's your name?"*

"Officer Goodnight," answered the cop and knocked my friend out cold with his nightstick.

I love that story.

So does my friend.

"Think about it. How often do you find a cop with a sense of humor?" he says when he tells the story.

This is the same friend, by the way, who once walked into a casino lounge in Las Vegas to meet me for a drink with his body wrapped head to toe in yellow police caution tape with one of those big orange traffic cones on his head, only to wonder out loud why the bartender wouldn't serve him. My buddy, who I know still has a few more Officer Goodnights in his future, would probably concur with Grover Whalen, the New York City chief of police during Prohibition, who astutely noted, *"There is plenty of law at the end of a nightstick."*

The second thing that stands out for me is how the inequality of the actions of any governing body or justice system or police force, all of which favor the rich over the poor and the haves over the have-nots, is not a whole lot different than the inequality that can be found in the minds and deeds of even the most noble and well intentioned of people. Tom and I had no problem asking for those badge numbers because we knew that police officers beating a handcuffed prisoner was not right. But we also had no problem allowing our social standing and connections to circumvent the laws that applied to everyone else so we could walk out of that police station. We didn't demand to be placed in the jail cell with Randy and Dennis, we didn't picket the courthouse when they were sentenced, and we didn't complain when the judge expunged our records.

Justice always takes a back seat to self interest and preservation.

The third thing that stands out from that night is my memory of how damn good that thin crust pizza was.

* * *

I take the binders with all of my financial records and the folders with the wills and the insurance policies and all that other red tape stuff and put them on the top shelf of the bookcase in my office so that they are not out in plain sight, but can be easily found later.

Then I swivel around in my chair and survey the rest of my office to see what other items might need to be taken care of or tossed out. I look through the rest of the folders in my filing cabinet to make sure I have not missed any important documents and to also make sure there isn't anything embarrassing that my staff or my wife may find when they go to clean out my office.

I find some letters from a few people saying nice things about me or one of my companies and also some photos of myself at industry events. I stick them all in a folder and place it on the stack. I toss out the folder that has printouts tracking how much money I have lost playing Internet poker over the past four or five years. My wife hates when I play poker online because she thinks she'll come home one day and find out that we no longer own the house, so I don't want her to find those printouts and say, *"Ha, I knew it! Your father lost a fortune on that goddammed Internet poker!"*

Yeah, but I had fun.

* * *

Dennis and Randy came up on my radar a few years later after I had become a reporter. I walked into the detective offices and one of the guys said, *"Have I got a story for you."*

Seems a burglar had shimmied a window and slipped into a first-floor apartment the night before in a particularly rough part of town. Just about any other apartment in the city would have been a better choice, because the one he picked had Dennis and Randy asleep in it.

"They beat the shit out of that burglar," said the detective in admiration. *"Man, he picked the wrong apartment. They thumped that boy good. Then they tied him up and called the police. I think they kept smacking him after he was tied up."*

He handed me the investigative report he had written up and I recognized Dennis and Randy's names. *"Hey, I know those guys,"* I said to the detective.

"Really? Those guys were so small. Looked like miniature hippies. But they were tough as barbed wire. And you'll love this. Guess what the patrolman who answered the call reported the burglar said when he walked into the apartment?"

"What?"

"Thank God you're here."

* * *

Continuing on my organizational spree, I turn my attention to my computer. I go through all the computer folders and throw away as much superfluous crap as possible since it's easier for me to know what is junk and can be trashed than for whoever has to go through the computer after I'm gone. I re-label a lot of the documents and folders to make it easier for my staff to know what's what.

them.

When I worked at the newspaper on those old Underwood manual typewriters years ago there was a reporter named Artie who had been at the paper for about five years and who was one of our star reporters covering City Hall. We had this special cheap-ass copy paper that was more tan than white that all the reporters used in their typewriters. We did not use white-out, and instead you actually marked in pen your changes and edits on that paper, and you could even add in whole paragraphs by ripping the paper across a ruler and hand pasting the new paragraph in between the ripped sections. We actually all had jars of glue on our desks. Sounds fucking archaic doesn't it.

Anyway, late one afternoon in the newsroom, as we started getting closer to the 7 pm deadline for turning in your articles, some of the reporters and editors noticed that Artie was not in the newsroom. They called his house and some of his newspaper contacts with no luck. As the 7 pm deadline came and went, everyone was worried about Artie because newspaper reporters seldom if ever miss deadlines. About an hour later one of the copyboys wandered over to Artie's desk and noticed that there was a single sheet of that crappy tan copy paper rolled into Artie's typewriter. He reached over and rolled the sheet up and saw that typed on the sheet were just two words:

I quit.

What a clever and classy way to quit. I loved it.

I need to think of something like that to leave on my computer.

* * *

The second time I was arrested I was twenty-four years old, and I was stoned out of my gourd.

Which would have been okay except that I was driving at the time.

In a very bad part of Dallas late at night.

And, unbeknownst to me, one of my tail lights was out.

And my car had a different state's license plate on it.

And I was a little drunk.

Oh, and I had an unregistered gun in the glove compartment.

So seeing those flashing lights in my rear view mirror at two in the morning was a definite buzz killer.

I watched in my rear view mirror as the two police officers cautiously approached my car, one on the driver's side and one on the passenger's side. For a minute I thought I might me overly-stoned because, unless I was imagining things, both of the officers walking toward me had nice shapely hips and full round breasts pushing out the front of their blue uniform shirts. The more I looked, the more I liked the one on the passenger side the best. Just about the time I told myself it was so very wrong to even fleetingly fantasize about having sex with a cop of undetermined gender, the one on the driver's side, thankfully in an unmistakably female voice said, *"License, registration and proof of insurance please."*

Both of my car windows were down because it was a cool fall night and I could easily see the curvaceous side profiles of the two female officers, who both positioned themselves per the police handbook in such a way that my car's metal door posts were between myself and them, the better to stop a bullet from an irate motorist.

"Yes, Ma'am," I answered and reached over to open the glove compartment.

I was leaning across the console and had my right hand on the glove compartment latch when some tiny inner voice was able to fight through the pot and alcohol fog in my brain just enough to suggest, *"Unless you want to be shot by two smoking hot chick cops, do not open that glove compartment you stupid, dumbshit motherfucker."*

I listened to the tiny voice.

Awkwardly stretched over the console and still with my fingers on the glove compartment latch, I turned my head to the left and said to the not quite as pretty police officer, *"I think I should tell you that I have a gun in the glove compartment."*

You have never seen two people move so fast.

They cleared holster leather quicker than an Old West movie gunslinger, and before the last syllable had rolled off my tongue I had two .357 Magnum pistols pointing straight at my head. By two sexy women. How fucking funny. And erotic.

Erotic or not, I did not move a muscle. And neither did they.

Truly a moment frozen in time.

Then the officer on my side opened the driver's door, yanked me from the car, bent me over the hood of the car, kicked my legs apart, pulled my hands behind me, cuffed me, and patted me down. I felt like together we had just set a world calf-roping record.

The other officer retrieved my gun from the glove compartment and unloaded it, stuck the gun in her waistband, then radioed for a tow truck to come get my car. The officers did not mention smelling any pot and getting stopped had sobered me up, so as they placed me in the back seat of their police cruiser I was happy to hear that were only charging me with carrying a concealed weapon.

That's it? No problem. Even if it was a felony charge, as opposed to a misdemeanor, and I was convicted, that only meant I could never be President of the United States, but it also meant I would never get called for jury duty. Sounded like a fair trade to me.

I turned into a chatterbox on the ride to the police station, explaining to the officers that I was a former police beat newspaper reporter and that the gun they had confiscated had actually been sold to me by a detective because in the state where I had been a reporter it was legal to carry a gun in your car as long as it was concealed.

"Not here," said the prettier officer.

I continued my cop shop talk with the officers and because of the police lingo I used, I could tell they knew I was telling the truth about having spent many hours with the boys in blue and I could also tell that they were amused by my predicament. It didn't mean they were going to cut me loose, but I was probably a welcome change of pace from the usual riffraff they had to listen to in their back seat.

We rode in silence for awhile and then the cannabis hunger pangs hit me and I realized that it would be late afternoon, a good fifteen or so hours into the future, before I would be bonded out of jail and could get something to eat.

"Any chance we can swing through McDonald's?" I asked.
The officers didn't answer.
"My treat."
They both laughed.
"Sorry, no can do."
"Are you sure?"
"Positive."
Damn. I tried another tactic.
"So are you two sisters?"
More laughs, and a *"no."*

"Well, you both sure are pretty. For cops, that is."
"We hear that a lot."
"You know ..."
"Listen, you're not getting a burger."
"Okay."

The police station and jail were in the heart of downtown. We had to wait in line in the underground garage like planes stacked up on a runway as patrol cars disgorged arresting officers and their suspects one after the other. It reminded me of high school seniors showing up at the prom, but these dates were wearing handcuffs on their wrists instead of corsages.

We finally made it to the front of the line and when we stepped through the door on the ground floor level to go to the booking desk, it was like stepping into the Eighth Circle of Hell in *Dante's Inferno* with *pimps, seducers, flatterers, simonists, sorcerers, corrupt politicians, sewers of division, falsifiers, alchemists, thieves, living in excrement, stuffed into holes, heads turned backwards, boiling tar, lead capes, snakes and flames.*

Okay, there was no boiling tar or lead capes, but it was still a nasty, chaotic place.

The prettier police officer went behind the booking desk and whispered into the desk sergeant's ear. He nodded without even looking up and the two female cops peeled me away from the line of suspects being booked and took me into a room off to the left where they patted me down again and then took off my handcuffs. I found out later that the suspects who went to the room to the right of the booking desk were strip-searched. The ladies had thrown me a bone.

"So you're gay," said the prettier officer, more of a statement than a question.

"What? Hell no. Why do you say that?"

"You wear your wedding ring on your right hand. That's where gays wear it."

"No, it's my grandfather's wedding ring. It's too big. I've always worn it on my right hand."

She fixed me with a raised eyebrow.

I stuck my finger into my mouth, coated the ring with spit, slid the ring off, and put it on my left ring finger faster than they had drawn their weapons a half hour earlier.

them.

"Better," said the officer.

We both knew that the jailers would be taking my ring, watch, wallet and other valuables soon enough, but until then it was better to be safe than sorry amidst all the prying eyes at the police station.

"Here," said the other female cop, tapping me on the shoulder and handing me two bags of potato chips she had gotten from a vending machine. *"Eat fast."*

I wolfed down the chips and then they walked me up some stairs to a holding cell on the second floor.

"Later, reporter boy," said the prettier cop as they turned to leave.

"Thanks."

"No problem."

The holding cell was the size of about eight phone booths and I was crammed into that small space with twenty other sweaty, smelly guys who had just been arrested. For those of you who have never had the pleasure of a leisurely chauffeured ride in the back of a police cruiser and then a night's free lodging at the local jail, you should know there is a big difference between a jail and a prison. A jail is where they temporarily house you right after you've been arrested, it is located within the city limits, and you might be there for a few hours or a week or two. A prison is where they send you to serve your sentence after you've been convicted, it is located in some barren area outside the city limits, and you might be there for a year or for life.

The bad news about jail is that it stinks.

The bad news about prison is anal rape. And maybe a shiv in your left eyeball.

Nobody ever goes to the local jail after a nice hot shower and a splash of Old Spice cologne, unlike prisons where inmates know where they are from day to day and shower accordingly. Most people have no idea that a night in jail might be on their agenda for the day. It's more like an unexpected surprise party. You just don't get any presents.

Chances are the guys you share space with in a jail will reek of alcohol, can you say DUI; or sticky runner's sweat, can you say fleeing the police; or dried blood, can you say barroom brawl; or vomit, urine or feces, can you say drunk in public. And they will all be oozing that funky smell that comes from fear and nervousness.

them.

My crew in the holding cell that night offered up an aromatic potpourri of all of those potent smells.

There was a phone in the holding cell and a young man was on the phone asking his father to come bail him out. He was crying. Bad move by him. The other guys were all making fun of him. A black guy asked me what I was in for and I said, *"concealed gun."* He nodded approvingly, and then asked how the cops found the gun, and I said, *"I told them it was in the glove compartment."* Bad move by me.

They took us out one by one, ran us through the mugshot, fingerprints and turn in your valuables routine and then placed us in jail cells. They put me in a two-bunk cell. The biggest, blackest motherfucker you ever saw was in my cell. Baby Huey was asleep, thank God, on the bottom bunk. I climbed into the top bunk and got as quiet and still as possible. I didn't sleep the whole night. It is almost impossible to sleep through the non-stop noise in a city jail. It's not like a hotel with established check-in and check-out times. Cops book people in and jailers let people out constantly, the jail cell doors clang open and shut every few minutes, and guys yell back and forth to each other from their cells all night long.

"That's nothing," I heard a familiar black voice yell. *"Some dumb white motherfucker actually told the police where his gun was."*

Hoots and hollers from one and all. So much for my street cred.

My huge cellmate never woke up, even when they brought us a horrendous lunch of stale bread and suspiciously colored baloney. I had called my wife earlier from the holding cell, and she spent the morning and afternoon finding a bail bondsman who would accept her engagement ring as collateral to get me bonded out. We were recent newlyweds, so this was a marvelous preview of what the little woman would be contending with over the next three decades.

When I was finally released and standing outside on the sidewalk, I gave my wife a hug, sucked down two cigarettes in a row, then hopped in her car.

"What now?" she asked.

"McDonald's, dear. And don't dilly-dally!"

In the car, she said, *"Is this going to be a problem?"*

"No, I can fix it."

"Sure?"

"Positive."

them.

And I did. I kept my nose clean for the next year, and at the end of the year, the gun charge was completely erased from my records. It was like it had never happened. They even gave me my gun back. They knew I had been a newspaper reporter, and for all they knew I might become one again in their fair city. And they knew better than to fuck with the press. Way too powerful. Justice may be blind, but she still plays favorites.

Burgers and fries in hand, we drove to our house.

"Halloween is next month isn't it?" I said to my wife.

"Yes?"

"Let's find a costume party to go to."

"Why?"

"I was thinking you would look great as a police officer."

*   *   *

Them versus us.

How can *them* have been in charge of *us* for so damn long, without *us* raising a ruckus and overthrowing *them*?

I have a theory.

Some time after we stopped living in caves and we got our very first kings and queens and emperors and pharaohs and sheiks and tycoons and emirs, a few of those muckety-mucks were laying around in their palatial digs, having peeled grapes fed to them by palm-fanning slaves while getting their dicks sucked by young virgins.

"This is the life," said Emperor Jed.

"No lie," said Pharaoh Willie.

"I'm a little concerned, though."

"About what?"

"Well, we have it made in the shade, yet our subjects are toiling away out there, starving to death and suffering under our unrestrained tyranny."

"Sounds good to me."

"Yes, but what happens when they realize that we are no better than them, that we are living it up while their life sucks and will continue to suck until the day they die? How do we keep them in line?"

them.

That question caused both rulers to pause for a few minutes. Even as they thought about the perplexing question, they still had time for their daily pleasures.

"More grapes," said Emperor Jed.

"More head," said Pharaoh Willie.

They continued to mull the dilemma over, and then Pharaoh Willie finally spoke up.

"I've got a great idea," he said.

"Do share."

"How about this. And don't laugh, because I'm just thinking outside of the box here."

"Go on."

"Okay. Let's tell them there is life after death."

"Why do that?"

"Because that way they will suffer through this life and put up with all our shit because they think they have another life after this one. We'll even promise them that their next life will be all peaches and cream."

"Damn Willie, that's a great fucking idea. What will we call this new thing?"

"Let's call it religion."

"I love it."

* * *

I get up from my desk and *walk the wall* in the rest of my office building. Walk the wall is a term used in the bar and restaurant industry and is where you stand in one corner of your business and then slowly walk along every wall in the business surveying everything in your path and making mental notes on all the things that need to be fixed or improved, from replacing lightbulbs to cleaning carpet spots to filling salt and pepper shakers to posting new signs. My buddy Jack taught me about that when we owned a sports bar together in Atlanta. We lost our asses on that venture. Bars are for drinking in, not owning.

The office building I own is about three thousand square feet with one large open room with desks for my secretary and the bookkeeper and a reception area with a couch where Boo holds court. Branching off from the main room are eight smaller offices for the rest of the staff. I poke my head in each office but don't see anything that needs to be added to the stack of files and folders for my wife. There is some cool artwork on the walls that is mine, but my guess is my wife will just leave it where it is.

I do notice that a few of the fluorescent ceiling bulbs need to be changed and mention it to the bookkeeper who will have one of the young guys on the staff replace them. *"He should probably replace all the air conditioner filters while he has the step ladder out,"* I tell her, wondering to myself as I say it why I give a fuck about an office environment that I will only be inhabiting for a few more days. Just my nature, I guess.

Speaking of Jack, he is the most prodigious drinker I have ever met, so having the two of us own our own bar was like putting a drooling fox in charge of the chicken coop.

Jack and I drink Johnny Walker Black scotch cocktails and between each of those rounds we order a shot, Crown Royal bourbon straight up for Jack with a Coke chaser and Jagermeister chilled for me. So it's cocktail, shot, cocktail, shot, all night long. We never have a bar tab less than $400 wherever we go, and that's just for the two of us. The difference between Jack and I is that Jack can drink all night and never truly get drunk, while I am the one most likely to wake up in a hotel stairwell the next morning as two maids smoke cigarettes on their break and ignore the passed out white dude sprawled on the concrete stairs. True story by the way.

We are probably the only two guys to ever get thrown out of the Star Trek Bar at the Las Vegas Hilton in the middle of the afternoon. In our defense, I think we got the boot not so much because we were drunk but moreso because the incredibly large-breasted chick who was with us kept flashing her enormous boobs at the bartender and occasionally at the young kids who walked past the bar to tour the Star Trek exhibits area. Captain Kirk wouldn't have objected, but management certainly did.

My best Vegas Jack story was the time we tried to find a restaurant for dinner on a late Saturday night without a reservation. Several places had already turned us away because they had no tables available when we walked into the third joint, a fancy steakhouse at one of the bigger casinos. We were greeted by a stern looking host in a tuxedo flanked by two young hostesses in matching black dresses. They stood behind a giant polished wood podium with a reservations book the size of a garage door spread out on it. The whole setup looked like a police roadblock.

"Name please," said the host.

"We don't have a reservation," said Jack. *"It's just the two of us and we're starving. Can't you squeeze us in?"*

The host looked like we had just asked him to shit in a cup.

"That's impossible, sir. We are completely booked up through the rest of the evening. We do not have a single table available now and won't for the rest of the night."

"But ..." Jack started to say.

The host cut him off. *"Sir, I would like to help you. But there is absolutely no way we can accommodate you with a table tonight."*

Jack's right hand was in his pant's pocket. He pulled his hand out, reached over the podium, slapped a $100 black poker chip down on the open reservations book, slid it toward the host and said, *"How about now?"*

And the host, without missing a beat, said, *"Will that be smoking or non-smoking, sir?"*

* * *

A hundred or so centuries later, Emperor Jed the 210th and Pharoah Willie the 209th were laying around the mansion sipping bootleg whiskey and getting their dicks sucked by some sweat shop ladies fresh off the boat.

"This is the life," said Jed the 210th.

"No lie," said Willie the 209th.

"I'm a little concerned, though."

"About what?"

"Well, I don't think the people are buying all that life after death religion crap any more."

"So, why do we care?"

"Because what happens when they realize that we are no better than them, that we are living it up while their life sucks, and that when they die, that's it, there are no peaches and cream? We need to come up with a brand new narcotic for the masses to keep them docile and to stop them from asking too many questions. And we need to do it quick."

them.

Willie the 209th, having come from a long line of great thinkers, didn't take long to come up with a solution.

"I've got a great idea," he said.

"Do share."

"How about this. Let's put something in every person's home so when they aren't sleeping or working or eating or screwing, they will just stare at that thing for hours on end. That way they will spend all of their free time thinking about that thing and not about us."

"Damn Willie, that's a great fucking idea. What will we call this new thing?"

"Let's call it television."

"I love it."

* * *

The third time I was arrested I was 50 years old and I said something very stupid. What I said to Officer Tipton was, *"I couldn't even do this if I was sober."*

* * *

Back at my desk I look at the stack of red tape folders.

And I think to myself that the guy who invented life insurance is an asshole and a genius.

He's an asshole because I don't like gambling my hard-earned money on whether I am going to live or die, and he's a genius for getting me and millions and millions of other schmucks to do just that. He's right up there with the guy who invented bottled water, the guys who started the Starbucks franchise, and the guy who came up with the concept of having us clean our own tables at fast food restaurants.

I'm speaking, of course, about *them*.

I am positive that there was a sales meeting a few decades ago where a company was trying to come up with some revenue generating ideas and the new guy who never said anything at the meetings finally got up the courage to raise his hand, and the boss, with a sigh, said, *"Yes Mortimer, what is it?"*

And Mortimer said, *"We could sell water."*

them.

And the boss said, *"Mortimer you're an idiot. Water is free. No one is going to pay for it."*

And everyone at the meeting laughed and the boss moved on to other discussion topics until about ten minutes later when Mortimer, who all of a sudden had grown a set of big, bouncy balls, raised his hand again.

And the boss said, with another deep sigh, *"Yes Mortimer, what is it this time?"*

And Mortimer said, *"Well, we could put the water in plastic bottles, and come up with a cool nifty name for the water, and tell everyone it is special water and it is so much better than regular water, and then charge a fortune for it so everyone will think it is indeed special."*

And the boss said, *"Mortimer, you're a genius!"*

Today we drink about forty billion gallons of bottled water a year, or, to put it more in perspective, 400,000,000,000 twelve-ounce bottles of water a year. It's a multi-billion-dollar industry.

I always buy a bottle of water before I get on a plane because, for some reason, I get particularly parched when I am thirty-five thousand feet up in the air and, God forbid, I have to buzz the stewardess to bring me an extra glass of water in one of those itsy-bitsy plastic glasses that hold three sips. The plane was delayed on one trip and when it came time to board I realized I had already drank my bottled water and there wasn't time to go to the newsstand to buy another bottle. I looked over and saw the sign for the restrooms and the water fountain next to them. Hey, I thought, I have a great idea. I went to the water fountain and filled up the plastic bottle and then took a sip. Tasted exactly like the bottled water I had bought earlier, and it was free. Imagine that. The funny thing is that I felt guilty doing it, and I actually worried that someone would see me and think I was a cheapskate. That's how trained and conditioned they have made us.

We are idiots.

So these three guys named Jerry, Gordon and Zev opened a little coffee shop in Seattle, Washington in 1971 and called it Starbucks. Two of the partners were teachers and one was a writer which meant they knew fuck-all about business so my guess is they just wanted a little place where they could sip some java and talk about how one day they would each write the Great American novel.

I'm pretty sure that they had a sales meeting and one of the partners, let's say it was Zev because you have to admit that's a pretty fucking cool name, raised his hand.

And the partners said, *"Yes, Zev-Man what's on your mind?"*

And Zev said, *"Let's franchise and open thousands of Starbucks coffee shops all around the world."*

And the partners probably said, *"Zev you're an idiot. People either drink coffee at home for a few pennies a cup or they drink it for free at the office. No one is going to pay us for it."*

And the two partners laughed and they moved on to other discussion topics until about ten minutes later when Zev, who was pumped up on a double espresso, raised his hand again.

And the partners said, *"Yes Zev, what is it now?"*

And Zev said, *"Well, we could put the coffee in these groovy cups with lids, and use our cool nifty name, and tell everyone it is special coffee and it is so much better than regular coffee, and charge a fortune for it so everyone will think it is indeed special."*

And the partners said, *"Zev, you're a genius!"*

Today there are more than 16,000 Starbucks coffee shops in forty-nine countries. There are over 50,000 coffee specialty shops in just the United States alone.

In fact, I am drinking a Caramel Macchiato made with nonfat milk and sugar-free vanilla syrup right now.

We are idiots.

In the late 1970s there was a management meeting at one of the fast food franchise companies and the chairman of the board was bemoaning the fact that the bottom line at their outlets was being adversely affected by labor costs, specifically the time employees had to spend cleaning up food wrappers and napkins and trays after customers ate their meals. That's when the new guy on the management team raised his hand and the chairman, with a sigh, said, *"Yes Gaylord, what is it?"*

And Gaylord said, *"We could make the customers clean up their own mess."*

And the chairman said, *"Gaylord you're an idiot. People come to our restaurants because they don't want to cook and clean. Besides they are paying us;, we aren't paying them."*

And everyone at the meeting laughed and the chairman moved on to other discussion topics until about ten minutes later when

Gaylord, who was an astute student of human nature, raised his hand again.

And the chairman said, with another deep sigh, *"Yes Gaylord, what is it this time?"*

And Gaylord said, *"All we need is for that first customer to clean up his mess and then walk over and toss it into the trashcan and then put his tray in the tray slot. After that, every other person will do it because they will be embarrassed not to do it. People are sheep. They'll do whatever we tell them to do. Trust me on this one, Big Guy."*

And the boss said, *"Gaylord, you're a genius!"*

Today you clean up your own mess at every fast food restaurant you go to, and you also pump your own gas and check your own oil and put air into your own tires at every gas station you go to, and now supermarkets are asking you to scan and ring up your own purchases and sack your own groceries. And, of course, they want you to pay them for the privilege of doing so.

We are idiots.

Which brings me back to life insurance.

Let me get this straight. I'm going to bet my own money on whether I am going to die or not. If I don't die, then I lost the bet because I spent money on insurance premiums and I got nothing in return. If I do die, I won the bet because my loved ones got more money back than I paid out in premiums, but on the flip side, I am fucking dead, which pretty much means I still lost.

WTF.

We are idiots.

Life insurance, extended warranties, and service plans are all a scam.

Let me get this straight. I just paid $4,000 for a 65-inch plasma TV and you want me to pay another $500 for a three-year extended warranty. If a TV that costs $4,000 is prone to break down in less than three years, then why the fuck are you selling me this piece of shit in the first place? Don't you stand behind what you sell? Didn't you just tell me that this was the best TV on the market? You can't have it both ways, Dickhead. Make up your mind.

Oh, you say that everybody else is buying the extended warranty? Okay, I guess I need to buy one too.

We are idiots.

them.

* * *

"Damn Willie the 209th, that television thing is a big hit. The people have turned into zombies."

"No doubt. Just wait until we go from black and white to color."

"No way."

"Yes way."

"But what if that starts to wear off, just like the religion thing did?"

"No worries, my brother from another mother. I've got another trick up my sleeve in case we ever need it."

"Great. What's it called?"

"Internet porn."

* * *

How to stop *them*.

Pennywise. LA punk band. The song, *"Fuck Authority."*

Play it loud.

"I say fuck authority

Silent majority

Raised by the system

Now it's time to rise against them

We're sick of your treason

Sick of your lies

Fuck no, we won't listen

We're gonna open your eyes

Frustration, domination, feel the rage of a new generation ...

We're livin', we're dyin', we're sick and tired of the endless liein' ...

No way, not gonna stand for it ...

It's time we had our say."

Real loud.

* * *

You would never think of Mean John as being patriotic. He is well known, though, and you might even say notorious depending on how you feel about cock rings and vibrators, in the major metropolitan city where he lives. He's no stranger to the front page of the daily newspaper, courtesy of his many high profile battles with City Hall over his right to operate retail stores that sell products for enhancing your sex life to consenting adults. His city is one of the murder capitals of this country and is ranked in the Top 20 cities for overall violent crime, yet the powers to be are more interested in stopping him from selling a bottle of lube than they are in locking up muggers and rapists. Mean John hates the legal bills, but loves the notoriety.

Every cop in the city knows who he is, and some secretly applaud his tenacity while others would like to get him in a backroom with some hot lights and rubber hoses. Problem is, he never knows which way a particular cop is leaning when he comes in contact with one.

Like the night he closed one of his stores and was driving home at three in the morning and got stopped for speeding. On a secluded stretch of road in a heavily wooded area with no street lights. In his very expensive Maserati. On his way to his very expensive mansion. A young guy who makes more money than any fifty cops' salaries combined stopped by an officer who makes 30K a year and is stuck working the midnight shift.

John knows all this as he rolls down his car window. He knows that the cop, if he was so inclined, could just shoot him and claim self defense, or he could radio for back-up and the boys could take turns doing the Rodney King dance on his head on that deserted stretch of road.

So, still knowing all this, when the cop asks for his license and registration and John hands them over and also tells the officer that he has a gun in the car and the cop sarcastically asks, *"Why do you have a gun in your car?"*, John just naturally says:

"Besides the fact that it's my constitutional right?"

Don't you just love it.

There are people who call Mean John a scoundrel, and like me he certainly is, but I say it in a complimentary way while they say it in a derogatory way. Those are the same people who keep their mouths shut when the powers that be increase their taxes or pass more laws infringing on their personal freedom. Mean John, like the guys who sent out invitations to the Boston Tea Party, won't put up

them.

with that shit. He'll fight *them* in a court of law or on a lonely stretch of highway.

Which, I think, is both admirable and ballsy.

I know a stripclub owner named Joe who became a millionaire opening and running a very successfull club, but with that success came a lot of unwanted attention from the media and the local cops. One night the cops went into his club undercover as customers and then arrested Joe and some of the dancers, alledging that the dancers had committed improprieties with the undercover officers while giving them lap dances. The cops made the club and the dancers give back the "marked" money they had spent on the dances, saying it was evidence for the case. Included in that marked money was $6 the cops had spent to buy six $1 bottles of water. Joe told the cops he wanted the $6 back because the cops had ordered and drank his bottled water and there was nothing illegal about the water. The cops said no, so Joe sued the city.

Joe's attorney, who I also know, told me that the case, because of hearings and what not, had been going on for over a year and had still not made it to trial, so he called Joe and said, *"Listen, this case has already cost you thousands of dollars in legal fees just to try to collect a measly six dollars. How much of your own personal money are you willing to spend to get that six dollars back?"*

"All of it," said Joe.

* * *

American Indians looked to the future when it came to their leadership responsibilities by considering whether or not each and every decision they made would benefit their children and their children's children and on and on for the next seven generations. It is an ecological concept that urges the current generation to protect and sustain the bounties of the earth for the benefit of the next seven generations.

"We must consider the impact on the seventh generation, even if it requires having skin as thick as the bark of a pine," reads the Constitution of the Iroquois Nations. *"In all of your deliberations in the Council, in your efforts at law making, in all your official acts, self interest shall be cast into oblivion. Look and listen for the welfare of the whole people and have always in view not only the present but*

also the coming generations, even those whose faces are yet beneath the surface of the ground."

Naturally, these people—who came up with a marvelous concept of abandoning self interest and instead making decisions that would take care of others into the future—were promptly deemed savages by us and then subjected to a massive campaign of genocide, with the broken survivors imprisoned on reservations. Where villages of teepees once sat we now have landfills of toxic waste.

Hurray for our side.

* * *

"Problems at home?" asks Albert.

"No. Why?"

"This is your fourth night in here. Not like you."

"I just enjoy your company."

"Bullshit."

Albert's cell phone rings and he walks outside the noisy club to take the call. He comes back inside a few minutes later and he doesn't look happy. With a little prodding he says that the call was from his attorney and that the county is trying to pass an ordinance requiring exotic dancers to be three feet away from customers which would eliminate lap dances, the bread and butter for strippers. Last year it was an attempt by the county to make stripclubs close earlier than other clubs, and Albert knows that next year it will be something else.

"It's all about ink," I say to Albert.

"Ink?"

"Yeah, ink as in newspaper coverage. Stripclubs are good ink. More ink means more exposure for the politicians. More exposure for the politicians means more chances for them to get re-elected. You're just the means to an end."

"That's not fair."

I nod my head in agreement, and then say, *"All of your problems would go away overnight if you had the right business partner."*

"Okay, I'll bite," says Albert. *"Who should I get to be my business partner?"*

First off, I say to him, it needs to be a she.

them.

Who is gay.
And black.
And over sixty-five.
And a vegetarian.
And a war veteran.
And an AIDS patient.
And a practicing Mormon.
And a Nazi party sympathizer.
And a survivor of childhood incest.
And she only has one leg.
And a hearing aid.

"*Now, if you can find a partner like that,*" I say to Albert, "*no one, and I mean no one, will ever fuck with your business again. You can have zebras wearing pink tutus fucking your dancers doggy-style on the roof of this club and nobody will say a word. They won't dare.*"

"*You're probably right,*" says Albert with a weary sigh.

We're both quiet for a minute and I swivel around on my barstool to watch the dancer on stage. I have just one word for her, Stairmaster.

I spin back around, take a sip of my cocktail and ask Albert a question.

"*What do you think about suicide?*"

"*Say what?*"

"*Suicide. What do you think about it?*"

Albert stares at me, his brow furrowed.

"*That's a fucking off-the-wall question,*" he says.

"*I know. But someone at my office mentioned it today and I was just wondering what your thoughts were on the subject.*"

"*Someone at your office mentioned it?*" he says.

"*Yeah.*"

"*Really? Interesting.*"

I plod on, despite his skepticism.

"*So, what's your take on it?*"

Albert looks at me, then looks at the mirror behind the bar, then back at me. He lifts his glass of Diet Coke off the bar and wipes the wet spot with a napkin, then sets the glass back down.

"*I guess,*" he says, "*just like you mentioned a minute ago, that it's just the means to an end.*"

157

them.

I know by the way Albert says that, by the tone of his voice, by the tilt of his head, that he isn't going to say anything more on the subject.

I spin around again and watch the next dancer.

* * *

In bed I reach for the book on my nightstand. Before my hand touches the book, Boo weighs in.

"I came to a conclusion today," says Boo.

"Which is?"

"Sucks to be you."

"What do you mean?"

"All that red tape crap you have to deal with. All that paperwork, all those rules and regulations. Wills and life insurance and licenses and bank accounts. Getting arrested, going to jail. What a pain."

"I agree."

"You should have my life. It's all good, baby. I don't have to work. I get to sleep all day if I want. You feed me, entertain me, buy me treats, make sure I have a nice warm place to sleep."

"Sounds marvelous."

"Listen, us dogs talk. We know we have it made. If you don't feed us or take care of us, or if you beat us, someone will rat you out to the red tape brigade. Until you cut our balls off, which by the way you are going to burn in hell for doing, we can screw anyone we want and we don't have to marry them or end up paying child support. You are stuck on this mean ass planet for seventy years or more but we get to enjoy the best of life for just twelve to fifteen years. Then you have to bury us in the backyard and we'll be fertilizing the lawn while you're getting Alzheimer's and colon cancer, and your kids never call, and you can't get a hard-on any more, and your savings start to run out, and you can only eat at restaurants that have early bird senior specials."

"You are one lucky canine," I say.

"Oh, it gets better. Here's how I start my day every day. In the morning the Little Lady lets me out of this cage and takes me outside into the front yard where it's nice and sunny and I can feel the dew on my paws. I get to pee a nice long stream that would make a racehorse proud onto your mailbox, and then I wander around the

*lawn and find just the right spot to take a dump. There are kids
walking to the bus stop and parents driving to work and they all
watch me and I don't care. I'm out there naked as a jaybird just
dropping my load and nobody thinks a thing about it. And I don't
have to wipe. Bet you wish you could do that."*

"Not really."

"You should try it sometime."

"I'll think about it. So you've got it made, huh?"

"You bet I do."

"What about the coyotes?"

"What coyotes?

*"The ones that have been in the woods inside our little golf
course community for the past year. The ones who have already
snatched up and eaten over a dozen pets so far."*

"What the fuck! And you're just now mentioning this?"

"I didn't want to scare you."

*"Scare me? Goddammit, I'm wandering around outside all the
time. Don't you think I should have known there were coyotes out
there?"*

"Sorry."

*"Dude, I'm fast, but not that fast. I can't outrun a fucking
coyote."*

"You're right."

*"I weigh ten pounds soaking wet. How am I going to fight off a
ninety-pound wild animal?"*

*"Actually, they travel in pairs so you would have to fight off two
of them."*

"Motherfucker!"

Boo is quiet for awhile. Then he asks a question.

"Is that what happened to Suzi?"

"Who's Suzi?"

*"You don't know her. She's that fly Pomeranian from around the
corner. I haven't eye-balled her in a month."*

"There you go."

The irony is that dogs, who would shit a brick if they walked
around a corner and came face to face with a coyote, are actually
descended from wolves. Domestic dogs originated from a single
species of wolf in East Asia anywhere between 50,000 and 100,000
years ago when one wolf said to hell with being hungry all the time

and freezing his ass off and sought the warmth and security of humans, which scientists call a domestication event. Whatever the hell they want to call it, it turned out to be a match made in heaven, with early wolf-dogs adopting humans as their protectors and providers, and humans using them for hunting purposes. Next thing you know they're buddies, and the canines are telling all the other animals, *"Yo dude, we're man's best friend."*

Modern man, the version that looks like you and not like an orangutan, has also only been around between 50,000 to 100,000 years which, as some scientists have pointed out, means that dogs literally walked out of the caves with us.

Man being man, he couldn't just be happy with a bunch of wolf-dogs sitting around the campfire telling ghost stories or helping chase down fleeing elk, so he started messing around with the mating process. Not man mating with dogs, you sick puppy, but dogs mating with dogs. Man realized he could breed dogs for specific tasks that would help make his life easier.

It's always all about us, isn't it.

Having two fast dogs do the dirty deed produced offspring that were even faster that their parents and could chase down other critters, and breeding big strong dogs together produced offspring that made great watchdogs or sled-pullers. I'm not sure what task they had in mind when they did mix and match breeding to come up with applehead Chihuahuas and Mexican hairless dogs. But there's no question there was a lot of rampant dog screwing going on over those thousands of years because today there are more than 300 recognized dog species, making Fido the most variable animal on the planet in terms of shape, size and color.

Lie down with dogs and you wake up with fleas would, on first telling, seem to be a slam against dogs, but it's actually the dogs who get the short end of the stick since living with humans and sharing their environment for thousands of years has caused dogs to develop many of the same genetic health problems that man has, from cancer to night blindness to narcolepsy. In fact, cancer is now the leading cause of death for dogs over the age of ten. And most of them don't even smoke.

If you don't think God has a wicked sense of humor, consider the fact that the canine narcolepsy problem—where dogs just all of a sudden fall asleep at inappropriate times—mainly affects Doberman

them.

Pinschers whose main job in life is to be vicious, wide awake, nothing-gets-past-me guard dogs.

And what about the history of cats? Who gives a shit. Cats suck.

Boo is quiet. I know the coyote thing has him rattled. He'll probably have nightmares tonight. Serves him right. It was about time I took him down a peg or two. I pick up my book and start to read.

Boo pipes up once more.

"I came to another conclusion today," he says.

"Which is?"

"I'm going to stick closer to the front door from now on whenever I go outside.'

"Stellar idea," I say.

life.

Life is good. For the most part.

But not for Boo. At least not this morning.

Because it's bath time. And he knows it.

How do I know that he knows? Because he's nowhere to be found.

I start the shower, call his name, and when he doesn't come running, I go looking. I take a shower every morning. How he knows that on this particular morning I plan to take him in there with me and wash him is beyond me, but he always knows when it's his bath time, even if I don't make the decision until I wake up that day. I find him under the covers in my wife's bed in the guest room. As I reach under the covers, he crawls deeper in. I get hold of one leg and gently pull him out. He doesn't look happy. I take off his collar and carry him under one arm back to the shower, grabbing his special dog shampoo from the towel closet.

I tell my friends that when I give Boo a bath in our walk-in shower that I use him like one of those loofah sponges, soaping him up and then scrubbing him all over my body to get myself nice and clean. He especially hates it, I tell them, when I do the crack of my butt.

life.

Truth be told, he is small enough to be used as a sponge, but this particular loofah sponge comes with very sharp teeth and I don't want them anywhere near the family jewels. Still, I am able to hold Boo with one hand, lather him up with the dog shampoo with the other hand, then rinse him off in the shower spray before tossing him out the shower door where he will run around the house a few times and rub his body on the carpet to dry himself off. What he is also trying to do is to get rid of the sickly sweet and incredibly strong, at least to him, scent of the shampoo. It's estimated that a dog's sense of smell is anywhere between one hundred to one thousand times stronger than a person's sense of smell. Dogs put their heads out of moving car windows not to enjoy the scenery, but instead because the smells that are inside your car when the windows are rolled up— from your bad breath to your body odor to your cigarette smoke to those stale french fries you didn't finish—are just too powerful for a dog. They stick their noses out the car window because, basically, you stink.

"My oh my, doesn't somebody smell good," I say to Boo as we drive to the office. He ignores me. Won't even look at me. Stares at the passenger side door. Pretends like I don't exist.

He'll get over it. When we get to the office, all the girls will fawn over him, telling him how sweet he smells, and he will lap it up.

He's so vain.

* * *

My Dad was a fanatic about not leaving any lights on in our house in any rooms that were not occupied. *"Quit wasting electricity. Who the hell do you think we are, the Rockefellers?"*

I never really understood his concern until one day he told me the story about when as a young child he was doing one of those paint-by-number pictures for his mother as a Mother's Day Present. He was upstairs in the bedroom he shared with his two brothers. It was evening and he had the bedroom light on. It was just after the Great Depression and everyone was still barely scraping by. His father saw the light on in his bedroom, walked into the room and told my Dad to turn the light off. My Dad protested that he needed the light to finish the Mother's Day painting, but his father said they could not afford to waste the electricity and turned the bedroom light off.

life.

My Dad then moved his chair over to the bedroom window, raised the blind and continued painting the picture using the light from a nearby street light that filtered in through the window.

The story said a lot about why my Dad was so frugal for the rest of his life—*"waste not, want not"* was his mantra—and it also said a lot about how industrious and clever he could be when he wanted to get something done.

I like to think that I am like him in that way.

Getting things done, and damn the obstacles.

Making a decision, and following through with it.

* * *

I pull up the *TCB List* on my computer and notice that I am a little behind schedule. Dad would not approve. According to the list, I was supposed to knock out the funeral arrangements yesterday. I move that chore over onto today's list. The rest of the list looks very doable, *"Get totally drunk and fucked up tonight, last chance to party."*

I add a few more items to today's list: get car washed, call drinking buddies and invite they and their wives over to the house, call wife and tell her I have put out the siren call, stop at the liquor store, order some pizzas and pasta for delivery, and get out the games.

Can't wait.

* * *

When I was a little kid, there was nothing in the world I loved more than candy.

More than Frosted Flakes cereal.

More than Saturday morning cartoons.

More than my brother and my sisters.

More even, dare I say it, than watching Lucas McCain dispatch the bad guys with his modified Winchester Model 1892 rifle with that special trigger that allowed him to rapid fire multiple shots on *The Rifleman*. Man, I loved that TV show. Lucas and his son Mark and the sheriff Micah were the good guys and just about everyone else was a bad guy, and before the thirty minutes were up each episode, the bad guys would be flat on their backs pumped full of lead. There was no gray area in that world, it was all black and white. The rules to life then were easy to understand and easy to follow.

But if I had a choice between watching the latest episode of *The Rifleman* or spending that half hour in the candy aisle at the local store, the candy perusing would always win hands down. I would steal pennies and nickels from the loose change on my Dad's dresser and slip off to the store where I could easily spend an hour studying each type of candy and analyzing their pros and cons. The actual eating of the candy was almost secondary to the thrill of the selection process.

But you had to be smart. You had to resist the temptation of immediate gratification.

Sure you could buy a Three Musketeers candy bar because there is nothing on this planet that tastes as good. Forget Beluga caviar or Chateaubriand or Baked Alaska or white truffles. I will put a Three Musketeers bar up against any one of those over-priced taste treats any day, and I'm not just talking about from a kid's perspective. Stick some Beluga caviar on a fine piece of china and the candy bar on another piece of china, hand them both to the world's greatest chef, tell him he can only eat one of the two and that no one will ever know which one he chooses, and my money is on that candy bar.

But if I picked the Three Musketeers bar I would have a few seconds of incredible enjoyment and then be left with nothing but an empty wrapper. Which is why, even after an hour of assessing the merits of every type of candy in the store, I would always buy NECCOs, which looked like a roll of quarters but were actually round, hard and flat sugary candies the width and diameter of a quarter that came in an assortment of flavors. I could eat them one at a time and make the whole roll last for several hours. I learned early on the art of stretching a dollar.

The first time I found myself in an aisle full of candy, I started grabbing every piece I could and stuffing the candy into my pockets just as I would have done if there was a plate of oatmeal cookies on the dining room table at my house. My Mom told me to put the candy back and explained that it was not free and that it would have to be paid for, which was my first introduction to the most basic and unpleasant tenet of life, which is that nothing is free and there is a price on everything you do and everything you want from the day you are born until the day you die.

Let's face it. Your whole life is really nothing more than standing at the counter of the world's convenience store. What do you want, and what are you willing to pay for it? What price happiness? What price love? What price success? There's always a toll to pay.

Complicating matters is the fact that the prices and the rules are constantly changing. As a kid, I knew the prices and I knew the rules. Without raising too much suspicion I could steal fifty cents a week from my Dad's dresser and I could buy five candy bars a week, which meant that two days of the week I went without. Which sucked. But that was my black and white world and those were the rules. I understood them and so did Lucas McCain.

So I would have been very confused if my Mom had said:

"Don't be upset. Do you know that one day you will have enough money to buy all the candy you want?"

"No way."

"Yes way."

"You mean one day I will be able to buy more than one candy bar a day?"

"Yes. In fact, one day you will be able to buy every candy bar in this store."

"No way."

"I promise."

"Can that day be today?"

"No."

"Why not?"

"You have to wait until you are older and are making money."

There's that damn *you gotta pay* thing again.

But Mom was right. As an adult I now have enough money to buy all the candy I want. But I don't particularly like candy anymore. When I wanted it, I could not afford it, and when I could afford it, I did not want it.

Just another of Mr. Life's cruel jokes.

Ha-ha, Mr. Life. Very funny. You are such a little jokester.

* * *

life.

Because you can't simply grab a shovel and clear out a nice patch of ground in your backyard to bury a deceased loved one, I go to the office mail room and get a copy of the Yellow Pages to look up funeral homes. I could search for them on the Internet but I'd rather do it old school style and actually flip through a book and look at all the ads. Seems more appropriate that way. But as I make some calls, everyone I talk to is reluctant to give me any pricing specifics over the phone and instead they put the hard-sell on me to schedule an appointment for a face-to-face meeting.

"Sure, I can come by," I say to one woman, *"but, and this is just out of curiosity, how much is it going to cost me to put Mom in the ground."*

Sorry Mom, but I had to use somebody's name.

"Is she deceased," the woman says.

"Isn't that a prerequisite for burial," I say. Sometimes I slay myself.

"Excuse me," says the woman.

"Oh, she's not dead yet. But any day now," I say.

"Well, now is the time to make the arrangements," says the woman. *"It is so much easier and less painful to do this in advance. When can you come by? We have some great special prices this month on our sixteen gauge sealer caskets. "*

"I'm not sure. Let me call Mom and see how she's feeling and I'll get back to you," I say and then hang up the phone.

Screw these people. I get a fresh cup of coffee and go to the Internet.

The National Funeral Directors Association says the average cost of a funeral is $6,500, but that's a real bare-bones, pardon the pun, cost. For a decent pop 'em into the ground package, here's the dent you will be looking at in your wallet:

$200	Transportation from the place of death
$1,200	Professional services from the funeral home.
$600	Embalming and other preparation.
$400	Supervision during visitation hours.
$300	Hearse and lead/flower car.
$1,400	Grave marker.
$275	Casket spray of flowers.
$1,500	Burial plot.

life.

$850	Digging the grave.
$3,000	Casket.

$9,725	Total

The Funeral Consumer Guardian Society has a website that tells you average burial costs state by state, and gives you three package choices in each state: Good, Better and Best. I kid you not. *We weren't too fond of Uncle Louie, so we just buried him good—not better or best.* On average you can get Good for $6,000, Better for $8,000, and Best for $10,000.

You can also add another $500 or more for a burial vault which is a four-sided container made of concrete, metal or hard plastic that the casket is lowered into, as opposed to being lowered directly into the ground. This prevents the ground from caving in around the casket or crushing the casket as it settles once the grave has been filled. Probably not a bad idea because there is nothing more embarrassing than having the grave cave in and take the teary-eyed widow with it when she goes to place a rose on the casket. *"Oh shit"* are two words you don't want to hear the pastor say at a graveside service.

Prices fluctuate based on how elaborate you want the wake, the church funeral, and the graveside services to be; how much you want to spend on the casket; and how much you want to spend on the burial plot. All cemeteries are not created equal and, just like in real life, you're going to pay more for a burial plot with a view. My Dad's burial plot was under a huge oak tree. *"How nice,"* someone said to me, *"your father is in the shade."* Are you fucking kidding me.

The cost for cemetery burial plots can range from $1,000 to $10,000, which may seem high, but land isn't cheap and your decomposing body will be taking up that space for the rest of eternity which means they can't build a Chucky Cheese on that spot. The average cost for a casket is between $1,500 and $6,500, but you can certainly spend a lot more, particularly if you want one that has a plasma TV and a wet bar in it.

Caskets are made of metal, wood, composition board, and even more exotic materials like fiberglass, plastic, compressed paper or natural marble. Metal caskets are usually painted and some are covered with a vinyl that can carry a variety of motifs or logos, like the Dallas Cowboys football logo or text saying, *Try Luigi's for the best deep dish pizza in town!* The most common interior materials for caskets are velvet and crepe, and occasionally rayon or tapestry-like weaves. The bed of a casket is spring supported from a metal frame that can be easily raised, lowered or tilted so the deceased can get positioned just right for what's going to be a very long nap. There are many options. You can go with a solid poplar wood with a polished simulated walnut finish and interior of rosetan crepe, or splurge on the eighteen gauge steel with a brushed blue finish and interior of silver taupe crepe. Mix and match is allowed.

One website that sells caskets online boasts that they offer Free Next Day Nationwide Delivery. How thoughtful. On their home page they even have a satisfied customer testimonial saying, *"The casket arrived at the funeral home at the exact time you told us it would. Thanks for getting it to us. We compared it to the funeral home's price for the same casket and we figure that you saved us about $1,200!"*—R.D.

It's not clear from the testimonial what R.D. was happier about —the timely delivery of the casket or saving the $1,200.

* * *

When I was about five years old, we went on a family vacation. As a military brat I had lived in seven states and two foreign countries by the time I was fourteen, so I don't remember where we went on that particular trip.

I do remember living in Baudette, Minnesota for a year, though, where it was freezing cold for 364 days out of the year and we had to have the fire department come to the house three different times to blow away the snowdrifts that completely covered the house just so we could open the front door. I always wanted to ask my Dad how he screwed up to get stationed at that remote Air Force Base, which was our military's version of Siberia, but he passed away before I had the courage to bring the topic up. I asked my Mom, and either she doesn't know, or she's just not telling.

On that particular family vacation I remember being at the airport standing in front of a vending machine. Behind the glass was a colorful assortment of candy bars, with a Three Musketeers bar front and center, just screaming my name. I looked at that candy bar for a solid minute and then walked over to where my parents were sitting.

"Dad?"

"Yes, son?"

"I need some money."

"Why?"

"To buy a candy bar."

"No."

"What?"

"I said no."

My Dad never beat around the bush. He was very decisive.

"Why can't I have some money?"

"Because we're going to eat lunch soon."

I thought for a few seconds.

"Dad?"

"Yes, son?"

"But I want a candy bar right now!"

"I said no!"

I paused for another few seconds, fixed my Dad with a five-year-old's angry scowl and said:

"That's it. From now on whenever we go on vacation, I'm bringing my own money!"

My Dad laughed his ass off. He told that story for years.

But he still didn't give me money for the candy bar.

Until about six months later.

On that day, he gave me a dime—and a nickel. We were walking to church. It was just the two of us. He pressed a dime and a nickel into my hand.

"What's this for, Dad?"

"One coin is for you to keep to buy some candy after church and the other coin is for you to put in the collection plate when they pass it around during Mass."

"Which coin do I keep and which coin do I put in the collection plate?"

"That's up to you," he said with a wink and a smile.

An hour later when the collection plate was in front of me, I dropped the dime into it with one hand and rubbed the nickel in my pocket with the other hand. After church we stopped and I bought candy with the nickel.

life.

My Dad could not wait to get home.

"*Honey,*" he said to my Mom as soon as we walked in the door, "*listen to this.*"

He told her the story about the nickel and the dime and was beaming with pride when he told her that I had given the church the dime and only kept the nickel for myself.

And then he stopped.

And looked at me long and hard before saying:

"*Let me ask you a question.*"

"*Sure, Dad.*"

"*Which coin did you keep?*"

"*The nickel.*"

"*Why?*"

"*Just because.*"

"*Son?*"

"*Yeah, Dad.*"

"*Did you keep the nickel because it was bigger than the dime?*"

I didn't say anything.

"*Son, do you even know which coin is worth more—a nickel or a dime?*"

He looked at me. I looked at him.

I had no clue what he was getting at.

Even today I can't remember what my reasoning was for keeping the nickel and putting the dime in the collection plate. What I did know was that I had my Dad stumped. Perhaps I was thinking about that day at the airport when he wouldn't let me buy the Three Musketeers bar, because what I did next was to look him dead in the eye, smile and say:

"*I'm not telling.*"

Man, did he ever laugh his ass off again.

He was so proud of being snookered by his own son.

* * *

I know exactly how I want my funeral and burial to go, and I have some rather odd twists planned for the affair that I know won't fly at a newer cemetery. What I need is a really old cemetery that is not as picky and doesn't mind making some exceptions just to get the business. The older and more rundown the cemetery, the better.

life.

Those types of graveyards have more history and more character anyway.

I search the Internet for old cemeteries in my part of the state, and find one that was opened in 1850 and that seems to fit the bill perfectly. A news article about it says, *"Homeless people wander aimlessly, red-tailed hawks swoop overhead. Nearby, commuters climb into public buses, chugging through life's everyday mundane tasks. This activity surrounds a decrepit cemetery with cracked markers and moss-draped oaks, a graveyard that appears to have been left behind by the city that grew up around it."*

Sounds perfect.

I place a call to the church that owns the cemetery and the secretary there promises me a woman named Maria will call me back to answer my questions. I wait for her call.

My daughter knows exactly what I want done at my funeral.

Granted, it's not her favorite topic.

I have tried to prepare and desensitize my children to my eventual death, and that of their mother. I don't want them blindsided like I was. So I wield phrases like, *"You're gonna miss me when I'm gone,"* and *"When I'm no longer around,"* like a police baton and beat them unmercifully with it to hopefully make them tougher and more accepting of what eventuality they will have to face one day. While the baton is always used in jest, in the lulls between it's use I have more serious talks about the fact that one day both their mother and father will be gone.

Because my daughter is a very artistic and creative person, her uneasiness about discussing my death is sometimes surpassed by her shared interest in the uniqueness of what I would like done at my funeral, and the fact that I have specifically asked her to make sure it is done as I have requested.

I want one of those cheap, old-time stone tombstones with the rounded top. It should be leaning back a little and chiseled into it should be just by name, the dates I was born and died, and the letters R.I.P.

I want a wooden coffin like the ones you see Wild West bad guys propped up in with their arms crossed over their chest in old black and white photographs. The nails in the coffin lid will only be hammered halfway in, and at the funeral the surviving relatives will

life.

each take a turn to hammer one of the protruding nails the rest of the way in.

I want the coffin to be lowered into the grave by hand using ropes, and I want everyone to take a turn with the shovel to fill in the grave.

Isn't that just the coolest thing you've ever heard of?

And the best part, the coup de gras, is that the song that will be playing will be a haunting song that my daughter and I both love called *Joey* by the punk band Concrete Blonde:

"Joey, baby, don't get crazy. I know you've heard it all before, so I don't say it anymore. I just stand by and watch you fight your secret war. All is forgiven, listen, listen. Oh, Joey, if you're hurting, so am I."

Trust me, there won't be a dry eye in the house.

My daughter agrees.

* * *

I love life. Life is a great thing. Just because I am ready to die does not mean that I haven't enjoyed the hell out of life. My wife tells me all the time that, despite my numerous faults, I am the one of the happiest people she knows. I smile a lot, I get excited about even the smallest things, I can be the life of the party, and I will sing songs out loud at any time and in any place, my favorite lyrics to sing being, *"You must remember this, a kiss is still a kiss, a sigh is still a sigh, the fundamental things in life as time goes by."* That's not exactly how that particular Johnny Mathis song goes, but that's the way I sing it.

"You do light up a room when you walk in," my wife will say to me every now and then.

I will remind her of that fact when I've fucked up really bad like staying out all night and then having a stripper call my cell phone at the house. *"You son-of-a-bitch! You are a horrible person,"* she'll yell and give me a smack and chase me around the house.

"Hey, what about that light-up-the-room thing?" I'll yell back over my shoulder.

"I take it back!"

life.

When I think of life, or at least enjoying life, I think of money and the things that money can buy, like those elusive candy bars when I was a child.

That is so wrong, I know, but it's the truth. At an early age I realized that money could get you the things that you want, whether it was that Three Musketeers candy bar or, later on as I grew older, an Armani suit or a Franck Muller watch or a Bentley GT convertible. They say that money can't buy you happiness, and I say that, if you believe that, then you probably just went to the wrong store. Try again. So I have been a hustler my whole life, chasing that almighty dollar, sometimes striking out, sometimes hitting a home run. Truth be told, I enjoy the game as much as I do the possible rewards.

In my defense, having money has also meant I could raise my children in a safe environment, and send them to good schools and colleges, and provide them with the best medical care, and I could financially help out family and friends when needed, which I have done many times.

So I agree completely with whoever said, "*I've been rich and I've been poor, and I can tell you being rich is much better.*" That guy was spot on. Hug all the trees you want if that's your gig, but personally I want all of those materialistic and capitalistic things that only money can buy.

Because I've been poor, or at least as poor as a white kid from suburbia can be. I always defined poor for me as not being able to buy something that I saw and wanted right when I wanted it, which was pretty much my case from birth through my early twenties. When I was a cub reporter in California there was a deli down the street where I would order my lunch, usually whatever sandwich was on special that day. They had the most incredible fucking cheesecake at that deli, huge wedges with fresh strawberries and sweet strawberry sauce dripping over the sides. Every time I ordered my special of the day sandwich I would look at those slices of cheesecake and lick my lips, but reporters are paid slave wages and a slice of cheesecake cost almost as much as my sandwich and so I could not afford it. Someday, though, I would tell myself.

Back in the day, after the last bars had closed, Dean and I would go to the convenience store next to my tiny rent house. We would each buy one of those two-item Swanson frozen chicken dinners, the ones that only have a dab of mashed potatoes and two shriveled up chicken thighs. They were right next to the Swanson Hungry-Man dinners that had three plump pieces of white chicken, mashed potatoes smothered in gravy, a colorful vegetable medley, and even an apple pie desert. We would look at those Hungry-Man dinners longingly, but they were way out of our budget. Back at my crib we would devour the tiny two-thighs-only TV dinners. All that would be left when we were done were some bleached white chicken bones, and the aluminum tray that the food had been in was so clean from tongue-licking that you could see your reflection in it.

Sometimes we went to Sambo's restaurant and got the $1.29 special, which was one egg, one piece of bacon and one piece of toast. Just one of each item. Talk about being broke.

Back in the 1970s Sambo's was a restaurant like Denny's or IHOP that served breakfast all day long, and they had more than 1,200 locations in forty-seven states. The Sambo's name was associated with the 1899 children's book *The Story of Little Black Sambo* which is about an Indian boy named Sambo who, to keep hungry tigers from eating him, gives the tigers his new clothes, shoes, and umbrella. But he gets his things back when the jealous tigers fight over the items and start chasing each other in a circle until they turn to butter. I guess the tie-in was butter, which is everywhere in a breakfast diner. The name Sambo eventually came to be considered a racial slur, and add in the fact that the Sambo's restaurants all had murals showing a black kid being chased by tigers, and you can figure out on your own why there aren't any more Sambo's restaurants in today's politically correct country of ours.

Too bad because they made a good egg. Not eggs, just egg.

* * *

Maria from the old cemetery calls me back.
It's good news.
They are still accepting bodies.
The cost for a burial plot is only $1,500. I don't mention my plans for a cheap wooden coffin and people hammering in nails. My daughter, who is much more persuasive than me, can handle that. Maria gives me all the contact info and other details that the funeral home will need to coordinate the burial and that my daughter will also need.

life.

"Did you know that thirteen mayors, the veterans of seven wars and the victims of five yellow fever epidemics are all buried here," says Maria.

"They're not still contagious are they?" I ask.

"I hope not," she laughs.

She goes on to tell me that Mr. James, the gentleman who donated most of the land for the cemetery back in 1850, was a lawyer, a legislator, a circuit judge, an editor, a publisher and, best of all, a notorious scalawag, which is defined either as a deceitful and unreliable scoundrel or a Southern white who supported Reconstruction following the Civil War. Apparently both definitions applied to Mr. James, who also could never say no to a stiff drink. He would partake until he passed out in the middle of the street, and on one such occasion the townsfolk poured molasses and cornmeal all over his body. During the night, hogs ate his clothes off and he woke up naked.

I'm going to fit right in at this cemetery. They know how to party.

I thank Maria and then call my banker and ask her to wire transfer a nice chunk of money from my personal bank account into my daughter's bank account so that she will have money to cover the funeral and burial costs and not have to bother my wife. I tell the banker not to do the wire transfer until next Wednesday. That way the money will not hit her account until the day after I am gone. I then type a note and include all the details and contact info from the old cemetery, details about the money transfer, and a reminder of all the things I would like done at the funeral. I print out the note, seal it in an envelope, write my daughter's name on the front, and put it on the very top of the stack of files and folders I have prepared and left in my office for my wife.

I feel like I've accomplished a lot so far today.

I head out for lunch and to get my car cleaned.

* * *

I did my first money-making scam when I was ten years old, which to me means I got a late start.

There were four workmen re-roofing the neighbor's house next door.

life.

"They look thirsty," I said to my best friend, Baron, after we had watched them toiling away in the hot sun for an hour or so. My parents weren't home, so I went into the kitchen and got four small Dixie paper cups, went to my Dad's liquor cabinet, pulled out a bottle of bourbon and filled each of the cups to the brim, a good double shot in each glass. Baron and I carried the four cups over to the workmen. One of the guys was standing by the ladder.

"Hey, are you guys thirsty?" I asked.

"What you got there?"

"Whiskey."

The guy laughed and said, *"No shit. How much?"*

"Fifty cents a glass."

He bought all four cups and called his coworkers down from the roof to enjoy.

"Care for another?" I asked.

"Sure," they all said.

I made three more roundtrips that afternoon and Baron and I split eight dollars, which to us was a small fortune.

Then my Dad came home. Not sure how he found out, maybe one of the workmen fell off the roof, but I found myself in the kitchen looking up at my Dad.

"Tell me what you did," he said.

I told him the story with pride in my voice and even pulled the four one-dollar bills out of my pocket to show him.

"Whose liquor did you sell them?" asked my Dad.

"Ours."

"Ours? Don't you mean mine?

"Yeah, I guess."

"Okay," said my Dad. *"First off, I am angry with you for taking something that does not belong to you without asking for permission. Don't ever do that again. Got it?"*

"Yes, sir."

"Second off, I'm very proud of you for being a smart businessman."

"Thanks!"

"But ..."

There is always a but. Even at the tender age of ten, I knew that.

"Yes, Dad?"

life.

"You owe me two dollars," he said and reached over and took two of the dollar bills out of my hand.

"Why?" I asked, a little startled and a little pissed off.

"Because that was my whiskey that you sold and I get my cut. If you are going to do business, then you need to learn to do it right. Got it?"

"Yes, sir."

"And son ..."

"Yes, Dad."

"Tell Baron he owes me two dollars too."

My next money making scam came a year later when I noticed that from eleven in the morning until one in the afternoon Monday through Saturday, the parking lot at our local convenience store was filled with day laborers who would come by for a lunch of packaged sandwiches or hot dogs, washed down with bottles of pop. They would eat, smoke and shoot the shit, then leave their empty pop bottles on the curb before rushing off to their job sites. Those empty bottles were worth five cents each if you turned them in. So every day at noon I rode my bike the mile and a half to the convenience store, sat in the parking lot, and over the next two hours collected all those empty bottles and turned them back into the store. I was there two hours a day, six days a week, just like a regular job. I just didn't punch a time clock. I was only eleven years old and I always had money in my pocket. Hell yeah.

Over the next few years I graduated to cutting lawns and washing cars in our neighborhood, and I even took an occasional babysitting job, which I loved, because as soon as the parents backed out of their driveway, I would start going through every closet and dresser drawer in their house. I never stole anything; I was just curious. I remember finding a ten-inch vibrator in one night stand which was a real shocker because you hardly ever heard about those types of sex toys back then. When the couple came back later that night, I kept staring at the wife, thinking to myself, *"I know a secret, I know a secret."*

I also sacked groceries at the commissary at the nearby Air Force base. You would pack ten brown paper bags, they didn't have plastic bags back then, full of heavy groceries, load them into the cart, push the cart a half mile in the blazing sun through the parking lot, unload those ten fucking heavy bags, and then the housewife

life.

would give you a dime. That's one thin dime, people! Sometimes you got a quarter. Every now and then one of the guys would come running back in back waving a dollar bill over his head like it was the winning betting ticket from the Kentucky Derby and we would all gather around and slap him on the back.

Today, now that I have money, I am an outrageous tipper. My friends get pissed and say that I do it just to show off, but they are wrong. I do it because I've been there.

When I was fifteen years old I got my first full-time job, working at the local gas station in the summer. I pumped gas, checked oil, washed windshields, put air in tires, cleaned the whole station, and even worked in the bay changing oil and replacing batteries, all for $1.25 an hour. Guys my age from the neighborhood would pull up to the gas pumps towing their parent's expensive ski boats. They would be in their cut-off shorts and their Ray-Ban sunglasses, always with the prettiest local girls wearing skimpy bikinis, and little grease monkey me would fill up their cars and wash their windshields and check their oil and air filters and then wave goodbye to them as they sped off to the lake.

That sucked. But I liked making money. And I liked relying on myself to get it. Goes back to that Three Musketeers candy bar I couldn't buy on my own when I was a little kid.

With that kind of early work ethic instilled in me, it was inevitable that I would go to college full-time and work full-time while I was in college, not a part-time job but a real forty-hours-a-week job, and I would graduate in four years, and I would pay my own way through college. Fuck student loans. Just seemed natural to me. Doesn't everybody do that?

I've been working ever since, well actually working, scamming and hustling, because hard work is good, but working hard with an angle is even better. I learned early on that thinking a few steps ahead of the next guy and not simply following the herd would move you to the front of the pack in this rat race. As my Dad used to say, *"Son, make sure you are always smarter than the average bear."*

When I was a sophomore in high school, at an all-boys Catholic high school run by no-nonsense Jesuit priests, we had a student assembly one day and the principal asked us to help sell raffle tickets to raise money for the renovation of the church on our campus. The raffle tickets were one dollar apiece and the prize was a big color TV. I tuned the droning principal out until he got to the part where he said that the student who sold the most raffle tickets would be given that exact same number of tickets for free, and could write his name on them and enter them in the contest for a chance to win the TV.

I looked at my buddy Tom and said, *"I've got a killer idea."*

That afternoon we went to the office of our head football couch who was in charge of the raffle. He was an older, crusty Italian guy who was a bit of a character but the priests gave him plenty of leeway since he took our team to state every year without fail.

"That's nice of you boys to get involved," said the coach. *"How many raffle tickets would you like?"*

"Can we get 500?" I asked.

His eyes popped open. *"Are you sure? That's a lot of damn tickets. Today is Monday and the ticket stubs and money need to be turned in to me by this Friday afternoon. The drawing is next Monday morning at student assembly. That doesn't give you much time."*

"No problem," I said.

"There's no way you can sell that many tickets in five days, but what the hell, I'll give you five hundred anyway. Just bring me the back the ones you don't sell."

Tom and I sold every single raffle ticket.

We worked our neighborhood for the next four days, going door to door from mid afternoon when we got out of class until late at night, using every ploy we could think of to get homeowners to buy the raffle tickets, saying it had been a dying priest's last wishes to see the church renovated, talking about the orphans that the church helped place in foster homes, getting a little teary-eyed when the occasion called for it. You name it, we did it.

On Friday afternoon Tom and I were back in the coach's office. *"Well, I'll be dammed, you did it,"* said the coach. *"You outsold everybody, nobody even came close. Here's your 500 free raffle tickets. If you want to write your names on them now and turn them in to me, I'll wait."*

I took the stack of raffle tickets and looked at the coach.

"Do we have to write our own names on these tickets?" I asked.

"I don't understand," he said.

"Does it really matter whose names are on these tickets?"

A light bulb seemed to flash on above the coach's head.

He smiled and said the tickets were ours to do with as we pleased.

"Cool," I said.

"Just get them back to me filled out before nine Monday morning," he said with a wink.

If you can't see where this story is going by now, then you probably failed *Becoming an Entrepreneur 101*.

Tom and I found another gullible neighborhood, worked our asses off all day and all night both Saturday and Sunday, and sold every one of those five hundred one-dollar tickets—pocketing all the money ourselves. And for two fifteen-year-olds in the early 1970s, that was a lot of fucking money. Did we feel guilty about taking money from people who thought they were donating to a charitable cause? Hell no. Plus those people all still had a chance to win the TV. We actually only sold 499 of the raffle tickets which meant we split $499 between us. We saved one ticket and wrote both our names on it and then turned all the tickets in to the coach Monday morning.

At the drawing later that morning, our one ticket didn't win the TV.

Now that would have been sweet.

*   *   *

At the car wash I sit outside with a dozen other people on benches watching the illegal aliens dry off our cars and clean the interiors after the cars have been run through the automated car wash. It's a mixed bag of people sitting on the benches, some housewives, some businessmen, some gray-haired retirees, and the cars being cleaned are a mixed bag too, some clunkers, some soccer mom vans, and some imports. I smoke a cigarette and relax.

As they finish polishing my car I notice that it looks beautiful. I am going to miss it. Over the years I have owned and then sold dozens of cars. Every time I was about to sell one of those cars, I would have any mechanical problems fixed and then have the car immaculately detailed. Without fail, I would then look at the car I was about to sell and realize what a great running and great looking car it was. Did I really want to get rid of it? Relationships are a lot like

life.

that, whether it's your relationship with your wife, or your relationship with your boss, or your relationship with yourself. Sometimes if you take a little time to repair and fix up and polish a relationship, you may find that it's really worth keeping.

I always speak Spanish to the guys cleaning my car. I think it's a sign of respect from me to them.

"Es finito?" I ask.

"Si."

"Las miradas perfeccionan. Gracias amigo," I say and give the worker a ten-dollar tip for a twenty-dollar car wash.

Again, not to show off, but because I have been there.

* * *

There are forums and chat rooms on the Internet for everything from global politics to antique cars to ant farms, so it stands to reason that the subject of suicide would have its fair share of websites, although most of them are geared toward thwarting suicide attempts and giving advice and counseling, the web version of suicide phone hot lines.

Except for ASH.

ASH is the acronym for a usenet group on the Internet called alt.suicide.holiday and started out as a chat room for talk about why suicides always increase on holidays. Today it is a rollicking forum for people with suicide on their minds to talk about everything from why they want to kill themselves to who they think is going to win the Superbowl.

"Welcome to ASH, and sorry you're here," is the typical greeting new users get from other posters on the site.

They have a sister usenet site called ASM which stands for alt.suicide.methods which gets into all of the different ways to off yourself. Instead of exchanging recipes, users discuss the pros and cons of the many ways you can CTB.

CTB stands for *Catch The Bus*, which is slang for, to kill yourself. If you've gathered up all the items you will need to successfully CTB, like a shotgun or a long rope or prescription pills, then you say that you already have your *Ticket*, as in a ticket to death. Many of the posters on ASH and ASM sound like amateur pharmacists as they discuss the merits of Valium, Midazolam,

life.

Diazepam, Chloroquine, Zolpidem, Zopiclone, Xanax, Nembutal, and on and on. While they all favor mixing different drugs together, called a suicide *Cocktail*, they will debate endlessly over which exact combination of drugs they think will make the best Cocktail, kind of like your two aunts used to do over who had the best pecan pie recipe.

So you don't ever say, *"I am going to kill myself tomorrow by taking some sleeping pills."* That's way too gauche. Instead, what you say is, *"I'm going to CTB manana, got my Ticket stamped first class, and will be sipping a yummy Cocktail of three grams of Phenobarbital, 300 mg of Midazolam and a dash of Chloroquine."* Much cooler and hipper.

Spend a few hours on the ASH and ASM sites and you'll be alternately laughing and crying. They have their fair share of posters who seem to be from another dimension, or maybe they are just undiscovered literary giants, as in, this post: *"I don't like the sound of the bells today. I want to make it out of the existential spectrum by midnight, preferably now. I just have no idea how."*

Or this jewel. *"All the snow is melting down. I don't like spring. The nausea sits like a heavy poison in my stomach and it's climbing up. The choking smell of life grabs my guts and shakes them until it makes me spew. I wish I could spill the existence out of me, or at least freeze all the motion."*

There is no shortage of jokesters: *"If you are planning to kill yourself, why are you still around?"*

Which netted these three replies:

"Just to piss you off."

"I tend to procrastinate."

"Cuz we haven't killed ourselves yet."

Some posters should make TV commercials: *"Holiday Inn Express, that's where I plan to kill myself. I'm gonna leave a suicide note to say my experience was so shitty, I decided to kill myself.*

Which brought a reply that would have made columnist Ann Landers proud: *"That sounds so tidy and expeditious! Express! And on holiday, too! Take ten grams of Pentobarbital and we'll clean up after you in the morning. p.s. Leave the maid a tip. It's just good manners."*

There are some excellent candidates for public office: *"There's about seven billion of us fuckers, and our planet can't fucking*

life.

support all of us. *The government should have a new law where every few months or so they just go on a killing spree, just killing random people. It could be like jury duty, you just get a letter through the post notifying you of your termination, and you can't get out of it!"*

Some tend to be whiners: *"What if I fail? I don't have the time, money or energy for a backup method. Planning a suicide is exhausting."* Some just need to invest in a bar of soap: *"It is officially Valentine's Day, the most retarded day of the year. Guess how long it's been since I showered?"*

The chuckles go on until you find posts that hammer home who is really on the website and how serious the intentions of some of the people are: *"I sure miss someone from ASH right now. I hope he is not dead yet,"* and, *"I wonder what happened to ... Alex."*

Some posters are suicide survivors who had second thoughts. If life prior to trying to commit suicide was tough, life after a failed suicide attempt can be even tougher, as pointed out by one poster, who wrote that these are the questions he gets that don't help his situation:

—How are you?

"There is no right answer. If I say I'm fine, they know that I'm lying. If I say I'm not, that is just something more to worry about."

—Just decide that life is worth living.

"Yeah right, it really is that easy."

—How come nobody saw this coming?

"You didn't either, so don't blame anyone else for not seeing this. And don't underestimate my acting skills."

—Just go to your shrink, just take some meds, etc.

"It is not that easy. I will try, but don't expect miracles to happen."

—People who are bipolar have productive lives.

"Sure, but are they happy? You just told me I have a mental disease that will last for the rest of my life."

—You have so many people that care about you.

"Yeah I know that. That was the reason I got out of the water, the reason I decided to get counseling, but that doesn't make it okay."

—I'm sorry I joked about ..."

"I'm not. I like it when people joke;, it gets my mind off things."

life.

And then there are the comments and questions that he thinks are helpful:

—I will kick the crap out of you when you're physically okay again.

"Thanks for informing me you're mad. You have every right to be, and it is better than pity."

—I'm sorry you're going through this, but I know I can't help.

"I know you can't, but just try to act normal."

—I might be stupid but at least, I didn't try to drown myself."

"Like I said, I don't mind a joke every now and then."

—Why the hell did you choose that method?

"I don't mind explaining why I chose that method, what it was like."

—Next time just jump off a high building; that would work.

"You really can't say anything to me to make me more likely to kill myself. Hell, you could shove a gun into my hand and tell me to shoot myself, and it won't make a difference. So I don't mind talking about suicide. Not when it is on my mind most of the time."

* * *

Many people who commit suicide or who attempt suicide aren't happy with their life, either their current life, the life they have already lived, or the life that is ahead of them. In that regard, I don't fit the norm because, except for those few parts of my life I would like to erase and do over again, I am, on the whole, very happy with and proud of the life I have been able to live up until now.

Like my life itself, which up to now has been unique and unusual and a bit quirky, my reason for wanting to commit suicide is also unique and unusual and a bit quirky.

I'm just ready to leave. It's that simple.

Many people who commit suicide or who attempt suicide aren't happy with their life, either their current life, the life they have already lived, or the life that is ahead of them. In that regard, I don't fit the norm because, except for those few parts of my life I would like to erase and do over again, I am, on the whole, very happy with and proud of the life I have been able to live up until now.

life.

Like my life itself, which up to now has been unique and unusual and a bit quirky, my reason for wanting to commit suicide is also unique and unusual and a bit quirky.

I'm just ready to leave. It's that simple.

My daughter says that when she thinks back on events we went to as a family, like a grade school play or a high school basketball game, she can still see me standing in the doorway at the back of the theater or the gym, ready to leave before the event was over. *"You never made it through to the end of anything,"* she says. *"You always had one foot out the door."*

"Well," I'd say, *"I'd seen enough. I was ready to go."*

"But I was still on stage!"

My bad.

Just recently I incurred the wrath of my wife because apparently I had pissed off one of her best friends whose son's wedding we had just attended.

"So what is she so upset about?" I asked my wife.

"You didn't let us stay until the end."

"It was practically over."

"They hadn't even cut the cake yet!"

Winston Churchill, one of the most well known statesmen of the 20th Century and possibly the main reason we are not speaking German today while eating dinner under a photo of Adolph Hitler, capped his string of great accomplishments by saying, *"I'm bored with it all,"* and then he died.

I wouldn't say that I am bored with life at this point. I've just seen enough and I'm ready to go. Again, it's just that simple.

* * *

I've always thought that the secret to living life is to accumulate enough interesting experiences along the way to keep yourself amused while you daydream in that rocking chair on your front porch in your final years. And I have no shortage of interesting memories.

Like the time the KGB stole my luggage.

Maybe I'm jumping to conclusions. But who else could it have been?

I was working in the concert business then and a real character named Larry was one of my top sales guys. Although he was ten years older than me, I was Larry's boss, but because he had traveled all around the world and was a top-rate hustler, we were good friends as well as co-workers. Larry and I were invited to Moscow by a concert promoter who said he needed our help to get U.S. rock bands to perform in Russia. We were in Europe for some business meetings, so we flew from Frankfurt to the Moscow airport which was a cold and barren place, much like most of Moscow itself. At the airport, Larry's luggage and everyone else's came down the carousel, but not mine. My suitcase was missing. *Motherfucker!*

One of the promoter's lackeys drove us to our hotel, mentioning that now that the Iron Curtain was down the city was packed with business entrepreneurs from around the world so there were literally dozens of very high-priced four-star hotels available. We had no idea which hotel the promoter had booked us into, but it turned out to be quite opulent. Larry and I sat in the lobby bar having our first drinks of the day, with me complaining nonstop about not having any fresh clothes or toiletries. *"Quit whining like a bitch. We're only here two days,"* said Larry. *"You can borrow some of my clothes, but you need to buy your own toothbrush and toothpaste."*

I was not happy. Larry weighed a good seventy pounds more than me so there was no way his tent-sized clothes would fit. I went up to my hotel room and took a shower. I was just about to put the same underwear and clothes that I had worn on the plane earlier that day back on when the phone in my room rang.

"Hello."

"I have your suitcase by mistake," said a heavy Russian voice in broken English.

"Where are you?" I asked.

"I am staying at this hotel. I will send your suitcase down to your room." Then he hung up.

What the fuck?

Two minutes later there was a knock at my door and a bellman brought my suitcase in. I tipped him, then opened the suitcase and went through every single item in the bag. Everything was there and was packed the exact same way I had packed the bag before we left Frankfurt.

How did the person who called know which hotel I was staying at since even I didn't know until we got here? What were the chances he would be staying at that exact same hotel? How did he know I was in my room? Where the hell was Jason Bourne when you needed him?

I met Larry downstairs in the lobby bar and told him what had happened and his concern was heartwarmingly overwhelming. *"Really? That's interesting,"* he said. *"How a cocktail?"*

The promoter himself picked us up that evening in a brand new, black Mercedes Benz with dark tinted windows and drove us to a three-story building he owned in downtown Moscow. On the third floor were his lavish offices, on the second floor was a fine dining restaurant, and on the first floor was a nightclub which the promoter said was currently the most popular disco in Moscow. He owned it all.

In the conference room on the third floor we sat around a beautiful mahogany table with the promoter and a half dozen scary looking guys who didn't say a word the entire meeting. Larry did all the talking for us, telling the promoter about the current state of the concert industry in the U.S., which bands were drawing the biggest crowds, things like that.

"So," said Concert Larry, *"is there a particular band you are interested in?"*

"Can you get us guns?" asked the promoter.

"Guns N' Roses? I'm not sure. They are the hottest band touring right now. They would be very expensive."

"No," said the promoter, *"not Guns N' Roses. We want guns."*

"You mean gun guns?" asked Larry.

"Yes. We would like Uzis mostly. Can you get them for us?"

These guys were not even remotely interested in booking the Captain & Tennille. Apparently we were in Moscow as the guests of the Russian Mafia. They were driving us around, they knew what hotel rooms we were staying in, they probably even had keys to our rooms. All of which might explain why the KGB was looking through my suitcase.

Larry quickly glommed on to what was happening and the danger we had blindly stumbled into, so what he said, naturally, was, *"Of course we can get you guns!"*

Which was a bald-faced lie. But it got the promoter and the other six scary guys sitting at the conference table all excited. We listened as the promoter reeled off other types of guns he wanted and in what quantities. *"Price,"* he said with a big smile, *"is no object."*

We all shook hands and the promoter took us to his restaurant on the second level where we had a gourmet meal. I tell people all the time that the best carpaccio I have ever eaten was at that restaurant, which is surprising, it being in Russia and all. After dinner we went to the disco on the first floor. It was the first nightclub I had ever seen with a metal detector at the front door that patrons had to walk through. Security also included a dozen or so beefy Ruskies who all looked like that Russian dude who beat the shit out of Stallone in *Rocky IV*. They wore nice suits, and had nice guns under those suits.

The promoter sat us at a VIP table, brought some ladies over, instructed the waiter to give us whatever we wanted on the house, told us that our original driver would be outside waiting for us when we were done partying, and then he disappeared. Three hours later, Larry and I were absolutely snockered. I had my feet up on one of the coffee tables in front of our VIP couches. It was a very fancy coffee table and on my feet were very old cowboy boots.

One of the security goons walked over, tapped me on my shoulder, pointed to my cowboy boots scraping up their nice, ornate coffee table and shook his head. I looked up at the giant and said the first words that came to my mind, which were, *"Go fuck yourself."*

I thought Larry was going to shit a brick.

The goon walked over to another goon whose suit was a little more expensive which meant he was the head goon. They both walked back over to me and repeated the process, but this time it was the head goon who did the tapping, pointing and head shaking. I knew then that this had just escalated into a very serious, and possibly violent, situation so I looked up at the head goon and said the first words that came to my mind, which were, *"Like I just told the other guy, go fuck yourself."*

The next thing I knew I was jerked straight up into the air like a rag doll. But it wasn't by one of the goons. It was by Larry, who then put me in a head lock and dragged me through the club, out the front door, through the snow on the sidewalk, and over to our driver's car. He tossed me in the back seat and the next thing I remember after that was waking up in my hotel room with all my clothes on and a headache from hell.

life.

That afternoon I met Concert Larry in the hotel lobby and he was steaming mad. *"You are such a dick. You almost got us killed last night. I fucking saved your life."*

"Really? That's interesting," I said. *"How about a cocktail?"*

* * *

On the way back to the office from the car wash, I use my cell phone to call an Italian restaurant near our house and place a large order for delivery of pizza, pasta and salad, and ask that they bring it by around eight o'clock. I then call Happy John and Dan the Beautiful Snowflake, more on that name later, and invite they and their better halves over to the house for some casual dinner, lots of drinking, and some gambling. I'm not big on personal chitchat on the phone, so I call my wife and let her know I've started the invitation process and she needs to give the rest of our friends a jingle.

We'll end up with a dozen or more people outside on our lanai with the stereo blasting and the liquor flowing until about three in the morning. A lanai, for those of you who don't live down South, is a Hawaiian word for a backyard patio, although in this case it involves a huge concrete deck, some outdoor ceiling fans, a swimming pool, and a screen enclosure that is as tall as the house and covers the entire outdoor area. The screen enclosure lets the sun in and keeps the bugs out.

The guys will play poker or backgammon for money, because we are gambling whores one and all.

We'll bet on anything.

The only thing Perfect Paul likes better than winning at gambling is beating me at gambling. He and I are gambling nemeses. And yes, that is the correct spelling for the plural of nemesis, although you would think that the plural would be nemesises. Try saying that word ten times in a row real fast.

Paul is *perfect*, according to all our wives. First off, he is tall and handsome with a full head of salt and pepper hair. The full hair thing pisses the shit out of the rest of us guys. When he comes to a party he makes sure to go up to every one of our wives and gives them each a warm hug and a discreet kiss on the cheek. He will actually stop and talk with each one of them and appear to be interested in whatever they have to say. He is very attentive to his wife, pulling her chair out for her, fixing her drinks, checking on her throughout the course of the party, calling her honey and sweetie. Sometimes he even holds her hand. That also pisses the shit out of us guys. *"Dude, seriously, cut it out. You're making the rest of us look bad."*

Paul never swears around the women and is as polite as can be when in their presence. But after he's got all the ladies swooning and asking themselves why their husbands can't be like Perfect Paul, he will move over to the table where us guys are and say, *"Okay you motherfuckers, whose turn is it to deal the cards? I'm ready to kick some ass you cock-sucking sons of bitches."* So not only is he a lady's guy, he's also a guy's guy. And he has that full head of hair. *Motherfucker!*

Perfect Paul and I were at the country club swimming pool once watching our two eleven-year-old daughters compete in a swim meet. We were there under duress, the wives having gone off to play tennis. We were laying in two lounge chairs bored to tears and getting burned to a crisp. We had been there a half hour or so when I said to Paul, *"Ten dollars on number three."*

Anybody else would have been confused, but not Paul. *"I'll take number six,"* he immediately said.

Now we were interested. We sat up and looked at the six eleven-year-old girls who were lined up at the edge of the pool, their knees bent and their arms out in front of them. Someone blew a whistle and the girls dived in and swam to the end. The third girl in the line, my number three, won.

"Okay, you're down ten," I said to Paul. *"Your turn to pick first."*

This time Paul's daughter was one of the six. She was number two.

"I'll take number four," he said.

"You aren't betting on your own daughter?" I asked, surprised.

"Hell no," said Paul, *"look at the thighs on number four."*

Back and forth it went, with us betting on every race. Soon Paul and I were both on our feet, running along the side of the pool cheering on our picks. *"Swim, baby, swim,"* we would yell and then jump up and down if our pick won the race, two large sweaty guys in their forties bouncing up and down like maniacs. Eventually, we noticed that all the other parents were staring at us. The pedophile police were just one phone call away. We sheepishly walked back to our lounge chairs. But we kept betting, only this time in whispers.

life.

Paul worked for a huge international corporation and his boss was a prick, as most bosses are prone to be. One of the salesmen under Paul had been with the company for more than twenty years, but his sales had declined because he was trying to take care of his wife who had been bedridden for months with a serious illness.

"Fire him," said Paul's boss. Paul argued that the man had been a major producer in the past and was now just on hard times. Paul said he would spend his own time after-hours helping the man increase his sales.

"Okay, spend a month helping him," said Paul's boss. *"Then, at the end of that month, fire him."*

Paul refused. He quit the corporation and, believe it or not, ended up getting hired as the CEO of a competing corporation at quadruple the salary. The first day at his new job Paul called the salesman with the ill wife, hired him and doubled his salary.

So, maybe Paul is perfect after all. *Motherfucker!*

While Paul and the rest of the guys gamble at our party, the wives will sit at another table and verbally eviscerate any of the wives who are part of our social group and who made the tactical error of not being at the party.

I bet you think I'm kidding about that last part.

I'm not.

* * *

Then there was the time I sat across from Wolfie.

Sounds like a cartoon character, doesn't it? But Wolfie was anything but a funny cartoon. Wolfie was a chapter president for the Bandidos outlaw motorcycle gang, and one afternoon I sat in his house with three other full-patched club members, all of whom were looking at me like I was Bambi who had just bounced into a den of hungry wolves.

Outside, the house was surrounded by an eight-foot high chain link fence topped with strips of razor wire, with a half dozen Doberman Pinschers and Rottweilers nervously pacing in the fenced area. Inside, were four guys in dirty blue jeans, steel-toed boots, full scruffy beards, and leather vests, called patches or colors, with the Bandidos logo stitched on the back. And there was clean shaven, smiley-faced me in a freshly washed pair of jeans and a bright yellow

life.

Izod golf shirt. All it would take was a word or a glance from Wolfie and, no questions asked, the three club members would happily and enthusiastically use those steel-toed boots to stomp me into a puddle of mush.

Which was very possible since I had just pissed Wolfie off.

The Bandidos are part of what law enforcement calls the Big Four, the four largest and most dangerous outlaw motorcycle gangs, or OMGs, in the world, the other three clubs being the Hell's Angels, the Outlaws, and the Pagans. There are hundreds of other outlaw motorcycle gangs worldwide, like the Mongols, the Warlocks, the Vagos, the Sons of Silence, the Gypsy Jokers and the Devil's Disciples. Gotta love those names.

The Bandidos Motorcycle Club, also known as the Bandido Nation, was started in San Antonio, Texas in 1966 by Don Chambers, a former U.S. Marine and Vietnam veteran. Their motto is, *"We are the people our parents warned us about,"* and the club's colors feature a fat, colorful Mexican bandit wielding a machete and a gun. Today they have more than 2,400 full-patched members in over 200 chapters in sixteen countries.

The Bandidos, like other OMGs, say they are merely a social club for guys who like to hang out together and ride Harley-Davidson motorcycles on the weekends. The cops say bullshit on that, and claim that certain factions within the Bandidos are involved in drugs, prostitution, extortion, arson, car bombings and contract murders. Whether or not they are a social club or a criminal enterprise, one thing both sides agree on is that nobody, and I mean nobody, fucks around with the Bandidos, not even the Mob. They are badass motherfuckers and damn proud of it.

Consider the Shedden Massacre which is the worst mass murder in the history of Ontario, Canada. Eight patched members of the Toronto chapter of the Bandidos were shot to death and their bodies dumped on a rural farm. Who were their killers? Would you believe six of their very own brother Bandidos from the nearby Winnipeg chapter. At least, that's what cops and prosecutors claim, saying that national Bandidos officers were displeased with how the Toronto chapter was running their business and decided it was time for some *"internal cleansing."*

No boring pink slips for these guys.

I didn't know all of these little details when a detective mentioned to me one day that our city was headquarters for one of the most active chapters of the Bandidos.

"What's a Bandido?" I asked.

"Are you kidding me?" he said. *"They're as big as the Hell's Angels."*

"Really! I want to do an article on them. How do I reach them?"

"Are you fucking serious? You don't just call them up out of the blue."

"Why not?"

"Because they are vicious and they don't like press."

"Oh, they can't be all that bad."

The detective smiled, flipped through his Rolodex and gave me a phone number.

"Who do I ask for?"

"Ask for Wolfie. He's the President."

Back in the newsroom, I called the number and spoke briefly to Wolfie, who said to come by his house that afternoon. I poked my head into the photo darkroom and saw Wayne, one of our three staff photographers. He was a really old guy who mostly did photos for our society and lifestyles sections.

"Yo Wayne, want to come with me to shoot some photos for an article?"

"Sure," he said, and together we walked out of the news building to the parking lot to get our cars.

"What's your article about?" asked Wayne.

"The Bandidos."

"What's a Bandido?"

I told him it was about some nice guys who like to ride motorcycles on the weekend.

"That sounds like fun," said Wayne.

Thirty minutes later Wayne was saying in a very shaky voice, *"Okay, I'm good. I got all the shots I need. Thank you all very much. I'll see you back at the newsroom."* And then he pretty much ran out of Wolfie's house to his car, giving me a weird look on the way out, the kind of look you give someone who you aren't sure you are ever going to see again. He had shot three rolls of film and he was outta there, baby, post haste.

life.

When we had arrived at Wolfie's house and I knocked on the front door, it was opened by a huge, 250-pound, mean as shit looking guy.

"Wolfie?"

"No. Come in."

Wayne and I stood in the middle of the living room. Another guy walked in from the kitchen. He was bigger and meaner looking than the first guy.

"Wolfie?"

"No. Sit down."

We sat. Quickly.

The front door opened loudly behind us and Wayne and I jumped. A brute who could barely fit through the doorway walked in and slammed the door shut.

"Wolfie?"

The brute didn't even answer me. He just sat down with the first two guys. We all sat there looking at each other, no one saying a word for what seemed like a good five minutes.

Well, isn't this awkward, I thought to myself. Wayne, meanwhile, looked like he was about to pee his pants.

At the back of the house we heard a door close and a few seconds later a guy walked into the living room. He was tiny, about five-foot-six and no more than 120 pounds, with a long black ponytail.

"Wolfie?" I asked, somewhat incredulously.

"That's me," he said.

No way, I thought. How in the world could this little guy be the boss? How could he be in charge of the three monster dudes sitting in the room with us and the dozens of other bone-crushers in their chapter?

I stood up to shake Wolfie's hand and when I started to let go, he gripped my hand even tighter and it felt like I was holding a twisted piece of steel cable, and he pulled me a few inches closer to him, and he looked straight into my eyes and I can tell you that in the over five decades that I have lived on this planet I have never seen eyes as dead fucking cold as Wolfie's. In Latin America they call it *ojos de diablo*, the eyes of the devil. And those eyes answered all my questions about why he was the boss.

"Let's do this," said Wolfie.

I pulled out my reporter's notepad and started firing off the interview questions. Wolfie had well rehearsed and polished answers for all of my questions, and for the next half hour he faithfully promoted the company line of the Bandidos simply being a social club of misunderstood motorcycle enthusiasts. The interview was winding down and I had just a few more questions.

And that's when I pissed Wolfie off.

Because what I said was, *"But isn't it true that police consider the Bandidos a criminal group that is involved in everything from manufacturing and distributing crystal meth to murder for hire?"*

Wolfie just stared at me and didn't say a word.

For a very long time.

Oh fuck, I thought to myself, what have I done now? I had not told my city editors where I was going, I had not told the police where I was going, I had not told my wife where I was going. The only person in the world who knew that I was sitting in a house with four members of one of the most ruthless outlaw motorcycle gangs in the world was Wayne, who was not only long gone, but for all I knew he had sped home and was hiding under his bed.

"Let me rephrase that," I said.

Thankfully, Wolfie let me rephrase it, and I tossed him a nice slow underhand pitch of a question which he smacked into the bleachers.

I closed my notepad, stood up and thanked Wolfie for the interview.

"I'll walk you out," said Wolfie.

The three bikers stood up and started to follow Wolfie.

"Did I fucking tell you to get up," Wolfie said in a low growl.

They sat right back down.

Wolfie walked me to my car and watched as I got in and started it up. He kept standing next to my door, so I rolled down the window. He leaned in, his tattooed arms on the door frame, his face just inches from mine, and he smiled for the first time.

"I'm going to be real interested to read your article," Wolfie said. *"I know you're going to do the right thing."*

I smiled back, said goodbye again and drove back to the newsroom. They ran my article a few weeks later as the front cover story on the special pull-out magazine section of the Sunday paper, along with a huge spread of photos and text on the inside. The photos were very powerful, although my article, which I think Wolfie liked very much, was a bit tame, but in my defense it was not supposed to be an expose on the Bandidos but rather a human interest piece about me spending an afternoon with some very heavy duty badasses. I had to show a little backbone, though, so I ended the article telling the readers about how Wolfie had leaned in my car window and warned me to do the right thing. I'll bet he liked that part too.

I never saw or talked to Wolfie again. About five years later, someone in a pickup truck blew his head off with a shotgun while he sat on his Harley at a stop light.

Made me sad to hear that. He seemed like a nice guy.

*   *   *

I stop at a liquor store near the office and buy a bottle of my favorite scotch, a single malt brand called Lagavulin which is very powerful with a peat-smoke aroma. Not for the faint of heart. I buy a bunch of cocktail mixers and three handles, or half gallons, of Stolichnaya vodka. All of our friends drink vodka almost exclusively.

And they drink like fish.

Which is one of the reasons why they are our friends.

Every house in our subdivision has the exact same, homeowners association-approved twelve-foot tall lamp post in the front yard. It's a thick, painted wooden post that has some special type of light bulb at the top encased in a huge, fancy plastic covering. A mailbox is perched on a wooden arm that sticks out from the post. Our lamp post is located in the patch of grass between the sidewalk and our street and it is a good six feet away from the end of our driveway.

The lamp post costs over fifteen hundred dollars.

I know because we have had to replace it four times after our friends have knocked it over with their cars leaving one of our parties. I won't mention any names, Scott, Happy John and Maggie (twice). Now my wife makes sure to walk all of our departing guests to the front door so she can stand in the doorway and thank them for coming and then shout, *"Watch out for the lamp post!"* as they get into their cars.

Needless to say, we throw a pretty good party at our house.

life.

Then there was the time in Costa Rica when Mean John and I spent the night with twelve naked lesbian hookers covered in baby oil and armed with huge, multi-colored dildos, and then with a short, fat, throat-cutting bandit named ChiChi who we kept encouraging to yell, *"Badges, badges we don't need no stinking badges,"* and then with twenty hard-as-nails Costa Rican cowboys who wanted to kill our gringo asses in a saloon showdown worthy of the OK Corral.

Perhaps I should explain.

Mean John and I were in San Jose, Costa Rica with a half dozen of our mutual friends. John and I had been to Costa Rica many times before, but it was the first trip for our buddies, which meant that we had no choice but to take them to this infamously seedy hotel which had an even seedier lounge where they would barricade the doors at ten o'clock every Friday night to keep the cops out, and whatever customers were left inside were treated to a two-hour lesbian show. A dozen attractive young ladies of the night would get completely naked and dance on the long bar in the lounge and use the dildos in the most creative of ways. It was an audience participation event and the customers were given squeeze bottles of baby oil that they could squirt and rub on the ladies as they danced and poked each other with the toys.

Our friends loved it because you just don't get that type of quality entertainment at your local TGI Fridays. But for John and I, it was the old been there, done that, got the T-shirt kind of thing.

The lounge was located in the roughest part of downtown San Juan. We had a hard time even finding two cab drivers who would bring our group to the lounge in that part of the city. The two cabbies who did, sped off as soon as we stepped out of the cabs.

"I'm bored," I said to Mean John fifteen minutes into the lesbian show.

"Me too. What do you want to do?"

"Let's go explore."

"Are you sure? It's a little rough out here."

"Scared?"

"Fuck you. You know better. Let's go."

life.

We told our buddies we would be back before the show was over and headed for the front door.

"Maybe we should get someone to watch our back?" I said to John.

"Good idea."

We turned around and went to find Doyle, an American guy we had met on our earlier trips who owned the hotel and lounge. He'd been in Costa Rica for twenty years which meant he must have come down when he was about fifty because the motherfucker was now as old as dirt and fat and baldheaded and had the personality and social graces of a lump of coal. You run into a lot of Americans in Latin America and a good percentage of them aren't down there by choice. They're either there because Uncle Sam strongly suggested that they find another country to hang their hat, or they're there because they know if they go back to the U.S. someone will be waiting for them with a key to their very own prison cell, or maybe a baseball bat or a bullet. So you learn not to ask an ex-pat what brought him south of the border and instead you just buy him a drink, catch him up on what's been happening with the Yankees and the Red Sox, and ask him how long he's been dating the cute eighteen-year-old Colombian who is sitting in his lap and calling him *pappi*.

We found Doyle in his office slash living room slash bedroom on the bottom floor. Four hookers, two of them topless, were sitting at a card table playing some type of confusing card game, two more were dancing together in the corner to a slow Spanish song, and one was at the stove cooking something that smelled horrendous. A shirtless Doyle was laying on his bed getting a massage from two young women who, funny enough, were squirting him with the same squeeze bottles that our friends were having a field day with down the hall in the lounge. The room had no air conditioning so the door and all the windows were open and everyone was covered in a sticky sheen of sweat. The mixture of exotic and decadent sights and sounds and smells in that room was pure Brando as Colonel Walter E. Kurtz from *Apocalypse Now*.

"What the hell do you boys want?" said Doyle, not even looking up from his massage.

"Our buddies are busy molesting your lesbians. We're bored, we want to go outside and explore. You got someone who can walk

around with us, make sure we don't get stabbed? We'll give him fifty bucks."

One of the girls squirted baby oil on Doyle's bald head and slowly massaged it in.

"Tatiana," barked Doyle, *"vaya encuentre ChiChi."*

One of the hookers dancing in the corner hurried out of the room. We waited.

"How's biz, Doyle?" I asked.

"Can't complain."

A few minutes later Tatiana walked in, followed by a five-foot-tall Mexican. Well, he was probably Costa Rican, but he looked like the stereotypical short and fat Mexican bandit bad guy that you see in every action movie. He was wearing ironed to a sharp crease Wrangler jeans, ostrich skin cowboy boots with sterling silver toe guards, a leather belt with a gigantic mother of pearl belt buckle inlaid with sterling silver steer horns, a starched, white cowboy shirt buttoned at the collar, a bolo with a turquoise clasp, and a humongous black cowboy hat with a rattlesnake head band around it. Oh, and he had a handlebar moustache and a gold front tooth.

"Hello senors. I am ChiChi," he said.

Of course he was. But this wasn't what we had in mind.

"Uh, Doyle, not sure if we're on the same page here," I said. *"Don't you have a big guy we can use?"*

Doyle lifted his head up from the bed and turned to look at us. He smiled like we had just questioned whether Jack the Ripper knew how to handle a blade. *"Don't you boys worry about a thing. All you need is ChiChi. You'll be as safe as a baby in its mother's arms."*

John and I both looked at ChiChi, or rather, down at ChiChi.

"I am ChiChi," he said again with a big smile, that one gold tooth just a shining.

If Doyle had tried to sell us on what a tough guy ChiChi was and that he had done this badass thing and that badass thing, we would not have believed him. But when he said, *"as safe as a baby in its mother's arms,"* I mean, come on, how can you even question that. Talk about underselling.

We went outside and started walking down the main drag that had all the dive bars and bodegas and cantinas. The street was packed with old cars honking and spewing exhaust and the sidewalks were jammed with people bumping into each other. John and I were the only white faces in any direction. ChiChi walked two steps in front of us, his thumbs stuck in his belt on either side of his hips, and he kind of rocked back and forth, left to right, as he walked. And as we walked behind ChiChi, we noticed that all the men, young and old, big and small, would step aside as ChiChi approached, and they would all nod their head at him in a very respectful manner. Some of the hombres farther down the sidewalk would see ChiChi and quickly cross the street to the sidewalk on the other side.

It was like being with Moses when he parted the Red Sea.

John and I looked at each other, and John said, *"Dude, I don't even want to know what this guy has done."*

Hearing us talking, ChiChi looked back, smiled and said yet again, *"I am ChiChi."*

No shit, ChiChi, you da man.

We started hitting the dive bars and at each one guys quickly cleared away from the bar counter so we could belly right up. John and I began downing cold beers and shots of cheap tequila. We tried to buy ChiChi a drink, but he just shook his head. We had four bars and a half dozen beers and a number of tequila shots under our belts and were wobbling a little when we saw a joint on one of the deserted side streets.

"One more round and then we'll head back," I suggested to John.

When we got close to the front door, ChiChi stopped to talk to two men standing outside. I tapped ChiChi on the shoulder and pointed at the bar door and he nodded.

John and I walked into the bar alone.

And it was like a scene out of a movie. Actually, more like a scene out of two different movies.

The first movie is the one where the two cowboys have been riding the range for months and roll into a new town and walk through the swinging doors of the town's only saloon and it's packed with rowdy cowpokes and gamblers who don't know the two cowboys and who aren't happy about them walking in. The joint we walked into had a hard packed dirt floor and a square bar that was constructed from sheets of plywood resting on wooden barrels. Sitting around that bar were twenty Costa Rican cowboys, the real deal, with dirty clothes, straw cowboy hats with sweat stains for hat bands, calloused hands holding bottles of the local beer, and faces like rawhide leather from working in the sun from sunup to sundown. It's safe to say that two guys with lilly white skin and forty dollar haircuts had never walked into their bar. And the shit, just like in that movie Western, was about to hit the fan.

The second movie is the one where two guys who don't fit in with a particular bar's clientele go running into that bar and everything just comes to a complete, you-can-hear-a-pin-drop stop. Think black as coal Eddie Murphy and angry cop Nick Nolte going into that redneck cowboy bar in *48 Hours*. When John and I walked into the joint, every head in the place swiveled to stare at us, everyone stopped talking, beers on their way from the countertop to open mouths froze midway, the bartender looked at us like he had just seen a group of nuns step off the curb into the path of a speeding Mac truck and, I swear to God, the music on the jukebox just quit. It was a freeze frame moment. Nobody moved. All you could hear was the heavy breathing of twenty very surprised and slowly becoming pissed off Latin cowboys.

"Uh-oh," said John.

"No shit," said I.

We both looked at the door hoping to see ChiChi come swaggering in. But Mr. *I am ChiChi* was a no-show.

Out of the corner of my eye I saw the only female in the place, a cute waitress who, like everyone else in the bar, was frozen in place. She was actually balancing her tray standing on just one foot, the other foot having been in mid-step when we walked in. I caught her eye and motioned to her. She walked over a bit hesitantly and when she was next to me, I pushed two twenty dollar bills into her hand and whispered into her ear, *"Cervezas por favor entodo hombres,"* which I was hoping translated to, give the house a round of beers on me. The waitress walked over to the square bar, slipped under one of the sheets of plywood and then started pulling bottles of beer out of the freezer, popping the caps off and setting the bottles in front of each of the cowboys at the bar one at a time. As she placed each beer, the cowboy sitting there would look at the beer, then at the waitress and then back at John and I. A few of the cowboys, still looking right at us, started to get up from their bar stools. But just then the waitress placed a beer in front of the last cowboy sitting at the bar, and that cowboy asked her a question in Spanish.

She answered, and pointed at John and I.

life.

It was quiet for a few more seconds as her answer sunk in, and then in unison all twenty of those Costa Rican cowboys lifted their bottles of beer up into the air and toward John and I in a toast, hollered out, *gracias amigos,* and the jukebox came back on nice and loud, and the cowboys who had stood up sat back down, and all the cowboys went back to talking to each other in rapid-fire Spanish, and the bartender breathed a big sigh of relief, and the waitress had a big smile on her face because twenty beers in that joint only cost $20 which meant she had just made a $20 tip. So everybody was happy.

But no one more so than John and I.

"That was fun," said John.

* * *

I drive past Jimmy's on the way home, but I don't stop. I've already been to the bar four times this week, and since I normally only stop in once or twice a week, I know that showing up a fifth time would be way too strange. I realize it means that Monday will be the last time I go to Jimmy's since Tuesday is the big day. It dawns on me that I am more than halfway through the ten-day timetable I have given myself.

Trite as it sounds, that realization gives me fixed feelings.

Excitement and fear.

Sadness and relief.

And emptiness.

* * *

"How embarrassing."

It's Boo talking.

He has a look of disdain on his face. I know because I am laying on the floor trying to put him in his cage. Actually, he's already in his cage, but I've spent the last five minutes trying to close the cage door. Not lock the door, just shut it. My brain does not seem to be communicating with my fingers.

"You are so shit-faced. Just go to bed you drunken fool."

That's Boo again.

life.

What I say back to him, or at least what I think I say, is, *"Just give me a minute, and I will get this damn door closed and we can both get a good night's sleep."*

But what comes out of my mouth is, *"Jiss gimme mint I giz diz damador cluzed an wee bote kane go nighty-poo."*

"Oh, that sounded charming."

Boo again.

"You are going to feel like shit tomorrow. Trust me on this one."

Needless to say, the party at our house was a success. It's four in the morning, my wife is asleep in the guest bedroom, and I am laying on the floor in just my underwear trying to close a dog cage door that has a simple latch on it. And Boo is not helping the situation.

"Jesus Christ, you stink. You smell like a brewery. Do you have any idea how strong my sense of smell is? Can we open a window or something? Come on, man!"

The Lagavulin had gone down so smooth. I remember seeing the empty bottle on the kitchen counter when I headed for bed.

"Yeah, it was empty," says Boo. *"And guess what, you were the only peckerwood drinking scotch tonight, so you know what that means."*

"Fuck me," I say.

"Brother, you already fucked yourself. You drank a fifth of scotch tonight."

"Oh, thaz note toooo bod," I say.

"And you had three beers before everyone came over."

"Oh."

"And four shots of Jagermeister later on."

"Uh-oh!"

I leave the cage door open, stand up, a bit too quickly, and dizzily fall onto the top of the bed. The room starts to spin ever so slowly, picking up speed on each rotation, and I realize that not only am I dying of thirst but I have to piss something fierce. But I can't move. So I just go to sleep.

And the last thing I hear before I enter dreamland is Boo's loud voice.

"Yo, you left the goddamm bedroom light on!"

wonder.

Boo was right.

I feel like shit.

So I say *Prayer Number 19* out loud as I lay in bed.

My Dad told me a joke one time about a new guy in prison. He was sitting there with a dozen longtime convicts when one of them said, *"twenty-two,"* and all the convicts broke up laughing. A few minutes later another convict said, *"ninety-five,"* and again all the convicts howled. When a third convict said *"seventy-six,"* and was met with a chorus of giggles, the new guy couldn't take it any longer and turned to one of the old cons and asked him what the hell was going on.

"Son," said the old-timer, *"we've all been in the joint so long and heard every con's favorite joke so many damn times that now you just say the number of the joke and spare everyone all the joke details."*

The new guy sat there for awhile and then yelled out, *"forty-two."*

And nobody laughed, or howled, or giggled.

wonder.

The new guy was confused. He turned to the old con and said, *"What's wrong? Why isn't anyone laughing?"*

"I think it's how you told it," said the old con.

That's how I say my prayers.

I have woken up so many mornings with a bone-crushing, stomach-turning hangover and have prayed to God so many times to make the hangover go away, and promised him that if he would do that for me, I would quit drinking, quit smoking, quit being a dickhead, go to church every Sunday, feed the poor, and on and on. I've also laid in bed a fair number of times in the early morning hours covered in sweat, with my heart racing, and my fingers starting to freeze into paralytic claws from one too many eight balls of cocaine and prayed to God so many times that if he would not let me die, I would promise to quit snorting drugs, quit smoking, quit being a dickhead, go to church every Sunday, feed the poor, and on and on.

There had been so many prayers and promises over the years that at some point it just made sense to number them. It's easier to lay there in the fetal position and just chant, *"Prayer Number 19, Prayer Number 19,"* over and over than it is to remember all the words to the Lord's Prayer, also known as the Our Father.

Cocaine, by the way, in case I haven't said it before, is the devil. Not the devil's drug, but the devil himself.

A friend once asked me if I had ever smoked crack cocaine and I said I had tried it once, and so the friend asked me what it was like.

And even knowing that it was the devil magnified, I said that smoking crack cocaine was like, *"Touching the face of God."*

And I meant it. That's fucked up.

* * *

I tell my kids all the time that my three favorite words to hear come out of another person's mouth are, *"Did you know?,"* because it means that, hopefully, I'm going to learn something new.

Sometimes I am disappointed. *"Did you know that if you mix the colors yellow and blue you will get the color green?"* No shit, Sherlock.

And sometimes I am pleasantly surprised. *"Did you know that James Wright invented Silly Putty in 1942?"* I did not know that, but know I do, so thank you very much.

wonder.

It didn't dawn on me until I was about thirty years old that the word *afternoon* actually meant *after* (pause) *noon*, as in that time period that comes after twelve o'clock during the day.

I remember exactly when and where I realized this fact. I was driving a rental car in Nashville and the DJ on the radio used the word and for some reason on that specific day at that specific time something clicked in my mind and the realization hit me. I mentioned this to a group of music industry people at dinner that night and they all looked at me like I was from another planet, and they laughed at my foolhardiness. But it got the conversation going and soon everyone took turns tossing out words and what their obvious and not-so-obvious meanings and origins were. We talked about how *midnight* means the middle of the night, and how *breakfast* means you are breaking your fast after sleeping all night, and how *brunch* comes from combining the words breakfast and lunch and refers to a meal that is eaten between the times when you normally eat breakfast and lunch.

Nobody ever says give me a driver for this screw, they say *screwdriver*. You put your cigarette out in an *ashtray* and never think of it as a tray for ashes. You put on your boxer briefs or your tiny thong and call it *underwear* and don't think of it as an article of clothing that you wear under your other clothing. *Weekend* means Saturday and Sunday to most people, who seldom think of it as the end of the week. That wacko guy is your *brother-in-law*, which to you just means he is married to your sister, but he is actually your brother based on civil law. You don't go out to the driveway in the morning to get a paper that has all the news in it, you get the *newspaper*. You use your *toothbrush* every night and have since you were a child, but as a child you never asked your mother where that special brush was that you use on your teeth. Did you ever think that an *earring* is actually a ring you wear in your ear?

As the list of words got longer at that dinner in Nashville, everyone at the table started to admit that they had never really thought about how some of those words came about and eventually every single person there said, *"You know, I never thought about that."*

And that was the key. Not thinking about it, or thinking anything of it. I'm not an idiot. If you tell me to meet you in the afternoon, I know what you're talking about, but to me, for as long as I can

wonder.

remember, that word simply referred to a time of the day that I knew about. It wasn't necessary for me to dissect and analyze it.

I just accepted it.

Imagine that you walk into your backyard tomorrow morning and you see an animal that is taller than the roof of your house, is covered in bright green fur with purple spots, has a forty-foot-long tail shaped like a corkscrew, has two eyes the size of manhole covers, and has a huge candy striped tongue sticking out between two front teeth that are bigger than your whole body.

You will freak the fuck out.

You will run into your house and call the police and the fire department and animal control and the local TV station and then all your family and friends, and you will say the same thing to all of them, *"You are not going to fucking believe what I just saw!"* And you will peek out your window at that strange animal and you will have a million questions and you will be so scared and excited that you can't sit still.

Now let's say that at that exact same time your three-year-old daughter is at the zoo with your wife and she walks around the corner and she sees an animal that is taller than the roof of your house, is covered in bright yellow fur with brown spots, has a narrow twenty-foot long neck, has front legs that are twice as long as its back legs, and has a tiny little head the size of a lunchbox.

Will your daughter run away? No. Will she call the police? No. Will she have a million questions? No.

She will simply say, *"Look mommy, a giraffe."*

Not thinking about it, or thinking anything of it because she knows about giraffes from books and cartoons. It's natural. Nothing special. She will just accept it.

Like all of us do.

Because we are oblivious, one and all, to the wonders around us.

I went to the American Museum of Natural History in New York with my daughter last year to see the dinosaurs exhibit. The place was packed. Dinosaurs and humans were hanging out together and no one was acting like it was anything special.

We looked at the skeleton of a forty-foot long and twenty-foot tall Tyrannosaurus rex, seven and a half tons of unbridled fury that could run twenty-five miles an hour and eat 500 pounds of meat, or four slow-running cavemen, in a single bite. We looked at the skeleton of a Brontosaurus that was more than seventy-five feet long —which is the length of two school buses—and weighed more than twenty-five tons—which is the weight of ten Lincoln Continentals. We looked at the skeleton of a Pteranodon, a flying dinosaur, with a thirty-foot wingspan and a long, sharp beak made of hard bone. I mean, come on now people, we're talking about a flying lizard that was thirty feet long!

Those things used to roam our world, not some far off planet. They actually walked on the same soil that we are walking on today. They were gigantic monsters, scarier than any alien you have ever seen in a science fiction movie. They lived right here. And everybody thinks that dinosaurs are just as natural and common as the sun coming up every morning.

So my daughter and I looked at all those dinosaurs.

And then we went across the street to get an ice cream.

* * *

Saturday is my favorite day of the week.

Always has been.

It started with Saturday morning cartoons when I was a youngster. After that, every week in school, from grade school all the way through to college, I could not wait for Saturday to arrive, and after I started working in an office, Saturday was again that light at the end of the tunnel. For me, Saturday signalled an end to the turmoil of the week for a brief period. Come Saturday, I was off the hook. All those pressures, from doing homework to paying credit card bills to answering to an asshole boss, were put on hold. Saturday was like a cease-fire during warfare. *Okay guys, let's take a short break. Everybody let their hair down and enjoy the next few days. Come Monday, we'll go back to killing each other.*

I never had a teacher call me on a Saturday and say, *"Hope you're enjoying watching Tom & Jerry, because on Monday your ass is mine."* And I never had a bank call me on Saturday to ask if I was familiar with the term overdrawn, or the IRS call me on Saturday to ask why my tax return listed twenty-three African pygmy dependents.

My nephew, when times are tough, likes to say, *"Make the bad man stop."* It's really funny when he says it because he is built like

wonder.

an NFL middle linebacker and could probably knock out a steer with one punch. But that's what Saturday is to me; it's the one day that the bad man stops. Sunday is also nice because you don't get hassled by those annoying people who clutter up your life Monday through Friday, but it is never as enjoyable and relaxing as Saturday because you know that you have to go back to the grind the next day.

I get out of bed and start the shower. I brush my teeth for a long time, using the *toothbrush* to scrub the three packs of cigarettes I smoked yesterday off my tongue. It takes a solid two minutes of scrubbing and rinsing before I can finally spit nice clear, non-nicotine colored saliva into the sink. I get in the shower and let the hot water beat down on the top of my hungover head, and I take a nice long luxurious piss right in the shower. There's nothing better. Trust me, every guy does it. It's not like it's a bathtub. I have a large walk-in shower with two showerheads that have the force of a fire hose so everything goes down the drain at a rapid pace.

In the kitchen I wash down three extra strength aspirins with a huge glass of ice water followed by a bottle of Gatorade.

"How do you feel?" asks my wife.

"Just dandy," I say with a smile.

And after I inhale two cigarettes, one right after the other, and drink a cup of hot coffee while sitting outside on the lanai, I actually do start to feel better.

It's time to make some eggs and sausage

Another Saturday favorite for me.

* * *

Let's do another imagine. Come on, it's fun.

Imagine that you wake up in bed tomorrow morning and you have total, absolute amnesia. Not only do you not remember who you are, you don't remember anything at all. Not your childhood or your past, not what day or night are, not what trees or cars are, not what time or space are, not what apples or butterflies are. The only thing you can still do is walk and talk. Everything else is unknown. Your brain is a completely blank canvas.

You get up and you walk into the next room which just happens to be your living room, but you don't know that, and sitting and

wonder.

standing around are about twenty creatures who look somewhat like you and they are your family and friends, but you don't know that. You sit down on the edge of the sofa and you watch all of these creatures talking and laughing and milling around. You clear your throat and a few of the creatures stop talking and laughing and milling and look at you with an expectant smile on their faces. You stand up and raise your hand in the air as one does before asking a question and the rest of the creatures in the room stop talking and laughing and milling until every creature in the room is staring at you, waiting for you to speak.

If that were to happen, then you—just like every single other person that was ever born or will ever be born on this planet—would ask the exact same three fucking questions.

How did I get here?
Why am I here?
What's next?

You wouldn't ask the creatures in the room if there was any spinach and mushroom quiche left. You wouldn't ask them what the day's weather forecast was. You wouldn't ask them how their mutual fund portfolio was doing. You wouldn't ask them their thoughts on global warming. You wouldn't ask them who they think will win the World Series this year. You wouldn't ask them any of the numerous trivial questions that make up our daily social banter.

While you are standing there, the house could catch on fire and rabid wolverines could come crashing through the bay window, but as your fellow creatures started to scatter, you would grab them and shout, *How the fuck did I get here? Why the fuck am I here?* and *What the fuck is going to happen to me?*

Nothing else would be of more importance to you.

Not the raging flames.

Not the razor sharp wolverine teeth.

Not the tasty spinach and mushroom quiche.

Before you took another breath, before you took a sip of water, before you combed your hair, before you took a piss, before you rubbed that sleepy out of your eye, before you did another single thing, you would demand answers to those three questions. And you would not stop asking those questions until you got answers.

Okay, now you don't have amnesia. You are just normal you. But now you are at a family reunion, or a crowded bar, or a PTA

wonder.

meeting, or a neighborhood cocktail party, or your office conference room. Wherever you are, there are twenty or so people within earshot of your voice. You clear your throat, you stand up and you wave your hand in the air. When you have everybody's full attention, you ask them three questions.

Who created the universe and what was there before it was created?

Where did man come from and exactly why am I here right now?

Is there life after death?

And watch the looks on their faces.

Watch them laugh nervously.

Watch them move away from you.

Ask those three questions again, and again, and again, and again.

Until someone calls the police and they Baker Act your ass to the nearest mental health facility.

What's wrong with this picture? There is an 800-pound gorilla sitting in the living room of our lives and we are ignoring him and instead asking someone to pass the chips and dip. We are watching inane sitcoms and reality shows on television instead of addressing the gorilla. We are spreading malicious neighborhood gossip instead of addressing the gorilla. We are talking about our favorite guys who throw leather pigskins or hit little white balls into holes instead of addressing the gorilla. We are giving our children advice about homework and curfews instead of talking to them about the gorilla. We are clicking off the days of our lives by riding a numbing treadmill of work and home life, speeding to the end of those days without ever stopping to address the gorilla.

I'm not talking about God and religion. Everybody talks about that crap all the time. That stuff is not truly real; it's just speculation and conjecture.

Take your right hand and lightly tap your forehead. That's real. Put your head on your young son's chest and hear his heart beat. That's real. Go outside and scoop up a handful of soil. That's real. Gently pull a leaf off the tree in your front yard. That's real. Feel the heat of the afternoon sun on your cheek. That's real. Watch a lizard scamper across your driveway. That's real. Listen to the sonic roar

wonder.

of an overhead jet plane. That's real. Later, at night, look at the thousands of pin prick stars in the sky. That's real.

If we all acknowledge that those things are as real and as common as the air we breathe in our daily life, then shouldn't the questions of where do those things (and you) come from, why are they (and you) here, and what is going to happen to them (and you) be just as real and common in our daily life.

I guess not.

Because we are more interested in the question of what's for dinner tonight than we are in the question of how and why we exist on this planet.

The emperor is not wearing any clothes.

Even the gorilla knows that.

* * *

Dan is a beautiful snowflake.

But don't tell him that. It really pisses him off.

Dan is an enigma. And if you make that statement to his wife, she will say, *"You aren't telling me anything I don't already know, baby."*

He's an enigma because he is a conservative trapped in the body of a liberal. Dan grew up as a New England hippy, did his fair share of drugs including lots of riding the Peruvian rails, loves to drink and party until the early morning hours, is a wine connoisseur, enjoys cooking gourmet meals and frequenting fine dining restaurants, loves rock and roll music and playing the guitar, is against the war, thinks most politicians are inept, is not particularly fond of cops or any other authority figures, has read all the literary classics, and can be very generous with his time and his money with others.

And he is also a rabid, just to the right of Senator Joseph McCarthy Republican conservative.

Makes no sense to me.

"That's because you just don't understand," he will say to me. *"You need to fucking grow up."*

I'm over a half century old. How much more growing up is left?

wonder.

Dan told me about standing outside a restaurant in Manhattan one night smoking a cigarette when a street bum walked up to him and said, *"You look like a twenty dollar guy."*

"Excuse me?" said Dan, who is very large and who has the patience of a NYPD cop. He can be very surly and intimidating.

"I said you look like a twenty dollar guy," said the bum.

"What the fuck does that mean?" said surly and intimidating Dan.

"I ask for money all day long," said the bum, *"so I am a good judge of people. I look at their clothes, their shoes, their watches, their attitude. And I can tell when a guy is a dollar guy, when a guy is a five dollar guy, or when a guy is a ten dollar guy. But you, my friend, you look like a twenty dollar guy."*

What did you do, I asked Dan.

"I gave him twenty fucking dollars."

What on the surface seemed to be a liberal reaction, the rich giving to the poor, was really a conservative reaction, the rich rewarding capitalistic business acumen. *"I should have offered that bum a job. He was better than any of the airheads on my sales team."*

Dan, Happy John and I and our wives were at a restaurant having dinner one night when, during one of the infrequent lulls in the conversation, I mentioned the snowflakes. I knew the subject would go over like a lead balloon with this group, particularly with Dan, but I forged ahead because, as my wife is fond of pointing out, I like to stir the shit up.

So I told them about Japanese scientist Dr. Masaru Emoto's before and after experiment with snowflakes.

Using a very powerful microscope in a freezing cold room along with high-speed photography, Dr. Emoto took "before" photos of some snowflakes and the resulting photos showed beautiful, intricate pure white snowflakes. The snowflakes were then split up between two groups of university students. The first group stared at the snowflakes and had pleasant thoughts about them and spoke positive words to them in soothing voices, saying they were beautiful snowflakes. The second group stared at the snowflakes and had evil thoughts about them and spoke negative words to them in angry voices, saying they were ugly snowflakes. Dr. Emoto then took "after" photos. The after photos showed that the snowflakes from the positive group where even whiter and more beautiful than before. The snowflakes from the negative group had turned black and ugly. Dr. Emoto did other experiments using negative/positive music, images, prayers and even handwritten notes and came up with the same results. His point was that thoughts and feelings and speech and images can affect physical reality.

When I finished telling the story, Dan looked at me like I had just told him that a Martian wearing a purple cowboy hat and a feather boa was going to deliver our next round of drinks.

"That is, without a doubt, the most ridiculous thing I have ever heard in my life," said Dan. *"Everybody knows snowflakes don't have ears."*

I think Dan was over analyzing and too quick to discount.

The world is not all black and white.

Let some colors in, my brother.

As Albert Einstein said, *"Imagination is more important than knowledge. Knowledge is limited. Imagination encircles the world. The important thing is not to stop questioning; curiosity has its own reason for existing."*

After dinner, we all stood outside the restaurant waiting for the valet to bring our car up. Happy John doesn't smoke, but the other five of us pulled out lighters and packs of cigarettes and fired away. Dan and I smoke the same brand so I offered him one of my cigarettes and even lit it for him.

As he leaned over to accept the light, I said, *"You know Dan ..."*

Everybody looked over at us as I spoke.

"... to me you are a beautiful snowflake."

Dan gagged.

* * *

I toss a quarter stick of butter in the frying pan, and get the eggs and sausage out of the refrigerator. I like the link sausages the best, the ones that have maple syrup in them. I cook the sausages first and then cook the eggs in the grease from the sausages. I slice a tomato and put the slices on two plates that will soon hold the over-easy eggs, sausages and buttered toast. The fresh tomatoes with morning eggs thing I learned when I went to London. A tall glass of really cold orange juice rounds out the meal. The whole thing takes me ten minutes tops.

I love to cook. I just don't know how.

I can make a mean egg, though.

My wife is a great cook. She learned from her mother, home style cooking at it's best. If food is not falling off your plate, then Mamaw feels like she didn't fix enough. So my daughter, technically, had access to a great teacher when it came to home cooking, but she never learned. She was always too busy. She knows how to make Congo Bar brownies and that's about it.

Last year my daughter, who now lives in Manhattan, called my wife to ask her for instructions on how to cook a turkey since she was inviting her friends over for Thanksgiving dinner later that week. My wife had a stunned look on her face, like our daughter had just called to ask how to fly a Boeing 747. The look of shock then went to a look of concern and I wasn't sure whether it was a mother's concern for a daughter who was about to be embarrassed in front of her friends by presenting them with an undercooked or charred turkey or a mother's concern for a daughter who was about to burn her apartment building to the ground.

But my daughter surprised us both.

"Dad, you wouldn't believe it. I cooked the best turkey I have ever eaten in my life," she said when she called us Thanksgiving night.

She excitedly explained how she had soaked the turkey in brine overnight and then placed pads of butter under the skin and then put orange slices inside the turkey and then added a bunch of different spices and then basted the turkey every twenty minutes, and watched it cook with the loving attention of a mother with a newborn baby.

"It was incredible," said my daughter with a mixture of wonder and pride.

My daughter is a very sharp, very charismatic and very adventurous person with a circle of friends that revolve around her like she was the sun. When she went away to college it was like the life was sucked out of our house. What my wife and I noticed most was the quiet. The nonstop ringing of the telephone was gone. The sound of the front doorbell chiming day and night as a parade of her friends came over was gone. The sound of laughter and excitement and wild ideas and lively debates that had filled the house from sunup to sundown was gone. Our talented daughter had been a cheerleader and a class president and had given the salutatorian speech at her high school graduation. She went skydiving and didn't tell us about it until years later. She was one of only twenty applicants out a field of thousands who was accepted to film school at one of the country's largest universities, and while other students learned how to do boring business accounting she learned how to make movies. She spent three months one summer backpacking across Europe with her best friend, smoking pot in the hash bars of Amsterdam, haggling with merchants over knickknacks in Turkey, partying on the beaches of Ibiza in Spain, and punching out a thief who woke her up while she was sleeping under the Eiffel Tower when he tried to rob her by slitting open her purse with a razor blade. She climbed Machu Picchu in Peru, one of the tallest mountains in the world, and during the hike hid in an outhouse made of branches and palm fronds for two hours one night as a mountain lion prowled just outside. As I write this, she is directing a full-length feature film from a script that she wrote and which she is producing with one of her best friends.

She's only twenty-two years old.

And making that turkey was one of the highlights of her life.

"Dad, it made me so proud. It gave me such a sense of accomplishment," she said.

"It's the little things in life," I said.

"You are so right," she agreed.

I read the incredible WWII novel *From Here to Eternity* by James Jones almost forty years ago, and the part I remember, the one that stands out the most, is the part where a sergeant decides to commit suicide. He jumps from a pier into the ocean and when he has settled on the bottom, he puts a .45 automatic to his head and pulls the trigger. The book is more than eight hundred fucking pages long, so no, I am not going to take the time to leaf through that monster of a book to find the exact text, all apologies to Mr. Jones. In a nutshell, from what I can recall, the exact second after the sergeant pulls the trigger, he regrets his action and thinks of all the things he will now never be able to do again, like bang some hot chicks, drive a new Cadillac, raise a loving family, or eat a fat, juicy T-bone steak.

wonder.

That's the part that got me.

The part about the steak.

It really put his suicide, or more specifically the importance of life and death, into perspective for me. It is the little things in life, like the five minutes of joy that eating a perfectly grilled steak can bring you, that can truly define what the best of life is. Or cooking a perfect turkey for the first time.

Because you don't have to write the Great American novel. You don't have to find the cure for cancer. You don't have to invent a better mousetrap. You don't have to captain a winning professional sports team. You don't have to win an election. You don't have to make the cover of *Time* magazine. You don't have to struggle your whole life for that fifteen minutes of fame.

You can simply plant a seed and grow a rose.

Or cook a really fine egg.

*   *   *

Happy John and I were playing backgammon, for money of course, on my lanai when he asked me about a book I was reading that was sitting on the patio table where we had set up the backgammon board. We both had a tumbler filled with single malt Scotch whiskey in front of us, and the wives were off doing something, so we were in a good place. I picked up the book and told him it was a great read and was loaded with interesting observations about the wonders of the world around us.

"Let me give you an example," I said.

"This isn't about snowflakes is it?" said John.

I thought about the many intriguing topics in the book, trying to determine which one would best hold John's interest. John is a realist in the truest sense of the world. If he can't see it, touch it, eat it, drink it, fuck it, bet on it, or punch it, he's just not interested. John grew up rich, in a big mansion with servants, but he is street savvy, not necessarily book smart. His father was a wheeler dealer who owned a piece of some of the first casinos to go up in Las Vegas and who was a fixture at many of the country's top horse racetracks, often betting on his own stable of thoroughbreds. John recalls his father paying him and his best friend fifty bucks each when they were teenagers to sit outside the racetrack stables where his

wonder.

thoroughbreds were kept, from early evening until the next morning, to make sure no one tried to drug the horses before that day's races. It wasn't unusual for John to answer the doorbell at their house as a kid to find a couple of FBI agents asking to chat with his father. A friendly, older black guy who was his father's driver and who John recalls was almost like part of his family growing up was found with his throat slit, floating in a river near one of the racetracks, the victim of a bookie who got tired of waiting to be paid. So John grew up knowing the score.

John and his younger brother hit the ground running as hustlers. They sold name brand knock-off velour tracksuits out of the trunk of their car in the poorest, blackest parts of the city. They sold gray market cigarettes. They had kiosks in shopping centers. They had beachside gift shops. They had used car lots. And through all those ventures they fine-tuned their insight into what sells and what doesn't and how best to get the American public to buy, until they ended up running one of the country's largest distribution companies of small dollar items to convenience stores and drugstores from coast to coast. Now, like their father did, they live in big houses and drive expensive imports, but that doesn't mean they have forgotten their roots. Just recently John got a few threatening leg-breaker phone calls about some long ago business dispute and had to go to a meeting to straighten things out and at that meeting instead of bringing his briefcase he tucked his .38 Smith & Wesson into his pants waistband.

So, like I said, John knows the score.

With that in mind I took string theory, parallel universes, nanotechnology, wormholes and quantum mechanics off the possible discussion list.

"What do you know about gravity?" I asked.

"Nothing."

I told John about gravity and anti-gravity, about how gravity impacts time, about how gravity only pulls and doesn't push, about how gravity affects plants and people, about how the universe is continuing to expand because of gravity but one day will collapse back into itself. John's eyes glazed over and he started to gulp his drink. He looked furtively to the left and the right like a mouse trapped in a corner by a cat. I was losing him. He needed to be able to bite into something.

wonder.

"Let's say you and your brother were born as identical twins and the day you were born someone kidnapped your brother and took him to live at the very top of the tallest mountain in the world. And then thirty years later, the kidnapper brought him back and you were reunited."

"Okay, I'm listening," said John. He liked the kidnapping part.

"Well, believe it or not, when you meet your identical twin after thirty years, he will look younger than you and actually be younger than you."

"Get the fuck out of here," said John. *"You just said we were identical twins born at the exact same time. So how could he be younger than me?"*

I explained that gravity affects the passage of time and that the farther you get from the surface of the Earth, the less the gravitational pull is, and that time slows down as the pull of gravity decreases. In reality, after thirty years your twin brother might only be a few minutes younger that you because mountains aren't that high. But it you had a rocketship that went fast enough and far enough, it would be possible to put your twin brother on that rocketship and blast him into space and have him come back thirty years later and have only aged by one day.

John started to get that glazed look again.

He's a sports nut, so I go that route.

"Did you know that if you dribble a basketball, the ball itself never actually touches the ground?" I said.

That was a good one. That one I knew he would appreciate.

"I think you are touched in the head," said John.

So, I explained how when you bounce a basketball, as the ball heads toward the ground it compresses the air between the bottom of the ball and the ground. As the compressed space becomes smaller and smaller, the density of the air in that space becomes more packed and energy charged, so that when the ball comes back up, it is actually the compressed air and its relation to gravity that is shooting the ball back up, and it's not because the ball hit the hard surface of the ground and bounced back up. Which also means, I said to John, that when we are walking on the ground, our feet are never actually touching the ground.

"And it's all because of gravity," I said. *"Isn't that so cool?"*

"You scare me," said John. *"You really do."*

wonder.

John took a nice long sip of his single malt Scotch, wiped his lips with the back of his hand, nodded his head a few times as he mulled something over in his head, looked at me, and said, *"Let me ask you a question."*

"Go ahead."

"Let's say I am up to bat at Wrigley Field."

"Okay."

"And I crack the very first pitch and the baseball goes flying over the second baseman's head, hits the grass in the outfield, bounces three times, and then the center fielder catches it."

"Okay."

"When the centerfielder looks at that ball in his glove, will there be green grass stains on that white baseball?"

"Of course."

"Well, if, like your basketball story, the baseball never actually touches the ground, how can there be green grass stains on the ball?"

Shit.

He had me.

"Well, Mr. Smarty Pants?" he asked.

He smiled and took another sip of scotch.

"Can I freshen your drink, John?"

"No, I'm good."

John stopped smiling and got a serious look on his face.

"Actually," he said, *"I have to admit that this is some really interesting stuff. Can I look at that book for a minute?"*

"Sure," I said. Apparently he did appreciate the subject matter. I handed him the book, a brand new hardback copy.

John held the book and looked at the front and then turned it around and looked at the back. Then, without even turning around, he threw the book with a mighty heave over his right shoulder into my pool.

"That," said Happy John, *"is what I think of your fucking book. Now can we please play some backgammon."*

A few months later all the couples went to the beach. We boated out to a small island a few miles offshore. The women knocked down margaritas under an umbrella while Happy John and Dan the Beautiful Snowflake and I sat in lawn chairs on the beach. I was sitting between the two of them. Our toes were in the wet sand and the waves were gently lapping at our feet.

"You know," I said. *"Isn't it amazing that the ocean always ends at the same place on every shore all around the world? These waves are ending right at our feet and way over there on the mainland they are ending at the same place. The ocean is thousands of miles long in every direction and many miles deep but the waves always end up on shore at the exact same spot. There is never more than a thirty yard spread between low tide and high tide. I mean, come on, if you shake a bowl of water, the water will spill over the sides, but people build beachfront high rise towers just a few hundred yards from the water every day and never worry about it. It's so incredible. I just don't understand how it all works. Why aren't there waves crashing over our heads right now? What do you guys think?"*

Neither of my two buddies answered me. They didn't even look at me. They both kept staring straight ahead at the ocean. Then one of them spoke.

"Personally, I think we should just kill him," said Dan the Beautiful Snowflake.

"Count me in," said Happy John.

* * *

I don't have the *TCB List* on any of my computers at home, but before leaving work yesterday I had looked at the list to remind me what my suicide chores for the weekend would be. On tap for today is deciding where to do the deed this coming Tuesday, the time of day to do it, and what to wear while doing it. Also, today I need to throw away my porn collection and any other things that are in the house that might prove to be embarrassing after my departure. And I need to go to the store to get something for the slow cooker.

"Be back in a few," I say to my wife as I grab my car keys. *"Do you need anything at the market?"*

"Nope."

Boo follows me to the door, his tail furiously wagging back and forth. He thinks we are going to the office. For such a smartass dog you would think he would know what day of the week it is.

wonder.

"I'm not going to the office, Goober. Just relax. I'll be back shortly."

He keeps whining as I go out the front door and shut it. On the drive to the market, I think about what to buy for what will be my last meal using my handy-dandy slow cooker. Some tender veal shanks for a tasty osso buco with capellini noodles and a spicy marinara sauce? Some braised short ribs smothered in tangy barbecue sauce accompanied by two baked potatoes loaded with butter, sour cream, chives and bacon bits and a Caesar salad? A whole cut up chicken in teriyaki sauce with pineapple slices, onions, carrots, green and red peppers, and some homemade Jasmine rice?

Don't be fooled, I am not a gourmet chef. I am but an egg cooker.

But my slow cooker, which is basically a very expensive and very huge crock pot, can make a gourmet cook out of anyone. I just buy all the ingredients, toss them into the slow cooker, put the setting on low and let the mishmash cook for eight hours. The recipes say I should dredge the meat through flour and brown it first, and deglaze the drippings, and add in various spices at different times, and put the vegetables into the pot after the meat has been cooking for a few hours, blah, blah, blah. Fuck that, I just throw everything into the slow cooker at once and then go outside to the lanai and chain smoke and play Internet poker, stopping every few hours to go inside and lift the cooker lid up for a good whiff, a few stirs with a big wooden spoon, and maybe a dash or two of salt and pepper.

I think long and hard about my options and decide on the chicken.

My brother-in-law Ricky, who is married to my wife's sister, is a master at cooking barbecued ribs and chicken on an outdoor grill. Being a good old Southern boy, he calls chicken *yard bird* which just amuses the shit out of me.

"Why don't ya'll come out to the house this weekend for some yard bird," he would say when my wife and I were newlyweds. We always accepted, mainly because the food was incredible but also because my wife and I didn't have a pot to piss in when we were first married and so never turned down a free dinner. We ate a lot of dinners and went to a lot of parties at Ricky's house in those early years and I would always buy just one six-pack of very cheap beer on the way over to their house. I knew I would end up drinking two

wonder.

or more six-packs of beer at those dinners and parties, but I could only afford one six pack, so when the beer I bought was gone, I would start drinking Ricky's beer. I did that for years, eating all his food and drinking all his beer.

And Ricky never said a word. Not once.

Which is why after I finally stopped being a broke ass newspaper reporter and put on my entrepreneur hat and started making money, I would fight Ricky over every dinner bill or bar tab. Whenever possible, everything was my treat. I would give Ricky the shirt off my back, and I think he knows that.

At the market I point to a nice plump whole chicken and ask one of the butchers behind the counter to cut it up, then I grab some white onions, whole carrots, green and red peppers, a pineapple, a bag of jasmine rice and a bottle of teriyaki marinade. A thick New York style cheesecake covered with strawberries catches my eye in the chilled display case and into my cart it goes.

I once asked Happy John, who is a big tipper like me and who is also a frequent shopper at this particular market, if he ever gives a tip to the butcher who slices, dices and wraps up his order.

"Hell no," said John. "Why, do you?"

"I always do," I said. "I slip the butcher who does my order a five or ten dollar bill depending on how big my order is."

"Why would you do that?"

"Well, sometimes it's a lot of work. Like if I have him hand make hamburger patties, or if he has to carve some special cuts of meat."

"You are crazy."

"Well, what do you do when you go to the market," I asked.

"I go inside, I take a number ..."

"Oh," I said, interrupting him, "you have to take a number?"

* * *

I was at my friend Kevin's house for a barbecue recently. Kevin, who is Jewish, had cooked pork ribs. None of my friends play by the rules. The women were inside the house daintily picking at their food and the guys, about a half dozen of us, were outside on the lanai.

Since it was ribs on the menu, that meant that the sounds coming from the guys grouped around the table on the lanai sounded like those from a pack of hyenas tearing apart a still breathing antelope, with barbecue sauce covering faces and hands, and a pile of bleached white discarded rib bones growing higher and higher in the center of the patio table.

All of us live in the same golf course community in expensive houses that cost more than any house our parents ever owned. We are all college educated with high-paying corporate jobs. The wives all have on multi-carat diamond tennis bracelets; the husbands all wear Rolex or Cartier watches.

At that moment a 727 passenger jet flew over the house. I could see, but not hear, the plane as it crossed over the top of Kevin's screen enclosure, a trail of snow white exhaust cutting a straight line through the light blue of the mid-afternoon sky.

Which made me think of something interesting to share.

I set the rib I was working on down, and said, *"You know, isn't it amazing. There is a giant plane flying through the air above us. We have walked on the moon. We now have cars and cell phones and the Internet and cable TV. We've found cures for almost every disease. We have X-ray machines and nuclear bombs. We've made all these technological advancements, and still, we sit around this table gnawing on animal bones just like the cavemen did a million years ago."*

All of the guys stopped chewing, biting and tearing at the ribs in their hands and looked at me for a moment.

No one said a word.

Then they all went back to chewing, biting and tearing at the ribs in their hands.

Case closed.

* * *

"What's for dinner?" my wife asks when I get home.
"Chicken."
"With the pineapple?"
"You bet."
"Sounds good."

As she asks these questions, Boo is bouncing up and down at my feet like his legs are made out of pogo sticks. He won't stop bouncing until I reach down and pet him and acknowledge his existence. He is so excited that I am back home. His protector from the coyotes and his food provider and his skilled belly scratcher has returned, so now he can relax. I read somewhere that dogs have no concept of time, so when you leave, they think you are never coming back. Boo sees that I am back, he goes through a few uncontrolled moments of canine hysteria to show how excited he is about not being an orphan, and then two minutes later, it's like I don't even exist. He won't give me the time of the day. It's back to his regular routine, which for Boo means chasing the squirrels who taunt him from the other side of the screen enclosure that surrounds the lanai, sleeping on the couch, in our bed, in his cage, and in another half dozen of his favorite spots in the house, making a circuit around the kitchen floor once an hour to see if any crumbs have been dropped, and occasionally watching a little bit of TV. You should see him work the remote control.

I pull out the slow cooker, peel and chop up the veggies, toss the veggies, the cut-up chicken, the teriyaki marinade and a can of chicken broth into the cooker, put the setting on low and hit start.

Yummy.

* * *

When you start ticking off the list of wonders of the world, you can't leave out the human body which, like the human spirit, is both the most indestructable and the most fragile thing on our planet.

I wrote a news article once about a guy who was shot nine times by his brother after an argument over who was going to get to eat the last porkchop at the dinner table. Hey, before you judge, I can promise you people get shot over a whole lot less. The fight started at the dinner table when both brothers reached across at the same time and stabbed their forks into the last porkchop on the plate. The two brothers, who were in their mid twenties, started yelling at each other, which then went to fisticuffs and an overturned dinner table, and then one of the brothers grabbed a .22 rifle and started blasting away. Think Cain and Abel, but instead of fighting over who God likes best, the bone of contention, pardon the pun, was over one of Mom's tasty grilled chops.

The brother with a gun started chasing the brother without a gun through their parent's small shotgun house. They call them shotgun houses because they are long narrow houses, only about twenty feet wide, where you can stand in the front doorway and fire a shotgun all the way down the hallway and right out the back door without hitting anything. In this case, though, as the brother without a gun ran down that long hallway, he was getting hit plenty. He was shot, fell down and got up running, and repeated that process again and again, until he crashed through the screened back door and collapsed in the back yard with nine .22 caliber bullets in him.

And he lived.

A month later I wrote a news article about a young kid who accidentally shot his fourteen-year-old sister in the neck with a pellet gun.

And she died.

Made no sense. A guy gets shot nine times with a real gun and is out of the hospital in less than a week, and a girl gets shot once with a glorified BB gun and dies.

I saw that kind of stuff all the time when I was a reporter. A guy slams his Corvette into a bridge abutment at ninety miles an hour, totals his car and walks away without a scratch, while across town a soccer Mom runs into the back of another car at thirty miles an hour and dies from a broken neck and her SUV isn't even dented. Of course, true to form, the guy in the Corvette was an asshole who was drunk and being chased by police for beating the fuck out of his girlfriend with a tire iron, while the soccer Mom was the loving mother of two on her way to the school to pick her kids.

I was waiting in a hospital emergency room once to get an injured toe looked at when two young guys came rushing in. One of the guys told the admissions nurse that he had just been struck by lightning. I remember he said it very calmly.

"It's true, it's true, I swear to God," said his overly excited buddy. *"We were playing football, he went up for a pass and while he was in the air a bolt of lighting hit him smack dab in the head."*

Mr. Excitable stopped, took a breath and added, *"We even had to stop the game."*

The admissions nurse looked at the first guy and asked, *"How do you feel?"*

"I feel all right, I guess."

"Okay. Take a seat. We'll get to you when we can."

wonder.

I thought that was the coolest thing I had ever heard. Every guy wishes he had a story like that to tell. *Oh yeah, well that's nothing. Did I ever tell you about the time I was struck by lightning?*

Forget about serial killers, head-on collisions and AIDs. Our world all by itself can be a pretty rough place to live in. We may have posturepedic mattresses, fabric softeners and Valium, but this planet is as harsh for humans today as it was millions of years ago. Just in the past six months in the city where I live, a woman was killed and eaten by an alligator, an infant was killed and half swallowed by her family's twelve-foot long pet python, and a young child was mauled and killed by a neighbor's pit bull. Even my niece, the one who was bit in the face by a pit bull when she was a youngster, ended up in the emergency room last month with her hand swollen to the size of a cantaloupe after she was bit by a water moccasin while working in her garden. I mean, really, how many people do you know who have been attacked by a pit bull and also bitten by a water moccasin. *"If I were you, I wouldn't be going to the zoo any time soon,"* I told her.

Then there are hurricanes and earthquakes and tornadoes. Just when we were getting complacent, God reached into his bag of tricks and introduced us to a wonderful new word called tsunami. Granted, tsunamis have been around since the beginning of time, but before that huge tsunami tidal wave, actually a series of tidal waves, hit and killed over 150,000 people sunbathing on the shores of the Indian Ocean in 2004, most people couldn't even spell the word much less define it. My favorite part about that tsunami was the part where all of the animals, from dogs to elephants to flamingos to monkeys, started running inland long before the tidal wave hit. More than 150,000 human bodies ended up bobbing like pieces of chum in that ocean water, but very few animal bodies were found. So, who's really smarter, us or them? I know what Boo would say.

All the nuclear bombs in the world don't have the power, or the vindictiveness, of that mischievous strumpet Mother Nature. Her weapons of mass destruction make ours look like Tinkertoys.

So we need to learn our place.

"This we know: the earth does not belong to man, man belongs to the earth. All things are connected like the blood that unites us all. Man does not weave this web of life. He is merely a strand of it," -were the words of wisdom from a Native American leader from the

early 1800s. His real name was "si al" but the white man called him Chief Seattle. Go figure.

A reporter I used to work with told me about an attorney we both knew when I called the newspaper years after leaving and we had one of those whatever happened to so-and-so conversations. I don't know if the entire story is true but, like most media people, I never let the truth get in the way of a good story.

The very flashy, but also very talented, defense attorney she was talking about was always on the front page of our newspaper because of the high profile cases he handled. He was very liberal and open-minded and handled lots of common people against the evil system types of cases, so it was kind of surprising what happened to him.

He was a real maverick and knew how to make waves. One afternoon he was making waves again, but this time it was because he was on his expensive ski boat with his latest nubile young girlfriend. They were doing a little bit of water skiing and a whole lot of hammering down of cocktails at the huge beautiful lake on the outskirts of our city.

The attorney, who was three sheets to the wind, stood up on the bow of his speedboat, pulled his dick out and stared peeing into the lake.

"You really shouldn't do that," said his girlfriend, who was sitting at the back of the boat sipping her cocktail.

"Why not?" slurred the attorney.

"Because it's not nice to do that to Mother Nature," said the girlfriend.

"Fuck Mother Nature," said the flashy, yet talented, attorney.

Whereupon, a bolt of lightning came out of the clear blue sky, struck the attorney in the head, and killed him deader than a doornail.

"You have got to be kidding me," I said to my former co-reporter.

"I shit you not," said she.

There are just so many great things about that story. The power of Mother Nature. The look on the girlfriend's face. The fact that the attorney spent his life helping the poor and less fortunate but he still got zapped. The first thought that you know ran through his girlfriend's head, *Nobody is going to fucking believe this story.*

wonder.

It defies belief. As do flying dinosaurs and beautiful snowflakes and basketballs that never touch the ground and tidal waves that spare monkeys.

Which, I think, is kind of wonderful.

* * *

Time to trash the porn.

"I think I'm gonna clean my closet," I say to my wife.

She rolls her eyes. I clean and organize my closet every month. I am a neat freak, bordering on OCD.

My buddy Vegas Jack is also a very organized guy. I was walking through a casino with Jack when he pulled out his Italian wallet to see how much cash he had on him. An Italian wallet is simply a thick rubberband. You take all of your bills and fold them in half, then slip your credit cards and drivers license into the middle of the folded bills, and then double wrap that thick rubberband around the whole packet. As Jack counted the money, I watched as he flipped each bill so that the bills were all facing the same way and then he organized the bills by denomination, with the hundreds on the outside working their way down to the smaller bills on the inside.

"Hey, I do the same thing," I said. *"I put all my bills in order by denomination too."*

"Yeah?" said Jack. *"But then I organize mine by serial number."*

Jack can be a very funny guy.

He and I were playing craps shoulder to shoulder at a table packed with high rollers one night and I had lost five times in a row.

"I am an idiot. I totally suck," I said.

"Please," said Jack. *"Do not belittle yourself. That's my job."*

Like I said, a funny guy.

In my closet I find my porn stash and toss the assorted magazines and DVDs into a trash bag.

Okay, two trash bags.

When I was about thirteen years old, I was riding my bike in our neighborhood one afternoon and I rode right over the top of a book that someone had apparently dropped in the street. It was actually more of a digest, or whatever the hell you call something that's not quite a book and not quite a magazine. As I rode over it, I looked down and because the digest was facing away from me I had to read the title upside down and I thought I saw the word *Photography* in the title.

I had ridden another few blocks when I had one of those *wait a minute* moments, and when you have one of those moments, you always stretch out the words like a comedian setting up a punch line. So what went through my mind was, *"Waaaaiiiittttt a minute. That didn't say Photography, that said Pornography!"*

I made a quick U-turn and raced back to where the digest was, saying a prayer to God that the book would still be there. It was. Straddling my bike in the middle of the street, I leaned over, picked the digest up and flipped to the middle pages. Yes indeed, it was all about pornography, or else the photo I saw of a woman on her knees with a giant cock in her mouth was illustrating some new type of camera lens technique.

I raced home, bolted into my bedroom and locked the door. A few hours and many, many tissues later I came out of the room. My Mom saw me in the hallway and said, *"Son, you look wore out."*

"Mom," I said, *"you have no idea."*

When you find the Holy Grail as a young teenager you can't keep that secret to yourself. Soon my friends were making daily visits to my bedroom to look at the digest and they all asked if they could take it home for a night or two, you know, just so they could read the educational text. I said no to all of them except to my good buddy Pat who lived across the street. When he returned the digest a few days later, I didn't notice that one of the pages was missing. He took that page with him to school and it was a big hit at his middle school because on that page was a photo of a woman giving a dog a blowjob. Why he chose that canine love photo to tear out of the digest out of all the photos he had to choose from I really can't say, so you'd have to ask Pat yourself about that. Of course Pat got caught by one of the teachers and the school called his parents and he got into a lot of trouble, but, to his credit, he didn't rat me out and instead made up some story about how he had found the photo at the park. He was big man on campus at his middle school for the rest of the semester, although he told me that all of the girls stopped talking to him.

I hid the porno digest under the carpet under my dresser. To get to it you had to move the heavy dresser and then lift up the carpet, which was wall to wall carpet that I had cut a small flap into.

wonder.

Over the coming years other porno mags would find their way there and I was sure my secret hiding spot was safe, although my Mom wondered why we were always out of tissues. Many years later at one of our family reunions, I told my little brother, who I had shared that bedroom with, about my secret hiding spot.

"*Secret? Bro, I read every porno mag you ever hid there,*" he said. "*And by the way, you're a pervert.*"

I know the part about the photo of the woman and the dog sounds gross, but it actually happens. Charles, one of my friends from high school and then college, became a doctor and in the process had to work weekends in the emergency room at the city's public hospital where the results of all sorts of incredible mayhem end up. He would regale us with stories about the horrors he saw come into that emergency room, but his best story would have to be about the night the ambulance attendants wheeled in a middle-aged woman who was flat on her back and pinned on top of her was a ninety-pound German Shepherd.

That's Shepherd as in the dog, not a guy from Germany who herds sheep.

Charles explained that, when enlarged, a dog's penis can end up with a huge knot the size of a tennis ball at the end of the shaft, and apparently the woman on the stretcher discovered this peculiar trait a little too late and could not get Rover's happy stick out of her most personal opening. Thus the call to 911, the very embarrassing trip to the emergency room, a hypodermic needle stuck by Charles into the dog's butt to make his erection disappear, and the woman probably saying to herself, *Free at last, free at last, thank God Almighty I am free at last.*

"*So,*" I said to Charles, "*did you ask the woman why she was fucking her dog?*"

"*No, we never ask those types of questions.*"

"*Was she hot?*"

"*Yeah, kind of.*"

"*Do you think her medical insurance covered it?*"

"*Good question.*"

Charles was a born and bred Southern boy but he was still a smart motherfucker. You have to be to make it through all those years of medical school.

wonder.

He and a half dozen other Southern boys were at my tiny apartment one night, crammed into a living room with less seating space than a mini van. We were all there for a bachelor party that I was throwing for a guy I worked with at the newspaper. With ice cold Old Milwaukee beers in their hands, they waited as I spooled the first of three 8mm stag films onto my Dad's borrowed projector and flashed the pornos onto a white sheet taped above my front door. The first film was a lesbian flick and the second film was of a couple screwing in a hotel room. The guys all hooted and hollered and joked through both films.

Then I put on the third 8mm film.

Which was a film of a huge black dude screwing the everlasting shit out of a white chick with pale skin and blonde hair. The room got real quiet. All you could hear was the whirring of the old projector. Nobody was drinking their beer. Nobody was talking. I suddenly realized that showing this particular film to a room full of guys for whom the word nigger rolled off their tongues with no hesitation was probably not the best idea for a liberal like myself who, as a military dependent, had lived all over the world and was a bit more open and accepting of such things. One by one, each of the Southern boys turned to look at me sitting behind them working the projector. I started wondering if I could get to my bedroom located right behind me and out the window before they grabbed me. My finger inched toward the stop button on the projector, and that's when Charles said:

"You know, I don't mind when he fucks her. But it really pisses me off when he kisses her."

The Southern boys all turned to look at Charles.

And then they all started laughing their asses off.

And we watched all three films several more times, and each time we played the interracial flick one of the Southern boys halfway through would say Charles' line and they would all start laughing again.

Like I said, Charles was a smart motherfucker.

* * *

I carry the two trash bags of porn out to the garage. I place each bag of porn into two more green plastic trash bags so they are triple wrapped and then tie them up tightly before putting them into one of the two huge trash cans on wheels that we take out to the curb each week. The trashmen come on Tuesday and I don't want them tossing the flimsy single bags into the truck and having one of them break open, and they see all that porn and then want to come back and rape my wife late one night because they think we're into the kinky lifestyle.

I'm thoughtful like that.

It dawns on me that the trashmen will come by Tuesday morning to take the trash away, and then later that day the police and the coroner's office will come by to take my body away. My porn will be taken to a dump and buried in the ground. And my body will be taken to a cemetery and buried in the ground. My body and *Butt Bangin' Babes Volume 9* sharing the same earth. Ashes to ashes, dust to dust.

I come back in, wash my hands, which I always do whenever I am even near a trash can, and then I make the circuit of my house, checking every room and closet and drawer to see if there is anything else incriminating that I need to toss out.

"What are you looking for?" asks my wife.

"Oh, nothing. Just puttering," I say.

I don't find anything else. I turn on my laptop computer. I'm not sure what might be on the laptop, so I just start deleting everything, from bookmarks to contact lists. Better safe than sorry. I grab both my iPods and do the same thing to them.

I go outside to the lanai for a cigarette. My wife joins me.

"What are we doing tonight?" I ask.

"I don't know. Want to go to a movie?"

"Sounds good to me."

I love going to the movies. So does my wife and so do our kids. Sounds relaxing after the chaos of last night's party.

"What's happening this week?" I ask. I need to know where my wife will be on Tuesday.

"Well I have a tennis match Tuesday morning," she says.

Bingo.

She mentions a country club that I know is an hour's drive away which means she will be up and gone Tuesday morning before I wake up and she won't be back until after noon. That gives me a three-hour window. She mentions other things going on this coming week but I don't pay attention because, what the fuck, I won't be around.

"You know Tuesday is your birthday," she says.

"Yeah, I know."

"Do you want to celebrate it on Tuesday or wait until the weekend and go out to dinner with the crew?"

"Let's wait until the weekend. Even for the presents and everything," I say. My wife is a very thoughtful person and she is very good about birthdays and holidays. There are always lots of gifts and a cake and candles and special cards. I don't want her planning all of that for this Tuesday.

That would be awkward.

* * *

I actually got in to see the emergency room doctor that day before Lightning Boy did.

"What's the problem, young man?" he asked.

I took the tennis shoe and sock off my right foot and showed him my big toe. The toe was swollen, but what really hurt was the giant blood blister under the entire toenail that had turned an ugly shade of blackish red. My foot had been in the wrong place at the wrong time when a very large guy from the other basketball team went up for a rebound and came down smack dab onto by big toe with his size thirteen Converse sneakers.

"Ouch," said the doctor.

I had been in that same emergency room six months earlier when I had a bad reaction to some penicillin I was taking for a strep throat. By bad reaction, I mean I was laying in bed and just stopped breathing. Completely. I went into the living room where my parents were watching TV, and since I couldn't talk, I started pointing at my mouth and my throat. My Dad tossed me into the car and rushed me to the base hospital just a few miles away. By then I was a lovely shade of blue, somewhere between royal blue and ultramarine blue. They put me on the table and I looked around at all the millions of dollars of high tech medical equipment in the bright white emergency room. Then the doctor came walking through the door. He was dressed all in white and I swear to God there was a white glow all around him. He slowly walked over, in no rush whatsoever, placed

wonder.

his hand on my forehead, smiled down at me and said, *"You are going to be all right, young man."*

And I started to breathe again. Just like that.

So I felt good to be back in that emergency room with those millions of dollars of high tech medical equipment and a doctor who had spent a bazillion years in medical school just so he could provide me with the best and latest in medical care.

The doctor started whistling a tune, reached over to a nearby counter and grabbed a paperclip, unfolded the paperclip into a long straight line, pulled a Zippo lighter out of his pocket, flicked out a nice fat flame, put one end of the paperclip into the flame until the metal glowed red, grabbed my big toe with his other hand, slowly pushed the tip of that fire hot paperclip through the top of my toenail, and then quickly pulled the paperclip out as a geyser of blackish red blood shot out of the hole a good foot into the air.

"All done," he said.

Made me wonder what he had in store for Lightning Boy.

* * *

I light another cigarette as my wife goes back inside to fold the laundry on the couch while she watches a tennis match on TV.

Gives me time to think. I know the day of the deed, Tuesday, and now I know the time, anywhere between nine in the morning and noon. Now the only question is where. I know it will be messy so I think about the back yard. That would certainly be easy to clean up. All you would need is a garden hose. But my neighbors might hear the shot and come outside and find my body. That's too much of a public scene for something that is meant to be private.

So it needs to be inside the house. I finish the cigarette, go inside and wander from room to room. I do it several times and always end up back in our huge master bathroom. It's perfect. It has the giant mirror across the two sinks that I can look into to make sure the barrel orientation is perfect, and it has easy to clean stone tile on the floor, not carpet. I form my right hand into a gun with my index finger straight out and my thumb sticking over the top like a hammer and put the make believe gun up to the side of my head and look into the mirror.

Gives me a bit of a chill.

wonder.

In the mirror I notice the huge sunken bathtub behind me. I carefully step backwards into the tub, with my finger still pointing at the side of my head, and I look in the mirror again. Much better. Much easier to clean up.

Finally, a use for the bathtub. I have lived in this house for twenty years and have never once used the tub. I always use the walk-in shower instead. If I take the overall square footage of my house and what my monthly mortgage used to be and then break out the square footage taken up by the sunken bathtub, I figure I was paying about fifty bucks a month for that tub, or about $12,000 over the past twenty years. And the first time I will ever use it, I will be using it as a receptacle to blow my brains out in. That's an expensive receptacle.

I decide I will fill the tub up with twelve inches of water so that the blood does not congeal on the sides of the white porcelain. I am right-handed, so if I stand in the tub and face the mirror, that means the bullet will exit the left side of my head and hit a half wall that separates the tub from the walk-in shower. We spent a lot of money to renovate that shower, so I also decide that I will hold two bunched up beach towels to the left side of my head with my left hand to hopefully keep the bullet from blasting through the wall and chipping the ridiculously expensive shower tile. I could hold a thick piece of lumber or a metal plate instead of a soft towel, but that would look silly. And I shouldn't be chuckling when I'm looking in that mirror and pulling the trigger.

I step into my walk-in closet and look through all my clothes for what I will wear on Tuesday. I want to be comfortable, but also fashionable.

At the top of my closet is a light fixture that holds two of those long, forty-eight-inch fluorescent bulbs. I turn that light on every single day. Sometimes I leave it on all day. And in the twenty-plus years I have lived in this house, I have never had to replace either of those two fluorescent bulbs. I have replaced the fluorescent bulbs in my garage and my kitchen hundreds of times over the past twenty years, but those two bulbs in my closet have never gone out. Remember those Ford Pinto and Maverick cars from the 1970s? When was the last time you ever saw one? They made millions of them and today they have just evaporated. Whole cars from just

wonder.

thirty years ago have turned to dust but my twenty-year-old light bulbs still keep chugging along. That is so fucking weird.

One night I started to tell Happy John and Dan the Beautiful Snowflake about my mystery fluorescent bulbs and got the words, *"Isn't it amazing ..."* out of my mouth before I thought better about it and instead asked them if they had watched the previous night's ball game.

I turn on the closet light and, after more than two decades, it again comes on nice and bright. *"Right on motherfucker,"* I say to the light. I pick out my favorite pair of blue jeans.

And a black Tommy Bahamas shirt.

Because I look really good in black.

* * *

There's a game everyone plays at one time or another, along the lines of, *"If you could have a private dinner with any person, either living or dead, who would it be?"*

For me, it would be Albert Einstein. I think he was the greatest thinker to ever walk the planet. I like that he made sure the most famous scientific equation of all time was easy to remember, $E = mc2$. And I like that he took a really cool photograph, what with that wild ass Three Stooges hair of his.

Einstein actually came up with two killer theories, special relativity and general relativity, and they have to do with gravity and space and time and speed and, of course, energy and mass. After becoming the first rock star in the world of science, Einstein spent the last years of his life trying to come up with the universal theory, which is the theory of everything. You know, that whole where did we come from, why are we here, is there life after death, is there a God, where do those missing socks from the laundry really go thingamajig. I love that last word. It should be called the thingamajig theory, not the universal theory.

Einstein died before he solved the thingamajig puzzle, but he spent many years tackling it and so I think he would probably have a lot of great thoughts to share on that subject and many others if we were to get together for a cozy dinner. *Why* may be just a tiny three-letter word, but it is one of the most provocative words in the history

238

wonder.

of humanity, and I would relish the chance to bring that word up in a private dinner with Albert Einstein.

"Albert, my man ..." I would ask, after we had finished our Caesar salads and were both nice and relaxed and waiting for our entrees.

" ... why are there fifty-two cards in a deck? I mean, really, why not forty-eight or fifty-six or ..."

* * *

My wife and I eat the slow cooker chicken while watching TV. It tastes scrumptious. I am a proud chef.

I lock Boo in his cage and my wife and I drive to the movie theater. I buy the biggest bag of popcorn they have and a giant diet Coke.

My wife is a little unhappy.

Because she knows she has to sit next to me.

When we go to the movie as a family, my wife and my son refuse to sit next to me. I always take a seat on the aisle and they make my daughter sit in the seat next to me. Apparently I am a loud popcorn eater. I eat the popcorn one kernel at a time and make the bag last until the end of the movie. The nonstop crunching drives everyone in the family absolutely fucking crazy, but my daughter loves me, so she takes the hit and sits next to me. I reward her several times during every movie by closing my mouth to capture a truly odoriferous popcorn belch and then slowly blowing the belched air out of my mouth sideways into my daughter's face as she stares ahead at the movie screen.

"Daaaaaddd!" she'll yell out loud in the theater, and my wife and son will smile, happy to be two seats down from me.

"If you burp in my face, I will fucking hit you," my wife says as we take our seats.

It's a good movie, the popcorn is nice and fresh and salted perfectly, the diet Coke has just the right amount of ice in it, nobody was talking or crinkling candy wrappers behind us, and I eat the very last popcorn kernel just as the end credits come up on the screen.

All in all, a perfect outing for the last movie I will ever see.

* * *

wonder.

"Guess what?" says Boo

"What's that, Snooks?" I answer. I call Boo Snooks a lot, which is short for Snookems. I also call him Monkey-Boy quite often. Don't even ask me why. Just seems appropriate. Mostly, I call him Boo, but if I'm angry at him, like when he's taking too long doing his thing in the front yard, I will call him Boudreaux, and say his name nice and loud and stretch out all the syllables.

"I saw a UFO once," says Boo.

"Sure you did," I say, my sarcasm thick as maple syrup.

"I'm telling you, I did."

"Oh yeah, and when was that?"

"Just the other day."

"Well, why didn't you tell me about it?"

"We weren't on speaking terms back then."

"So, why bring it up now?"

"Because you've been talking about the wonders of the world, and I've seen some pretty crazy stuff." Boo sounds really excited.

"What color was the UFO?" I ask.

Boo hems and haws for a bit and then says, *"It was purple. Yeah, that's right, it was a real pretty purple."*

"You don't say."

"And it had green lights on it. Lots and lots of green lights."

"Wow, that's incredible."

Boo is quiet for a few moments and then says, *"I don't think you believe me. I detect a certain skepticism in your voice."*

"You are mistaken. I absolutely believe you. Tell me more. What was it like when they abducted you and then flew off and did all those experiments on your bellybutton?"

"I'm not talking to you any more."

I roll over on my side, switch on the nightstand light and grab my book. I read a few sentences and then feel bad. What the hell, maybe Boo did see a UFO, or what he thought was a UFO, or maybe he didn't see anything and just wants to be the center of attention for a little while. He is my best buddy, so what harm is it for me to humor him and make him feel important.

"I'm sorry, Boo," I say, *"perhaps you indeed did see a UFO."*

"Apology accepted," he says.

I can sense his contentment. I read a few pages of the book.

240

wonder.

"*Riddle me this Batman?*" says Boo.

"*Shoot.*"

"*If life is full of wonder, does that mean life is wonderful?*"

"*I guess so.*"

"*Well, if life is wonderful, why do you want to end yours?*"

"*Lobster is wonderful. But if I ate it every single day, after awhile I would get tired of it.*"

"*So, this is all about food?*" says Boo.

"*Maybe.*"

Boo is quiet for a solid minute. Then he says, "*You have no idea what an aggravating human being you can be.*"

Sunday, June 28

god.

"*I think I'm going to go to church this morning,*" I say to my wife.
"*Are you serious?*"
"*Yes.*"
"*Why?*"
"*I don't know. I just feel like it.*"
My wife gives me a perplexed look. We are C&E Catholics, which means we only go to church on Christmas Day and Easter Day, and even then it's like pulling teeth to round up the family.
"*Do you want me to go with you?*"
"*No, that's okay. I'm just going to pop in real quick.*"
"*Okay,*" says my wife, her eyebrows still raised.
I jump in the shower, get dressed and head for the door.
"*You're not going dressed like that are you?*" my wife asks. I am wearing faded jeans, a polo shirt and my ever-present Birkenstock sandals.
"*Jesus was big on sandals,*" I say.

* * *

god.

Tom, my buddy who I got arrested with that time outside the pizza parlor, and I drove my 1965 cherry red Mustang down to New Orleans when we were just sixteen years old. Don't even ask me how we convinced our parents to let us spend a weekend on decadent Bourbon Street at that impressionable young age.

It was during that trip that I came to the conclusion that there is no God, at least not the all-seeing, full of mercy and wisdom God who had been spoon fed to me over the past ten years of Catholic school attendance, the one who is in all those side profile paintings with a little halo around his shaggy mane. That realization did not come after witnessing the debauchery in the French Quarter, of which Tom and I partook our fair share, but instead it was because of the nuns.

Just south of New Orleans is the Lake Pontchartrain Causeway which, at twenty-four miles, is the longest bridge in the world. It is supported by 9,500 concrete pilings and connects the Louisiana cities of Metairie and Mandeville. It looks more like a highway than a bridge and is suspended about forty feet above the water the entire length of the bridge. At the halfway point you see nothing but flat highway in front of you, flat highway behind you, and water all around you. It's like you are floating on a road over the water. Very spooky.

Tom and I drove over the causeway that weekend to visit a friend of his. *"Be careful on the causeway,"* said his buddy after giving us directions.

"Why?" asked Tom.

"Because of the accident."

Several barges floating on the lake had smashed into some of the concrete pilings during the middle of the night two months earlier, and a whole section of the bridge had simply dropped into the lake. Police sealed off both ends of the bridge, but some cars were already on the causeway, and one of them went hurtling into the lake. The people in that car were happily driving along on a nice flat surface and then that surface just disappeared. They could probably see the continuation of the bridge on the other side, but between that spot and where they were was nothing but a forty-foot drop, in a car going sixty miles an hour, into the cold dark water of Lake Pontchartrain.

That car, said Tom's friend, was a brand new Cadillac.

god.

And it was full of nuns.
Which, I hate to admit, amused the fuck out of Tom and I.
"Can you imagine the look on their faces?"
"I wonder of one of them yelled, 'Jesus-Fucking-Chirst!'"
"What were nuns doing in a brand new Cadillac?"
And on and on. Granted, as we made those comments, we both leaned forward in our car seats to peer down the causeway as far ahead as possible to make sure we didn't suffer the same fate.
"Slow the fuck down," Tom would say to me every few minutes.
Poor taste jokes aside, it did perplex me that of all the cars that could have gone into the lake, it was a car full of nuns. Those women had given up the intimacy of a man's touch, the joy of raising their own children, and the comfort and warmth of a traditional family to live a spartan existence toiling away in God's name. And he had rewarded them by allowing them to die. Not by peacefully passing away in their sleep, but instead in a horrific and painful accident.
"It was God's will," Christians will say.
Nope. Not buying that.
If you tell me that the death of those nuns, and the deaths of million of children every year from the lack of clean drinking water, and the rape and murder of women and children every single day by the many sick fucks who walk this earth, and the hacking off of the arms and legs of children by machete-wielding tribesmen in South Africa, and the worldwide spread of AIDS are all part of God's will, then I don't want to have anything to do with that particular God. I'd rather you tell me that all that shit happens while God is taking a nap and he feels really bad about not being on top of things.
That I'll buy.

* * *

I get to the church a few minutes before the service is scheduled to start and sit in the second to last pew. I'm on the aisle, so I am tickled pink. But just as the organ music kicks in and the priest and his little altar helpers start walking down the aisle, a late arriving couple scoot into my pew and I have to move over so that claustrophobic me is now sandwiched between worshippers.
Motherfucker!
Did I just say, or think, that at church? My bad.

244

god.

I was about ten years old when I asked my Dad if he believed in God. I was thinking about that crap at a very early age. For some strange reason; when I asked him the question I was standing in our backyard and he was standing on the landing of the outside stairs that went to the second story of our house, so I was looking up at him when he answered. Kind of like a voice from on high.

He said that yes he believed in God.

"Why?" I asked.

My Dad thought for a minute before answering. He took his time because he knew that his son, the one who had just last month sold Dixie cups full of liquor to construction workers, was, like him, a pragmatist who would not suffer any religious pablum.

"If you look at the human body, at how all the organs and fluids and molecules inside our bodies work so well together, you just have to believe that someone or something much greater than us made us," said my Dad.

I went to Catholic schools for twelve years and have gone to church for fifty years and over all that time I have never had a nun or a priest or a parishioner explain to me why they believe in God in a more down to earth and believable way than my Dad did. Just tell it to me straight, baby.

For centuries priests said Mass in Latin which meant that no one sitting in the pews knew what the hell they were talking about. That was a smart move on their part. Keep the congregation in the dark so they don't ask any questions when the collection plate comes around. When priests eventually had to start saying Mass in the language of whatever country they were preaching in, it started tongues wagging.

"Did he just say that Mary was a virgin and gave birth to a child? That's physically impossible!"

"It gets better. Wait 'til he gets to the part about raising some guy named Lazarus from the dead."

"No shit. What's next, somebody turns water into wine?"

god.

When it's time for communion I stand up and get in line for that tasty wafer. I feel a little guilty because, technically, you are not supposed to put the body of Christ on your tongue if you have unconfessed sins in your heart. The last time I went to confession Nixon was President, so my heart is pretty much bursting with sins since I have not taken the time to sit down in a tiny closet with a priest and tell him about all my infractions and ask him to throw some Hail Marys my way to expunge them.

So the Big Guy will just have to add this latest sin to my list.

If he can find room.

When my Dad was ten years old, he and his younger brother, Teddy, were raking leaves in their front yard when their mother told them it was time for them to go to church and then to confession. As they started to leave, their father came out and told Teddy he had to stay and finish the raking chore. My Dad went to Mass, then went into the confessional booth. He told the priest his sins, and when he had finished, he said, *"Father, Teddy couldn't make it today, so these are his sins,"* and he proceeded to tell the priest what sins he thought his younger brother had committed since his last confession. Is that cute, or what.

They say that 99 percent of the men in the world masturbate and the other 1 percent lie about it. That may come as a shock to women, along with the news I passed on earlier about how every guy in the world also pees in the shower. Here's another truly horrible thing that most guys do. You know that part during the church service when people stand up and then walk down the runway to the altar to get a communion wafer or a sip of wine or a chunk of bread? Well, when young ladies and women walk up there, looking all nice and spiffy in their Sunday best, every guy who is sitting down watches them. And when those women get their wafer or wine or bread and turn around and walk back to their seats, as they pass by, every guy says to himself, *Her, I would fuck; Her, I wouldn't; Oh yeah, I'd definitely bang her; That one's a maybe.* And on and on for each and every woman, young or old, who walks by, even though we are sitting in church.

Yeah, we're pigs.

You're not telling us anything we don't already know.

Today I refrain from such debauchery. After I get my communion wafer, I sit in my pew and keep my head down until everyone else has sat down. Okay, I do take a quick peek at this one chick who could be a Victoria's Secret model.

It's just my nature.

* * *

The only bad thing about being a C&E Catholic is that those two Masses are the longest Masses of the year and the church is always packed to the rafters. One Easter the Mass that the family and I went to was even longer than usual because there were a dozen or so youngsters who were receiving their First Communion that day. They all sat in the front row wearing pretty spring dresses or little person suits and their beaming parents sat proudly in the pews behind them. The smiling priest came down from the altar, put his hands on the children's pew, and started telling them the importance of accepting the body of Christ for the first time.

"I'll bet all of you were so excited that you couldn't sleep last night," said the priest.

The children all nodded their heads.

"Did any of you dream about Jesus Christ last night?" asked the priest.

One young boy raised his hand.

The priest smiled an even bigger smile, looked around at all the people in the packed church, nodded his head knowingly, and said to the boy, *"Yes, my son, and what was Jesus doing in your dream?"*

"He was stabbing me in the head with a knife," said the boy.

Now I know what five hundred people gasping in unison sounds like.

His poor parents.

I laughed so hard that I had to go outside for a few minutes.

Priceless.

* * *

I pull my wallet out when they start passing the collection basket down the pews in front of me. I always carry $1,000 in $100 bills folded up in one of the pockets of my wallet. I used to give my kids a $100 bill each and tell them to fold it up and hide it in their wallet or purse.

god.

"There are very few problems you will get yourself into in life that a $100 bill won't get you out of," I would tell them.

My son asked me why, if that was true, I carried $1,000 in my wallet.

"Because the problems I get myself into are a whole lot bigger," I said.

The last time I got arrested, which was for DUI, Officer Tipton was nice enough to call my house, even though it was two in the morning, to see if anyone wanted to come get my car so he would not have to have it towed to the pound. My daughter was in town from New York so she drove to where I was sitting handcuffed in the back seat of Officer Tipton's patrol car, as did my son who lived just a few miles away. I twisted my body around and looked through the back window of the patrol car and saw Officer Tipton talking to my son and daughter, the red and blue flashing lights from his cruiser bouncing off their bodies. I smiled a big ass drunk smile, and my daughter smiled back and waved at me. Neither my son or my daughter looked upset, or even mildly surprised. Nobody will ever accuse me of having been a boring father.

Later that afternoon they both came to pick me up from the jail, along with my wife, who was so pissed off she didn't say a word the whole drive home, and even Boo, who was happy as could be to see me. In the car my daughter handed me my wallet, which Officer Tipton had given to her and my son when he turned my car over to them. She told me that when Officer Tipton handed her the wallet, he said, *"Do you know that there is $1,000 in your father's wallet. That's a hell of a lot of money to be carrying around."*

"No shit," said my daughter.

I pull the ten crisp $100 bills from my wallet, fan the bills out with Ben Franklin facing up and then drop all ten bills on top of the other money in the collection basket when the guy to my left passes it to me. I hand the basket to the teenaged boy who is sitting to my right and who is holding a one dollar bill that his father gave him. When he sees all those hundred dollar bills, his eyes about pop out of his head. As he hands the basket to his father with one hand, with his other hand he tugs hard on his father's sleeve to get his attention, motioning with his head toward the basket. His father doesn't respond, drops a ten dollar bill into the basket without even looking at the basket, and then passes it on. I know that on the ride home,

god.

the teenager will say, *"Dad, I can't believe you didn't see it! That man next to me put thousands of dollars into the basket!"*

"Sure he did, son," his father will say.

I pick up a hymnal on the pew next to me, open it and slowly and quietly tear out one of the pages. I fold the page several times into a small square and stick it into the pocket of the wallet where the money used to be. At some point, after I'm gone, one of my kids or my wife will have to go through my wallet, and when they get to the pocket where they know I hide my big bills, they'll find the page from the hymnal and have a clue about where the money went.

"Dad, then he stole a page from one of the hymnals!"

"Sure he did, son."

As the priest drones on, I wonder why I just dropped all that money into the collection basket, and I wonder why I am even sitting here at this church service. I don't believe in religion, I don't believe in God, and I don't believe in life after death. I do know, though, that in less than forty-eight hours I am going to kill myself. So maybe subconsciously I'm hedging my bets in case I'm wrong about the whole afterlife thing.

My good friend Ben the Chinaman and I were deep sea fishing last year when about thirty yards from our boat a scuba diver in a black wetsuit exploded like a shot straight up out of the water and started yelling for help. He scared the fuck out of us, because we were so far out in the ocean that you could not see land in any direction, everything had been so quiet and serene just a few seconds before, and the last thing we expected to see was another human being in the middle of nowhere.

Ben, who used to be in the Coast Guard which he says means he served in the military and which I say is bullshit because the only real military is the Army, Navy, Air Force or Marines, went right into Coast Guard mode, dropping his fishing pole, firing up the boat engine, and speeding over to the scuba diver who at that point was just barely floating on top of the water. When we got to him, he was so exhausted that he couldn't climb into our boat, he just hung onto the side. We finally pulled him into the boat, but not before I had Ben take a picture of me sitting next to the diver holding my clenched first above his head like he was a fish I had caught.

"So nice of you to pop in," I said.

god.

Ben asked the diver where he had come from, and the diver pointed off to the west, where we could just barely see another boat more than a half mile away. Turns out he was part of a scuba diving group, had became separated from his dive partner, and was swimming in the wrong direction trying to get back to the dive boat. We took him back. The dive boat captain didn't even know he was missing one of his divers.

On the way back to our fishing spot, Ben said, *"You know that guy would have drowned if we hadn't been there. He was too fatigued to swim any more and the dive boat was too far away to save him."*

"That's wonderful for us. We are so lucky," I said.

"What do you mean?" asked Ben.

"We saved that guy's life. So that means we are guaranteed to get into heaven."

My buddy Mean John doesn't think about getting into heaven as pearly gates that you walk up to and then ask if you made it onto the guest list. He looks at heaven like it is at the top of a very tall ladder that you must climb up. Whenever I am out and about with him and he sees a panhandler, he will give the bum a twenty dollar bill, then turn and smile at me and say, *"I just made it up another rung."*

My guess is I put that money into the collection basket and I went to the church service today for the very same reason that I buy a one dollar lottery ticket to try to win a multi-million dollar Lotto jackpot. I know that the chances of winning the lottery are about one in a billion, just like the chances of there being a heaven are about one in a billion, but it doesn't hurt to buy a ticket and hope for the long shot.

Because you just never know.

My lottery ticket would have God's custom designed logo on it, though, and not a particular religion's logo on it.

People tend to confuse God with religion.

Which makes no sense.

They are two different things.

God is what your personal answer is to the Big Question of why are we here, where did we come from, and where are we going.

Religion is simply a gang you join.

If you think using the word *gang* is a little harsh to describe organized religion, then you have apparently never opened a history

god.

book. Religious gangs make the Hell's Angel's and the Bloods & Crips look like Cabbage Patch kids. That is, unless I missed the news stories about biker and street gangs burning women at the stake, beheading men in the street, stoning children to death, hanging entire families on crosses, running concentration camps, practicing genocide, blowing up twin towers, convincing kids to be suicide bombers, and sending their gang members off to fight in Crusades that last more than two centuries.

If you trot out the adage that more people have been killed in the name of religion than for any other reason, Christians will answer that God doesn't kill people, people kill people. Sounds suspiciously like the excuse of gun enthusiasts who say that guns don't kill people, people kill people. God and guns, now that's a happy combination.

In an Internet forum someone actually answered the question of how many people, since the world was formed, have been killed in the name of religion by writing, *"My guess would be around 1,000."* The only thing scarier than that was that he didn't put one of those yellow smiley faces after his answer.

Belief in a personal God is much more exclusive than membership in an organized religion. The first item is something that only you can do, because when you die and either go to meet your Maker or go to rot in the ground, it will only be you making the trip. The second item is something that anybody can do who has the price of admission.

I suggest scrapping the whole religion thing. If being in a gang and having a secret handshake and getting dressed up every Sunday and singing goofy songs together and having somebody stand up and lecture you once a week is really that important to you, then join the Kiwanis Club or start selling Mary Kay cosmetics.

As Ben Kingsley said, *"God has no religion."* Well, actually it was Mahatma Gandhi who said it, but wasn't Sir Kingsley fucking great in the movie.

"When one person suffers from a delusion it is called insanity; when many people suffer from a delusion it is called religion," said American author and philosopher Robert Maynard Pirsig, who wrote the bestseller *Zen and the Art of Motorcycle Maintenance: An Inquiry into Values*. Dude, try a shorter title next time. Pirsig also had an IQ of 170 at the tender age of nine. Precocious little bastard.

god.

Remember that book, *Brave New World*, that we all had to read in high school? Thank God for Cliff Notes. Anyway, the book's author, Aldous Huxley, said, *"If we must play the theological game, let us never forget that it is a game. Religion, it seems to me, can survive only as a consciously accepted system of make-believe."*

German philosopher Karl Marx stirred up a real shit storm with a tome called *The Communist Manifesto* with the end results being the Berlin Wall, the Cold War, and some really great James Bond villians. He didn't just restrict his comments to how much he thought capitalism bites a big weenie. *"Religion,"* KM said, *"is the sigh of the oppressed creature, the heart of a heartless world, and the soul of soulless conditions. It is the opium of the people."*

I agree. Let's fire up the pipe.

When you think about it, the three words that have caused the most grief and misery in the world since man first walked upright are, *"Let's get organized."*

For our physical world, the *let's get organized* concept worked well for a while, like when all the cavemen got together to help Thor build his own hut, but in the ensuing centuries that loss of individuality and acceptance of the group dynamic brought us our social caste system and wars and dictators and prisons and nuclear bombs and seat belt laws.

Today, ten percent of the world's population owns eighty-five percent of the world's assets. More than eighty percent of the world's population lives on less than ten dollars a day. Half of the 2.2 billion children in the world live in poverty. Over ten million children die every year before they reach the age of five, two million of them simply because they do not have access to safe drinking water or adequate sanitation. Globally we shell out $780,000,000,000 on military spending which is $767,000,000,000 more than we spend on basic health and nutrition for the people of our world. In other words, we spend sixty times more on bombs than on rice and beans.

Comedian Bill Hicks had the right idea: *"Here's what we can do to change the world, right now. Take all that money we spend on weapons and defenses each year and instead spend it feeding and clothing and educating the poor of the world, which it would pay for many times over, not one human being excluded, and we could explore space, together, both inner and outer, forever, in peace."*

god.

Unfortunately, Hicks couldn't sell that plan, which prompted him to note that, *"We are experiencing a reality based on a thin veneer of lies and illusions. A world where greed is our God and wisdom is sin, where division is key and unity is fantasy, where the ego-driven cleverness of the mind is praised, rather than the intelligence of the heart."* Damn, that guy had a way with words.

So, it appears the *let's get organized* thing has not been a raging success for most of the people in our day to day physical world.

It gets even worse when you apply the *let's get organized* concept to our spiritual world, and give birth to that bastard stepchild called organized religion. Or, as I like to look at it, the debate over whose God has the better beard.

If you table organized religion, and all the ceremony and pomp and circumstance that comes with being in a religious gang, then that just leaves the focus on God. And there is only one reason that people believe in God.

Just one.

People believe in God because they want to get into heaven.

Screw all that *treat thy neighbor as you would have them treat you* bullshit, and all that *it is better to give than to receive* tripe, and all that *turn the other cheek* drivel.

What most people are thinking is this: *Sure God, whatever, I'll pretend to do all that silly crap, but I mainly want to make damn sure that there is life after death. For me.*

That's it. Period. End of story.

Personally, I'm certain there is no life after death.

But there is one thing that concerns me on the subject. Over the years when I have tried to lure my Mom into discussions about the ludicrousness of religion and the debatable existence of God and the laughable notion that there is life after death, she never takes the bait, and instead simply says, *"You need to believe."*

Which is the part that has me concerned.

I know there are two parts to me—a physical body and a nonphysical consciousness, which, for the sake of argument, we can call my soul.

I know that when I die my physical body goes straight into the ground, but I'm not totally positive about where my soul goes.

And that bugs me. Because I don't like loose ends.

god.

If my soul simply gets absorbed into the cosmic energy of the universe, that's fine and dandy with me.

But, what if, as my Mom says, my soul will only go to the place in my mind that I *believe* it will go?

If I *believe* my soul will just become part of a cold black hole in space, then it will.

And if I *believe* my soul will become part of a heavenly paradise of puffy white clouds, peaceful tranquility and eternal life, then it will.

What I believe, will be.

Black hole. Or white heaven.

"It's your choice," my Mom says to me.

"I hope not," I say to her.

* * *

Three things stand out in my memory from my days of being in Catholic school.

The first is the priest who liked his wine. I was an altar boy. Yeah, I know, of all people. At one point during every Mass the priest whips around with a chalice and one altar boy pours some water into it and another altar boy pours some wine into it. I was always the wine guy. I would pour wine into the chalice and start to pull the wine decanter away and this particular priest would tap it with his chalice, signalling me to add more wine. He would do this about three more times until the chalice was almost overflowing, then he would drink it all down and actually smack his lips when he was done, while the whole congregation looked on. My kind of priest. He also swore like a sailor which all of us altar boys thought was mighty cool.

The second was my non-white shirt. We had to wear uniforms in Catholic school that were comprised of blue dress pants and white, short-sleeved shirts. I, and every other boy who sweated in school, would bend his head down to the left or the right and wipe his greasy face on the sleeve of his shirt a hundred times a day. No matter how much bleach our mothers used, those sleeves were always a dingy gray the entire school year. The first time I went to a department store, I said, *"Hey Mom, look shirts that are all white. I didn't know they made them."*

The third also involved a school uniform at that Catholic school. The girls wore blue plaid jumpers over a white blouse with white

god.

socks and saddle shoes. When I was thirteen I walked by the girl's restroom at school just as one of the girls opened the door and as I glanced in I saw three girls fixing their hair in the big mirror. A fourth girl was also looking in the mirror, but she had the skirt part of her jumper pulled up over her stomach and she was straightening out a really skimpy pair of leopard print bikini panties. The juxtaposition of religious serenity with budding sexuality was almost too much to bear for either of my two thirteen-year-old heads. Ten minutes earlier I had been shooting marbles in the school playground and now I was realizing that, whoa nelly, girls are hot. And they know it.

After that I stopped shooting marbles.

And started combing my hair.

* * *

As the priest wraps up the service, I get serious for a minute. I bow my head and say a prayer to whomever might be up in those clouds and ask him or her, or it, to please look out for my wife and my two children after I am gone and to please make sure that their lives are filled with as much happiness as possible. I'm not big on praying, but today, right now, I pray. For them.

I walk out of the church behind the teenaged boy and his family. He keeps turning his head to look back at me. The third time he does it, he walks right into the back of his father, so I take that opportunity to flash him the peace sign and a wink and then peel off to where my car is parked.

"How was church?" my wife asks when I get home.

"It was great. They sacrificed a virgin. They should do that more often."

"I knew I should have gone with you." It's tough to get laughs when, after thirty years, your wife is immune to your twisted humor.

Today's *Taking Care of Business List* is easy. Write my suicide notes.

I take my laptop outside to the lanai and fire up a cigarette. A few months ago I was at my dentist's office to get my teeth cleaned. When the dental tech was finished sandblasting six months of nicotine off my now pearly whites, I went to the front desk to pay the bill and schedule my next appointment.

god.

"*Mary would like to see you again in four months,*" said the one of the receptionists.

"*Does she know that I'm married?*" I asked.

"*Ho, ho, ho, that is so funny,*" said receptionist number one with a fake chuckle, and then turned to receptionist number two and said, "*We haven't heard that one in a while, have we.*"

Liars. They must hear that line ten times a day. I was so embarrassed because I consider my humor anything but pedestrian. But right then I had been tossed in with the rest of the rabble.

So I don't want the same fate to befall me when it comes to my suicide note. God forbid, I come up with a clever concept for the note or some snappy phrasing, only to have coroner number one read the note and turn to coroner number two and say, "*Ho, ho, ho, we haven't heard that one in a while, have we.*"

So it's Internet time again. I punch *suicide notes* into the search box.

Psychologists say the most common reason for leaving a suicide note is to ease the pain of survivors by letting them know that they are not to blame for your death, or—*and I love this part*—to increase the pain of some of the survivors by letting them know that it was all their fault that you killed yourself.

Other motivations for leaving a suicide note include spelling out the reasons why you decided to kill yourself, giving instructions on how you want your burial to go and who you don't want in the front row, or confessing some other crime or indiscretion of yours that may have been a contributing factor in your decision to commit suicide. *I should never have screwed that sheep without a condom.*

On the flip side, there are a number of reasons why people don't leave a suicide note. One of the most common reasons is that the suicide candidate is so focused on accomplishing their task that they don't even think about leaving a note. *Why don't these bullets fit?-*

Or the suicide is an impulsive, last-minute decision so there is no time for a note. *Hey look, a train!*

Or they have nobody who cares enough about them to say anything to. *Dear Mr. Postman, you may notice my junk mail starting to stack up ...*

256

god.

Or they don't feel like they can put into adequate and proper words what they wish to say--. *Me dont no how rite im sory note fo yewz.*

Or they are engaging in some tomfoolery and hope their suicide will be considered an accidental death or homicide so their family can collect the insurance. *It was a guy with one arm who did me in!*

Or they simply don't want to leave a note. *Fuck you, don't tell me what to do.*

Committing suicide and not leaving a note is like giving your best friend a really great mystery novel to read, and he doesn't find out until he gets to the end of the book that you tore out the last chapter before you gave him the book. *Motherfucker!* When people are told that someone they know committed suicide, the question they will always ask first without fail is whether or not the person left a suicide note. Then they will ask how the person killed themself. It's always in that order. Inquiring minds just want to know.

I used to call Happy John, who is six months older than me, every Sunday after I read that day's newspaper.

"How many today?" he would ask.

"Four out of thirty-three."

"That's not bad. Better than last Sunday."

What I was calling to tell him was the total number of obituaries in that day's newspaper and how many of the people who croaked were younger than us.

"You guys are sick puppies," my wife would say.

"Inquiring minds just want to know," I would answer.

Back in the old days when I used to write obituaries for the newspaper, we always included the cause of death. They don't do that any more, which sucks. Whenever Happy John and I read about someone, particularly if it was a guy, who died and who was younger than us, it would put us in a real tizzy.

"Damn, I wish we knew what he died from," Happy John would say.

"I know, I know. It's not fair. They should have to tell us."

Because if the dead guy's obituary said that he put on his red striped Greg Norman golf shirt and drove his 2007 Hyundai Civic to a Roadrunner gas station and bought a Hostess Twinkie and then keeled over in the parking lot, I can guarantee you that, from that day forward, you would never see John or I wearing a red striped Greg

god.

Norman golf shirt, or driving to a Roadrunner gas station, or eating a Hostess Twinkie. We would both stick hot pokers in our eyeballs before getting into a Hyundai Civic.

Suicide notes can actually be pretty cool if they don't blather on too much about the *why* of the act, which, frankly, can be a little boring because if I wasn't interested in your problems and what was bugging you before you pulled the trigger, what makes you think I'm interested after you pull the trigger. The best suicides notes are the ones that tell us what was foremost on the person's mind at the time they decided to end it all.

"Football season is over," complained gonzo author Hunter S. Thompson.

"My work is done. Why wait?" wrote George Eastman, inventor of the Eastman Kodak Camera. How about a photo before you go, George?

Newscaster Chris Chubbuck chose the verbal version of a suicide note. On live TV she said, *"And now, in keeping with Channel 40's policy of always bringing you the latest in blood and guts, in living color, you're about to see another first—an attempted suicide."* Then she blew her brains out. I always miss the good shows.

"And so I leave this world, where the heart must either break or turn to lead," wrote French author Nicolas-Sebastien Chamfort. Anybody got a tissue?

Some people go out swinging. *"They tried to get me; I got them first!"* wrote poet Vachel Lindsay before drinking Lysol. Wrote British actor George Sanders, *"Dear World, I am bored. I have lived long enough. I am leaving you with your worries in this sweet cesspool. Good luck."*

My favorite suicide note, was actually more of a fuck-you poem. Poet Sara Teasdale left this note for the lover who had abandoned her:

"When I am dead, and over me bright April
Shakes out her rain drenched hair
Tho you should lean above me broken hearted
I shall not care
For I shall have peace
As leafey trees are peaceful
When rain bends down the bough

god.

And I shall be more silent and cold hearted
Than you are now."

In other words, fuck you and the horse you rode in on for leaving me.

Actually, I have a second favorite, which I love both for its brevity and its sense of spirit, which was left by Clara Blandick, better known as Auntie Em from *The Wizard of Oz*, who wrote, *"I am now about to make the great adventure ..."*

Suicide notes aren't just the purview of famous people. Regular folk tend to write suicide notes which speak to the heart of the matter. No flowery prose in these notes from coroner files:

"May her guts rot in hell. I loved her so much," from a man, age 47.

"I hereby bequeath to my father the sum of one dollar ($1)," from a woman, 35.

"You cops will want to know why I did it, well, let us just say that I lived 61 years too many. People have always put obstacles in my way. One of the great ones is leaving this world when you want to and you have nothing to live for. It has been a long day. The motor got so hot it would not run so I just had to sit here and wait. The breaks were against me to the last," from a divorced woman, 61.

Wives crop up quite often.

"No more will I pay the bills. Her grub I can not eat. At night I can not sleep. I married the wrong nag-nag-nag and I lost my life," from a married man, 55, who added a postscript to his note, *"Dear undertaker, we have got plenty money to give me a decent burial. Don't let my wife kid you by saying she has not got any money."*

A 45-year-old man left this suicide note for his wife, *"You win, I can't take it any longer. I know you have been waiting for this to happen. I hope it makes you very happy. A little bit of kindness from you would have made everything so different, but all that ever interested you was the dollar. Well, it's all yours now and you won't have to see the lawyer anymore."* And a second note for his daughter, *"Don't go in the bedroom. Call your mother, she will know what to do. Love, Daddy."*

It's not all negative. From a 51-year-old single man: *"Though I am about to kick the bucket, I am as happy as ever. I am going over to see the other side."*

I wonder what that guy did with the $1 his daughter left him?

god.

He must have been a real shitbird.

*   *   *

Most religions turn thumbs down on suicide.

Buddhists don't condemn suicide, but since they are against the destruction of life, be it yours or someone else's, they do frown on suicide.

Hindus consider suicide the same as murdering another person, and they toss in another wrinkle. They say that if you commit suicide, you will become a very unhappy ghost and have to wander the earth every day until you get to the exact day you would have normally died had you not pulled the plug yourself. They used to make an exception, though, for the now outlawed practice of Sati, which is where a recently widowed woman either voluntarily or through use of force climbs onto her deceased husband's funeral pyre and burns to death. I'm not one to quibble, but I think some grieving wives might see a world of difference between the concepts of *voluntary* and *use of force.*

"*So, Aishwarya, you planning to climb up on that burning pyre?*"

"*Nope, think I'll pass.*"

"*Are you sure?*"

"*Positive.*"

"*Aishwarya?*"

"*Yes?*

"*I think you dropped something by your left foot.*"

"*I don't see anything. Hey, hey, hey, let me go!*"

Islamics view suicide as one of the worst sins you can commit and a major roadblock on your spiritual journey to that place where you get to tap all those virgins, a fact they do not go out of their way to remind suicide bombers about. Jews also say suicide is a big no-no. Wow, Islamics and Jews actually agreeing on something. Maybe they can stop throwing rocks at each other now.

Christians consider suicide a grave sin because it is self-murder and no different that you murdering another person, plus they say that your life is actually the property of God and a gift to the world, so if you kill yourself you are asserting dominion over what is God's property and stealing a gift from the world. "*Do you not know that your body is a temple of the Holy Spirit, who is in you, whom you*

god.

have received from God? You are not your own, you were bought at a price."

I was bought? My wife wants a refund.

With all of the violence that is in the Bible, from brother slayings —*Take that Abel!*—to human sacrifices—*Poppa Jephthah, what's that fire for?*—to crucifixions—*Peter, I can see your house from here*, it's surprising that there are only seven suicides mentioned in the Bible.

One. Abimelech was a king who went around doing his fair share of conquering and was laying siege to one particular town when a woman in a tower tossed a piece of millstone down on top of his head and damn near killed him. No, sorry, I don't have a clue what a millstone is. Abimelech, being the macho conqueror that he was, could not bear the shame of being killed by a woman, so he yelled to his armor bearer to finish the job, saying, *"Draw thy sword, and slay me, that men say not of me, a woman slew him."*

Two. Samson, the original pussy-whipped guy with the hots for Delilah who cut off his superman hair to get into her pants, purposely killed himself and a shitload of evil Philistines by collapsing a house on top of them and himself.

Three. Saul was fighting those same evil Philistines and not doing too good of a job. They had already knocked off his three sons and put a few arrows in his ass when, like Abimelech had done, he called for his armor bearer to finish him off, saying, *"Draw thy sword, and thrust me through therewith; lest these uncircumcised come and thrust me through, and abuse me."* But his armor bearer chickened out, so Saul had to do the job himself, falling on his own sword.

Four. Believe it or not, Saul's armor bearer got the fourth coveted suicide spot in the Bible, falling on his own sword right after Saul did himself in. Copycat.

Five. Ahithophel wanted to raise an army of twelve thousand men and go out and kick King David's ass, but he couldn't get anyone else on board with that plan, which just pissed him off to no end, so, *"He saddled his ass, and arose, and gat him home to his house, to his city, and put his household in order, and hanged himself."* He gat himself home. Now that's funny.

Six. Zimri was the king's bodyguard, and one day when the king got a little drunk, Zimri whacked him and took over his reign. Zimri was only in power for seven days before the people said,

god.

"Dude, that wasn't cool," and they picked someone else to be the king, so a despondent Zimri, who had been living it up in the king's old house, set the house on fire with himself and his whole family in it.

Seven: Judas ratted Jesus Christ out, then hung himself. Never even got to spend those thirty pieces of silver.

I may be going out on a cross here, but personally I think there are really eight suicides in the Bible, not the seven I just highlighted.

Number eight is Jesus Christ himself.

He committed suicide by cop.

Think about it.

Suicide by cop is defined as when an *individual deliberately acts in a threatening way, with the goal of provoking a lethal response from a law enforcement officer, such as being shot to death.*

Jesus was smart enough to know that if he kept wandering the countryside raising the dead, feeding thousands of people with a few loaves of bread and some stale fish, curing lepers, and making the blind see again, somebody in charge was going to start feeling a little threatened. And if while doing all those cool miracles, he was also preaching that everybody should stop worshipping false Gods, not worry about paying taxes any more, stop kowtowing to those pain in the ass Romans, and, worst of all, just love thy neighbor and treat them how you would have them treat you, well, he had to know he was about to be in a world of shit.

But even knowing that, Jesus continued to *deliberately act in a threatening way* which *provoked a lethal response* from Roman centurions, who were the boys in blue back then, and instead of a bullet to the head, he was nailed to a cross and had a spear stuck into his chest a few times.

Not saying he deserved it, but he certainly knew it was coming.

* * *

"Hungry?" my wife asks, setting a bowl of salted whole cashews in front of me.

"Thanks," I say. I work the laptop keyboard with my right hand and the nuts with my left hand. And I have a cigarette burning in the ashtray. I am a multi-tasker.

My wife lights a cigarette.

262

god.

"What are you looking at?" she asks.
"Naked pictures of you."
"Very funny."
"Hey, I don't recognize that bedspread."
"Shut up."

My wife eats a few of the cashews, then says, *"Is it a gold bedspread with black stripes?"*

"Ha ha. Leave the jokes to the professional please."

She finishes her cigarette and gets up. *"I'm going to run some errands. I'll be back in a few hours. I'll pick up some steaks for tonight."*

"Later gator," I say.

That means I will have some solo time to write my suicide note. But first, I type *famous last words* into the Internet search box, looking for a little more inspiration. I am a journalist after all so everyone is going to expect me to be somewhat clever in my suicide note.

People who know they are about to die from a grave illness or injury or an imminent execution don't write suicide notes, so it's their last spoken words that can make a lasting impression on family, friends and society and end up being recorded for posterity. The best of these death bed utterances tend to be brief and succinct, like that of Australian bush cowboy and outlaw Ned Kelly who stepped onto the gallows and simply said, *"Such is life,"* before they sprang the trap door.

Just as the particular method that a well known person chooses to commit suicide can be interesting in relation to what they did that made them famous, so too can be the final death bed words of famous people since it tells us what message they deem to be the most important to impart before they die.

The best one-liners come from criminals about to be executed.

"I'd rather be fishing," said Jimmy Glass before he was fried in the electric chair.

"I'd like to be in hell in time for dinner," said Edward Ruloff before being hung.

"Hurry up, I could kill ten men while you're fooling around!" said Carl Panzram while waiting for the hangman.

But the winner has to be Thomas Grasso who was killed by lethal injection, but not before saying, *"I did not get my Spaghetti-O's; I got spaghetti. I want the press to know this."*

Humor does well.

"I should never have switched from Scotch to Martinis," said tough guy actor Humphrey Bogart.

Asked for his final words of wisdom, Conrad Hilton, founder of the Hilton Hotels chain, said, *"Leave the shower curtain on the inside of the tub."*

Some famous people were a little pissed off as they took those last breaths.

"Goddamn the whole fucking world and everyone in it except you, Carlotta!" said comedian W.C. Fields, whose mistress was Carlotta Monti.

Edith Piaf, France's greatest popular singer, complained that, *"Every damn fool thing you do in this life you pay for."*

Some last words just don't seem to go with the person saying them.

"I have offended God and mankind because my work did not reach the quality it should have," said Leonardo da Vinci, whose lack of accomplishments included painting the *Mona Lisa* and *The Last Supper*.

Nostradamus, famous for predicting huge cultural changes and calamities way into the future, died with these I-might-be-stating-the-obvious words spilling from his lips, *"Tomorrow, I shall no longer be here."* Well duh, we could have told you that.

Personally I like those famous people who looked upon their impending death as the start of a new adventure. *"Now comes the mystery,"* said evangelist Henry Ward Beecher, while French writer Francois Rabelais said, *"I am off in search of the great perhaps."*

The *great perhaps*! Gotta love it.

Perhaps, I say to myself, I shall pop another cashew into my mouth.

* * *

Scholars say that in the early days, the Big Kahunas of Christianity did make a few exceptions for suicide, like when Christian women were allowed to kill themselves rather than be

god.

raped by pagan males. No pagan sperm in our Christian women, please. They also gave a thumbs up to anyone who wanted to kill themselves to avoid being arrested and tortured by those same pagans. *Hey, that's not a water board is it?*

So, back then if you were a Christian and wanted to kill yourself, you just needed a pagan pass, which were actually the first ever all-access VIP backstage passes, all apologies to the Rolling Stones.

"Yo Bathsheba, don't jump. Suicide is forbidden."

"No worries, I got me one of them there pagan passes."

"Wow. Very cool. Which apostle did you have to blow to get one?"

The question this raises, though, is why Christians would approve of suicide to avoid the pain and misery of torture by another human being, but not allow you to commit suicide if that pain and misery came from a disease that was torturing your body, like cancer. Suicide to avoid having your fingernails pulled out with pliers is okay, but suicide to avoid the slow, painful decay of your body's organs by a black rotting cancer is not?

Time for another vote on this. And we just might get a reversal. Because, frankly, both religion and government are like the same two wishy-washy peas in a pod, flip-flopping all the time on decisions that heretofore they claimed were carved in stone.

Government: You can't sell or drink alcohol. It is prohibited. We will arrest you.

—Oops, changed our mind, now you can drink. Bottoms up.

Church: You can't take birth control pills. You will burn in hell if you do.

—Oops, changed our mind, now the pill is okay. See you in heaven.

Government: You can't burn the flag. We will fucking kick your ass if you do.

—Oops, changed our mind, burn away. Especially you skinheads.

Church: You can't have girls helping priests at the altar. It's altar boys only.

—Oops, changed our mind, altar girls rock. Hands off, Father Tom!

Government: You can't have an abortion. That's murder. We will arrest you.

god.

—*Oops, changed our mind, screw that little rugrat. Here's a hanger.*

Church: You can't get divorced. We don't care if he beats you every night.

—*Oops, changed our mind, you can leave that scoundrel ... just make sure we get a nice fat envelope in the collection basket.*

* * *

In college I took a course on logic where at the very first class the professor told us that one plus one equals three and then proceeded to explain why that statement was true, and when he was done talking, every student in the class agreed with him that, yes indeed, one plus one equals three. I don't recall what his exact argument, or logic, was, but I'll be a son of a bitch if that professor did not convince every single one of us.

Today, I'm positive that one plus one does not equal three, so I would have to say that sometimes logic, or at least the arguments supporting a certain point, can be flawed. For now, though, let's just say that logic does make sense, and, just for shits and giggles, follow me through on this evangelical one-plus-one-equals-whatever-I-say-it-does equation.

Point One: If you believe in God, then you know that God gave us the gift of life. And life and death are not inseparable. You can't have one without the other. They are the two sides of the exact same coin. Life is the absence of death, and death is the absence of life. It is really quite that simple.

So if God gave us the gift of life, then at the very same time he also gave us the gift of death.

Point Two: If you believe in God, then you know that God gave us the gift of free will. God did not create us as pre-programmed robots. He said we can live our life the way we choose.

So if God gave us the gift of free will to choose how we live our life, then at the very same time he also gave us the gift of free will to choose how we end our life.

Conclusion: So suicide is okay—because God gave us the gift of death and the free will to do what we want with that gift.

Makes perfect sense to me.

god.

Personally, I think this argument, or logic, holds up even if you don't believe in God. Just replace the word *God* with whatever words you want, like *someone* or *something* or *Martians* or *space dust*, in the equation above and you will come up with the same conclusion.

Of all the wonders in our world, there is no question that life is the most incredible wonder of them all. My hat is off to God, or *someone* or *something* or *Martians* or *space dust*, on that one. Whoever it was gives a really great present. They could have given us a toaster, but instead they gave us life.

While nobody disputes how great the gift of life is, at the same time nobody ever talks about how great the gift of death is. It's like identical twins where one twin, Life, is the parents' favorite and the other twin, Death, is banished to the basement. Everyone knows that the Death twin exists, because they can hear him bumping into things in the dark down in the basement, but nobody wants to invite him upstairs to sit at the family dinner table.

When you are alive, you may have free will, but you are a naive fool if you think you control your life. Society, government, religion, family, the earth's elements, your mental state, and the health, or lack thereof, of your own body control your life. God may have promised us life but he didn't promise us that it would necessarily be a good life. That's why he also gave us the gift of death. Of those two sides of the coin, it is actually the death side that we have the most control over.

If life becomes too much for you, you yourself can stop the ride. That is a gift that is as magnificent as the gift of the ride itself. There are so many examples. Your body is being eaten away by cancer and every waking moment of your life is filled with intolerable pain. You are imprisoned for life and beaten and tortured every day because of your political or religious beliefs. Your entire family has been killed by a drunken driver, or you are the drunken driver who has killed someone else's entire family. You can't control or change those things, so you are at the mercy of life every single minute of every single day until death comes walking around the corner. Do you wait for death to come calling on his own sweet time, or do you call and invite him over yourself?

Before you answer, remember there is a world of difference between theoretical debate and real life. Writer, sociologist and

god.

feminist Charlotte Perkins Gilman's 1935 suicide note explained why she chose a quick death by chloroform over a slow death by cancer, *"When all usefulness is over, when one is assured of an unavoidable and imminent death, it is the simplest of human rights to choose a quick and easy death in place of a slow and horrible one."*

The *simplest of human rights*. So incredible, and so obvious.

Forget her eloquent prose for a minute and let the reality sink in of what this talented, creative and caring humanitarian faced and how she dealt with it. She wasn't choosing between wearing a red dress or a blue dress. Her dance with Death was certain, and she on her own chose the exact day and time that she and Death would dance. That took a strength and courage not found in most people.

Imagine you go to an amusement park and take a seat on the roller coaster. As the attendant straps you in, you notice there is nobody else on the ride. The ride starts up, and for the next few minutes you are speeding along the track, taking sharp turns and making upside down loops, and just having a grand old time. But then a few minutes turns into fifteen minutes and now you are starting to feel dizzy and queasy. As you speed by the attendant you yell, *"Okay, I'm done. I want to get off now."*

"Sorry, no can do," he yells back.

When you swing by again, you yell, *"When is this fucking thing going to stop?"*

"I have no idea," yells the attendant.

"Who does know?"

"Nobody knows. It will stop when it stops."

"But I want it to stop now!"

"Too bad."

If you have your choice between getting on a ride where you have no idea when it will ever end or getting on a ride where, if you wanted to, you could stop it yourself, which ride would you choose? God gave us a ticket to the ride of life, but what's so wonderful, and so overlooked, is the fact that he also gave us the button to push to stop the ride whenever we want to.

Most people never think about that, much less appreciate it.

* * *

god.

Life and death. Death and life. Like the lyric from that saccharine song "Love and Marriage"—*you can't have one without the other*.

My wife and I and a few other couples went to the circus recently, which is not something we normally do, but we were offered free tickets by Bill the Handholder. Bill, who holds his wife's hand way too much, is Perfect Paul's main competition, and like Paul, he makes it really hard for the rest of us non-affectionate husbands. *Mofo!* Our whole row, except for my daughter who was in town and who joined us, was made up of 50-somethings, while sitting all around us were families with children, both big and small. The age difference didn't matter though as we all gasped, and occasionally shrieked, as the trapeze artists swung on thin ropes four stories above us, as the lion tamer stuck his head in the mouths of tigers and lions, as the dozen motorbikes spun round and round in the steel sphere, and as acrobats jumped through hoops of fire.

I had seen circuses before, granted mostly on TV in the last few decades, but for some reason on this particular night it dawned on me what the central theme was of circuses which made them so popular.

I turned to my daughter just as one of the clowns slid a two-foot long saber down his throat and asked her, *"Do you know what all these circus people are doing?"*

"Entertaining us?"

"No. They are cheating death."

"What?"

"Think about it. Every act that is done on that circus floor involves someone escaping death. That's what we are celebrating. Them not dying."

My daughter's brow was furrowed.

I helped her along: *"The trapeze artists not falling, the lion tamer not getting eaten, the motorcyclists not colliding in the steel ball."*

"Oh my God," said my daughter, *"you're right."*

We both, almost on cue, looked at all the children sitting around us with big smiles on their faces, bouncing up and down in their seats and clapping their hands in glee.

If I had asked the same question of all those parents who brought their little kiddies to the show, they too would have all said they were at the circus so their children could have fun: *"It's just so entertaining!"*

"Watching people almost die is entertaining?"

"What?"

"Your kids are laughing and clapping because people in colorful costumes are cheating death. Don't you think that's a little macabre?"

"Security!"

* * *

An argument could be made that, while God did give us the gift of free will, there were some strings attached to that gift, specifically the Ten Commandments, one of which says murder, even self-murder, is a sin. We know about those Ten Commandments because they are in the Bible.

Funny thing about the Bible, though.

If you asked God who wrote it, he just might say, *"Well, first off, it wasn't me.*

I didn't write the bible.

Man did.

In fact, many men did.

At many different times.

In many different ways.

In many different languages.

For many different reasons.

When there were no tape recorders.

And no computers.

And no copy machines or cell phones.

And no Internet."

Then God might take a sip of his Colombian espresso, and maybe a drag off his Cuban cigar if he is so inclined, and say, *"Considering what I just pointed out, you might not want to believe everything you read."*

Buddha is on the same page with the Big Guy on that one. Buddha, which is actually just his stage name, was born Siddhārtha Gautama in India about 563 BC and he wandered around getting everybody hip to Buddhism. One of the things he told his followers while they sat around cross-legged with their hands folded was,

god.

"Believe nothing, no matter where you read it, or who said it, no matter if I have said it, unless it agrees with your own reason and your own common sense."

Love the part about using your own common sense.

The next time you find yourself laying in bed in one of those cheap roadside motor lodge type hotels, with or without your secretary, reach over and open the drawer on the nightstand and pull out that copy of the Gideon's Bible. Read a few pages. No problem, right.

You know why that Bible is so easy to read?

Because it's in fucking English!

Here's a biblical newsflash boys and girls, nobody spoke or wrote English back when Noah was loading up the Ark and Moses was parting the Red Sea. The Old Testament was written in Hebrew and the New Testament was written in Greek. On scrolls.

Really, when was the last time you saw a scroll?

On the Internet there are websites that will do free language translations for you. In the box on the left you type a sentence, say in English, then you select what language you want your sentence translated into, say Spanish, you hit the translate button, and your sentence pops up in the box on the right in Spanish. I own a business in Central America and the guy down there who runs the shop for me only speaks and writes a little bit of English, so sometimes I use one of those translation websites to send him an email in Spanish.

"Senor, are you mad at me?" he said one day when he called.

"No, why?"

"The email you just sent."

"What about it? I told you to make sure the permits had been approved for the remodeling."

"No senor, you told me I am a lizard who fucks wild goats."

"Oh sorry, my bad."

So, far all we know, what ended up in the Bible as, *"In the beginning God created the heaven and the earth,"* might have actually started out before multiple translations as, *"Later that night God fixed himself a peanut butter and jelly sandwich. And a nice cold glass of milk."*

The translation issue is only part of the problem. All that neat stuff in the Bible actually started out as oral history, meaning that the

god.

stories were passed down from generation to generation through word of mouth, until some people with way too much time on their hands thought, *"You know, maybe we should be writing this shit down."*

Remember when you were in kindergarten and the teacher had all the students sit in a big circle and the first kid whispered a short sentence into the ear of the kid sitting next to him, and then that kid whispered the sentence, or at least what he heard, into the next kid's ear, and so on and so on until it made it to the last kid in the circle? Then the teacher would ask the first kid to say the sentence out loud and then she would ask the last kid in the circle to say the sentence out loud, and of course, the two sentences were never even remotely similar.

And that was with just ten kids and one short sentence.

So what happens when you have thousands of people whispering thousands of parables and verses and speeches and prayers and prophecies into the ears of thousands of other people over a period of hundreds of years? That's how we got, *"Blessed are the meek, for they shall inherit the earth,"* but what Jebediah might have said when he whispered in that very first person's ear was, *"Dude, I took the most awesome crap today."*

Even my dinner buddy Albert Einstein thinks the Bible should be on the comic book rack. *"The Bible is a collection of honourable, but still primitive, legends which are nevertheless pretty childish. No interpretation no matter how subtle can change this. These subtilised interpretations are highly manifold according to their nature and have almost nothing to do with the original text."*

By the way, *subtilised* is a derivative of the word *subtilize*, which means subtle arguments or definitions. Don't feel bad; I had to look it up too.

Back to murder being a sin according to the Bible. I don't wonder so much about the specific transgressions that made the Top 10 List of the commandments, but I do wonder who put them in that particular order.

Not to throw anyone under the bus, but if it was indeed God who came up with the rankings, then does he have a big ego, or what? The first four commandments are all about him—he's the only God that counts, his image is the only image that counts, don't swear using his name, and be sure to celebrate his birthday every Sunday.

272

god.

Not murdering people, not banging anyone else if you're married, not stealing, not lying, not honoring your parents, and not wanting what you don't have all ranked lower on the commandments chart.

Listen, if God is the guy who started this whole ball rolling, then he has every right to ask that our top priorities be worshipping him and constantly thanking him. If he needs to be fawned over, that's his prerogative. But is saying Goddammit when you stub your toe, the third commandment, really infinitely worse than beating your boss to death with the coffee maker in the break room, the sixth commandment? Some people might argue with His Holiness on that one.

While we're on the subject, I think God could have been a little more clear on the second commandment, *"Thou shalt not make unto thee any graven image."* What exactly is a graven image, and does it involve Adobe Photoshop?

And for somebody who is supposed to be omnipotent, I don't think God was looking ahead to the future when he came up with the tenth commandment, *"Thou shall not covet your neighbor's house; you shall not covet your neighbor's wife, nor his male servant, nor his female servant, nor his ox, nor his donkey, nor anything that is your neighbor's."*

Trust me, I know a lot of people, but I don't know a single person who owns an ox. And what's up with that male servant part? *"Ezekiel, pardon me for coveting, but I must say your male servant Jeremiah is looking mighty fine today in that loincloth."*

I also don't know anyone who has read the entire Bible. Priests and ministers reel off the same stale parts every week, usually the parts geared to make us tow the religious line and get out our wallets when the collection plate comes around. If you were to read the entire Bible, not only would you be left with a shitload of new unanswerable questions, you would be mighty depressed because the Bible is full of more homicidal mayhem than most horror movies.

Thomas Paine, one of our nation's Founding Fathers, said, *"Whenever we read the obscene stories, the voluptuous debaucheries, the cruel and tortuous executions, the unrelenting vindictiveness with which more than half the Bible is filled, it would be more consistent that we call it the word of a demon than the word of God. It is a history of wickedness that has served to corrupt and brutalize mankind."*

god.

When he wasn't busy upholding his crown as one of the most popular and prolific science fiction writers of all time, Isaac Asimov also weighed in on the Bible, saying, *"Properly read, the Bible is the most potent force for atheism ever conceived."*

Taking a shot as well was flamboyant Irish author and poet Oscar Wilde, who said, *"When I think of all the harm the Bible has done, I despair of ever writing anything to equal it."* Wilde was one wild cat. He also said, *"I think that God in creating Man somewhat overestimated his ability."*

Clever. And true.

* * *

Enough about other people's famous last words. Time for mine. I open a blank Word document on my laptop and start typing my suicide note. I just finish the opening line, *It was the best of times, it was the worst of times ...* when my wife opens the lanai door.

"I'm back."

Damn. The note will have to wait until tomorrow. I can type it at work.

My wife throws the steaks on the grill and goes inside to make a Caesar salad. Dinner tastes great. Later I play some Internet poker and take my bank up to over two thousand dollars, and then lose it all playing Omaha high-low. An asshole with the screen name LayerCake212 fills an inside straight on the river and takes the last of my money.

Easy come, easy go.

The irony is not lost on me.

* * *

As if believing in some all powerful supreme being called God is not enough of a stretch, a handsome chap named Jesus Christ had to be born twenty centuries ago just to confuse the issue even more.

Let me see if I have this straight.

Of the billions of planets in our universe, God chose our tiny spinning rock to send his son to. And he sent him to spread the word about peace and love and harmony back when everyone was walking around wearing robes and sandals and the deadliest

274

god.

weapons we had were bows and arrows that could shoot about fifty yards before clattering to the ground. Might it not have been more prudent to hold off on his only son's summer vacation until now, when we have thousands of nuclear weapons capable of reducing this spinning rock into a pile of dust? I could be wrong, but right about now seems to be a much more appropriate time to preach the message about us all just fucking getting along.

I think Jesus would have agreed.

"Yo Pops, can't I wait awhile before I make my visit? At least until mankind gets deodorant, air conditioning and cable TV. What do you say?"

"No, I'm sending you now."

"Dad, you're not being reasonable. How many people am I realistically going to be able to reach with my message if I have to walk everywhere. Or ride a donkey. If we wait until I can get a nice set of wheels, like a Mercedes SL600, and fly on the Concorde, I'll be able to cover a lot more ground."

"Hmmm, you have a point, son."

"Hey, I'll even fly coach."

Jesus was thirty-three years old when he was crucified. Prior to that he gave a lot of pep talks to the people on a broad range of subjects. As the son of God, he knew everything, so people tended to listen to what he had to say. You would think that while he was advising people to love one another and performing an occasional miracle or two, he might have taken a little time to give us a more specific answer to how and why the universe was created, other than just saying, *"It was Dad's will."*

If Random House had been around back then and all the apostles had turned in their Jesus Christ notes to get their new book, working title *The Bible*, published, I can imagine one of the Random House editors saying, *"You know Peter, Andrew, John, Philip, Matthew, Thomas, Thaddeus, Simon, Matthias, James one and two, and Bartholomew, I think we got a hit on our hands here."*

"Great."

"I love the parts about the miracles. Good stuff."

"Great."

"One question, though. Did any of you think to ask him what the cure for cancer is?"

"No."

275

god.

"Okay, don't worry about it. By the way, Scorsese just bought the book rights."

* * *

Possibly the two best quotes ever about God and religion and science and the universe come from two of the greatest minds in the history of the world, Albert Einstein, who everybody knows, and Stephen Hawking, who everybody should know. If you don't know who Mr. Hawking is, then please look him up because I'm not going to insult the man by trying to describe his accomplishments in a few words. The quotes from these two magnificent theorists are wonderful because they are short and pithy, and the quotes both complement and contradict each other. Their genesis may be from quantum mechanics and the debate over probability versus certainty, but think outside the box for a minute and they actually address the big picture of why are we here, where did we come from, and where are we going.

Here's what Albert Einstein said:

"I am convinced that God does not play dice."

And here's what Stephen Hawking said:

"God not only plays dice. He sometimes throws the dice where they cannot be seen."

It doesn't get any better than that.

* * *

Boo pouts. Which is not an attractive look on a dog's face.

"So, what am I chopped liver?" says Boo.

"What, pray tell, are you talking about?"

"I didn't hear my name mentioned when you said that prayer at church this morning, asking God to take care of the family after you're gone. What's up with that? Why you dissin' me, homey?"

"Are you sure? I thought I included you." I know I didn't, but I don't want Boo to feel left out. He's sensitive that way.

"You didn't."

"Are you sure?"

"Positive."

276

god.

"I'm sorry. But what's the problem? You're already covered. Isn't there a movie called All Dogs Go To Heaven?"

"That's a movie, you moron. This is real life here."

"Oh."

"And even if the movie is right, that doesn't guarantee me getting into heaven. You're not the only one with skeletons in your closet. I get around, you know."

"Do tell."

"No way, playa. You can't keep a secret."

"Sure, I can."

"Really? Who ratted me out when I pooped in the little lady's closet last week?"

"Well, that was gross."

"Not my fault. It was something I ate."

I slip on my reading glasses and pick up my book. I read a few pages and then peer over the top of the book at Boo in his cage.

"You mentioned heaven. Do dogs believe in heaven?"

"Of course we do. It's a wonderful place."

"What makes it so wonderful?"

"Well, first off, there aren't any people there."

Boo laughs. Which is also not an attractive look on a dog's face.

"Funny," I say.

"I thought so, too" says Boo.

"What about God? Do dogs believe in God."

"Yes we do."

"What about religion?"

"No. Do you think we're stupid?"

I try to go back to my book, but Boo is not done.

"Dogs also pray. I say a prayer every single night."

"And what do you pray for?"

"For you to wake up with a kidney stone."

"Nice."

"Hey, you asked."

I know that Boo pretends like he doesn't like me, but deep down he really loves me.

"No I don't," says Boo.

Man oh man, he is on a roll. I am outmatched tonight.

"What page are you on?" asks Boo.

god.

I look at the book in my hands and tell him page 198.

"How many pages do you have left?"

I flip to the back of the book, do a quick calculation and tell him about forty.

"Better read fast. You don't have much time left."

I close the book and look at the blue plastic gun case on top of my dresser. I've seen it perched there so many times over the past eight days that I have become immune to its presence, to what is inside the case, to what I have decided to do with its contents. Suicide has seemed to be one long Internet search, more of a research distraction than a reality. It sinks in that Boo is right; I only have one more tomorrow night left in my life. I realize that I have not been devoting enough time to thoroughly thinking this decision through, but I also realize that that has been intentional. If I think too long and hard about it, I won't do it. I know that I have to limit my decision making to the span of a single second, the time it takes to pull the trigger. So until I get to the exact day and exact time when that single second presents itself, I can't think about it.

"I think your Mom is right," says Boo.

"About what?"

"When she said that whatever you believe will happen when you die is what will happen."

"But what if she's wrong?"

Boo pauses for a few seconds.

"More importantly," he says, *"what if she's right?"*

Monday, June 29

family.

The drive to work, my last one ever, is uneventful. I expect something more, like everything I do today should be spectacular because it will be the last time I am doing it. But the drive is blase, I hit the same stoplights as always, I've heard the same songs on the radio a hundred times before, and Boo sleeps the whole way to the office.

I get a cup of coffee, fire up my computer and call up the *TCB List* and study it for what will be the last time at the office. I notice that I didn't make the *"just saying hi"* phone calls to family and friends yesterday. Screw that. If I start calling my family members just to say hello, alarm bells will go off from coast to coast because that is so not my nature. I will make but one phone call, and that's to my Mom. The items on the list for today are short and easy; have a staff meeting, go out for a nice lunch, and take Boo for a walk.

Like I said, uneventful.

* * *

family.

Most people actually have five families in their lifetime, not just one.

Your first family is the one you are born into, with a mother and a father and maybe some brothers and sisters. For the first twenty or so years of your life, that is your most important family.

Your second family is the one you start when you find a spouse and burp out your own sons and daughters. For the rest of your life, that is your most important family.

Your third family is your circle of friends, which is usually an ever-changing and revolving cast of characters. Some are fair weather and some are sturdy as an oak. Some lead you down the wrong path and some show you the way. They are a mixed bag.

Your fourth family are the people you work with, because if you have a full-time job you spend more of your waking hours every week with those people than you do with your blood relatives or your friends.

Your fifth family is made up of every other human being on this planet who happens to be alive at the same time you are. That is the family you overlook the most.

* * *

My Mom has a voicemail that starts with her saying *"Hello?"* in a very cheery voice followed by a rather long pause and then her saying she's sorry she isn't there to take your call. The bad news is that when my Mom actually does answer the phone she also says *"Hello?"* in a cheery voice and then pauses. So initially you're never really sure whether you're talking to the flesh and blood Mom or the electronic Mom.

I dial her number. I hear the cheery *"Hello?"* and wait.

I hear a second *"Hello?"* and a muffled smoker's cough.

Yeah, I got the live one.

"It's your favorite son calling. How are you doing?"

"I'm fine. And to what do I owe the pleasure of a call from the son who never calls his Mom."

"I'm calling you now, Mom," I say.

We do this same exchange every time I call which, I would have to agree with her, is not often enough.

family.

She updates me on the goings on of my brother and three sisters and of any of her grandchildren, my nieces and nephews, who have done something noteworthy or something ridiculous since we last spoke. She asks me about my wife and my two children. She tells me what's she's been up to and lately many of those updates have to do with doctor visits.

"It sucks getting old," she will say.

"Tell me about it," I will answer.

Toward the end of the conversation she will ask me how I am doing and spoon out huge dollops of motherly advice. It doesn't matter that I am over a half century old. I am still her little boy.

Losing weight? Yes, Mom.

Cutting back on the cigarettes? Yes. Mom.

Drinking in moderation? Yes, Mom.

Not getting too stressed out? Yes. Mom.

Getting enough exercise? Yes, Mom.

Eventually we wrap up the conversation.

"I love you," I say to her.

"I love you too, son."

I hang up. I feel good about the call and bad about what I am planning to do tomorrow. For some reason I know that my wife and my two children will understand why I did it. They won't be happy about it, but they will understand.

Mom won't.

* * *

No one will ever know you better than your mother.

Not your father, not your husband or wife, not your kids, not your best friend.

And nobody will ever stick by you stronger and for longer than your mother.

My wife's younger brother was a wild child from his late teens until his early thirties, consuming drugs and alcohol to ridiculous excess, doing break-ins to feed his drug habit, stealing from family and friends, racking up DUI after DUI, spending nights in one jail cell after the other, and burning bridges left and right. The crystal meth devil had him by the throat and everybody, and I mean everybody, from family to friends to counselors, had given up on him.

family.

Everybody that is except his mother, or Mamaw as she is known by my children, her grandkids.

Mamaw was the lone soldier standing on that barren hill waiting years and years for her son to come home.

And he eventually did.

Just like she knew he would.

He conquered the devil in his head, had two beautiful daughters, and has been happy and healthy for more than twenty years. Mamaw never gave up, no matter how long it was going to take. If she had to, she would have gone to her grave still waiting, still believing in her child.

There is nothing in this world, or this universe, stronger than the bond between a mother and her child. Try taking a lion cub away from it's mother, or try saying something negative to my wife about one of my children. In either scenario, you will get your head ripped off.

I don't care how old you are, or how successful you are, or how tough you are, or how many of your own kids you have; if you are ever depressed or sad or lonely or hurt, there is no drug or therapy or remedy that will make you feel better than to have your mother pull your head to her bosom and pat you on the back and whisper in your ear that everything is going to be all right.

I tell my kids all the time that I know they love me, but that I also know if all four us were in the middle of a crosswalk at a busy Manhattan intersection and a gypsy cab ran a red light and was speeding straight at us, both of them would push my wife to safety without a moment's hesitation, and then, if there was some time left, they would turn around and see if they could save me.

"Dad, that's so not true," my daughter will say.

My son will say nothing, and instead just smile. He knows I know.

But I'm all right with that. That's how it should be.

On the flip side, no one will ever give you better advice than your father. A mother's perspective is more short term, as in, you look hungry can I fix you something to eat, did you sleep well, or let me iron that shirt so you look nice at school. A father's perspective is more long term, as in, if it seems too good to be true then it isn't, hard work never killed anyone, always plan ahead, and never bet a man at his own game.

family.

I have lived my life by the advice my Dad gave to me. I'm not saying I always followed that advice, and the times I haven't I have suffered the consequences.

One of my Dad's favorite stories was about a son and his father and the son's best friend. The son says to his friend, *"You know when I was sixteen years old you would not believe how stupid my father was. But now that I am twenty-six years old, it's amazing how much smarter my father has become in that time."*

My Dad would pose questions designed to stimulate his children's brain cells. He always made it fun, and there always seemed to be a joke or a catchy phrase associated with the life lesson he was espousing. When he left for work he would yell to us, *"See you later alligator,"* to which we would dutifully and happily reply, *"In a while crocodile."* My father gave me loads of practical advice, and I have shared every nugget with my two children. *"Use your head,"* was his constant refrain, and they are best three words of advice anyone can ever receive. Besides advice, he helped expand my narrow mind.

When I was twelve years old I watched my Dad working under the hood of his car. A neighborhood girl wandered over to also watch and to unsuccessfully flirt with me. After twenty minutes she left.

"Thank God, she's gone," I said to my Dad. *"She is so ugly."*

My Dad's head snapped up like a shot and he stared at me with those eyes that could go from soft baby blue to angry coal black in a heartbeat. He had a huge wrench in his oil and grease covered hand. At that moment he looked as intimidating as all fuck.

"Son," he said very slowly, *"there is no such thing as an ugly woman. They are all beautiful. Don't you ever forget that."*

And I never did. Because he was right. Women are the lifeblood of this human race and the only thing they ask of us for carrying that burden is that we treat them as truly beautiful creatures, regardless of what they look like.

If you don't believe me, the next time you walk by a woman who is overweight or not particularly attractive or older than you, give her a nice smile, or, better yet, give her a smile and a wink. Her face will light up, she will blush, and you will have made her day. And here's the wildest part, it will also make you feel good. Dad, as usual, was right.

family.

Some friends dropped me off in front of my house after high school one day and I walked up the walkway that cut through the middle of our yard to the front door. When I stepped into the house I saw my Dad standing at the bay window looking outside. He was not happy.

"Stand next to me, son" he said. I did.

"Look into the front yard and tell me what you see."

I looked out the window and saw two empty beer cans in our front yard. Somebody driving down the street had apparently thrown them into our yard.

"Did you see those beer cans when you walked up to the house?" asked my Dad.

"Yes," I answered.

"Why didn't you pick them up?"

I shrugged sheepishly.

My Dad put his hand on my shoulder and said, *"Son, this is not my house. This is our house. Take pride in our house. Take pride in our family. Take pride in yourself. Next time, pick up the beer cans."*

Twenty years later I had that same conversation with my son. And I hope one day he will do the same with his son.

I was standing next to the main bar in a huge country and western honky-tonk in Dallas when I was in my mid twenties. This was just after Debra Winger wore that wonderfully tight tanktop while seductively riding the mechanical bull in the movie *Urban Cowboy*, so this joint, along with other country bars from coast to coast, was packed with real cowboys and with weekend warriors in sharp creased Wrangler jeans, Resistol western shirts, Tony Lama boots, and black Stetson cowboy hats. The dancefloor was jammed with line dancers stomping away to the latest country music hit and the main bar and a dozen satellite bars were force feeding beers and shots to drunken cowboys and cowgirls. Two weeks earlier at this same joint I had watched one cowgirl break a bottle of beer across the face of another cowgirl, so if the ladies here were that rowdy you can imagine what their counterparts with the swinging balls were like. I have always warned my son to be careful in bars after the clock slips past one in the morning because that's when all the sexually frustrated guys who have struck out trying to hook up with a chick are going to want to fight.

family.

That night, the clock slipped past one in the morning and, right on schedule, the cowboy standing next to me said, *"Hey."*

"What's up?" I responded, turning my head to look at the very small cowboy next to me. And by small I mean the top of his cowboy hat came to a point halfway between my elbow and my shoulder.

"You know," he said, fixing me with a stare and punctuating his words by pointing the top of his beer bottle up at me, *"you are so tall and I am so small that you could just rest your beer on top of my head if you wanted to."*

Okey-dokey. Didn't take a rocket scientist to figure out where this was going. I remembered my Dad's constant admonition to just use my head.

So I stretched up to my full six feet and two inches, looked right back down at the small cowboy, tilted the top of my beer bottle toward him to punctuate my point, and I said, *"You know, sometimes it's no fun being as tall as I am."*

The short cowboy stared at me for a few seconds with a rather surprised look on his face, then he gave a slight nod of his head, clinked the top of his bottle of beer against my bottle, and turned back to watch the action on the dancefloor. Crisis averted, plus at that point if six bikers jumped my ass, I know that small cowboy would have dove right into the fray on my behalf. Because I used my head. Thanks, Pops.

They say the acorn doesn't fall far from the tree and, like most sayings, there is a wealth of truth there. My Dad was irreverent, which is why the Air Force never promoted him from major to colonel; he always saw the brighter side, which is why he scavenged materials and built a full-blown bar in his barracks during the Vietnam war; and he was occasionally goofy and silly, which is why his favorite joke was to ask someone, *"Does your face hurt?"*, and when they said no, he would shoot back, *"Well, its killing me!"*

My Dad loved his handheld 8mm camera and played movie director at all our family outings. Our living room would be packed with relatives and friends and my Dad would roll the movie footage he had shot and there would be all of us kids on the screen splashing away in the military base swimming pool, and then the camera would pan away and settle on the jiggly bikini ass of some hottie walking by. *"Dad!"* my sisters would yell, while my little brother and I would just smile and think, *"Way to go, Pops!"*

family.

At one point my Dad was transferrred from an overseas Air
Force base to a base in one of the Southern states where we had to
stay at a dump of a roadside motel for two weeks until he could find
a house to buy. After a stressful weeklong journey by train, boat and
rental car, we unloaded our family of seven's many suitcases into the
small motel. I just dropped the suitcases inside the front doorway
and I remember my Dad telling me to spread out the suitcases into
the different bedrooms so that my Mom would not walk through the
motel door into a mound of clutter and chaos after our weary
pilgrimage. That comment made a big impression, showing selfish
me that, one, it was possible to think about someone else besides
yourself, and, two, it can be the littlest of things you do that can make
another person happy.

The motel we stayed at was called the Kickapoo Motel. I shit
you not. Like other roadside motels, the motel was in the shape of
the letter "U" with a tiny pool in the middle courtyard.

It was at that pool that I had my first boner.

I was in the shallow end when a bleached blonde in her forties
with boobs the size of soccer balls and a thong bikini emblazoned
with rhinestones walked up and sat on the edge of the pool. Keep in
mind this was over forty years ago when very few women had breast
implants and no women wore swim suits the size of dental floss.
Turns out Miss Humongous Boobs was the featured star that week at
a supper club/strip club called the Stork Lounge just down the
highway.

I savored the view for about a half hour and when the little bulge
in my swimsuit had finally subsided, I jumped out of the pool and ran
to our motel room.

"Dad, come here. You gotta see this."

"I'm busy, son. Go away."

"Trust me. You're gonna want to see this."

He came, he saw, he stayed.

For the next week I heard the same three words from my Mom.

"Where's you're father?"

"At the pool."

"What, again?"

* * *

286

family.

I cheated every now and then in college.

I had to.

I didn't have time to study. I was going to classes from early morning to mid afternoon and then working from mid afternoon to midnight, first as a shoe salesmen, and then as a newspaper reporter. I was a full-time journalist going to college to get a bachelor's degree in journalism. The whole cart before the horse thing.

To me a college degree is just a formality. Over the years I have hired over a hundred people and looked at a few thousand resumes. I always check to see if the applicant has a college degree, but I never look at what college they went to. Who gives a fuck? I am more interested in what part-time or full-time jobs they had while they were in college trying to get that embossed piece of paper. I want to hire hard workers, not those assholes who always raised their hands first in class. If a job applicant includes their GPA in their resume, I toss their resume into the trash. How pretentious. I didn't like you A-plus fucks in school, so why would I like you working for me?

I also make sure to say the work *fuck* a few times in job interviews. If they flinch, be they man or woman, I don't hire them because, baby, they aren't going to fit in here. My bookkeeper, who is now a grandmother in her early sixties, has been with me for more than twenty years, and sprinkles her conversation with f-bombs every day, especially when she is making collection calls. Hey, that's just how we roll.

So I had roving eyes when it came to tests in college. I mean, really, what the hell does biology and calculus have to do with the ability to ask the right questions, take good notes and then write an accurate news story? I got caught cheating once and tossed out of class. That was a little embarrassing. But I did graduate. My final GPA began with the number two, but who's keeping score.

My son, my first born, did not graduate from college. He went for a few years, took a short break, and never went back. He was too busy playing Internet video games. It was a major source of consternation with me and I browbeat him about it for years, telling him how disappointed my Dad, his grandfather, would be. While he was becoming an expert at Internet video games, he was also reading books about computer programming and graphics design as a hobby and eventually he built a website from scratch, custom programming and designing it by himself. Two years later it was ranked in the Top 300 websites in the country based on traffic and he sold it to some Internet conglomerate for millions and millions of dollars. He was twenty-five years old. He has more money than me now, and never has to work another day in his life if he chooses not to.

"Son of mine," I say to him now, *"who needs a college degree? That shit is so over rated."*

My son had been sharing a cramped apartment with two of his buddies for years, so when he got that boatload of cash he bought a huge three-story house on several acres of wooded land. I went to the closing with him at the title company. There were only five people there; my son and I, the lady from the title company, and the couple in their early fifties who were selling the house. The husband was a contractor and had custom built the house himself and he and his wife had raised their children in that house. There was no one there from the bank because my son was not financing the house. He handed the couple a check for a half million dollars. He was wearing baggy shorts, a worn out t-shirt, flip-flops and a baseball cap on backwards.

The look on the faces of the couple selling the house was priceless.

That's my boy.

*   *   *

My stomach growls.

Time for lunch. I know the list says I am supposed to treat myself to a great lunch today, but I can't decide what I want to eat. And I don't really want to eat alone. And despite my stomach growling, I don't feel hungry. Truth be told, today I feel kind of blah. Which, I guess, is understandable, given the situation.

I love food, or, more specifically, I love to eat. Happy John tells me he has never met anyone who likes to eat more than I do. *"Your whole face lights up when you have a plate of food in front of you."* Which is true.

There was one of those single panel cartoons in *Playboy* magazine years ago that showed a starving bum in a science testing lab. He had been given his choice between a table piled high with

family.

turkey, dressing, mashed potatoes, vegetables and pumpkin pie or a stool upon which sat a scantily clad hooker in her late fifties with sagging boobs and a lit cigarette in her grotesquely lipsticked mouth. The bum has dived into the pile of food, ignoring the aged hooker, and the pleased scientist says that the test proves his theory that man's hunger for food is greater than his hunger for sex. I would argue that it really depends on what's being served.

Eating and screwing have a lot in common. They both arouse most of your five senses, they both can be quite enjoyable, and they both don't take very much time. You just get to do one of them for a lot longer during your life than the other.

So it suprises me when I find someone who doesn't enjoy eating. Like Gary. Gary has worked both with me and for me for over two decades, so I have shared a lot of meals on the road with him. He inhales his food and he does it at warp speed. The waiter will put our plates down in front of us and by the time I have put salt and pepper on my entree, Gary is wiping his lips with his napkin and tossing it onto his empty plate. *"How was it?"* I will sarcastically ask and Gary will just shrug. It's funny to see the look on the waiter's face if we are at an Italian restaurant and he comes back with the Parmesan cheese grinder only to position it over the top of Gary's empty plate. Gary used to be an air traffic controller which meant they had to eat fast, but that was years ago, and now I think it's time for him to enjoy that herb-crusted filet mignon and not worry about landing jumbo jets.

Gary, by the way, is probably the best salesman to have ever walked the planet. He's sixty-five years old now and he should be retired and playing golf with other Q-tips but instead he bounces up and down in his office chair and works the phone like a deranged stalker. If he calls a prospective new client and makes a sale on that first call, Gary is downright depressed. He will actually pout. He wants the client to say no and to keep saying no until Gary wears him down and he agrees to buy, and then Gary will come into my office with a big ass smile on his face and punch his fist into his hand and say, *"Ha, I finally got that motherfucker!"* If only Gary could get that excited about a nice plate of corned beef and cabbage.

I know other people who, when their plate of food is served, insist on eating all of one item on the plate before proceeding to the next item, as in eat all the peas, then eat all the scalloped potatoes, then eat all the chicken. Those are the most boring people in the world. They are the people who only have missionary sex, and only with the lights off. Then there are the people who can't have any of the different food items on their plate touch each other. Those are the people who eventually end up on the evening news as the police pull decomposing bodies out of their cellar, while there's always that one neighbor who says, *"I'm so surprised. He was the nicest guy in the world."*

Speaking of cartoons, my three favorites of all time are also single panel cartoons and I mention them because if you really want to find out what makes a person tick, you don't have to give them the Rorschach inkblot test; just find out what makes them laugh. Tells a lot about a person.

The first cartoon shows two guys fishing off a pier, their legs dangling over the side and their fishing lines in the water. The pier is ridiculously high above the water, like four stories high. The two guys look over and see three alligators defying gravity by climbing vertically straight up one of the pier's wooden posts toward them. And one guys says to the other, *"They're not supposed to be able to do that."*

The second cartoon shows a man talking to a woman at an elegant cocktail party. They are both holding martinis. The handsome man is wearing a suit. The attractive woman is wearing a short, black, low-neck dress. The man is looking down at the bottom hem of the woman's dress as more than a dozen small, perfectly round balls fall out from below her hem toward the floor. *"Either your strand of pearls just broke,"* says the man, *"or else you defecate beautifully."*

The third cartoon has no text with it. Just the illustration. That makes it even funnier. It shows three young kids in a movie theater which is jam packed. They are sitting in the second row from the front. There are only three empty seats left in the entire theater, and those seats are in the front row directly in front of the three kids. The movie has not started yet. The three kids each have a huge bag of popcorn in their laps and the expressions on their faces show how happy and excited they are as they wait for the movie to start. The kids can't see it, but walking down the aisle behind them toward the last three empty seats in the theater are three gigantic men. The men also have bags of popcorn and happy expressions on their

290

faces. There is no second panel to the cartoon to show the huge men after they take those last seats in the front row and completely block the view of the young kids. We know it's about to happen, but they don't.

What appeals to me about the three cartoons is that something that should not happen, happens in each of them. To me, that's more fun. Expect the unexpected, and deal with it when it comes.

As for lunch, nothing interests me. So I buzz my secretary, Teresa, and go the tried and true route.

"Yes?"

"Can you order me a Garibaldi? Please."

Which means whoever does my autopsy tomorrow is in for a pungent garlic treat.

Oh well, they wear masks.

*   *   *

I killed my grandfather when I was 14 years old.

I still feel bad about it, even now, forty years later.

My Mom says I didn't kill her father. In fact, she gets mad whenever I bring it up. But I know I did.

My grandfather, who we called Grampy, was full blooded Italian and his wife, Grammy, was full blooded Irish. I'll give you one guess who ran that house. I always thought Grammy was the sweetest little old lady but I remember being at their house once and overhearing my Mom and her only sister talking, and my aunt, after Grammy had done something particularly sweet for us grandkids, said to my Mom, *"They have no idea."*

So apparently Grammy, Irish temper and all, could be as mean as a three headed snake. She was a stern taskmaster who set rigid rules and was not afraid to use a switch on her two girls to enforce those rules, which is why my Mom gets pissed whenever I bring up the jump rope story from when I was growing up, which I can't go into detail on, although I think it's as funny as shit.

Grampy, on the other hand, was a friendly, affable sort, rail thin with a full head of thick salt and pepper hair, even into his seventies. I always hoped I would get his hair genes. No such luck.

I didn't see my grandparents much growing up because my Dad was being transferred from one Air Force base to the next all around the world. They came to visit us once or twice in whatever state we happened to be living in at the time and we saw them at a few family reunions. Every relative on both my Mom's side and my Dad's side lives up north. My Dad was the only one to leave the nest, kind of a prodigal son, albeit one in good standing. Grammy died when I was ten years old and after that I saw more of Grampy. He would come live with us for two months every year.

Every morning while I sat in the kitchen eating my cereal, Grampy would walk in, say good morning and then stand in front of the cabinets to the right of the kitchen sink. He would open the cabinet and from the top shelf take down a bottle of bourbon and a little green plastic glass that myself and my siblings had all drank out of when we were toddlers. The glass had teeth marks on it and it wobbled if you set it down, that's how old and beat up it was, but it served Grampy's purpose. He would open the bottle of bourbon and fill that little green glass all the way to the top. Then, while still standing and facing the cabinet, he would drink the whole glass of bourbon, rinse the glass out in the sink, put the glass and the bottle of bourbon back on the top shelf, close the cabinet, turn around, and say to me, *"Don't tell your mother."*

It was Grampy's daily routine. He would not drink the rest of the day.

I realized later that, just as I needed a bowl of cereal to get my metabolism going in the morning, Grampy needed that shot every morning to get his heart started. It was his morning medicine. He didn't pour the bourbon into a nice cocktail glass with ice cubes and then sit down and leisurely sip it. He took it just like you would take two aspirin. What made it all the more interesting to me was the little green glass. That glass had come full circle, providing milk and orange juice and Kool-Aid to us children and then providing a more potent form of liquid nourishment to our grandparent without whom we would never have existed.

Grampy was dapper and handsome. He was always dressed immaculately and I liked to sit next to him when he smoked his pipe, it smelled so good and made me think about bygone times that I had never even been part of. He was a diehard Red Sox fan and would play catch with me in the back yard, firing that baseball like a rocket despite his age.

family.

"Dad, don't throw the ball so hard. You're going to hurt yourself," my Mom would yell at him from the porch.

"Oh, leave me alone dammit," he would yell back.

Later at night, I would notice that he smoked his pipe with his left hand, his right arm limp at his side, strained from throwing the baseball. He would never say a word about it.

My two favorite stories about my grandfather revolve, as you might expect, around money.

Grampy worked for the railroad, first as a ticket taker, then as a conductor. He would walk through every car and collect the fare from the passengers. It only cost ten cents to ride the train, but one well dressed man told my grandfather that all he had on him was a ten-dollar bill. That was a lot of money back then and my grandfather did not have that much change, so he let the man ride for free. The next day, the man told my grandfather the same story. By the end of the week the man had ridden for free all week and my grandfather was pissed about it the whole weekend. On Monday when my grandfather approached the man, the man smiled, pulled a ten-dollar bill out of his pocket, waved it in front of my grandfather and said, *"This is all I have."*

"No problem," said my grandfather, who snatched the ten-dollar bill from the man's hand and then dropped a paper bag with 990 pennies in it into the man's lap. *"Here's your change."*

My other favorite Grampy story is shrouded in mystery, but the upshot is that he lost the family's house playing poker.

"How many time do I have to tell you. We did not lose our house," my Mom will say in an exasperated voice. They did, however, have to take out a second mortgage to cover my grandfather's gambling losses. He never gambled again after that.

I love that story. I love that the cool, calm, sophisticated old gentleman that I knew as Grampy had once had a wild streak that cost him his house. Not a week's paycheck, not his lawn mower, not his bowling ball, his fucking house. Now that's hardcore.

You would never have thought it looking at that old man.

Which is why gays, blacks, Hispanics, Jews, and all those other whiny groups are all so full of shit when they each claim that their's is the most discriminated against and overlooked segment of society.

That's bullshit.

family.

Old people are the most discriminated against and overlooked segment of our society.

No matter what their race, religion or sexual orientation.

Old people are the *Invisible Man*, all apologies to Ralph Ellison.

They are everywhere, sitting in restaurants, walking through shopping malls, driving cars really slow, and we don't pay any attention to them, we don't even see them. We pay more attention to the punk kid taking our hamburger order than we do to the old guy sitting in the next booth. I think it's because when we see wrinkled skin and silver hair and stooped shoulders, we see death. Which is wrong. What we are seeing is actually the well worn and wonderfully aged hardcover of a book and inside that book are hundreds and hundreds of pages of life, not death. But we never bother to open their books.

There was an article in the newspaper a year or so ago about five American couples in their seventies who were in a van on a tour of some beaches in Costa Rica as part of a weeklong vacation package. They had just pulled up to one of the beaches and stepped out of the van when they were accosted by two young robbers armed with knives. The article stated that the senior citizens froze in fear, all of them that is except for one of the elderly husbands. In a flash, he knocked one of the robbers out cold, then he disarmed the second robber and in the process he snapped the man's neck, killing him instantly. The elderly husband, in his seventies mind you, did it all with his bare hands.

"It happened so quick," said one of the seniors. *"We couldn't believe it. He killed that robber in less than a second."*

The article did not give the name of the old man and simply stated, *"He had a military background in special forces."*

No shit.

Those robbers simply saw ten old people with well worn and aged hardcover books and thought they were easy targets, but had they bothered to open that one old man's book and read a few pages of his life story, they would have run for the hills.

The next time you make eye contact with an old person and no words are exchanged, not even the courtesy of a nod of acknowledgement on your part, and you wonder what that old person might be thinking, I can tell you exactly what he or she is thinking, and that is, *If you only knew.*

family.

Grampy was staying with us when I was fourteen years old. He slept in my bedroom in my little brother's bed. My brother took the couch in the den. If my brother and I were to go back to our old house today and walk into that little bedroom we shared and try to picture both of us sleeping in there with two beds and two dressers, we would look at each other and both say the same thing: *"No fucking way."*

It was a very tiny bedroom. Actually it was a tiny house for a family of seven. A few times I could hear my parents going at it in their bedroom down the hall, and by going at it, I don't mean they were fighting. I know, it's the last sound you want to hear as a kid.

So when my grandfather in the middle of the night in our tiny bedroom called my name and said, *"Go get your father,"* I heard him nice and clear. But I just went back to sleep. I'm not sure if he said it again or not, and I hope like hell he didn't, but deep down inside I know he did. And I don't know how much time elapsed after he first called out to me, but what I remember next was the bedroom light coming on and my Dad standing in the doorway saying, *"Grampy are you okay?"* The ambulance was at our house five minutes later.

When I left for school that morning my parents were both still at the hospital. I was playing basketball in the school gym around lunch time when the assistant principal walked into the gym and put his arm around my shoulder and walked me to his car in the school parking lot and drove me home. I asked him what was going on but he didn't answer.

When I walked into the house, my Mom gave me a big hug and said, *"Grampy's gone."*

I don't like talking about it.

* * *

I wipe the last bit of garlic from my lips and toss the butcher paper that the Garibaldi sandwich had been wrapped in into the trash, and then I buzz Teresa and tell her to rally the troops in the main room for a staff meeting. I have a staff staff meeting every six weeks or so. I hate staff meetings. If my peeps don't know what they need to do and when they need to do it and how they need to do it by now, then shame on them, and me.

family.

Several of the ladies crowd next to Boo on the couch. He won't give up his spot for anyone. The other staffers roll their chairs from their offices into the main room. I blather on for awhile about upcoming projects and briefly think about saying something telling and significant that they will all remember after I'm gone, but I quickly jettison that notion, and just blather on for another few minutes.

"Any questions?" I ask.

Nobody says anything.

"What about you, Boo? I saw you had your hand up."

Everybody laughs.

Even though they've heard that line a dozen times before.

"Okay," I say, *"thanks so much for coming. See you later."*

If they only knew.

*   *   *

My buddy Vegas Jack was crazy about this chick when he was a young man. And she was crazy about him. After about six months he realized that the girl he was crazy about was just plain crazy. So he stopped seeing her and soon found out how truly crazy she was. She stalked him and made his life a living hell for months until one night when he was leaving a party and she crashed into the back of his car, trapping him in the parking lot. Jack got out of his car, walked back to her car, opened the passenger door, slid in, placed a .45 automatic to the girl's forehead, looked her straight in the eye, and said, *"I'll do the time."*

And he meant it.

And, crazy or not, she knew he meant it.

So she stopped stalking him.

Isn't true love grand.

My Mom used to tell me to never despair because there is one special person for everyone somewhere in this world. Mom, I said, what a fucking coincidence that my person just happened to live three blocks from my house.

People tend to confuse marriage with family. Marriage is an arrangement, family is blood. One is by choice, the other isn't.

Listen, I love my wife today as much as I did when we were married. But the way I feel about married life today, or anything else in this world for that matter, compared to how I felt about it thirty years ago are two different things. Everything changes.

My Mom, never one to hold her tongue, told my wife before we were married, *"I love my son, but you are about to marry the most selfish person in the world. Are you ready for that?"* Thanks Mom. That could have cost you your first two grandchildren.

I remind my wife of my Mom's warning whenever she calls me to task now for a variety of shortcomings. *"Listen, I was an asshole when you married me, and I'm still an asshole now. Is this some new revelation for you?"*

The problem is, that the answer is yes, it is indeed a new revelation for my wife and all the other wives around the globe.

Mainly because of those damn children.

Don't get me wrong. The greatest accomplishment of my wife and I is our two children. We did a good job on that little project.

But here's what happens. When you first get married you are oblivious to your partner's faults because you are both young and foolish. Just about the time your partner's idiosyncrasies start to irritate the fuck out of you, you start having kids, so for the next twenty years or so you focus on your kids and don't have time to be irritated by your spouse. But once the kids are gone, once you have that empty nest, once it's just you and your spouse staring at each other across that breakfast nook table, that's when the shit starts to hit the fan.

I knew a young woman who had been married for five years to a very nice guy, those were the very words she used to describe him, and together they had two wonderful little boys. But she still divorced him. When I asked her why, she said, *"Just the sound of him chewing his food drove me crazy."*

And that was after just five years. What happens when people are married for twenty or thirty or forty years, decades upon decades of living in such close proximity, sharing the same house, the same bed, the same shower day in and day out, finishing each other's sentences, watching each other slowly turn gray and fall apart, sinking hand in hand into that pool of crankiness and irritability that comes with old age. I mean, come on, whose idea was that? Can anybody really expect two human beings to spend that much time together without something exploding? Is that why half of all marriages end in divorce?

family.

When my wife and I periodically reach the breaking point and have one of our sitdown discussions, I will ask her if she loves her parents.

"Of course I do," she says.

I love them too. They are very easy going and low maintenance. When they come to visit, Papaw will fix anything that is broken at our house—the man could strip down the Space Shuttle and put it back together without leaving any extra pieces—and then quietly watch NASCAR in the living room. Mamaw will cook huge country style meals, clean the kitchen, wash and fold all the laundry, and then organize all the canned goods in our pantry.

"Okay, so when your parents come to stay at our house for a week-long visit, on what day are you ready for them to leave?"

"The fourth day."

"So," I say, *"five or more days with the people who raised you and who are so easy to be around is too much for you, yet you and I have been together on an almost daily basis for more than thirty-five years and you don't recognize how much friction that can create?"*

"Listen," I will say to her, *"most of the time, I don't even like me. So why are you so surprised that every now and then you realize that you don't particularly like me?"*

There is a joke about the three types of sex that married couples have, which are kitchen sex, bedroom sex and hallway sex. Kitchen sex is when you are first married and you have sex in every room in your house, even the kitchen. Bedroom sex is when you've been married for ten years and you only have sex in the bedroom. Hallway sex is when you've been married twenty years and you just pass each other in the hallway and say, *"Fuck you,"* to each other.

The best jokes are the ones that have a nugget of truth to them, like that one. When you are first married you screw like rabbits and your spouse is wonderful and you have not a care or worry in the world. After ten years you are weighed down with demanding kids and home mortgages and work pressures and you find time every now and then to knock boots in your bedroom after collapsing exhausted into your bed. Then when the kids are gone and neither of you have that same sex appeal that you had when you were young, and the wrinkles are showing, and the aches and pains are starting, and you realize that neither of you are as perfect as you once thought, then you would rather fight than fuck.

family.

If that's not enough of a roadblock to keep you and your spouse from enjoying years and years of wedded bliss before walking off into the sunset together, there's the problem of the on-and-off switch, just one more area where God, I hate to say, it, kind of fucked up.

There is a reason food tastes good. If it didn't, we wouldn't eat. And if we didn't eat, we would die and then there would be no more human race. So God made food taste good. Smart move.

And there is a reason that having sex feels good. If it didn't, we wouldn't fuck. And if we didn't fuck, there would be no more babies and then there would be no more human race. So God made having sex feel good. Smart move.

But God couldn't just stop there. He had to mess around with the sex thing.

Because many women tend to have headaches and prefer reading romance novels over having their sweaty mates huffing and puffing away on top of them, he gave men a triple dose of the sex drive to insure that babies would keep popping out. In his haste, he forgot that, to insure that men brought home the bacon to their hungry brood, he had already given men the hunter's instinct where the hunt is even more fun than the kill. And he forgot that, to insure that men didn't just bring home rabbits for dinner every single night, he gave men the eternal quest for variety. And then, bless his heart, he made sure to turn off the sex drive for women when they hit their late thirties, but just when he was about to do the same thing for men, he got a phone call, and he completely forgot about it until it was too late. *"Damn, I forgot to turn that sex drive switch off for the boys!"*

No shit, Sherlock.

So what he ended up with were women who are happily monogamous, who enjoy sex for a certain period, and who then just want to raise their children. But he also ended up with men who want to screw anything that squats to piss, pretty much from the day they are born until the day they die.

When God finally realized his mistake, he didn't go back and reverse that whole sex drive thing so that men and women would be on the same playing field and would live happily ever after with no broken hearts, divorces or kids growing up without two parents. Instead, his remedy was to make young secretaries, eager strippers and glitzy trophy wives. Oh, and also Corvettes, penthouse condos, hair dye for men, gold chest chains, and Viagra.

What was he thinking?

* * *

To get my writing juices flowing before tackling the suicide note that I did not get done yesterday, I go to the alt.suicide.holiday website again and read the latest posts. Some of them are just too funny.

"I once put my head in an enormous mound of fire ants, and proceeded to let them eat it. They crawled up my nose, into my mouth, and down my throat. Someone saw me and pulled me out before they could do me in. Healing took months. I could not talk, could hardly breathe, and was force fed through a pump like a vegetable."

Another poster ended up in the same emergency room after three separate failed drug overdose attempts and recalls a nurse saying to him, *"If you keep this up, you're going to kill yourself.'"*

Emergency rooms crop up a lot. *"The next thing I knew I was in ER with my crying brother over me saying, 'Why did you do that? You're not even fat.'"*

Some posters can be quite creative. *"I tried oleander, one of the most poisonous plants in the world, at least five times in a two-week period. Each time I had major projectile vomiting. I don't recommend oleander except for weight loss. I lost ten pounds in one week."*

If at first you don't succeed ...

First attempt: *"Drank bleach. It made me throw up. My stomach burned for weeks."*

Second attempt: *"Hanging. Did not know how to tie a correct noose, and my head slipped out after my throat was crushed. Could not swallow well for a few weeks. Painful."*

Third attempt: *"Prescription drugs. Did not have enough to complete the job. This method was pleasant. I am looking forward to trying it again with morphine, probably in conjunction with a plastic bag."*

They have persistence and diversity. *"I've tried to electrocute myself in the bathtub like in Groundhog Day using a hair dryer and a toaster but they both were grounded and didn't do shit. I've tried putting a tight plastic bag over my face but I panic when I can't breathe and end up ripping the bag off. It's the same with trying to hang myself outside my door. I can't force myself to stay there, plus all the weird sounds coming out of my mouth freak the shit out of me."*

The ASH stories are interesting, but deliver no fodder for my note. I open a blank text document, and stare at the computer screen trying to decide what the hell to put in the note. I'm not even sure how to start it.

Boy, I'll bet you guys are surprised ...

* * *

When my son was twenty years old, he and some of his buddies were at our house sitting in the living room watching a football game on television. They were all healthy, handsome white guys from affluent families who had gone to school together.

So I said to them, *"If you died and you could come back into this world, but only as a black man or as a white woman, which one would you choose?"*

Nothing against black men or women, but there is no question that their lot in life is, and probably always will be, a lot tougher than that of a white man. They say it's a young man's world, but what they really mean to say is that it's a young white man's world. Sucks, but it's the truth.

A lively debate ensued, and for the next half hour the football game was forgotten. But they soon came to a consensus, all of them saying they would choose to come back as a black man. When I asked why, they said they knew that as a black man they would have to deal with discrimination but that they could not even imagine going through life as a woman. Having periods, giving birth and being the weaker sex was too foreign a concept to hardy young guys who wake up every day ready to either fuck or fight.

I asked the same question a week later to a group of my buddies while we were playing poker one night. They too are white guys, well there is Ben the Chinaman and Will the Japanese guy but we consider them token whites, and they are all in their early fifties

family.

and they are healthy for the most part, but not really handsome any more, except for Perfect Paul, and they are all affluent.

Same thing happened.

A lively debate ensued, and for the next half hour the poker game was forgotten. But they too soon came to a concensus, all of them saying they would choose to come back as a white woman. When I asked why, they all said they were gay. Just kidding. What they agreed on was that, in the long run, race and not gender has a bigger impact on how your life unfolds. They said life is much easier if you are white, regardless of whether you are a man or a woman.

The key to their reasoning was their vantage point of being able to look at life in the long run. My son and his friends have not yet started their trek down the road of life. They have a hard time thinking any farther into the future than where that weekend's party is going to be. My friends, though, have traveled down the road of life and they know how treacherous and unforgiving it can be. They know that life is a hard enough journey on its own, but it can be so much harder if the color of your skin multiplies the obstacles in your path to the tenth degree.

Being born is your first roll of the dice: what color, what race, what country, what sexual preference, what physical and mental prowess, or lack thereof. Then your parents and your social environment come into play.

My buddy Tom's father, the Air Force colonel who got us out of jail that time, was a tough old bird. I was always nervous when I went over to Tom's house to hang out when we were teenagers. You don't get to be a full bird colonel in the military, the next rank up is general, without knowing how to crack the whip and bust some chops, and Tom's father could do both with his eyes closed. To let off steam he spent years restoring from scratch an antique 1930s era car in their garage and when he was finished it looked like it had just rolled off the showroom floor. The man was a perfectionist, wanted things done his way, was opinionated and bullheaded, and was a leader and not a follower, all traits that clashed head-on with a teenaged son just starting to feel his oats. The irony was that Tom had every single one of those traits himself.

After one blow-up with his father, Tom picked me up in his car and we headed out for some mischief. In the car I listened for ten minutes as Tom, who was so hot and worked up that his face was

family.

flushed, complained about his father. When he was finished, I waited a few seconds and let the silence in the car sink in before I said, *"I don't know what you're bitching about. You are exactly like your father. To a fucking-T, buddy."*

Tom didn't say a word but I could see his whole body slowly deflate. Then he smiled a wicked little smile and said, *"You know, you are so fucking right."*

* * *

"Where's the leash?" I ask Teresa about mid-afternoon.

"Why?" she asks back.

"Because I'm going to take Boo for a walk"

"No you're not.

"Yes I am."

"But you never take him for a walk. I've never once seen you walk him."

"I just feel like it today."

She takes Boo's leash out of her top drawer and hands it to me.

"Want me to show you how to put it on?"

My secretary is such a smartass. She's the youngest person on my staff and she is also the best worker I have ever had. She is the undisputed Queen Bee of the office and if she wasn't here, everything would pretty much fall apart. I hired her when she was twenty and she has been with me for more than ten years. She is almost like a second daughter to me. I cried at her wedding. She had her first baby a year ago. She will go to my funeral, and then she will never set foot again in this office. I know that.

"Be careful. He's awful strong."

Yeah right, I think, to myself. The leather leash weighs more than Boo. Outside, I find out she is right.

Boo takes off like a shot, dragging me behind him, which has to look ridiculous to anyone who happens to be watching, ten pounds of canine pulling two-hundred-and-forty pounds of human.

"Slow the fuck down," I yell at him and give the leash a jerk. Does no good whatsoever and for the next twenty minutes I do a fast walk to keep up with Boo. He's always in a rush to get to the spot three feet ahead of him and when he gets there he wants to go to the next spot three feet ahead of that, and on and on. He's never

family.

satisfied with where he's at and always wants to rush ahead to what he thinks is something even better. Reminds me of someone I know.

My plan was to enjoy a nice leisurely walk with my best friend on my last sunny day. Instead, I feel like I am running a decathlon looking up the ass of a squirrel the whole way.

I herd Boo back to the office, take off his leash and hand it to Teresa.

"Maybe you should lie down on the couch. You look a little winded."

"I'm fine."

"I'm just saying. Don't even expect me to perform CPR on you."

"You mean you wouldn't give me mouth to mouth?"

"Not even."

"Okay, you're fired."

"Promises, promises."

In my office, I lean back and put my feet up on my desk. Shit, I am winded.

*   *   *

"Make new friends but keep the old, one is silver and the other is gold," says my Mom.

I was having dinner in London with Concert Larry and two business associates who were friends of ours as well as being our clients. They worked in the concert industry promoting rock and roll shows in Canada. All four of us were hardcore drinkers, so we started with martinis and cocktails, had beer and wine with our meal, and then went to after dinner brandy and coffee as we smoked, which you could actually do in restaurants back then. The massive amount of liquor had loosened everyone's tongues. So when I made the clever observation that we had just had a United Nations dinner because Larry and I were from the United States, they were from Canada, we were all in London, and we had just eaten at an Indian restaurant, it opened the door for an observation from one of our two Canadian friends.

"We like you guys, but do you want to know what most Canadians think about Americans?" he asked, a slight slur in his voice.

family.

"Well, I'll tell you. Canadians thinks Americans are arrogant assholes. You control the global economy, you start wars whenever and wherever you want, you are bullies, and you have no taste or class."

The other Canadian, also slurring a bit, then chimed in.

"He's right. Canadians think that Americans are unintelligent, unattractive, uncouth and overweight. You would not believe how often we Canadians badmouth you Americans."

When they stopped, I took a sip of brandy, looked at both of our Canadian friends and said, *"That's funny because in America we never talk about Canadians.*

"To us, you don't even exist."

With a few well chosen words, I had reinforced their point and kicked them in the teeth at the same time.

"You are such a dick," Larry said to me later.

"That was good, wasn't it."

"Yeah, it was," said Larry.

I walked into Larry's office once to find him rubbing the wooden bowl of his unlit pipe on each side of his nose. He's finally snapped, I thought to myself.

"What the hell are you doing?"

Larry, who was born in Italy, explained that in his homeland the old-timers would rub the skin oil from their nose on their wooden pipes to keep them from drying out and to keep the wood nice and shiny. There was no Internet back then so I had to take Larry's word for it. It reminded me of the time I had a bad head cold and was on an airplane. The cabin pressure combined with my congestion made me feel like my head was about to explode. My ears were ringing and it felt like someone was stabbing sharp needles into my eardrums. I mentioned this to a stewardess who said she could fix the problem. She came back with two Styrofoam cups into which she had placed napkins soaked in hot water.

"Put these cups over your ears and just hold them there," she said.

I did as she suggested and after twenty minutes of holding the two cups on my ears I realized that the ringing and pain had not subsided one little bit. I also realized that every passenger who walked by me on the way to the restroom looked at me like I had just left the set of *One Flew Over the Cuckoo's Nest*.

family.

"Uh, are you sure this really works?" I asked the stewardess. She just smiled. I felt like a goofball.

Larry also told me that in Italy when they cook a steak on a grill, they never let steel touch the steak. They use wooden tongs to move the steak around on the grill. I found that interesting, just like the nose oil thing. That's why I liked Larry; he always had something new and intriguing to pass along.

Like my buddy Vegas Jack, Concert Larry could drink like a fish and never get wasted. He was a big solid guy who looked a lot like Wolfman Jack. He was always smiling and seemed to be a jolly soul, but if he got pissed off, with his full beard, long hair and huge build, he looked like a Hell's Angel. We were in a bar in California once and, of course, I was shitfaced. I bumped into some musclehead and spilled his drink. The guy squared off in front of me and I was about one second away from him smashing me in the face. I watched as he cocked his right arm back and then I watched as his eyes got as big as saucers and he quickly dropped his arm. He was staring at something over my shoulder. I turned my head and saw that Larry had stood up from the table where he had been sitting with two young ladies. He was staring right at the musclehead. Larry stood absolutely still, but one look at his eyes and you knew that if the musclehead laid a finger on me Larry would beat him down like a dog. The guy turned and walked away. Larry sat back down with the ladies and that big smile was back on his face in a flash.

Larry always had my back.

Except for one night when he himself almost punched me out. We were in downtown Nashville after a night of heavy drinking. It was about two in the morning and I was driving us in our rental car back to our hotel. I was driving very fast and very recklessly, the car radio blaring. Larry kept yelling at me to slow down. I turned down a one-way street going the wrong way. Now Larry really started yelling, so naturally the only thing I could do in response was to speed up and weave the car back and forth, seeing how close I could get to the cars parked on the side of the street without hitting them.

"I swear to God, if you don't stop the car right now, I am going to knock you out," Larry yelled.

family.

Which made me laugh, and drive even closer to the parked cars. The speedometer was at fifty.

"I'm gonna do it," screamed Larry. *"You better fucking stop."*

More laughs from me and I punched it up to sixty.

Then Larry grabbed my shoulder with his left hand and cocked his right hand back, and I took one look at that massive fist and slowly applied the brakes. I was still laughing when we came to a stop.

"You are fucking crazy," said Larry.

"It's all your fault," I said.

"Why?" he asked, pulling the keys out of the ignition.

"You should never have let me drive."

"One of these days," said Larry, but even as drunk as I was, I could see him smiling when he said it.

* * *

One more imagine. I promise it's the last one.

Imagine you are on a airplane, a huge fucking plane that is flying over the Atlantic Ocean midway between Europe and America. On the plane are some niggers, spics, kikes, wops, rednecks, camel jockeys, gooks, honkies, coons, frogs, limeys, goys, greasers, hebes, redskins, krauts, skinheads, niglets, dotheads, bikers, polacks, crackers, ragheads, shiksas, slopes, wetbacks, albinos, midgets, amputees, lesbians, fags, trannies, racists, democrats, republicans, libertarians, socialists, communists, baptists, catholics, muslims, hindus, buddhists, wiccas, atheists, the bully who stuffed you in your locker in fifth grade, and the former girlfriend who told everybody that you had a premature ejaculation problem.

It's like Moses was hard of hearing and instead of loading a motley assortment of animals onto the ark, he loaded a motley assortment of people onto your plane. And you hate every fucking one of those people. They don't look like you or think like you, they don't live like you or act like you. They all suck. Big time.

If you and all those asswipes were on the ground, you would be hurling insults, or fists, or bricks, or gunshots, or embargoes, or nuclear bombs at them.

But you're not on the ground. You are all together inside an object that is hurtling through the air at an incredibly rapid speed.

family.

You can't get off that object, and neither can any of those other peeps. There's nowhere to go. You can't just open the door and step outside. You can't just say you want to move to another airplane. You're stuck with the one that you're on. And you can't screw around with the stability and safety and longevity of that flying object by fighting row to row with those people you hate, or by setting fires in the aisle, or by using up all the jet fuel, or by knocking out the windows, or by eating all the tiny packages of salted peanuts.

So you realize at that point, as any sane person would, that it does not really matter any more what the gender, race, religion, politics or sexual preference is of the people on the plane with you because you no longer have the luxury of hating them. You have to get along, you have to work together, and you have to rely on each other to make sure that the plane keeps flying safely through the air. You simply have no other choice. You now have a shared interest with every other person on that airplane if you want to survive.

Because, like it or not, they are your airplane family.

Okay, now imagine that you are not on an airplane with all those people. Instead, you are on Planet Earth with all those people.

And Planet Earth is an object that is hurtling through space at an incredibly rapid speed.

And you can't get off that object.

And you can't just say you want to move to another planet.

Which means you can't screw around with the stability and safety and longevity of that planet by fighting border to border with those people you hate, or by not equally sharing all of the bounties of the planet with them, or by firing off nuclear warheads at them, or by using up all of the planet's natural resources, or by eating all the tiny packages of salted peanuts.

You have to get along, you have to work together, and you have to rely on each other to make sure that your planet keeps hurtling safely through space. You simply have no other choice. You have a shared interest with every other person on your planet if you want the human race to survive.

Because, like it or not, they are your planet family.

When you were a kid, you and your buddies owned your block. If guys from the next block came over, the rocks started sailing. We hate those fuckers, you would say.

family.

When guys from the next town cruised your neighborhood, you and your buddies and the guys from the next block would band together against those townies and the fists would start flying. Those guys from the next block aren't so bad after all, but we hate those other fuckers, you all said.

When guys from the next state came to your town for a football game, you and your buddies, and the guys from the next block, and the townie guys would band together against those out-of-staters and it was punch city. Those townies aren't so bad after all, but we hate those other fuckers, you all said.

When guys from up North came down South for a championship game, you and your buddies and the townie guys and the guys from your adjoining states would band together and start a rumble with those damn Northeners. Those guys from our adjoining states aren't so bad after all, but we hate those other fuckers, you all said.

When guys from another country really pissed your country off, you and your buddies and the next block guys and the townie guys and the adjoining state guys and the guys from up North all banded together and put the smackdown down on those foreigners. Those guys from up North aren't so bad after all, but we hate those other fuckers, you all said.

And when the spaceships from another planet entered our atmosphere and started blasting your block, and the townies, and the adjoining states, and the cities up North, and every country on our planet ...

Get it? One planet. One people. One family.

Like it or not.

* * *

I am proud to be Human.

Notice I didn't say proud to be American, or Swedish, or African, or Australian, or Martian, although, for the record, I am damn proud to be an American. Still, I consider myself a member of the entire Human Race and not just one geographical area. Think of all the wars and carnage and hate that has come from something as silly as people swearing allegiance to a specific chunk of real estate on this planet.

If you want to get technical, then I am proud to be Pangaean.

family.

We are all from Pangaea. Today there are seven continents
and about two-hundred countries on our planet, but many centuries
ago all of the continents were part of one huge land mass called
Pangaea. Then the Continental Drift kicked in and split Pangaea up
and huge land masses drifted away to form the continents we have
today. People who had been neighbors and friends and bowling
partners for years saw their buddies floating away on different pieces
of land which, of course, immediately made them their enemies.

"Don't be such a hater, Homer."

*"Fuck you and your chunk of land. One day I'm going to drop
an atom bomb on your head."*

*"But why, Homer? We used to be such good friends, almost like
family."*

"Not any more. You moved."

* * *

I buzz Teresa.

"What is it now?" she says. *"You're wearing me out."*

I remember when it used to be good to be The King. Today, it's
good to be the Queen Bee.

*"I am so sorry to have disturbed you. Can you please hold all
my calls and tell everyone to stay the hell out of my office for the next
hour."*

"You got it."

I write my suicide note.

It's not as easy as those five words make it sound.

Not even close.

* * *

At those popular parties that we have on the lanai at our house,
one of the big hits is always the Jello Shots.

My wife mixes vodka with powdered Jello, pours the mixture
into little paper shot cups, freezes them, and then passes the tray of
shots around at the party. You just squeeze the bottom of the paper
cup and the Jello Shot pops right into your mouth. It may seem like
a harmless, fruity concoction, but knock down a half dozen or more
of those puppies and you will be feeling no pain. All of our friends

family.

ask for the recipe, and my wife is happy to give it to them, never mentioning that the recipe was given to her by our next door neighbor.

The one who shot her husband to death.

While we slept two houses away.

That was twenty-five years ago when we lived in Texas. They were a married couple in their early thirties who both worked, who had no children, and who pretty much kept to themselves in the neighborhood. We knew them just well enough to wave at them when we were each outside doing yardwork. One year, though, they came out of their shell and invited us and the rest of the neighbors to their house for a New Year's Eve party and that's when we tried our first Jello Shots and my wife asked for and was given the cocktail recipe from the lady of the house.

A few months after that fun-filled party, Mrs. Jello Shot shot her husband twice in the back, killing him deader than hell.

The *shot* lady *shot* him. Don't you just love it.

She initially told police that her husband, who was found in his underwear lying in the middle of their driveway early in the morning, had been shot by two Hispanic men who were trying to break into his new pickup truck. Her story didn't adequately explain why, if her hubby was capped outside in the driveway, there was blood inside the house, in both the sink and on the refrigerator, and why there was a bullet hole in their hallway. Or why there was a plastic bag filled with bloody towels hidden under their bedroom mattress.

So she got life in prison.

And we got a cool recipe.

My wife still has that recipe card, which was handwritten by the murderess herself. It's like having Ted Bundy's autograph. I may sell it on eBay.

That murder really freaked my wife and I out.

Not because we lived in a nice subdivision of new, yet modest, houses, but because just six months earlier when we were renting a house across town, our next door neighbor's daughter was raped and murdered.

Yeah, that's two murders.

Those particular neighbors lived right next door to us and we shared a six-foot tall chain link fence. On their side of the fence they had kennels and dog runs for more than a dozen full grown and

family.

ferocious German Shepherds that they raised and trained as attack dogs. The couple's twenty-one-year-old daughter went out partying one night and never came home. Police found her car the next day and inside they found her body. She had been brutally raped and strangled to death. It gave my wife chills when police returned the murdered young woman's car, a bright yellow Volkswagen, and her parents left it parked outside in their driveway, a colorful and constant reminder to everyone on our street of what had happened. What gave me chills was thinking about how our neighbors had a dozen huge dogs trained to tear a grown man's throat out, and yet that had not helped their daughter one little bit.

I don't know if they ever caught the killer. A few months later, my wife and I withdrew what little savings we had for a down payment on a small house on the other side of town. We thought it would be safer there for us and our infant son.

So we bought the house next to Mrs. Jello Shot.

How were we to know.

It gets better. Or worse. Depending on how you look at it.

There was a young newlywed couple who lived directly behind our new house. Though we had a lot in common since they were about the same age as my wife and I and they too had an infant son, we didn't really know them other than to occasionally say hello over the tall wooden fence that separated our backyards. A few months after the Jello Shot shooting, the young newlywed couple were in their pickup truck on the way to a nearby supermarket in the middle of a sunny Sunday afternoon. Another pickup truck cut them off in traffic and so the husband gave the other driver the middle finger. A passenger in the other truck leaned out the window and fired a high-powered rifle at our neighbors. The bullet blasted through their windshield and hit the wife in the head, killing her. Their infant son was sitting in the front seat between them.

Nobody was ever caught. The widowed husband soon moved out of the house. The house went unsold for years, the empty structure slowly turning gray, yet again another visual reminder to my wife and I of what had happened every time we went into our backyard.

So yeah, that made three murders.

Of our immediate neighbors.

In less than a year.

family.

Not accidental or natural deaths, mind you, but flat out murders. Kind of fucked up, if you ask me.

The sad part is that more than being our neighbors, they had been families. Families that disintegrated.

Everybody hopes to one day have their own family. In your late teens through mid twenties you may sow some wild oats, bang a lot of chicks or dudes, dabble in drink and drugs, tour Europe for a summer, go to political rallies, and have heated discussions about how to change the world, but eventually your orbit of self discovery and independence will start circling back to the center and you will want to settle down with that white picket fence and the comfort and security of a loving spouse and the smiling eyes of your own children.

Our three neighbors had all of that one day.

And the next day it was gone.

It can happen that quickly.

Because life is fragile, and so are families.

The family life of the Jello Shot couple might not have been lovey-dovey, but I'm sure the husband would have preferred puttering in his family garden over being shot to death, and I'm sure the wife, after just a few months of starchy prison food and groping bull dyke cellmates, would have preferred helping her husband in that garden over a lifetime behind steel bars. For the neighbors who lost their daughter and the neighbor who lost his wife, and the infant who lost his mother, life will never be the same, their family unit will never be whole again, no matter how much time goes by.

Those three stories always make me think about capital punishment. I am a rabid liberal who is pro-people and anti-establishment and who believes that the state should be involved in my life and the lives of every other person on this planet as little as possible. And I also believe that every single person who is on Death Row right now should be executed at 9 am tomorrow morning. I'll even help pull the switch.

Give me the most anti-capital punishment person in the world and I will stick that person with a team of veteran homicide detectives who will spend the week letting them read homicide reports and view crime scene photos and videos, and after that week I will deliver to you a person who vehemently supports the death penalty. And if that doesn't quite do it, then I will send that person back for one more week of orientation with the cops and this time the crime reports and the crime scene photos and videos will only show children who were the victims of rape, torture and murder. After that, that person will stand right next to me and help pull the switch. Trust me on that.

We have no problem putting down a mad dog, but we balk at doing the same thing for a person. You can't rehabilitate a mad dog, and you can't rehabilitate a truly evil and vicious person.

Take a survey of prison inmates where their votes are kept secret and ask them if they support capital punishment. The majority of them will vote yes because they spend every day looking into the eyes of the most mad dogs on this planet. Ward and June Cleaver in their suburban house have no clue what evil lurks in the minds and deeds of some men and women, but that lifer in Angola State Penitentiary sure the fuck does. Justice in a prison is swift, with no room for theoretical debate. Try stealing in prison, or not paying back a debt, or not honoring your word, or stabbing someone in the neck, or being a convicted child molester and see how quickly your punishment is meted out by people not even remotely interested in trials or the appeals process.

I could bore you with a hundred true, make-your-skin-crawl examples of why the death penalty makes sense, but there is one story from ten years ago that stands out for me. A woman in California was viciously raped by a man who told her he would come back and cut her throat if she called the police. She called police, he was arrested, and at his trial, when the victim took the stand to testify, the man stood up in court and said that, if he was convicted, then the week he got out of prison he would find the woman and kill her. The man was convicted, served his ten years, and the week he was released, he tracked down the woman, broke into her apartment, beat and raped her, and then slit her throat. Just like he promised. The woman's teenaged daughter was also at home, and so the man beat, raped and slit her throat.

I remember that the news story said there was a trail of blood on the carpet from the woman's front door to her back door. The woman, knowing her daughter was in the apartment, had tried unsuccessfully to draw her killer out the back door, to protect her family, one of the strongest natural instincts in the world.

family.

Had that man been put to death after his first brutal rape, his death might not have been a deterrent to other criminals. I'll give you that. But, had he been put to death, then he would not have been able to come back and slaughter that woman and her child. You have to give me that. The death penalty is not supposed to be a deterrent to *all* criminals. It's a deterrent to *one* criminal. At a time. Come on people, this is some simple shit. Nothing complicated here. As my Dad used to say, *"Use your head."*

I think the problem has to do with semantics. People take issue with the government *punishing* someone, because punishment hints at retaliation, and we don't want the powers to be involved in that line of business. So instead let's call it what it really is. It's not *capital punishment*, it's *waste management.*

When I was a teenager, there was a family that lived across the street from us, and my parents were very good friends with the mother and father who lived there. They had three children the same ages as myself and my two oldest sisters, and I would pal around with their son, getting into neighborhood mischief and shooting hoops down at the local recreation center. Their father was in the Air Force with my Dad and their mother and my Mom would shop together and visit over coffee.

When my first dog died during an operation to have her spayed, I was devastated. I was twelve years old and I rode my bike to the vet's office and, sobbing, I asked the vet if I could have her collar. The vet started to cry as he handed me the collar. The whole thing was a fucking emotional mess. I remember my Mom's friend from across the street walked over to our house, came into our kitchen, put her arms around me and gave me a big hug and told me that everything would be all right. Like my Mom, she was a tiny little thing, but that hug from someone outside of my family meant the world to me. I can still remember it more than forty years later.

When I was twenty-one I moved out to Southern California to explore the world and to work at a newspaper there. One night I got a call from my Dad. He told me that the oldest son of their friends from across the street had been shot and killed. He had gone to a downtown area of nightclubs and restaurants and was walking through the parking lot with some buddies when one of them, not my friend, said something to a young woman seated in a truck. The woman's boyfriend took issue and confronted the group with a rifle.

family.

The gun went off and the bullet hit my friend in the head and he died right there in that parking lot.

So.

My childhood friend went out with friends and never came home.

My neighbor's daughter went to a party and never came home.

My neighbor's husband went to his driveway and never came home.

My neighbor's wife went to the supermarket and never came home.

My Dad went to play racquetball and never came home.

Familes intact one minute, and shattered the next.

When my Dad called me about the killing of my friend from across the street, he was not sad. He was angry. He was seething. My Dad had no tolerance for stupidity. And the stupidity of someone waving a loaded gun at another human being because of a harmless remark, and subsequently killing the first born child of two people who he knew and cared about, was just too much for him. It was the angriest I ever heard my Dad.

To lose a family member to death is the most heart breaking of tragedies. But to lose a family member to a senseless death takes it from heart breaking to soul crushing. How do you even go on?

That thought weighs heavy on my mind. Because I know that there is really no type of death that is more senseless than suicide. It is a stupid thing to do. My Dad would not approve. And to even consider taking my own life when the people I have mentioned above would give anything to have the lives of their departed loved ones returned, well, it makes me sick to my stomach.

This is not an easy decision.

So I tell myself I will think about it more later. Which I know is just an excuse.

Like most people, I do have regrets in life.

One of my biggest regrets is that when I came back from California a year after my friend was killed, I never walked across the street to my friend's house, went into his kitchen, put my huge arms around his tiny mother, and gave her a big hug.

I should have done that.

* * *

316

family.

I fold the suicide note and put it into a blank white envelope and seal it. I will hide it in my top dresser drawer when I get home. Before I put it into my briefcase, on the front I write three words.
Of quiet desperation.

* * *

Albert sits down on the stool next to me without saying hello.
The waitress brings him his diet coke. He tells her to bring me a drink. Albert has never bought me a drink.
I sip my scotch, he sips his coke.
"Tomorrow is your birthday, isn't it?" he asks, already knowing the answer.
"Yep."
I notice that Albert is not looking at me. Instead he is staring into the mirror behind the bar.
"So, you got big plans for tomorrow," he says, a statement, not a question.
I think for a few seconds and then say, *"Yeah, looks like it."*
Albert finishes his coke and stands up. He reaches his hand out. We shake hands.
"Don't fuck it up," he says.
I am not surprised. Albert is a smart man.
He starts to walk away and then stops, turns, and says to me, *"I robbed a bank. Actually, I robbed six banks."*
He smiles.
And then he walks into the club's back office.

* * *

My wife is cleaning the kitchen. She usually does the dishes late at night after we've eaten and watched our favorite TV shows. I turn off the light next to my lounge chair in the living room which signals that my evening is over. Boo hops off the couch and heads back to his cage in the bedroom. I walk into the kitchen.
"Calling it a night?" asks my wife, putting dishes into the dishwasher.

family.

"Yeah, I'm done. I'm tired tonight for some reason. I'm going to bed to read a little."

"Okay, good night."

"Good luck at your match tomorrow."

"Thanks, I need it. My game has sucked lately."

I walk up behind her and give her a hug, which surprises her. And before letting go, I say, *"I love you."* Which really surprises her. She gets a big smile, which reinforces for me how much just the tiniest bit of affection from me has always meant to her and how stingy I have always been with that affection.

I want my last memory of my wife to be that smile on her face, and I want her last memory of me to be that hug and those three simple words.

* * *

I finish the book I have been reading.

Boo notices.

"Took it right down to the wire didn't you."

"Yeah."

"Was it a good read?"

"It was okay. I couldn't really concentrate."

"Gee, I wonder why."

I turn off the light on the nightstand and lay on my back with my eyes open. It is very quiet in the room. And very calm too.

"Hey."

"Yes?"

"I didn't hear my name mentioned in your breakdown on the different types of families there are. Am I just left out in the cold?"

"Of course not. You are a major part of my family."

"Foreals?"

"Yes, foreals."

"Cool."

It's quiet again in the room for what seems like a long time.

I hear a light scratching, Boo's nails scraping the thin metal bars on the front of his cage.

"Yes?" I ask.

"Is there anything I can say to talk you out of this?" says Boo. His voice is oddly emotional, almost tentative.

318

family.

"No. I'm sorry."
"Are you positive?"
"Yes."
More quiet. More calm. Then Boo speaks.
"I'm sad."
"So am I, Boo," I say. *"So am I."*

leaving.

I wake up at 9 am. My wife has left for tennis. It's just Boo and I. He's still in his cage. He's awake and I can see that he is looking at me. A sliver of morning sunshine is coming in through the shades. It's going to be a beautiful day.

I am both nervous and calm.

I get the blue case from the top of my dresser and the box of ammo from my top drawer and sit back on my bed cross-legged. I take the gun out of the case, load all six chambers with the heavy bullets, and then hold the gun in both hands. The steel is so cold.

"Hey."

It's Boo. I'm surprised. I've never heard him talk during the day.

"*I have a request.*"

"Which is?"

"*Take me with you.*"

That throws me for a loop.

"Why?" I ask.

"*Because I don't want to be here if you are gone.*"

"I can't take you with me."

"*Why not?*"

leaving.

"Because that means I would have to kill you."

"So?"

"I am not going to kill you. I am not a monster. What would people say?"

"That's bullshit. You don't care what people say. We both know that. What's the real reason you won't kill me?"

"Because I love you."

"You love me?" he asks.

"Yes, very much so."

"Then you can't kill yourself," he says.

"Why not?"

"Because I am you. And you are me."

That throws me for a double loop.

"That's an interesting thought," I say. *"Give me a minute."*

"Sure," says Boo, *"but do you mind putting the gun down while we talk?"*

I set the gun down next to me on the bedspread.

"Thanks," says Boo.

I lay back on the bed and study the blades of the ceiling fan spinning lazily above me. Boo waits. After a few minutes, I sit back up.

"I get your point," I say, *"but I've made my decision. I've already come to terms with it in my head. It's a done deal. I am going to kill myself today."*

"I know you are," says Boo. *"It's already done. Congratulations."*

Now I'm confused.

"I haven't done it yet, you goofball."

"Yes you did," says Boo. *"You already killed yourself. In your own mind."*

"I don't follow you," I say.

"Have you given up on life?"

"Yes."

"Do you no longer care about anything?"

"Yes."

"Has your soul moved on?"

"Yes."

"Then you have already committed suicide."

"But I'm still here."

leaving.

"Your body is, but you aren't. Do you really think the only suicides are the ones where someone kills themself?"

I lay back on the bed. This damn dog is actually making sense. I try to think of a counter argument. I can't come up with anything except for more questions, which I ask while still laying on my back staring at the fan blades.

"So you are saying I am already dead, I have already killed myself?"

"Absolutely," says Boo.

"What about the gun?"

"Fuck the gun. Who needs that mess to clean up. Don't you get it? You've already done it."

"But ..."

"Listen, if you shoot yourself today then you have just committed suicide twice. Don't you think once is enough?"

I fix my eye on one of the four fan blades and try to follow just that one blade as it makes its rotations. When I finally lose sight of that blade and it becomes part of the spinning blur, I sit back up and look at Boo. He looks right back at me.

I just stare at Boo for a long time. I think about everything I have done over the past nine days to get ready for today. I think about checking off each item on the *TCB List.* I think about all the thoughts I have had over those nine days and how I have accepted and come to terms with my no longer being part of this enticing and aggravating game called life. And, as Boo has so astutely pointed out, I realize that I have done everything I said I would, with the exception of what would simply be a split second of time, the pulling of a trigger.

"You make some very valid points," I finally say.

"Of course I do. What else would you expect."

"I think you are right. On all counts."

"So we're done?" asks Boo.

I pick the gun up and hold it in my hand for a few seconds and then slowly put it back into the blue case and snap the case shut. I get off the bed and take the case to my walk-in closet, sticking the case on one of the top shelves. Then I lay down flat on the carpet in front of Boo's cage. I put my left hand on top of my right hand on the carpet, and place my chin on the top of both hands.

I stare at Boo.

leaving.

He stares at me.

A full minute ticks by.

"Yeah," I finally say to Boo. *"We're done."*

I stand up, pull on a pair of gym shorts, and open the top drawer of my dresser. I take out the note I had written to my wife and children.

"Be right back," I say to Boo.

"Take your time," says Boo.

I go outside on the lanai and sit at the patio table. The sunshine is brighter and warmer than what the sliver that had come through my blinds had hinted at. I light a cigarette and for some reason it tastes better than any cigarette I have had in recent years. I slowly read the note, then tear it into little pieces and drop the pieces into the large stone ashtray on the table. I light the pieces with my lighter and watch as they burn. As the last tiny slip of white paper turns to ash, I wonder, for just the briefest of seconds, whether my life has just ended or if a new life has just begun.

I go inside, back to the bedroom and open Boo's cage.

"How about we go outside and let you do your thing in the front yard," I say.

"I'm down," says Boo.

I smile. The little fucker has such a way with words. We head for the front door.

"By the way," says Boo.

"What?"

"Happy Birthday."

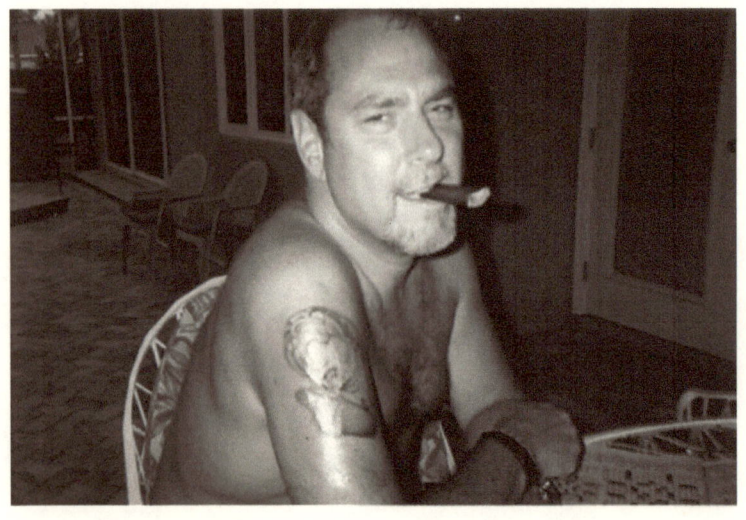

Don Waitt has been a newspaper reporter, journalist, magazine editor and accomplished ne'er-do-well for the past thirty years.

www.ingramcontent.com/pod-product-compliance
Lightning Source LLC
Chambersburg PA
CBHW030405030726
47497CB00002B/481